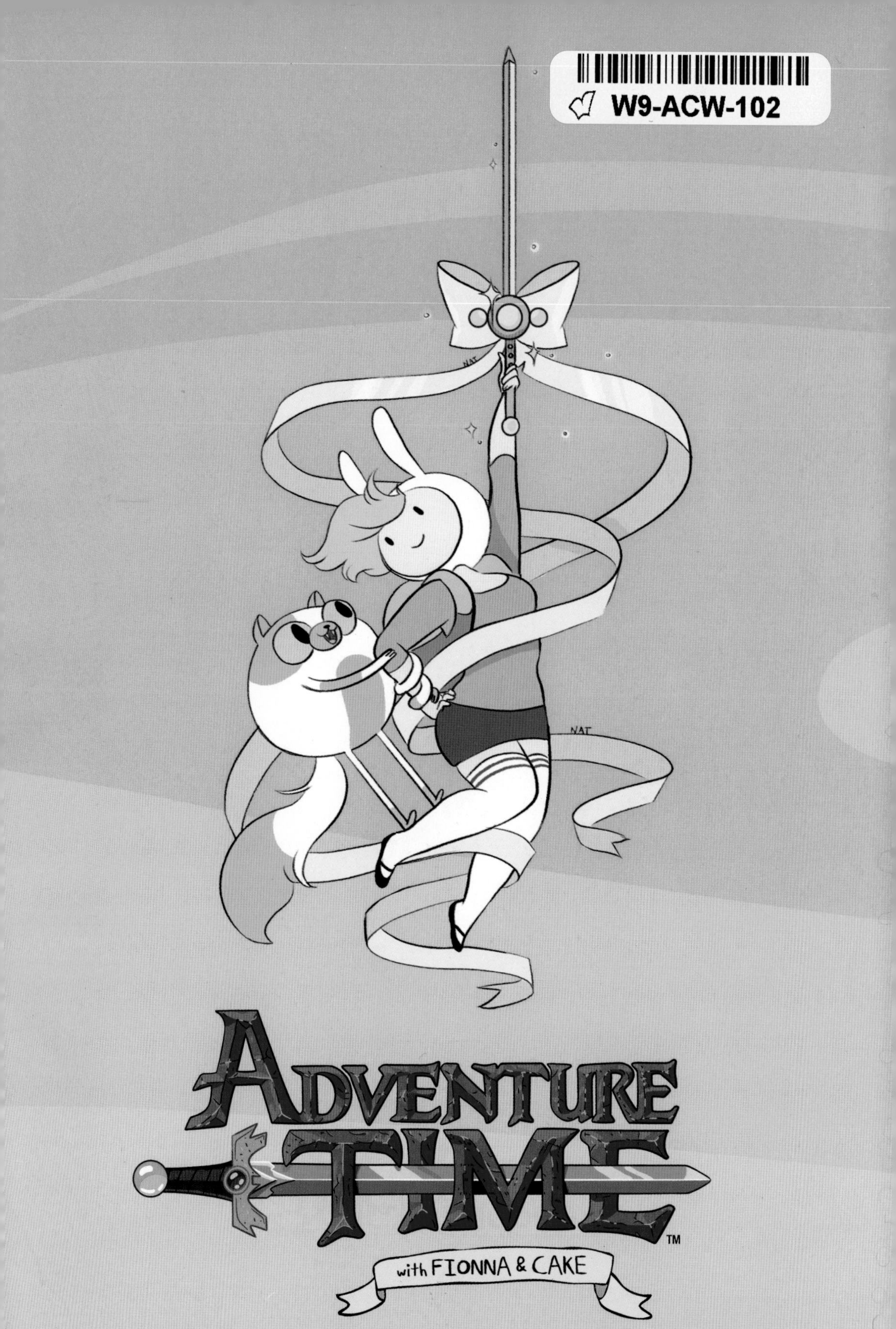
NAT
NAT

ADVENTURE TIME™

with FIONNA & CAKE

ROSS RICHIE CEO & Founder • MATT GAGNON Editor-in-Chief • FILIP SABLIK VP-Publishing & Marketing • LANCE KREITER VP-Licensing & Merchandising • MATT NISSENBAUM Senior Director of Sales & Marketing • PHIL BARBARO Director of Finance
BRYCE CARLSON Managing Editor • DAFNA PLEBAN Editor • SHANNON WATTERS Editor • ERIC HARBURN Editor • CHRIS ROSA Assistant Editor • ALEX GALER Assistant Editor • WHITNEY LEOPARD Assistant Editor • JASMINE AMIRI Assistant Editor
STEPHANIE GONZAGA Graphic Designer • MIKE LOPEZ Production Designer • DEVIN FUNCHES E-Commerce & Inventory Coordinator • VINCE FREDERICK Event Coordinator • BRIANNA HART Executive Assistant • AARON FERRARA Operations Assistant

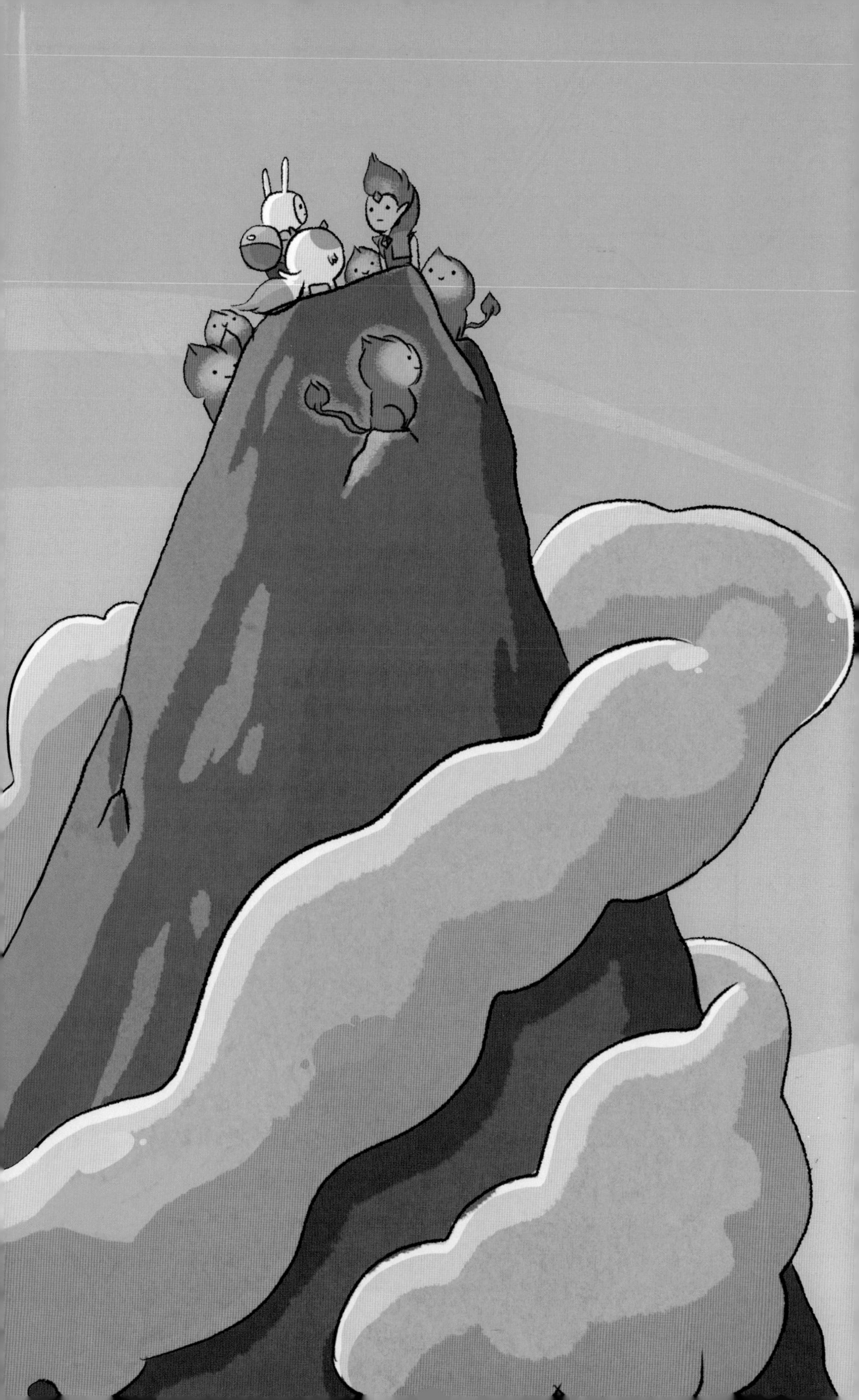

"ADVENTURE TIME" CREATED BY

Pendleton Ward

WRITTEN AND ILLUSTRATED BY

Natasha Allegri

Colors by Natasha Allegri & Patrick Seery

with Betty Liang (Chapter 6)

LETTERS BY
Britt Wilson

"THE SWEATER BANDIT"
WRITTEN AND ILLUSTRATED BY
Noelle Stevenson

"COOTIE POWER"
WRITTEN AND ILLUSTRATED BY
Lucy Knisley

"SOUR CANDY"
WRITTEN AND ILLUSTRATED BY
Kate Leth

COVER BY
Natasha Allegri

Colors by Amanda Thomas

ASSISTANT EDITOR
Whitney Leopard

EDITOR
Shannon Watters

TRADE DESIGN BY
Stephanie Gonzaga

with Hannah Nance Partlow

With Special Thanks to Marisa Marionakis, Rick Blanco, Curtis Lelash, Laurie Halal-Ono, Keith Mack, Kelly Crews and the wonderful folks at Cartoon Network.

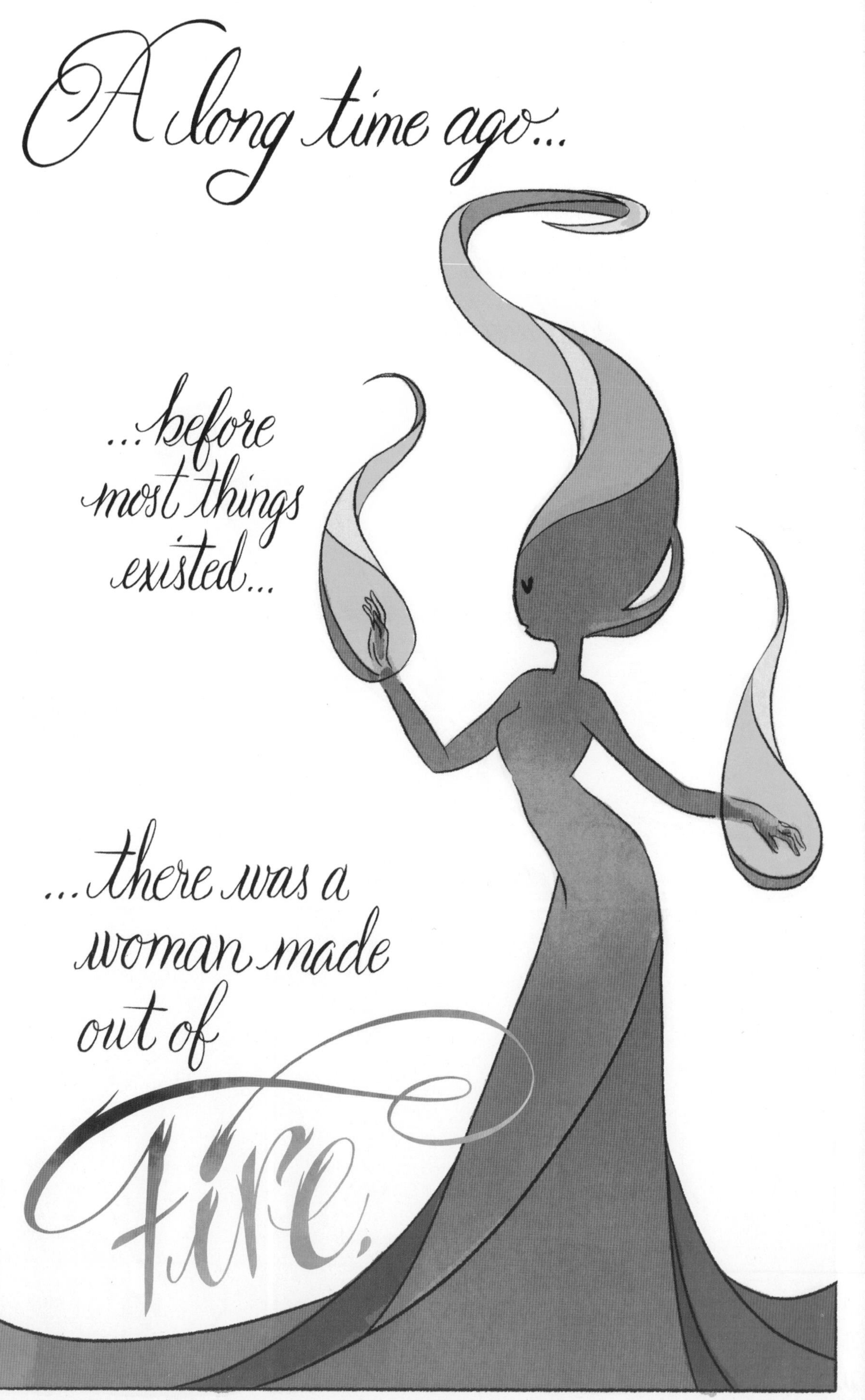
A long time ago...
...before most things existed...
...there was a woman made out of fire.

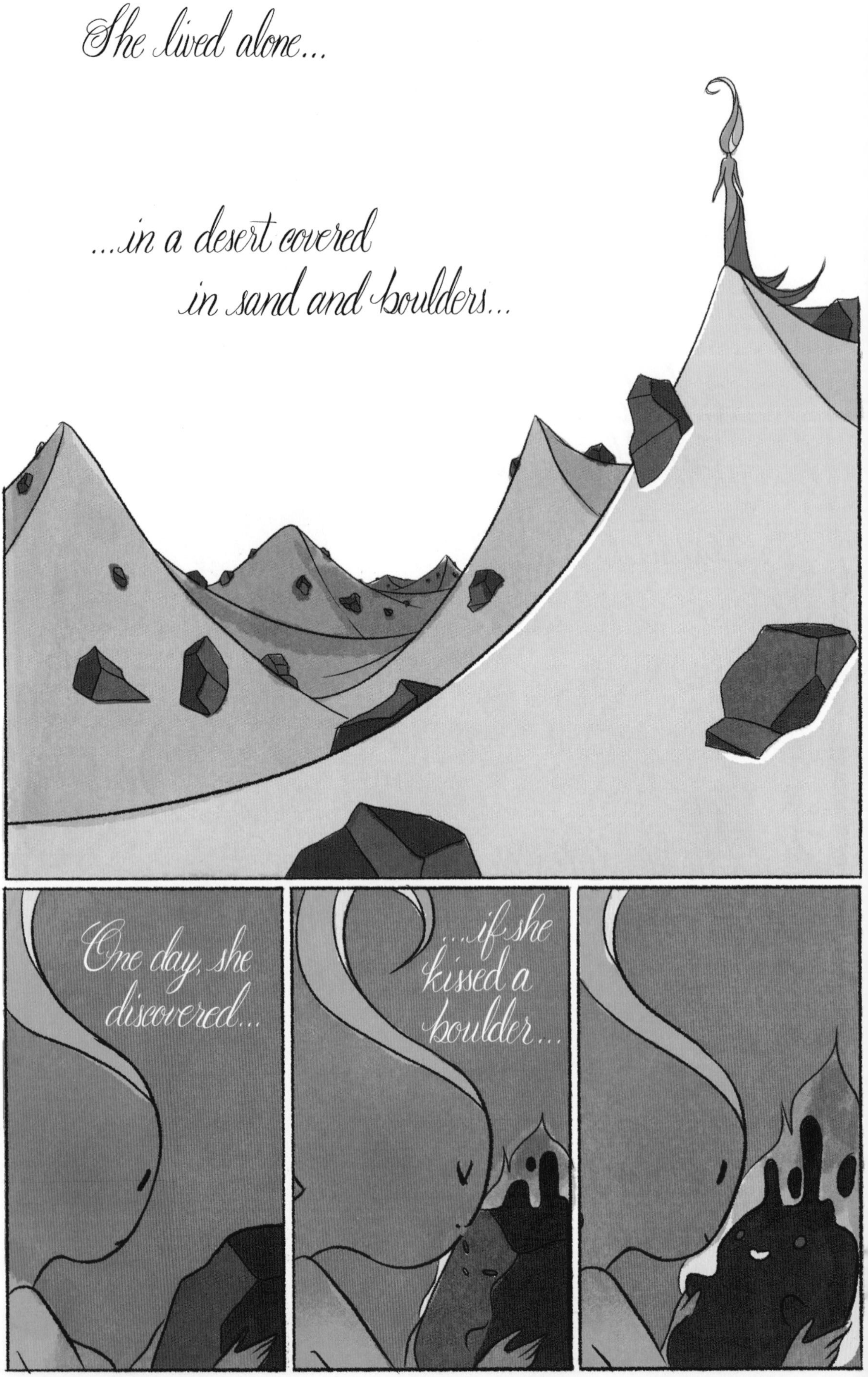
She lived alone...
...in a desert covered in sand and boulders...
One day, she discovered...
...if she kissed a boulder...

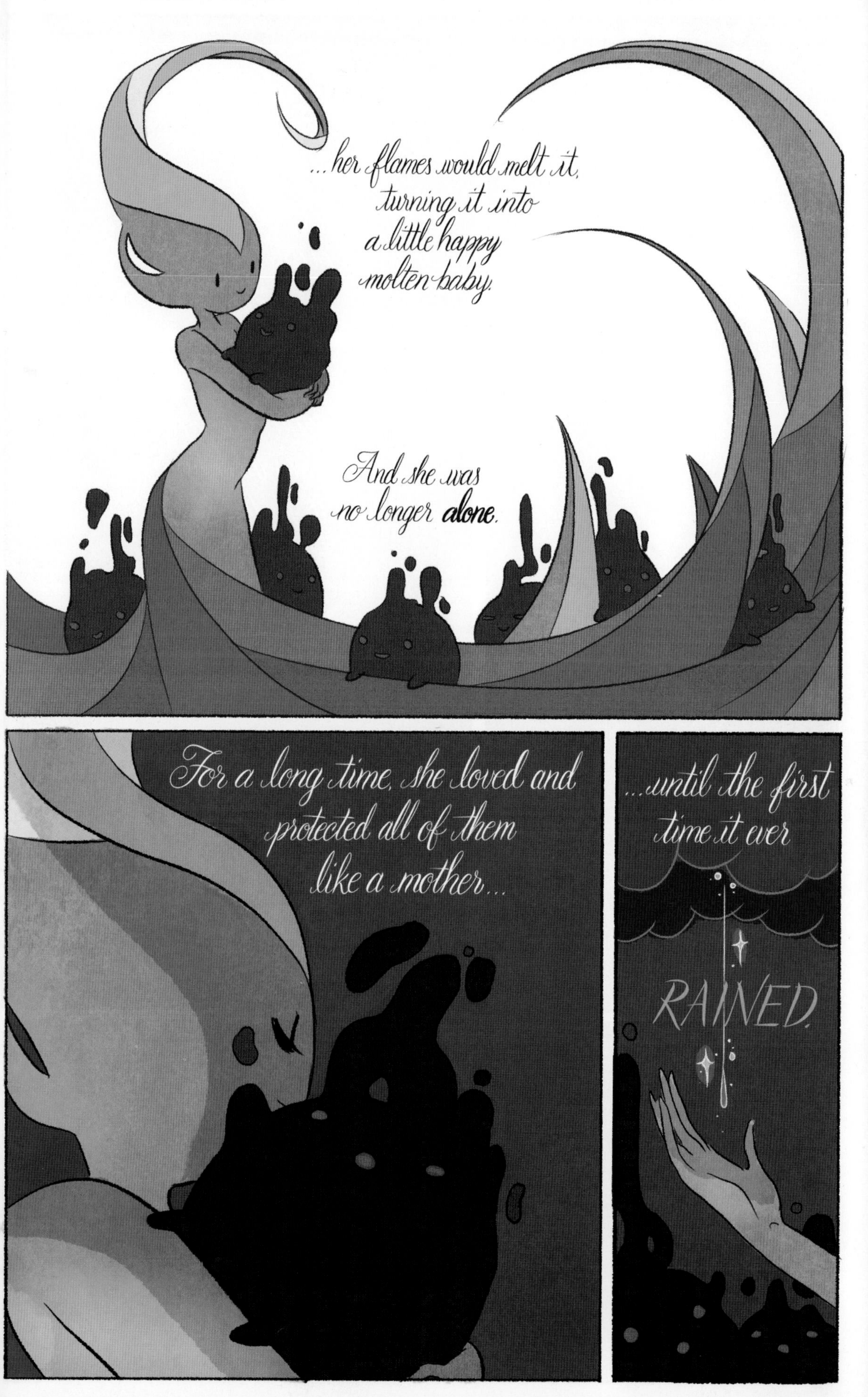

...her flames would melt it, turning it into a little happy molten baby.
And she was no longer alone.
For a long time, she loved and protected all of them like a mother...
...until the first time it ever
RAINED.

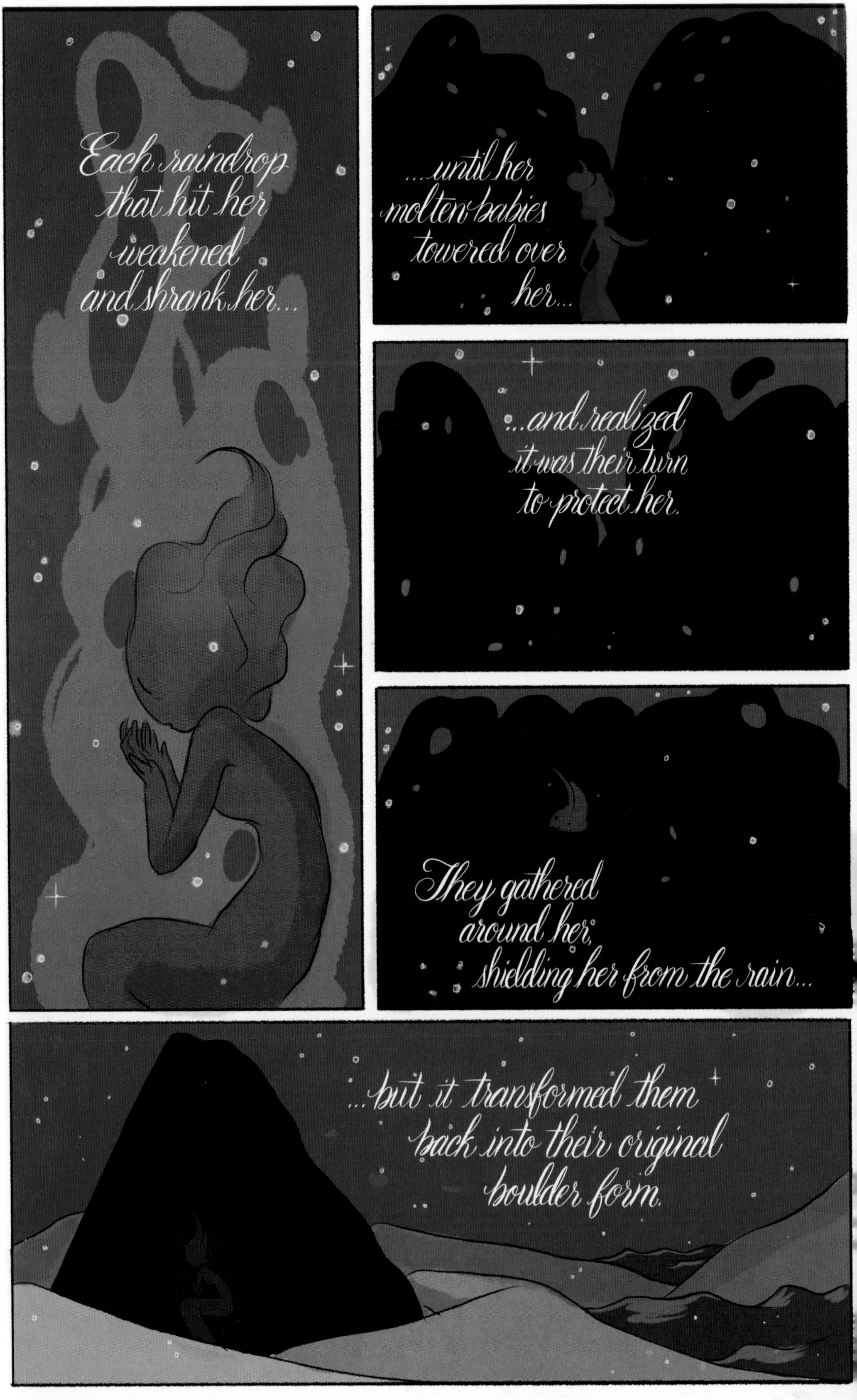
Each raindrop that hit her weakened and shrank her...
...until her molten babies towered over her...
...and realized it was their turn to protect her.
They gathered around her, shielding her from the rain...
...but it transformed them back into their original boulder form.

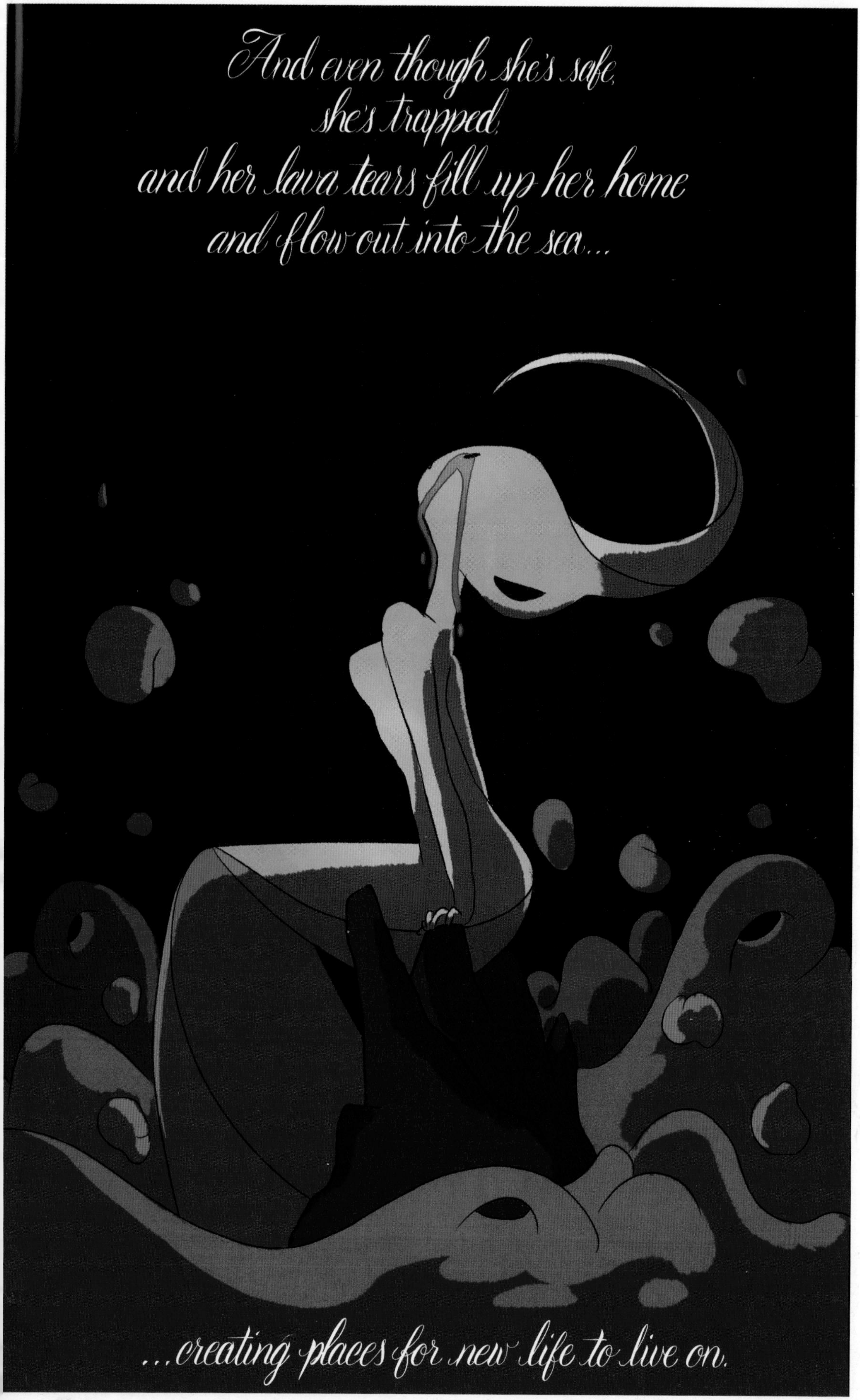
And even though she's safe,
she's trapped,
and her lava tears fill up her home
and flow out into the sea...
...creating places for new life to live on.

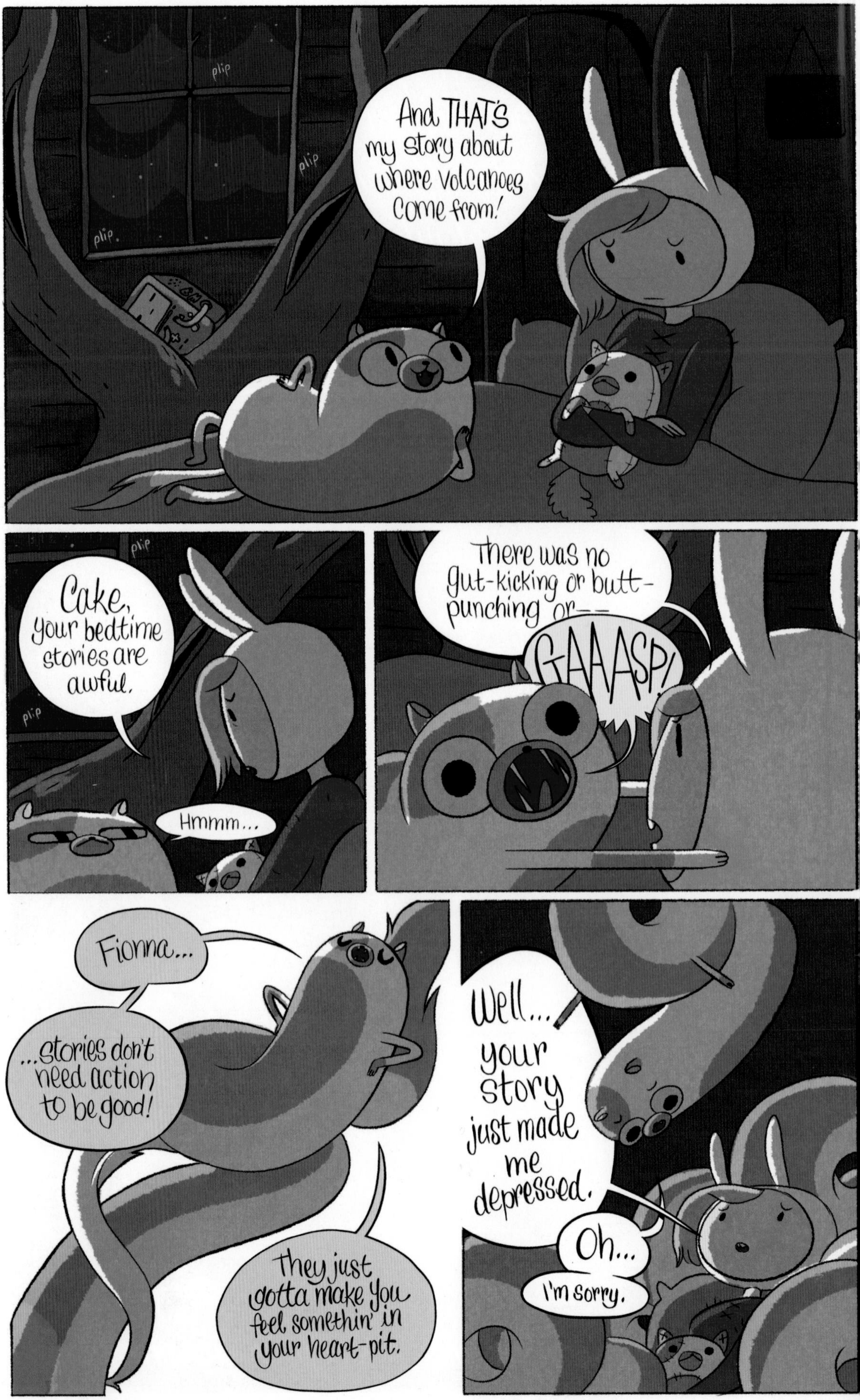
plip
plip
plip
And THAT'S my story about where volcanoes come from!
plip
plip
Cake, your bedtime stories are awful.
Hmmm...
There was no gut-kicking or butt-punching or--
GAAASP!
Fionna...
...stories don't need action to be good!
They just gotta make you feel somethin' in your heart-pit.
Well... your story just made me depressed.
Oh...
I'm sorry.

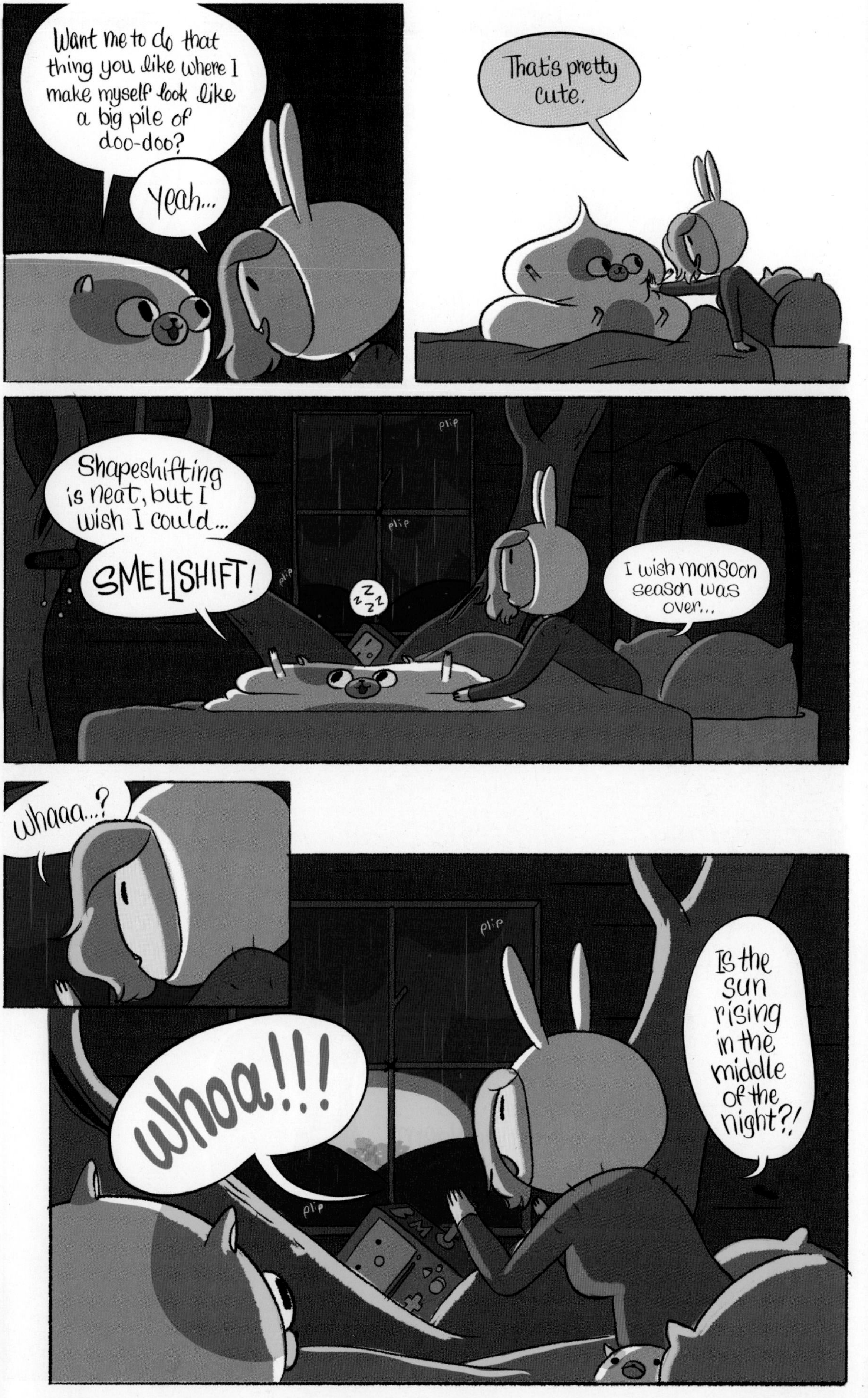
Want me to do that thing you like where I make myself look like a big pile of doo-doo?
Yeah...
That's pretty cute.
Shapeshifting is neat, but I wish I could...
SMELLSHIFT!
plip
plip
plip
Z Z Z Z
I wish monsoon season was over...
whaaa...?
plip
Whoa!!!
Is the sun rising in the middle of the night?!
plip

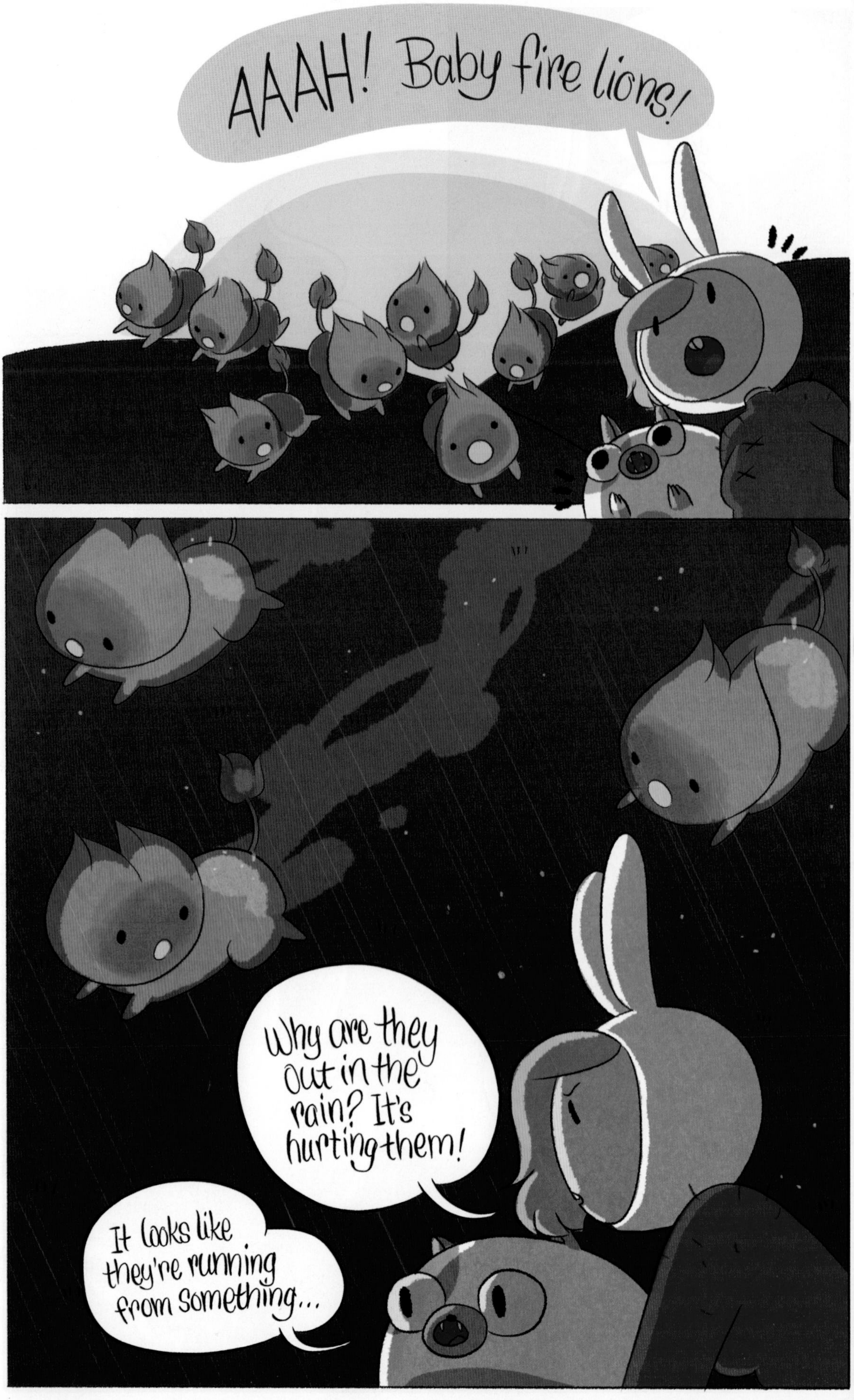
AAAH! Baby fire lions!
Why are they out in the rain? It's hurting them!
It looks like they're running from something...

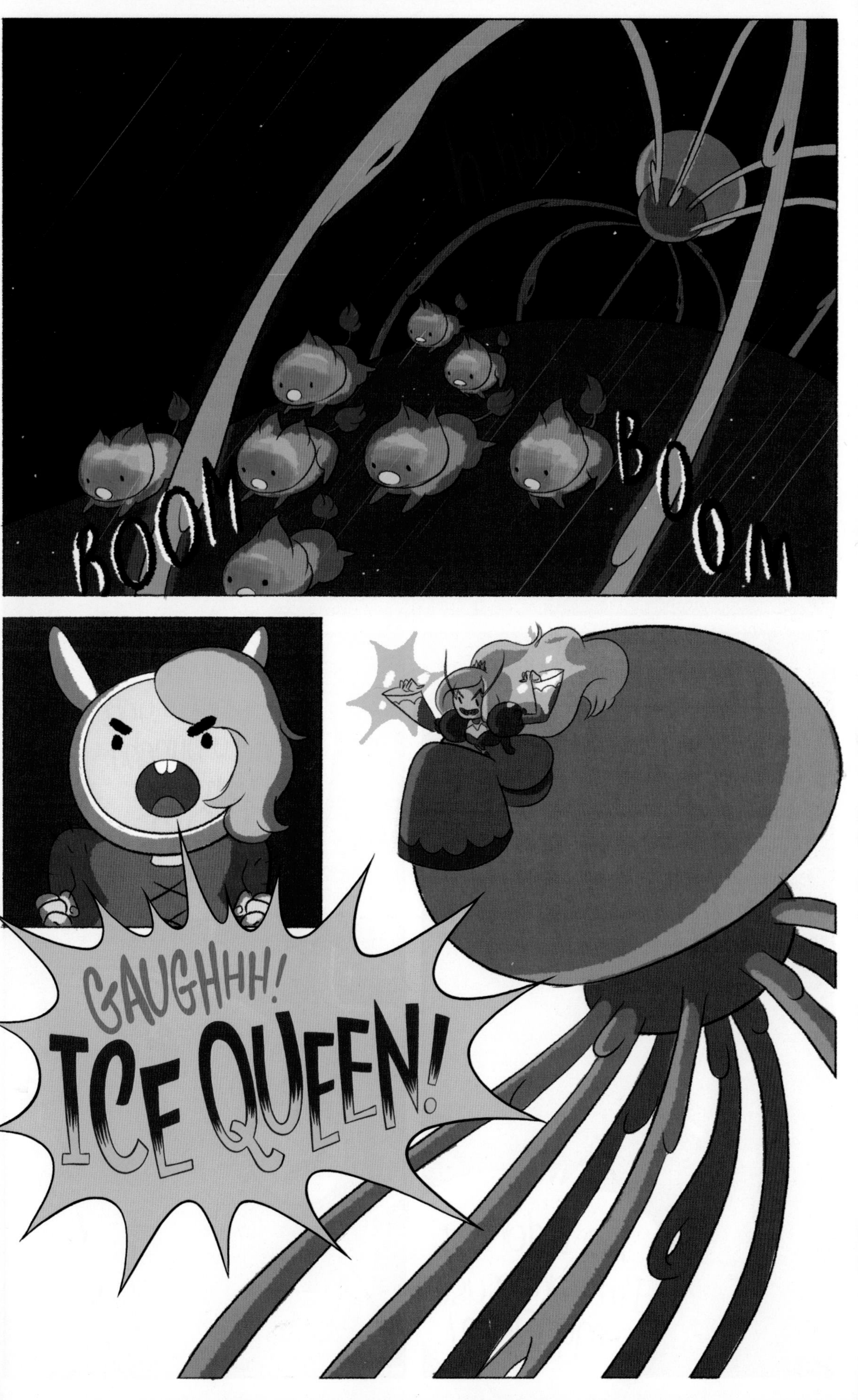

BOOM
BOOM
GAUGHHH!
ICE QUEEN!

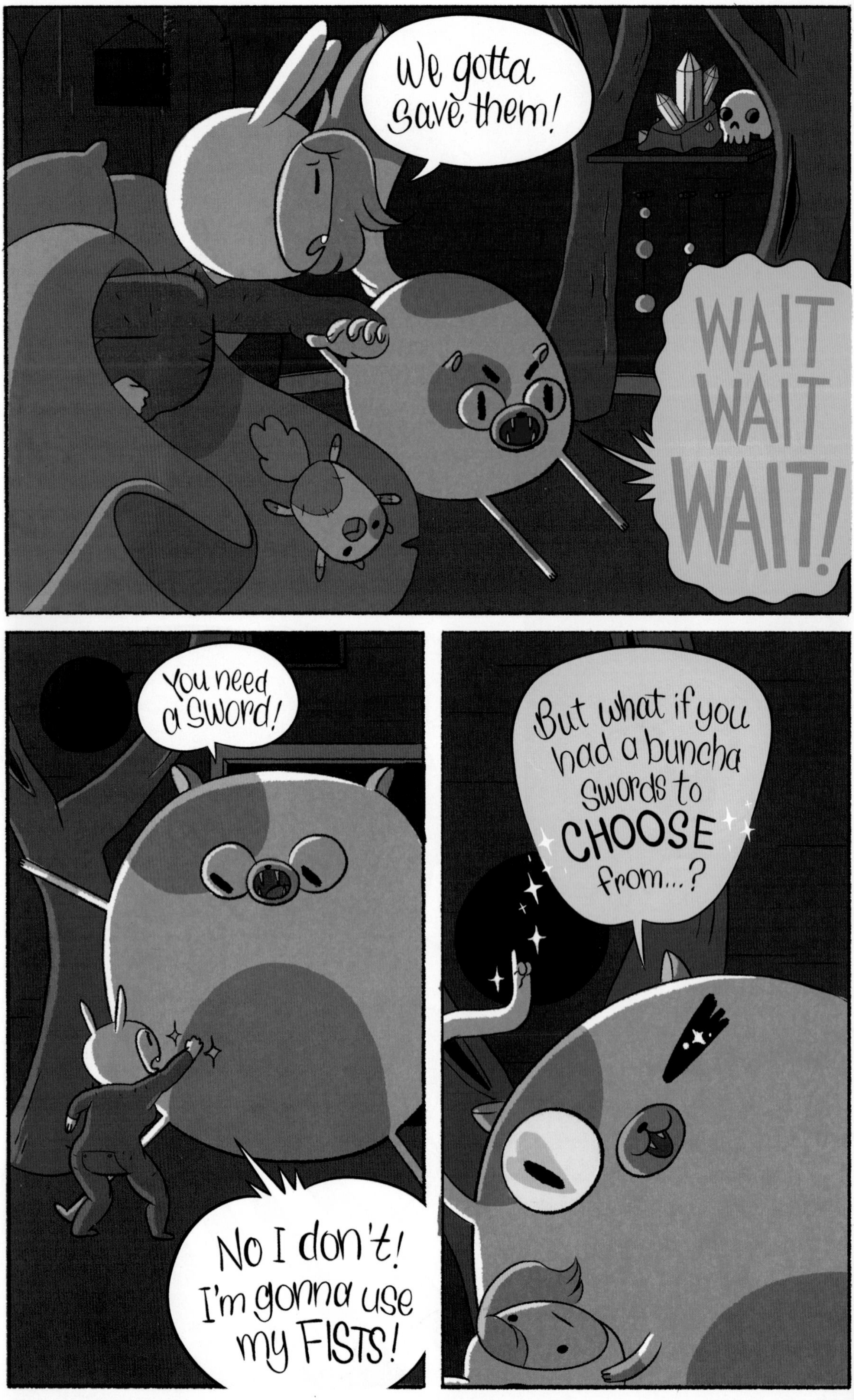

We gotta save them!
WAIT WAIT WAIT!
You need a sword!
No I don't! I'm gonna use my FISTS!
But what if you had a buncha swords to CHOOSE from...?

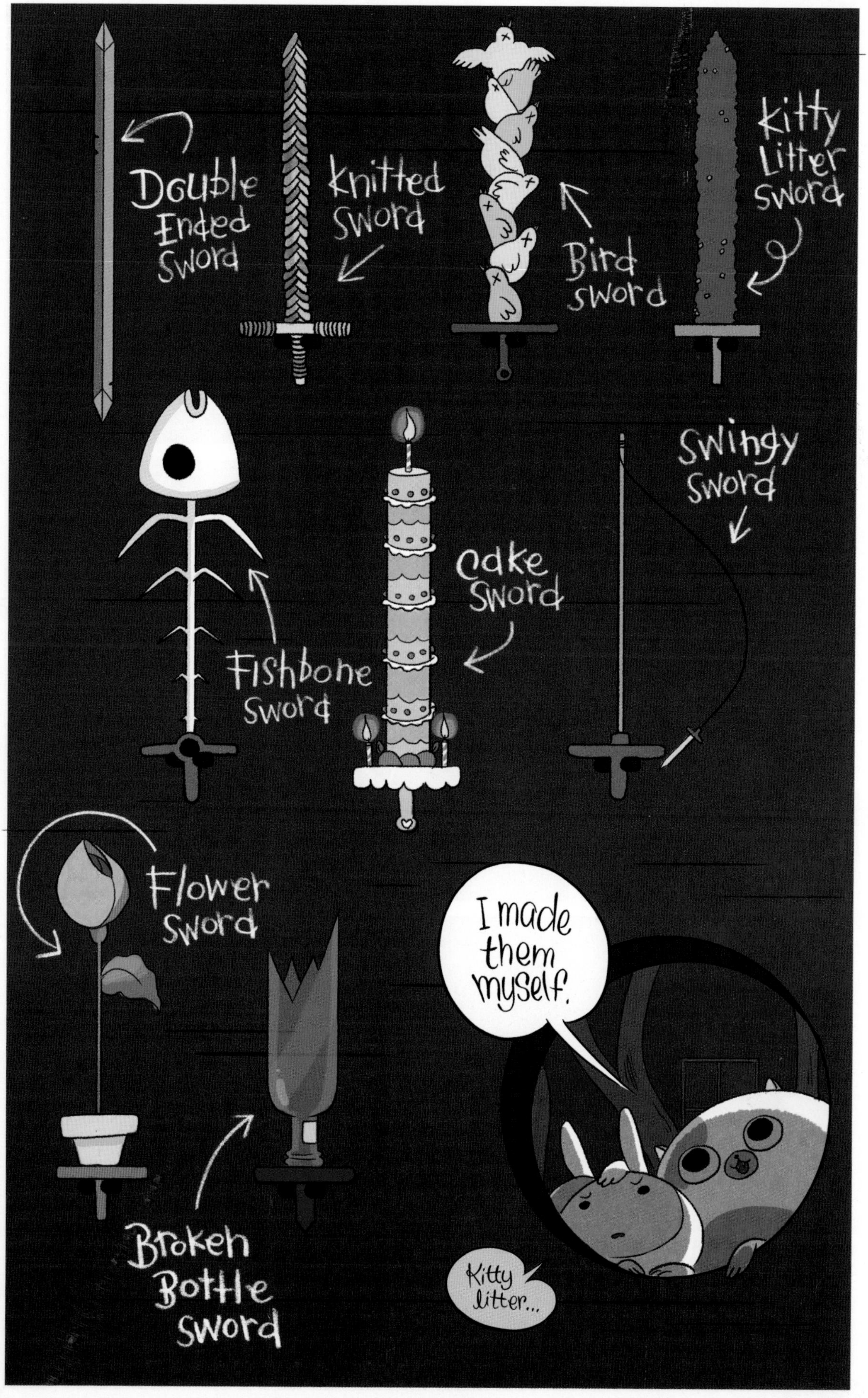
Double Ended Sword
Knitted Sword
Bird Sword
Kitty Litter Sword
Swingy Sword
Fishbone Sword
Cake Sword
Flower Sword
Broken Bottle Sword
I made them myself.
Kitty litter...

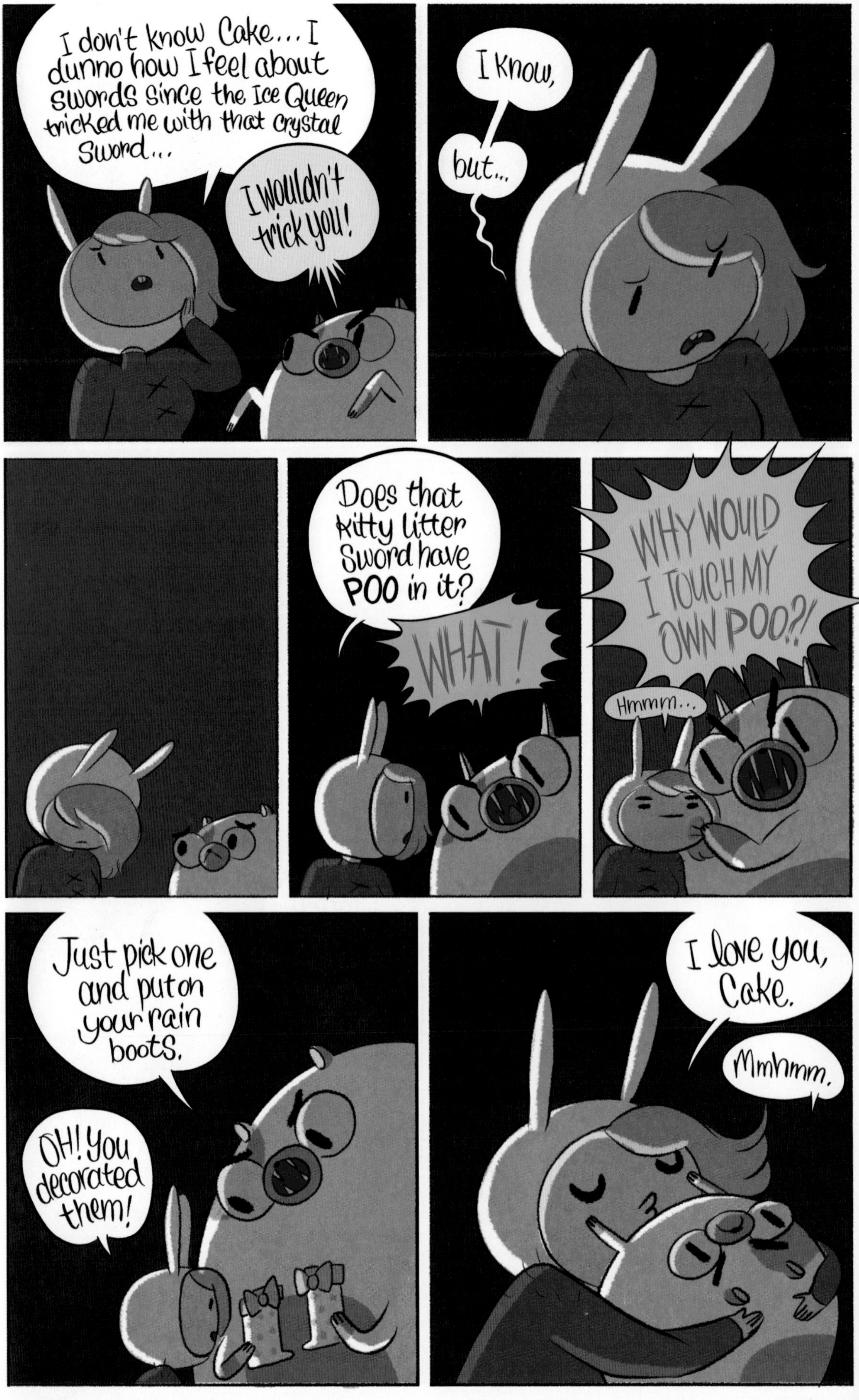
I don't know Cake... I dunno how I feel about swords since the Ice Queen tricked me with that crystal sword...
I wouldn't trick you!
I know,
but...
Does that kitty litter sword have POO in it?
WHAT!
WHY WOULD I TOUCH MY OWN POO?!
Hmmm...
Just pick one and put on your rain boots.
OH! You decorated them!
I love you, Cake.
Mmhmm.

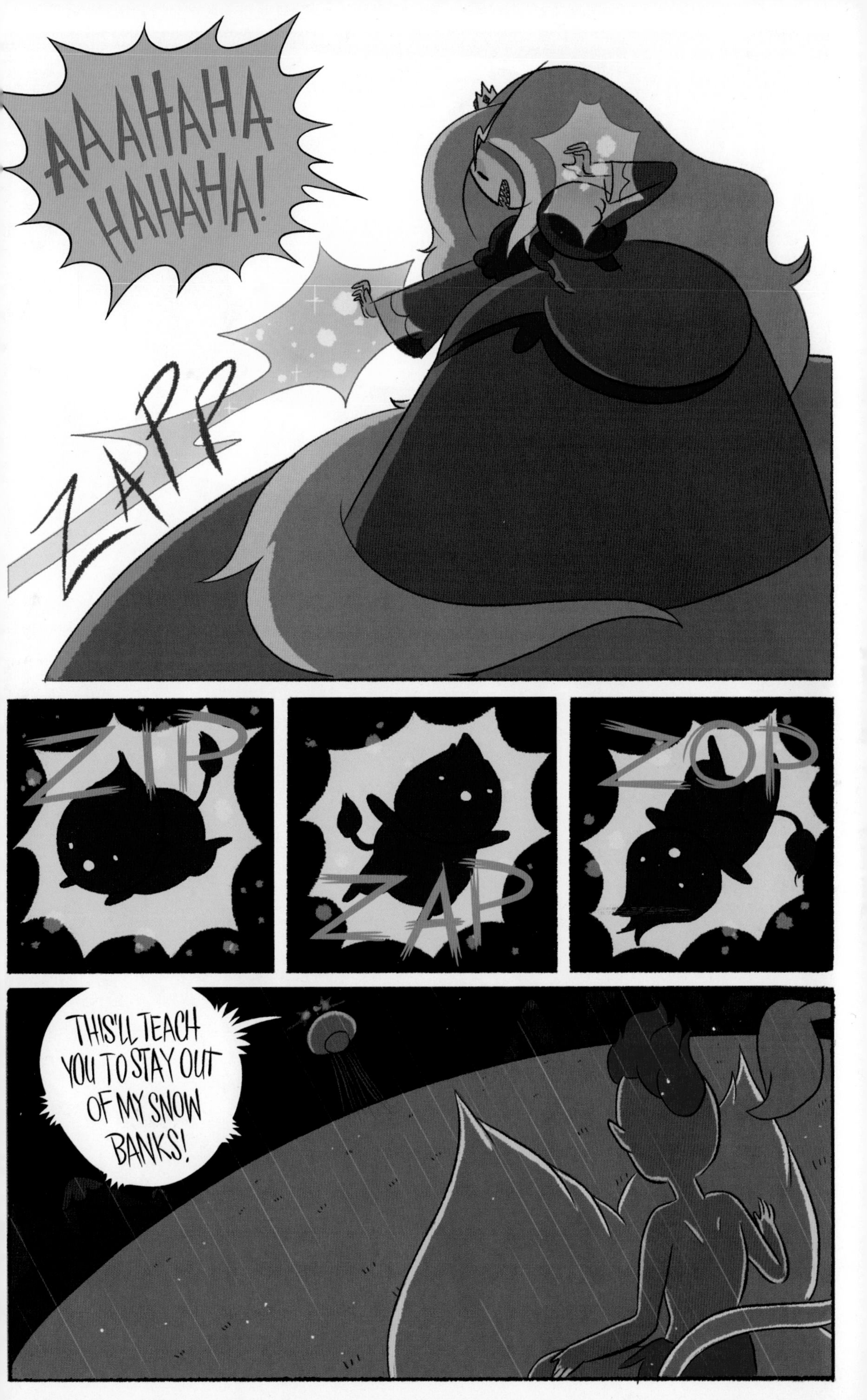
AAAHAHA HAHAHA!
ZAPP
ZIP
ZAP
ZOP
THIS'LL TEACH YOU TO STAY OUT OF MY SNOW BANKS!

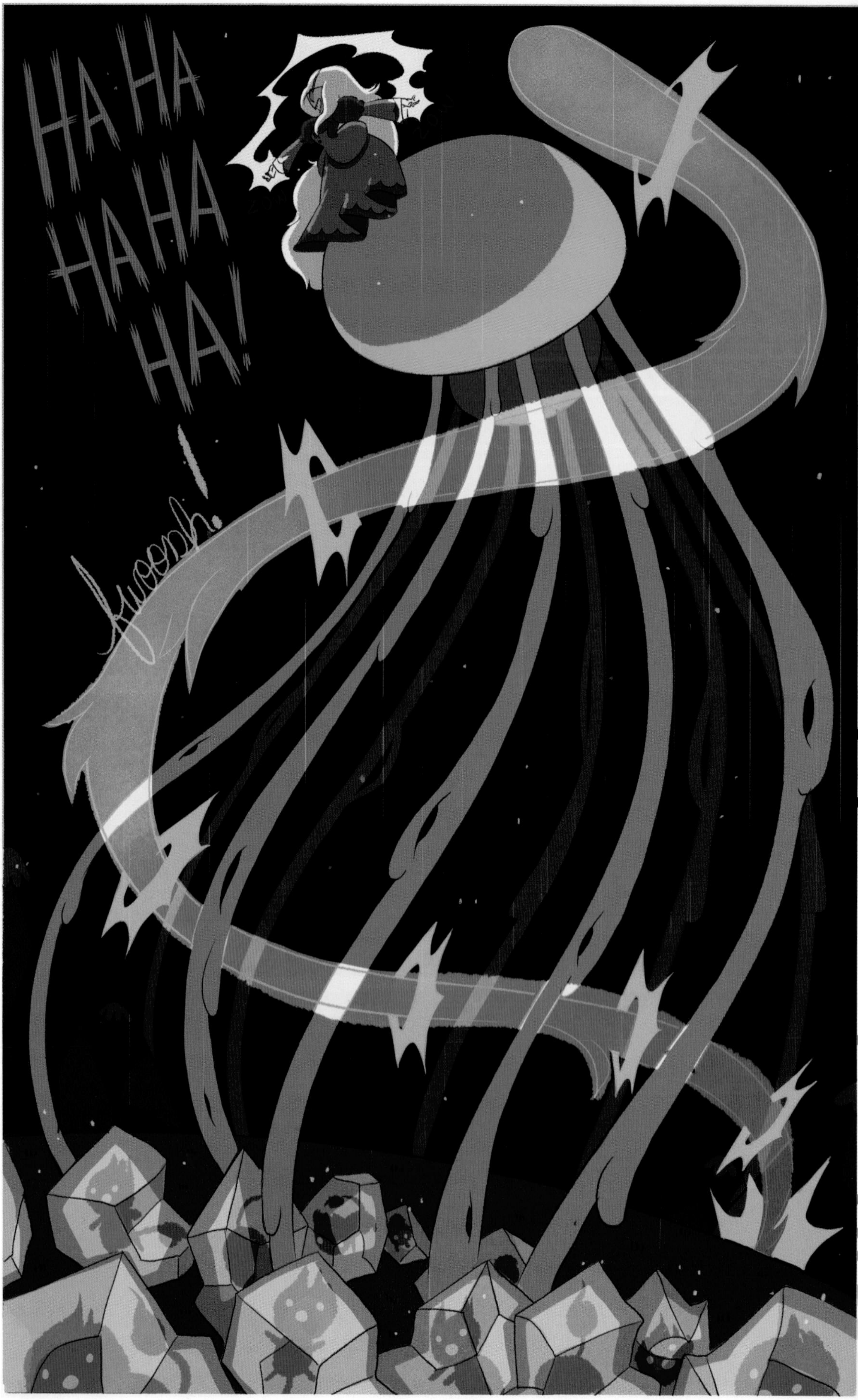
HA HA HAHA HA!
fwoosh!

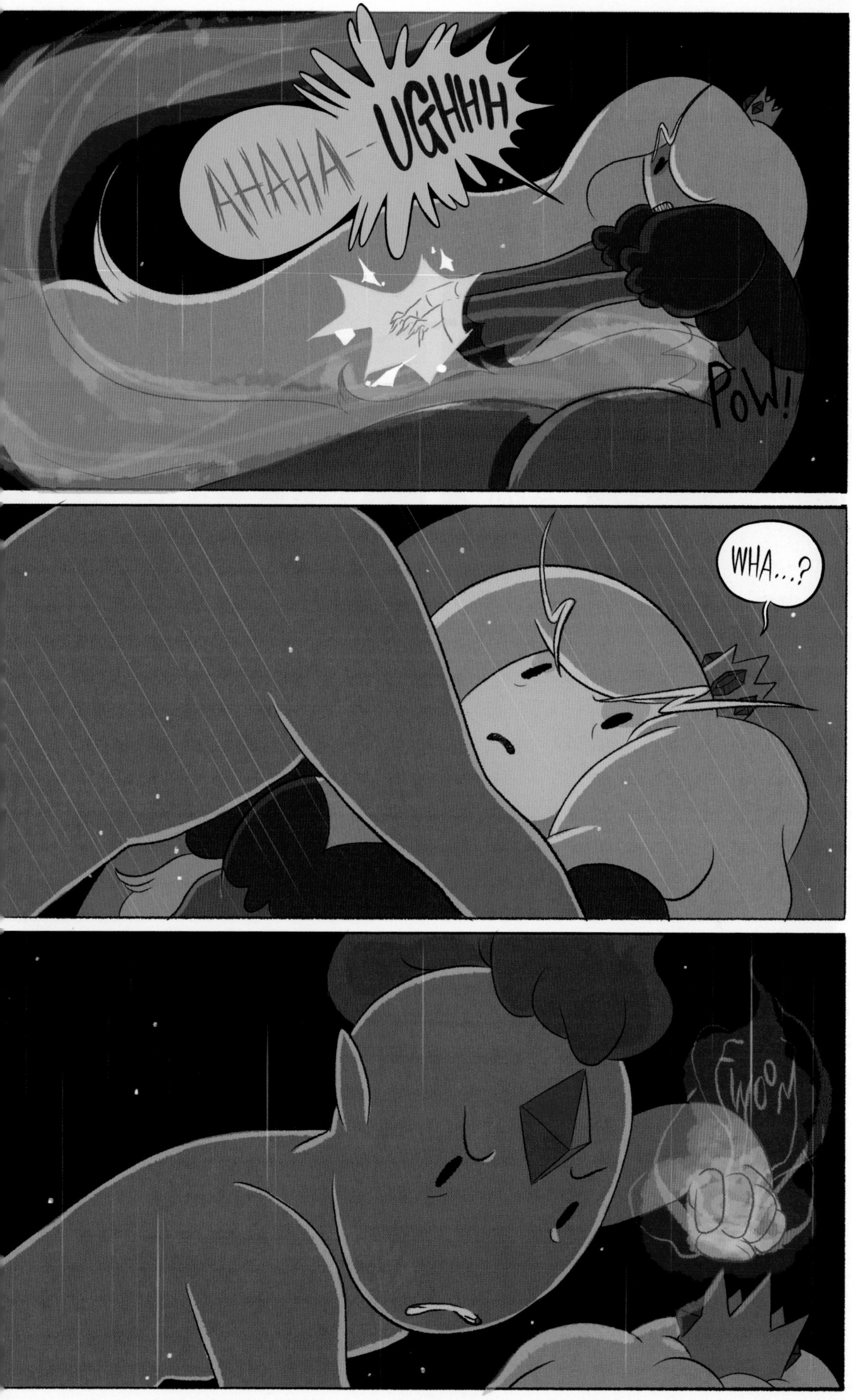
AHAHA--UGHHH
POW!
WHA...?
FWOOM

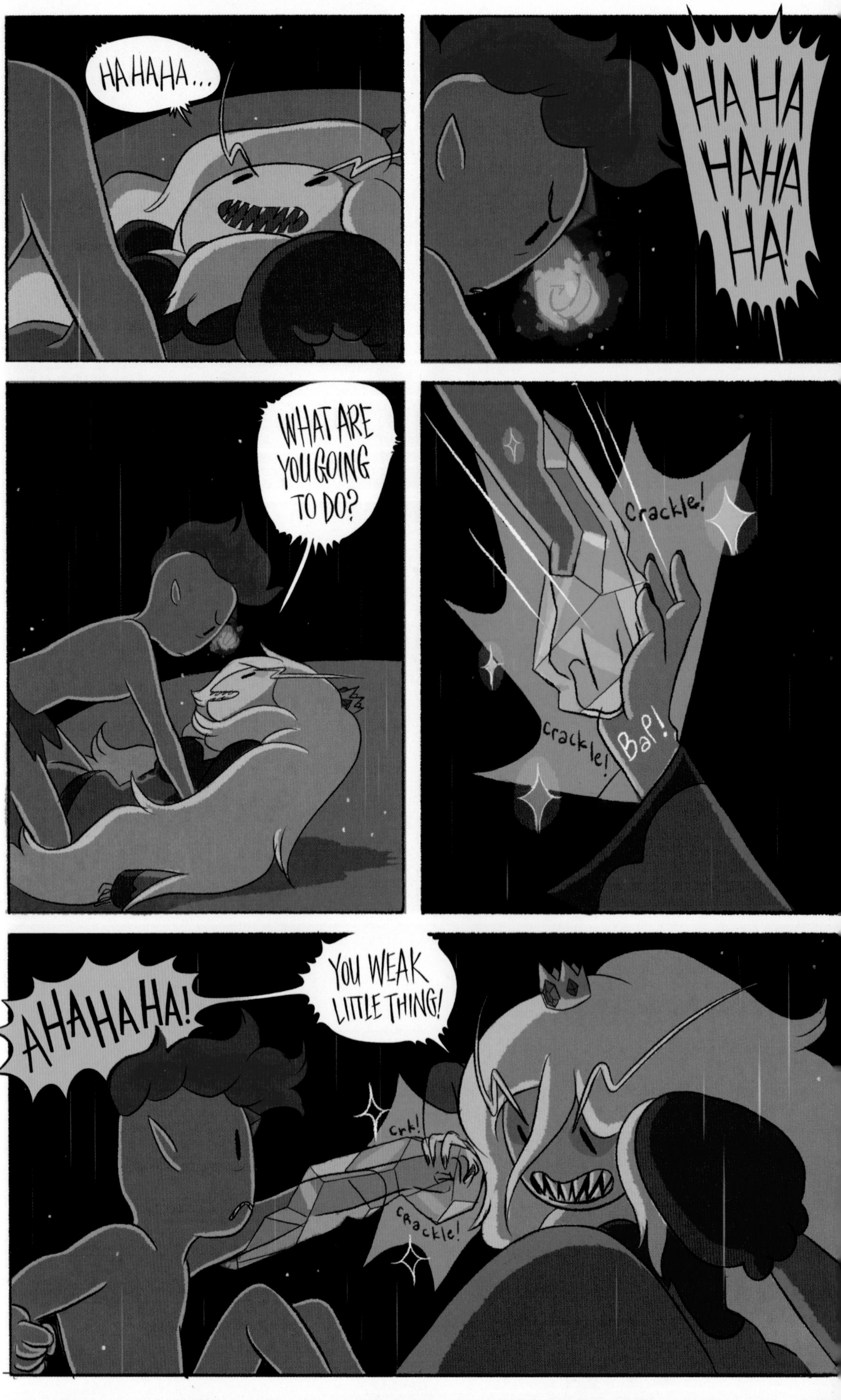
HA HAHA...
HA HA HAHA HA!
WHAT ARE YOU GOING TO DO?
Crackle!
Crackle!
BaP!
AHAHAHA!
YOU WEAK LITTLE THING!
crk!
crackle!

I WANTED TO TEST THIS OUT ON THOSE LITTLE FLAME RUNTS...

shimmer

shimmer

BUT I THINK YOU DESERVE A **TREAT.**

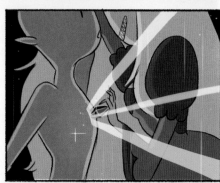

Vyooom

GOOD BOY.

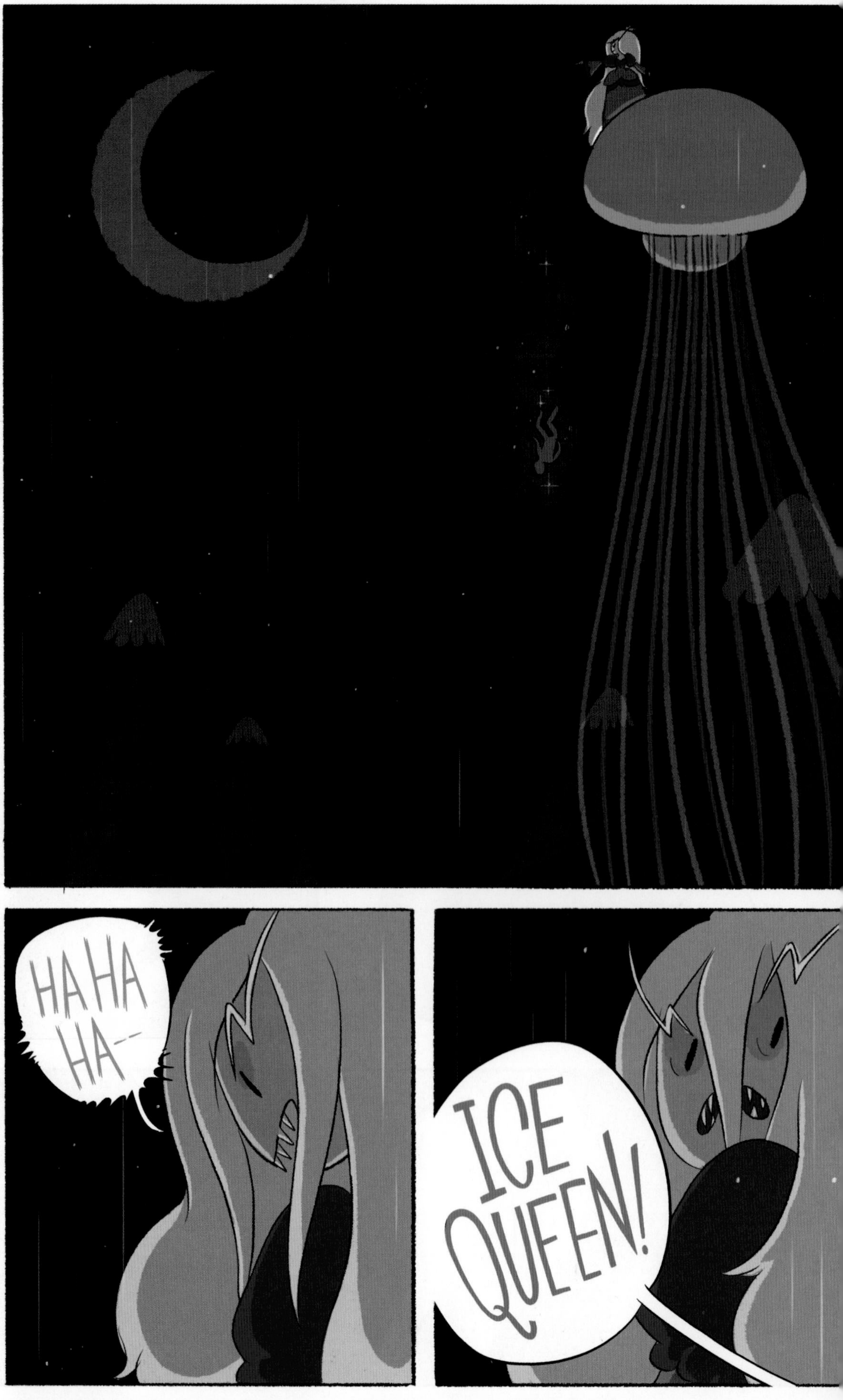
HA HA HA--
ICE QUEEN!

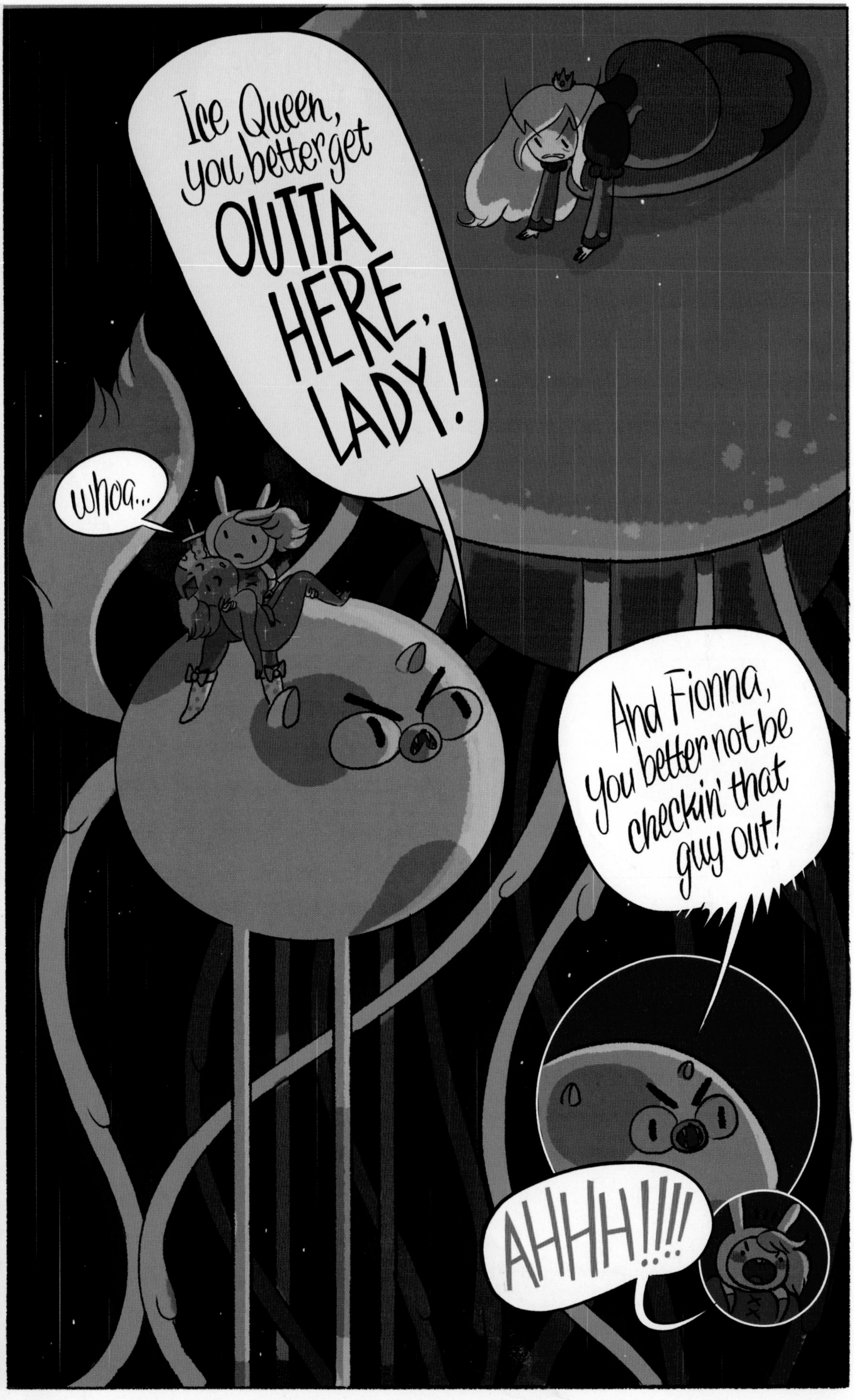
Ice Queen, you better get OUTTA HERE, LADY!
whoa...
And Fionna, you better not be checkin' that guy out!
AHHH!!!!

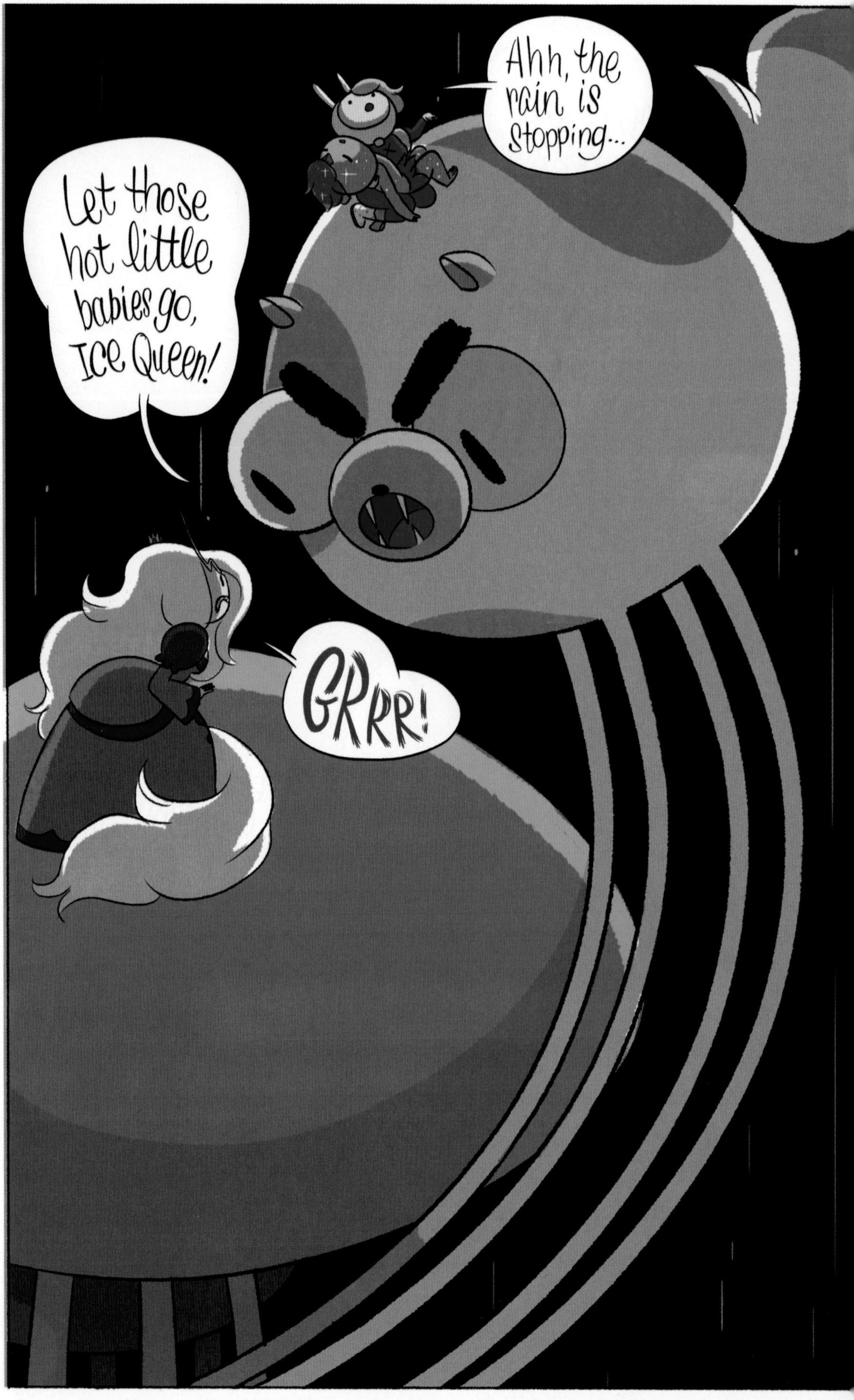
Ahh, the rain is stopping...
Let those hot little babies go, Ice Queen!
GRRR!

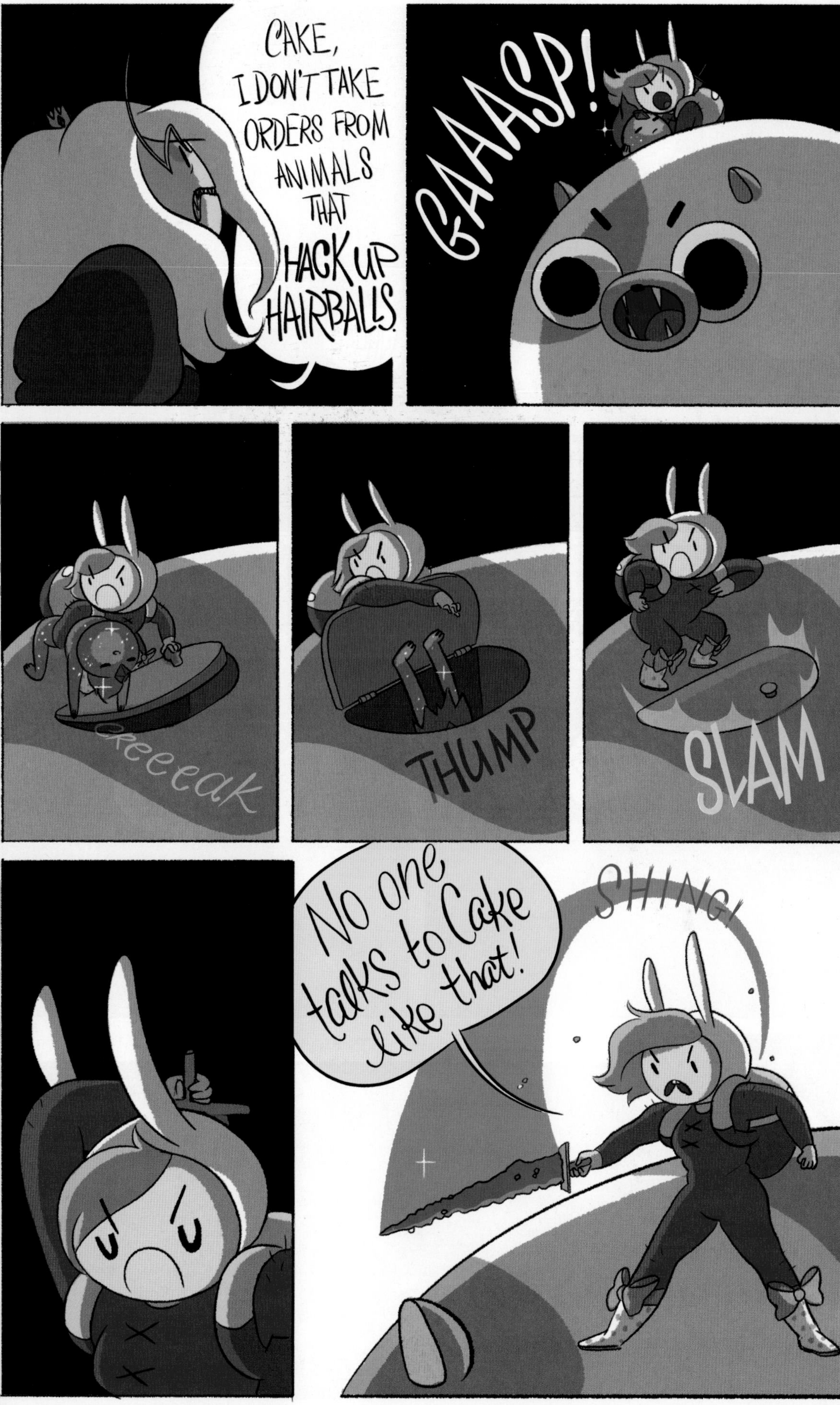
CAKE, I DON'T TAKE ORDERS FROM ANIMALS THAT HACK UP HAIRBALLS.
GAAASP!
Creeeak
THUMP
SLAM
SHING!
No one talks to Cake like that!

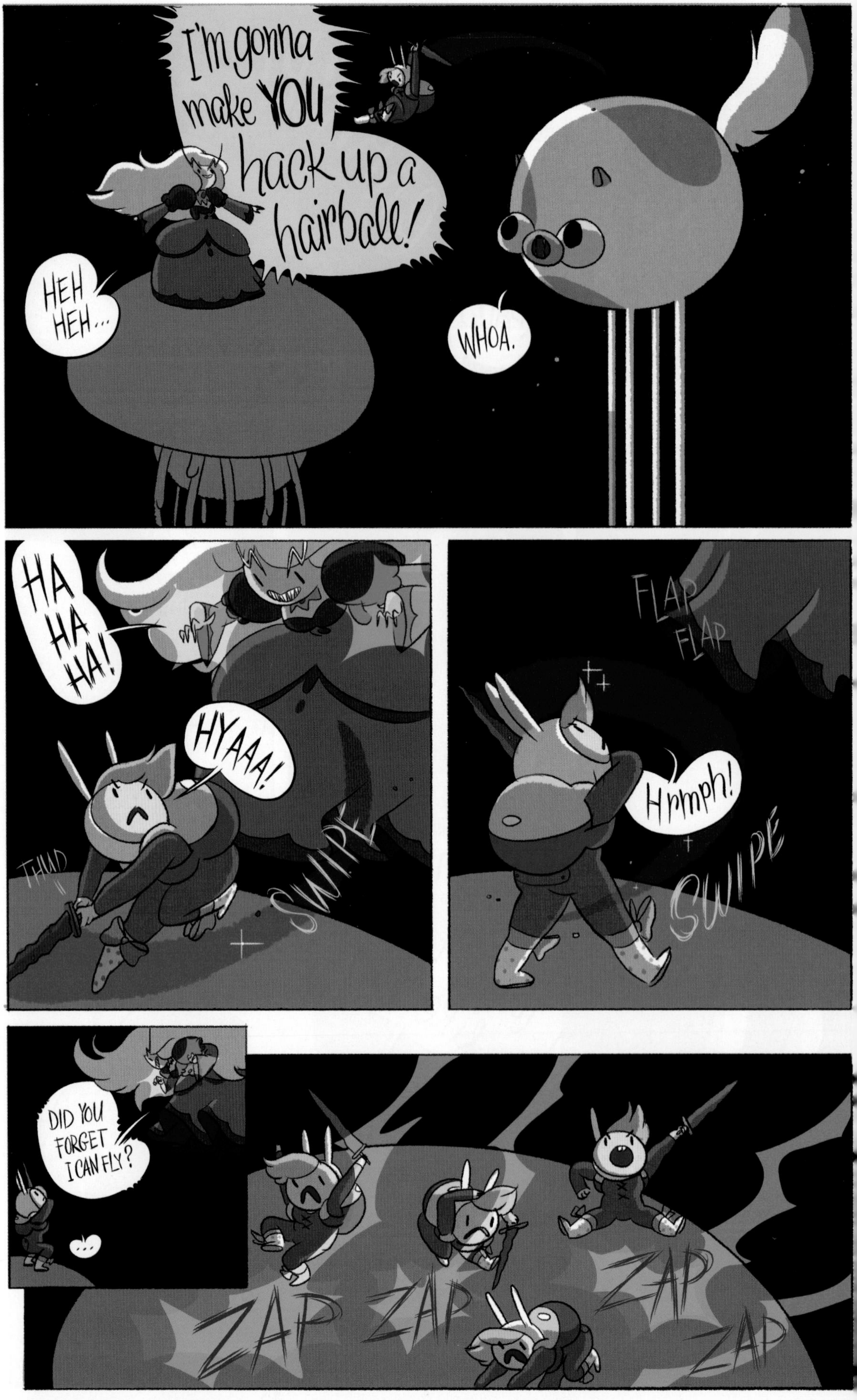
I'm gonna make YOU hack up a hairball!
HEH HEH...
WHOA.
HA HA HA!
HYAAA!
THUD
SWIPE
FLAP FLAP
Hrmph!
SWIPE
DID YOU FORGET I CAN FLY?
...
ZAP ZAP ZAP ZAP

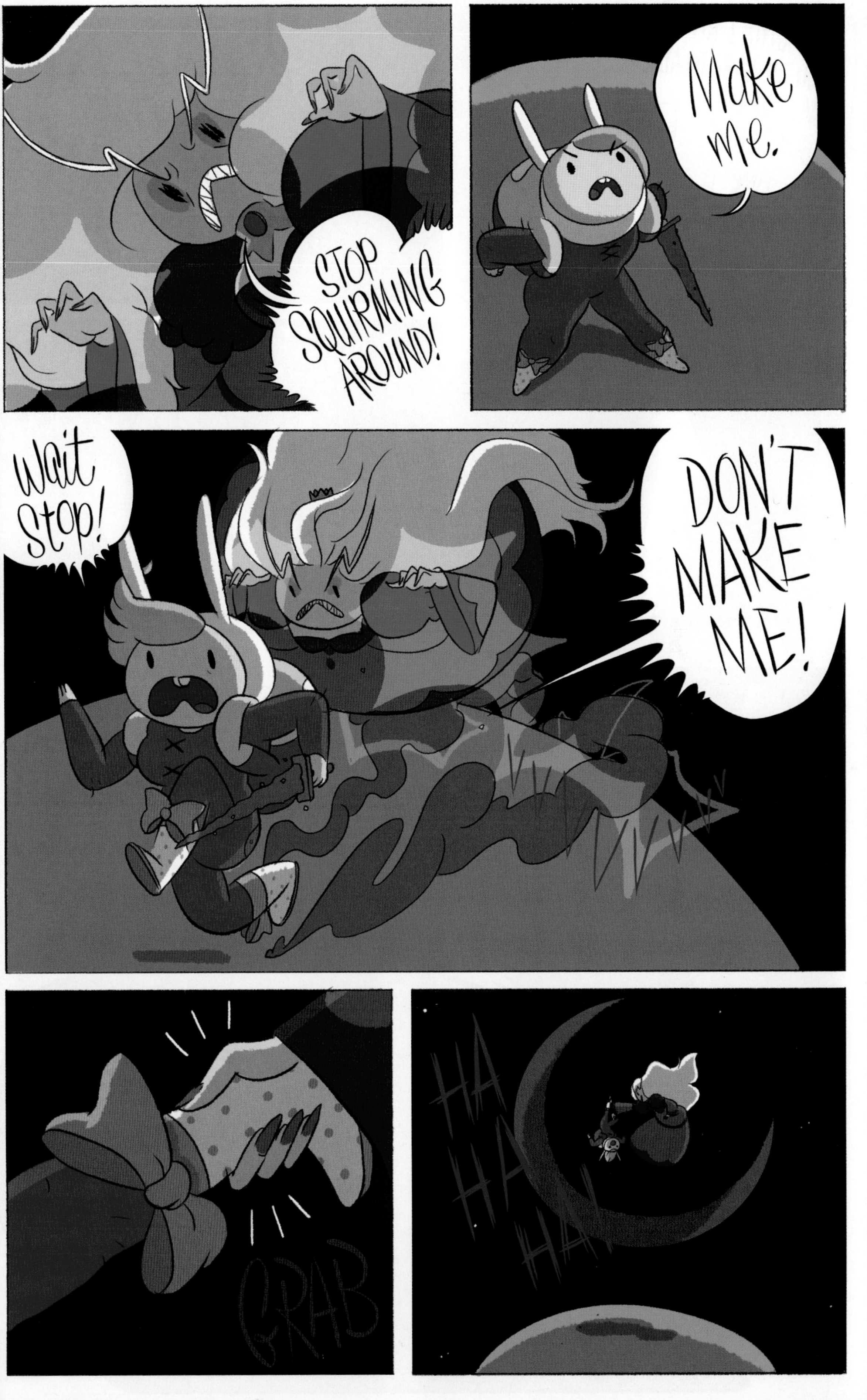
STOP SQUIRMING AROUND!
Make me.
Wait stop!
DON'T MAKE ME!
GRAB
HA HA HA

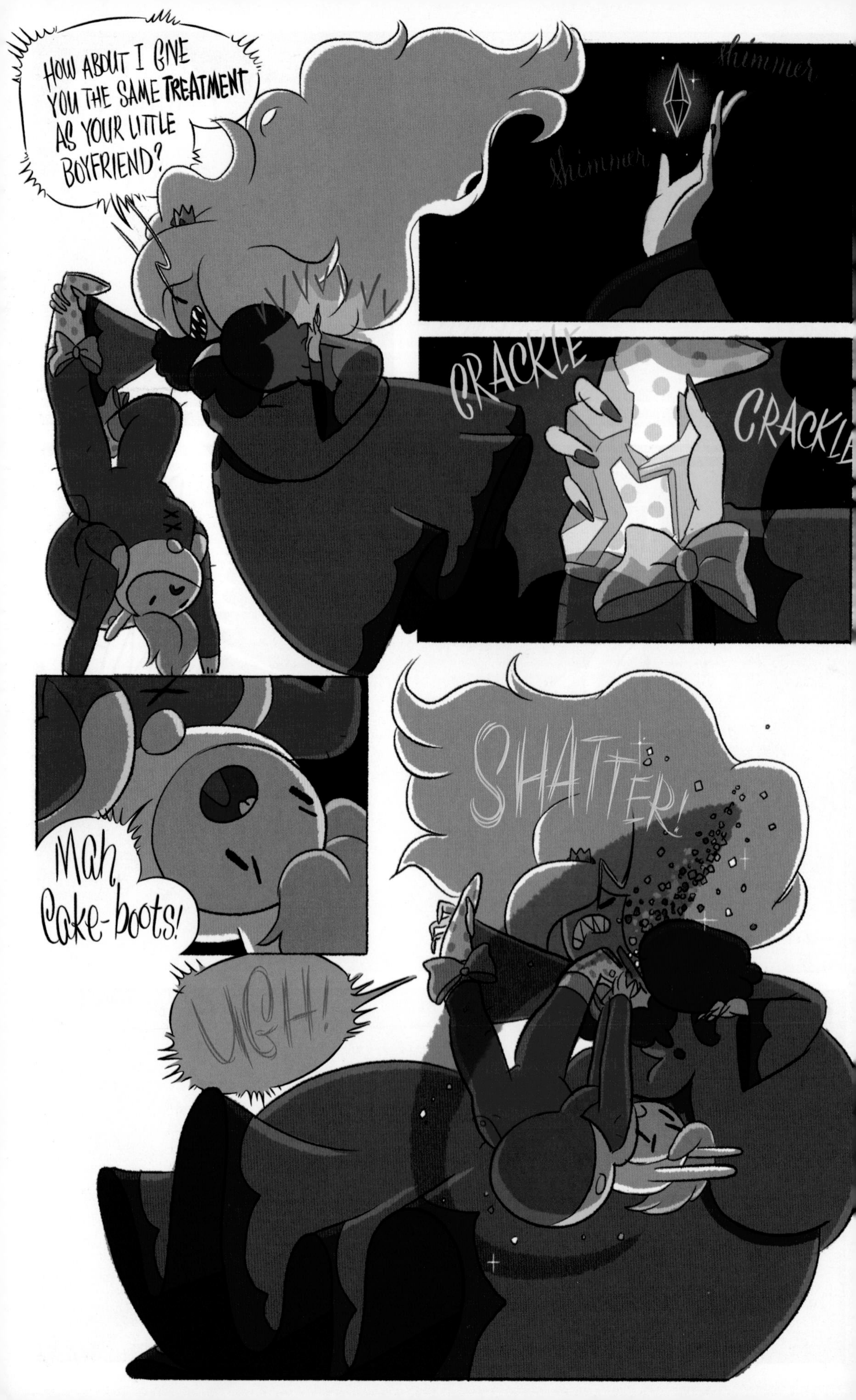
HOW ABOUT I GIVE YOU THE SAME TREATMENT AS YOUR LITTLE BOYFRIEND?
shimmer
shimmer
CRACKLE
CRACKLE
Mah Cake-boots!
SHATTER!
UGH!

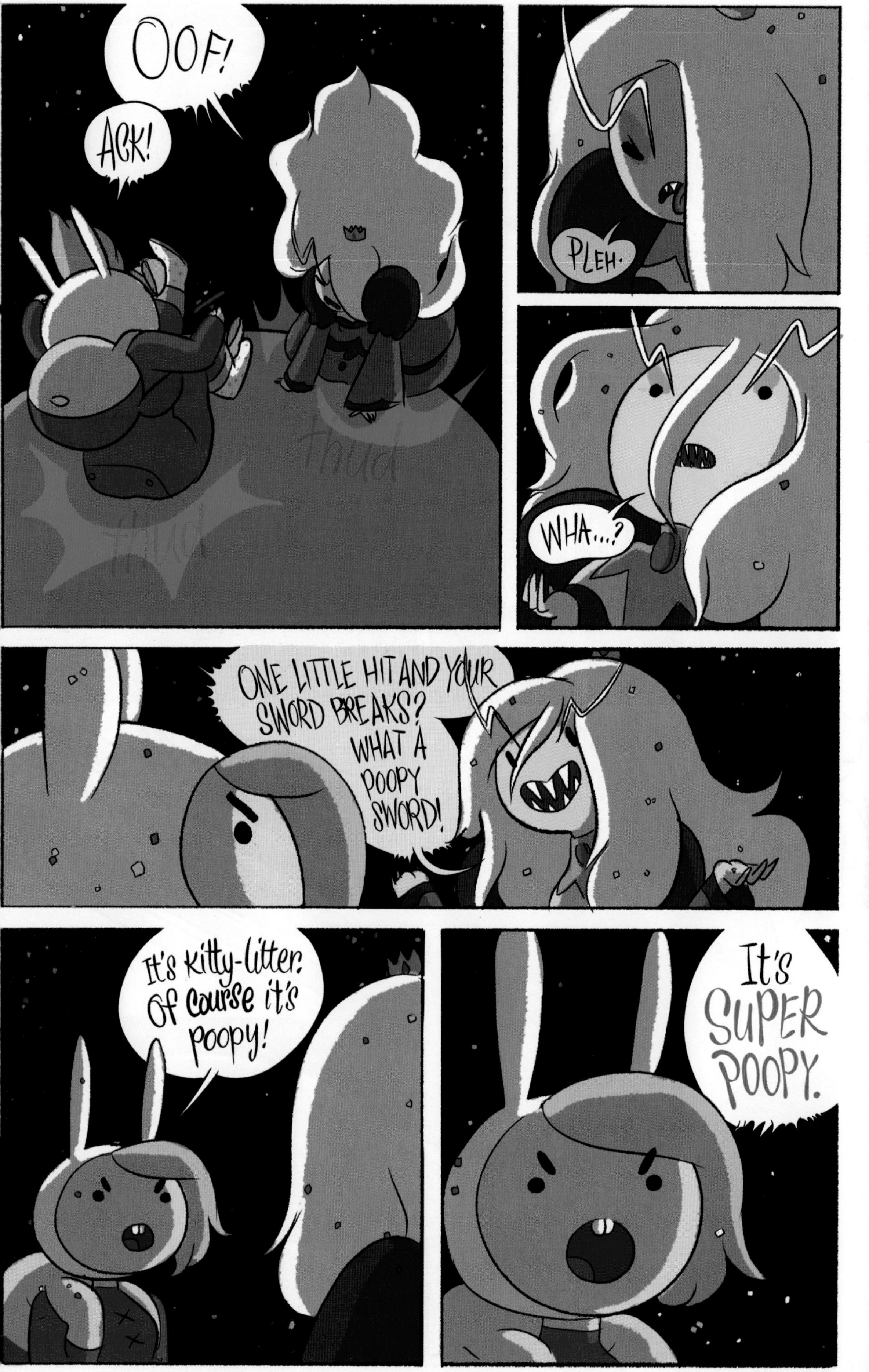
OOF!
ACK!
thud
thud
PLEH.
WHA...?
ONE LITTLE HIT AND YOUR SWORD BREAKS? WHAT A POOPY SWORD!
It's kitty-litter. Of course it's poopy!
It's SUPER POOPY.

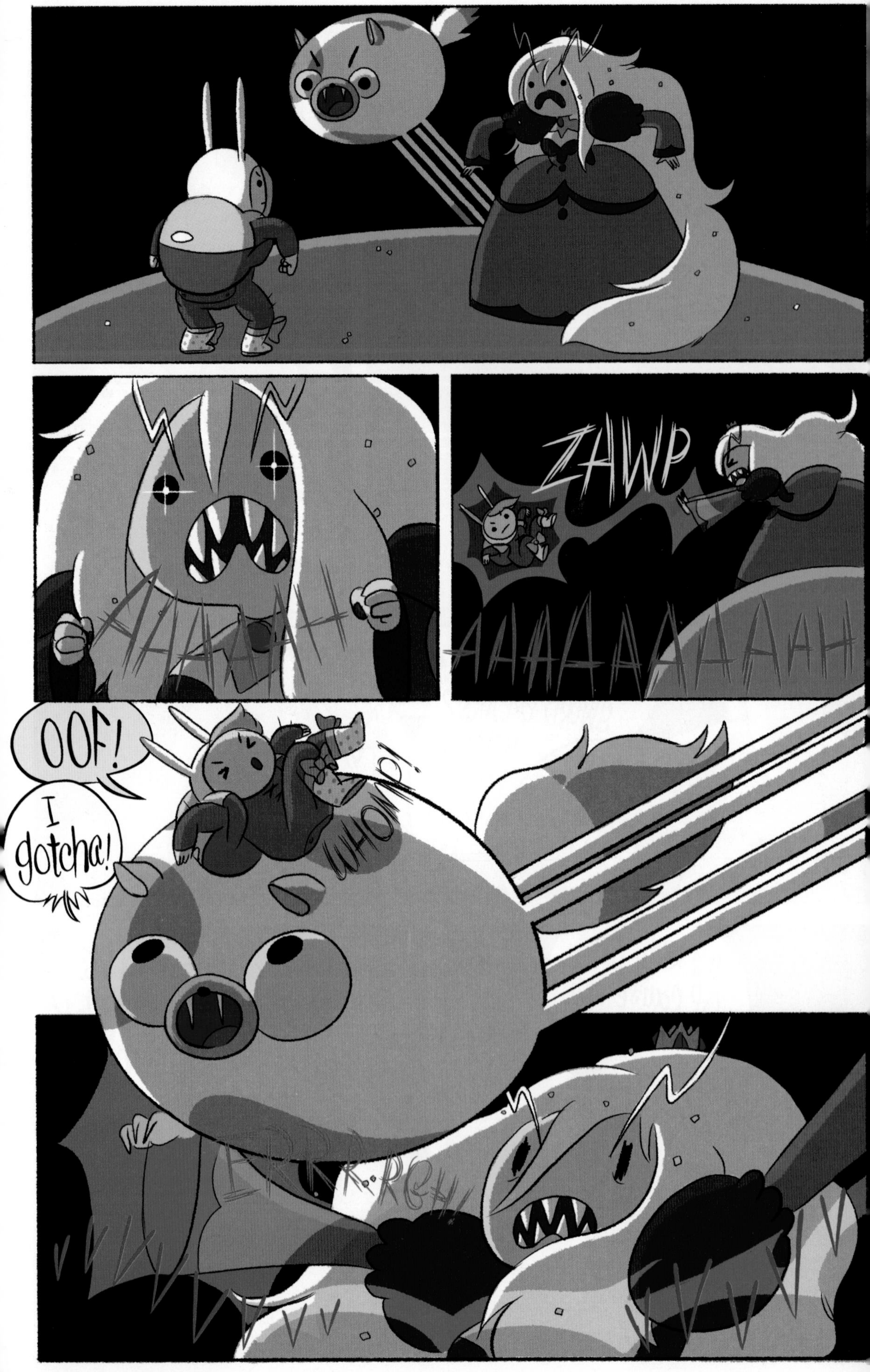
AAAAAAH
ZAWP
AAAAAAAAAAAH
OOF!
I gotcha!
WHOMP!
HRRRRCH!

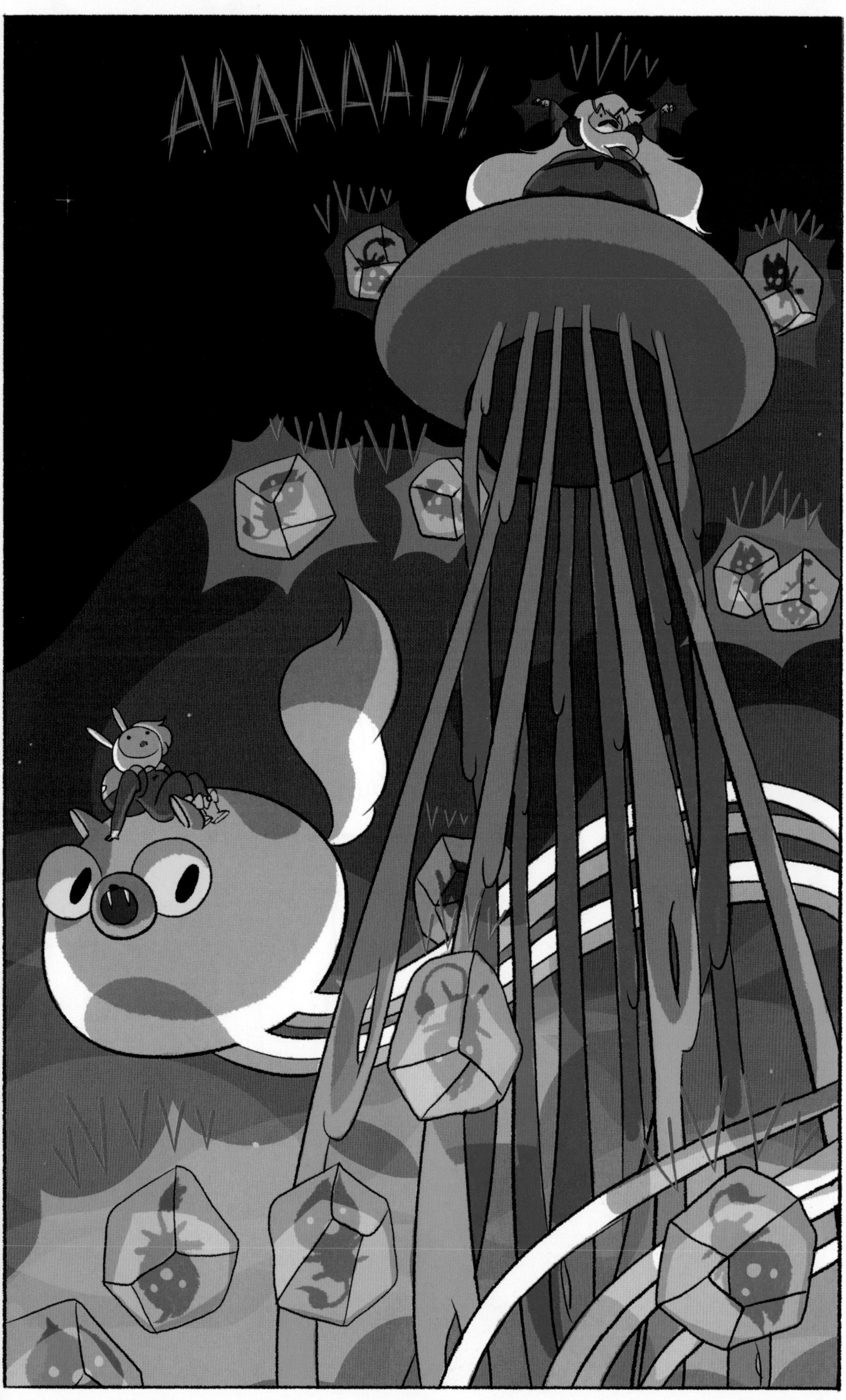
AAAAAAH!

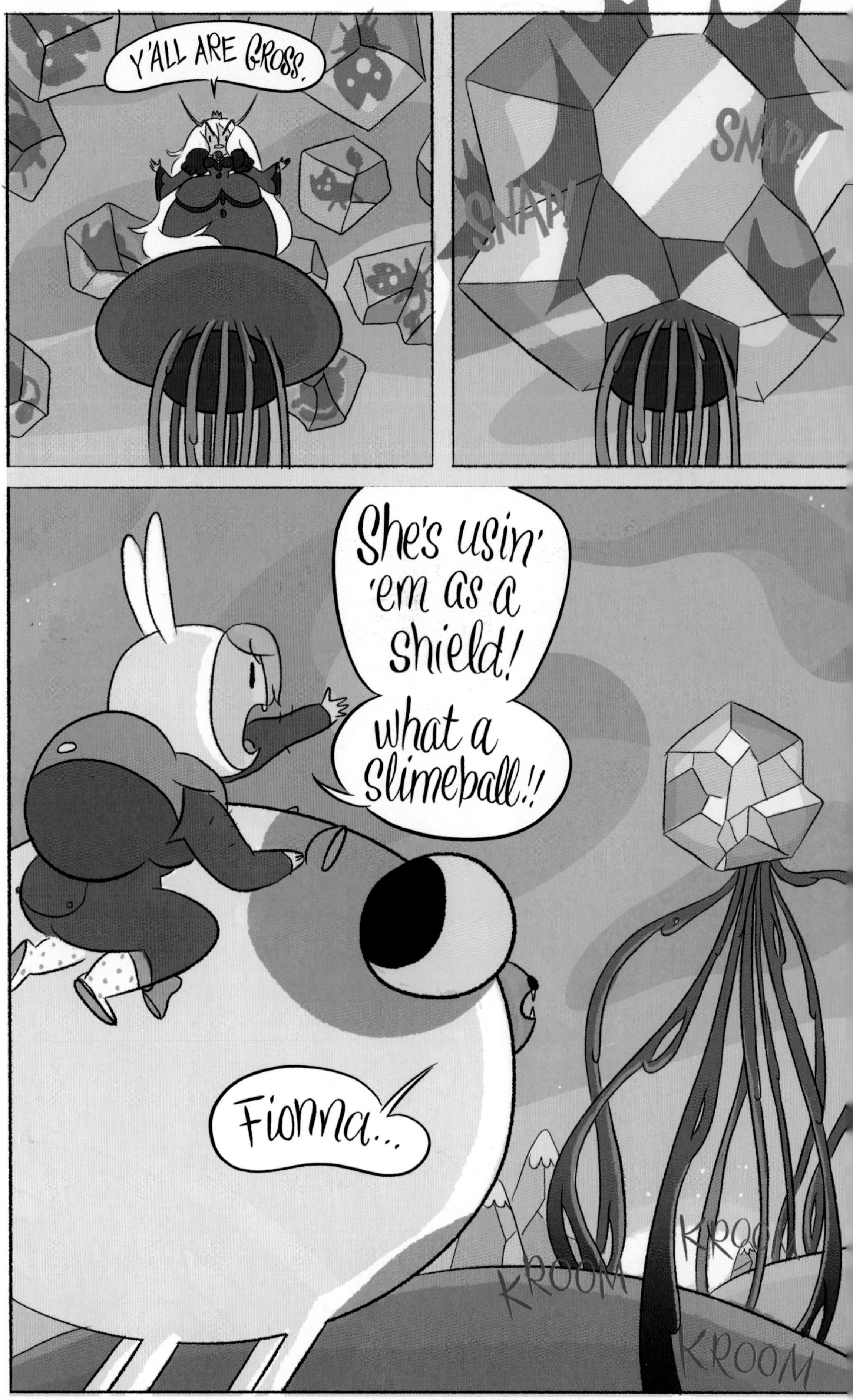
Y'ALL ARE GROSS.
SNAP!
SNAP!
She's usin' 'em as a shield!
what a slimeball!!
Fionna...
KROOM
KROOM
KROOM

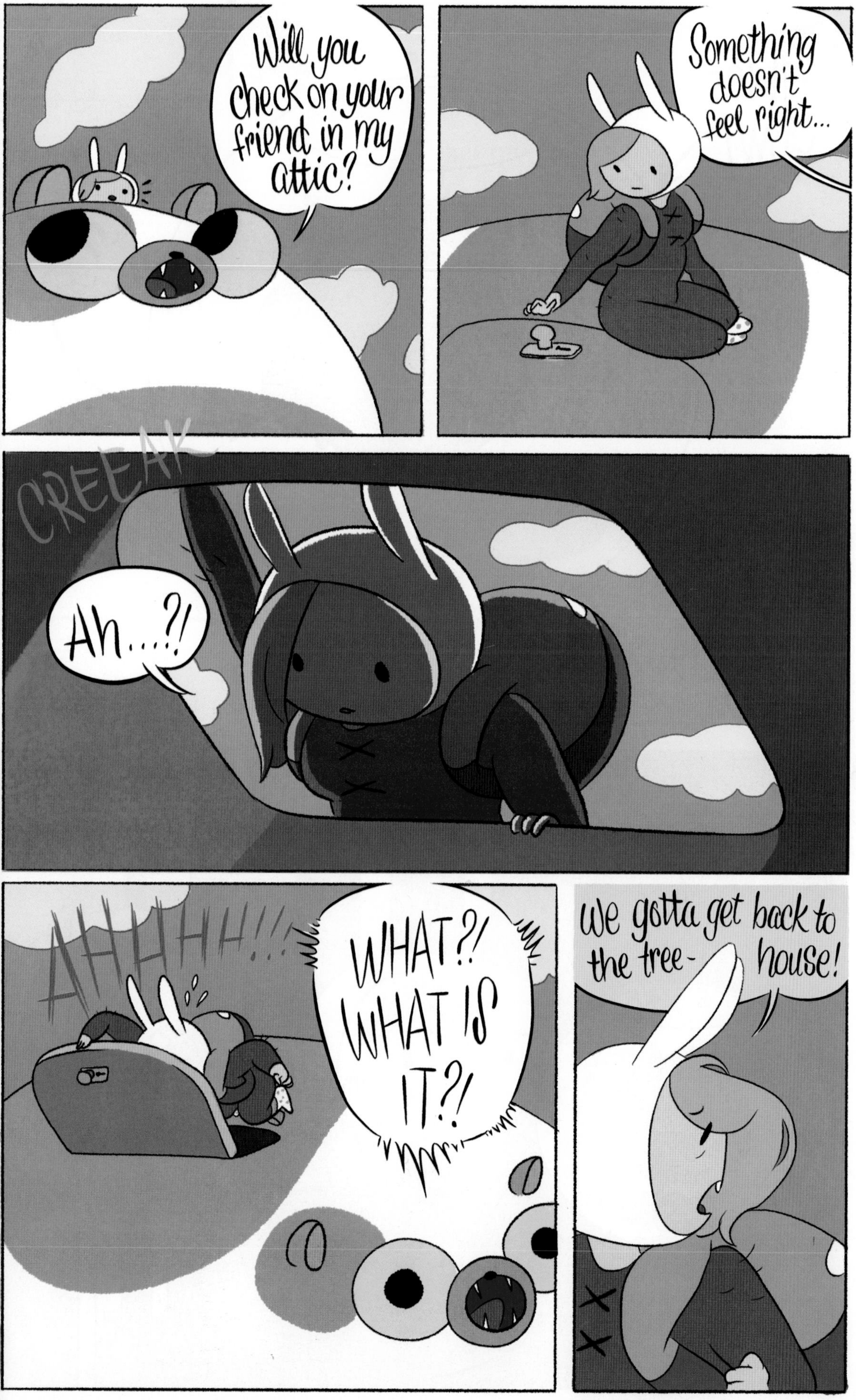
Will you check on your friend in my attic?
Something doesn't feel right...
CREEAK
Ah...?!
AHHHH!!!
WHAT?! WHAT IS IT?!
We gotta get back to the tree-house!

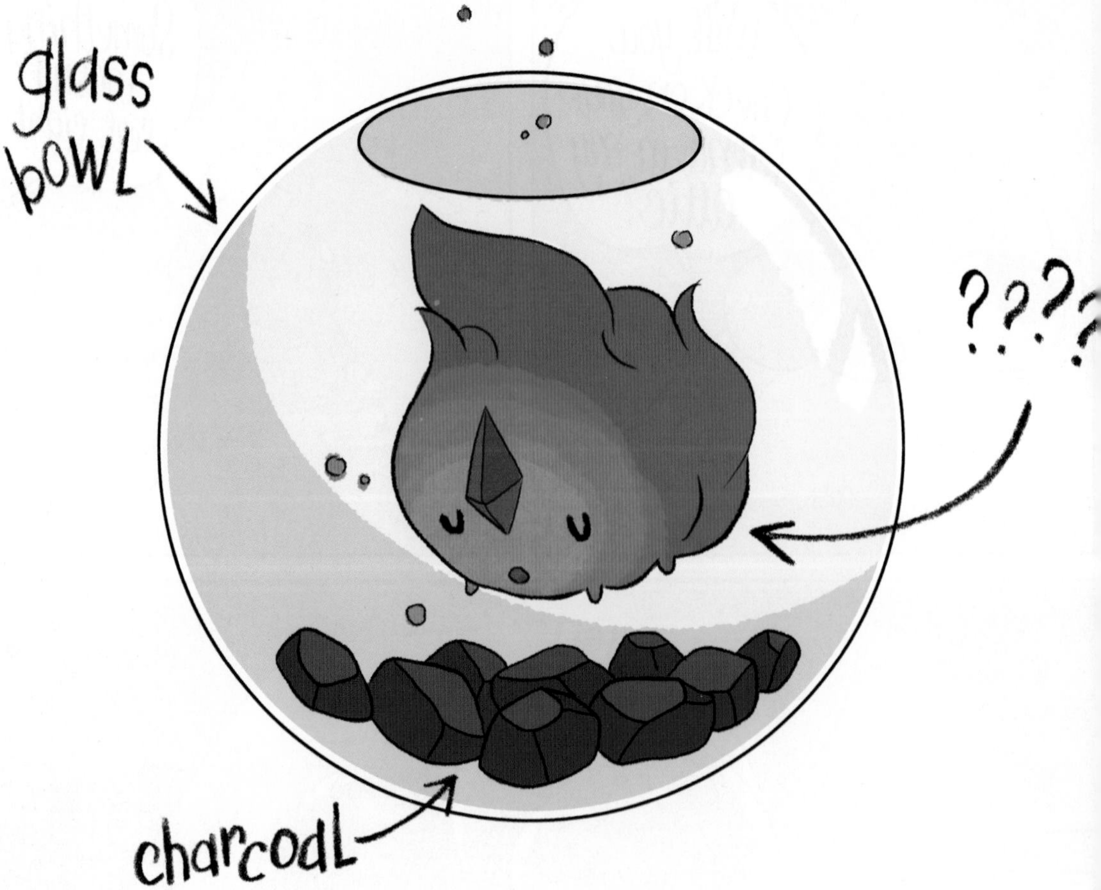
glass bowl
???
charcoal

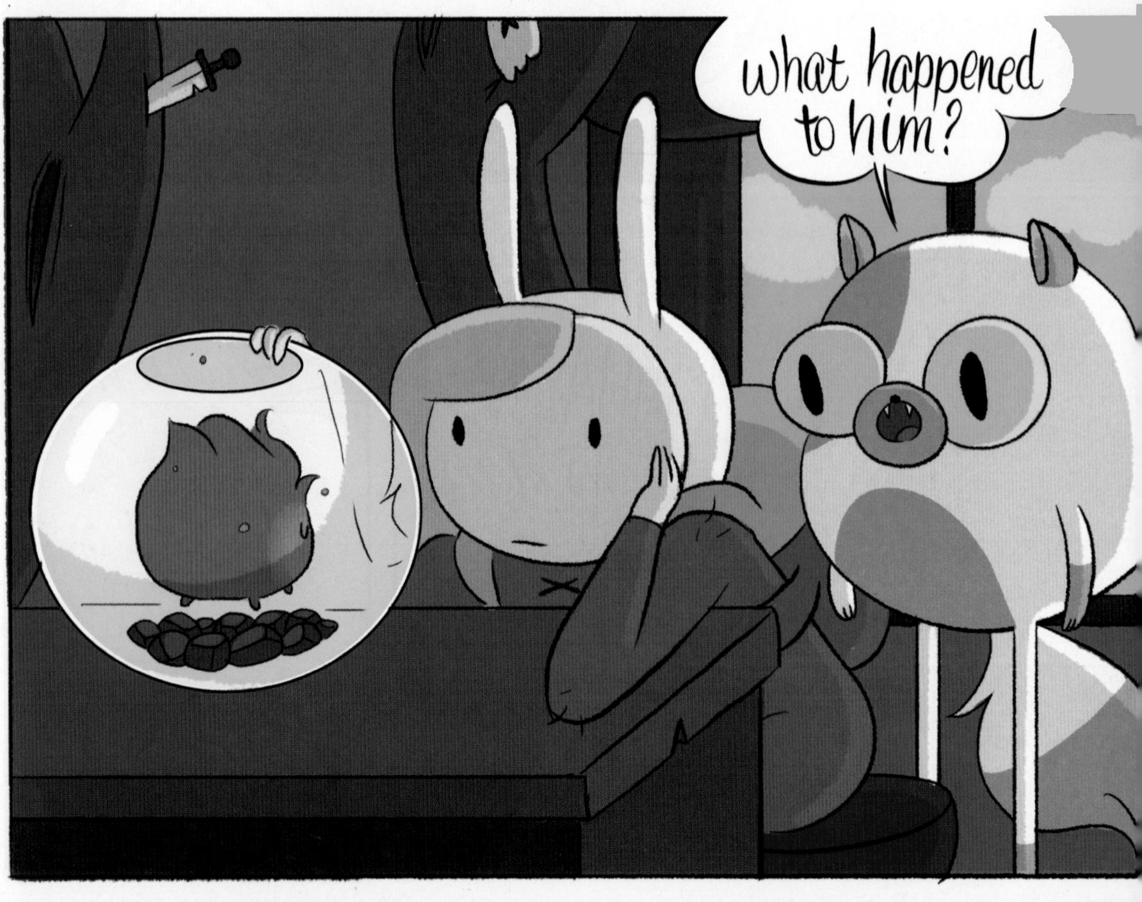
what happened to him?

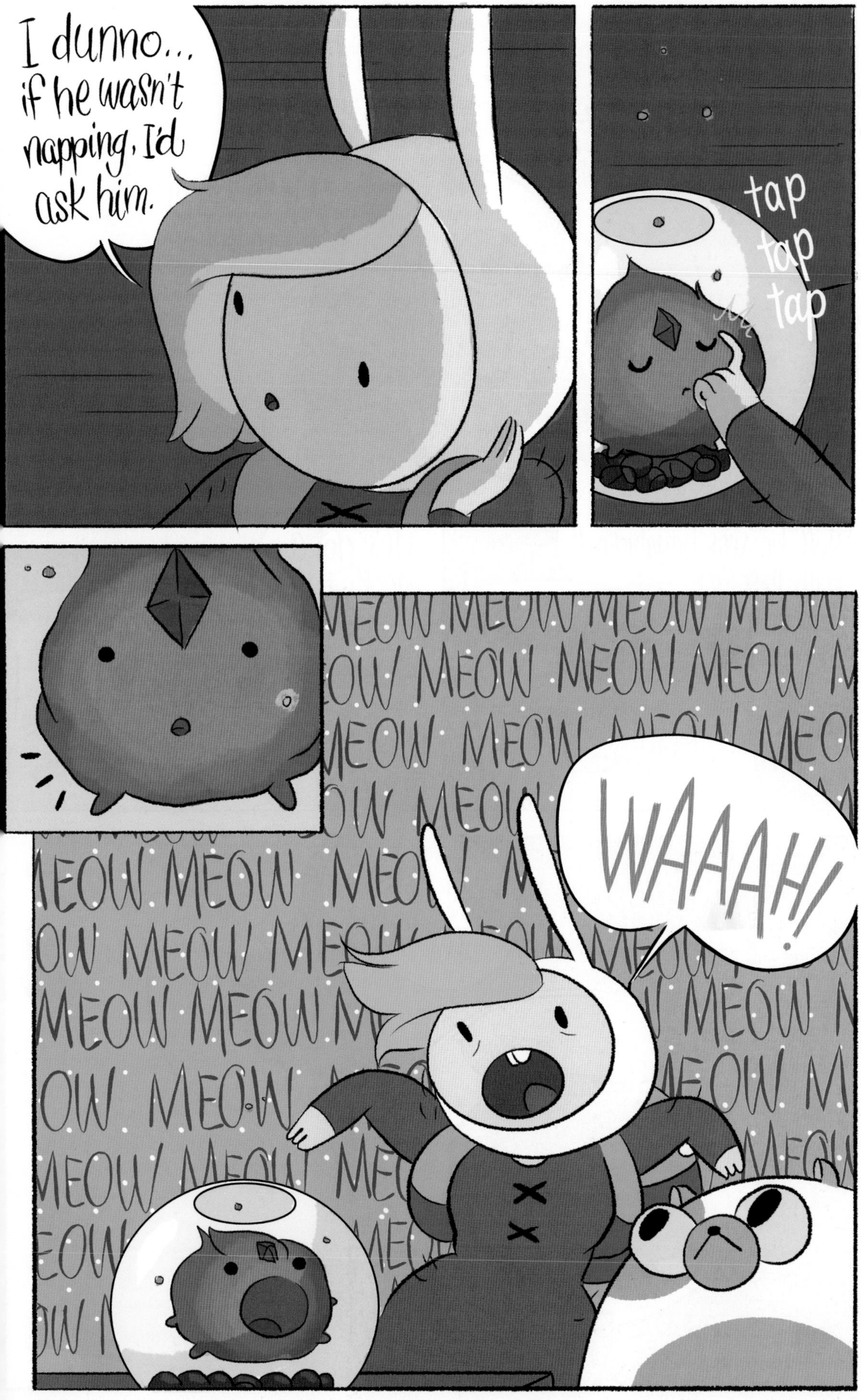
I dunno... if he wasn't napping, I'd ask him.
tap tap tap
MEOW MEOW MEOW MEOW
WAAAH!

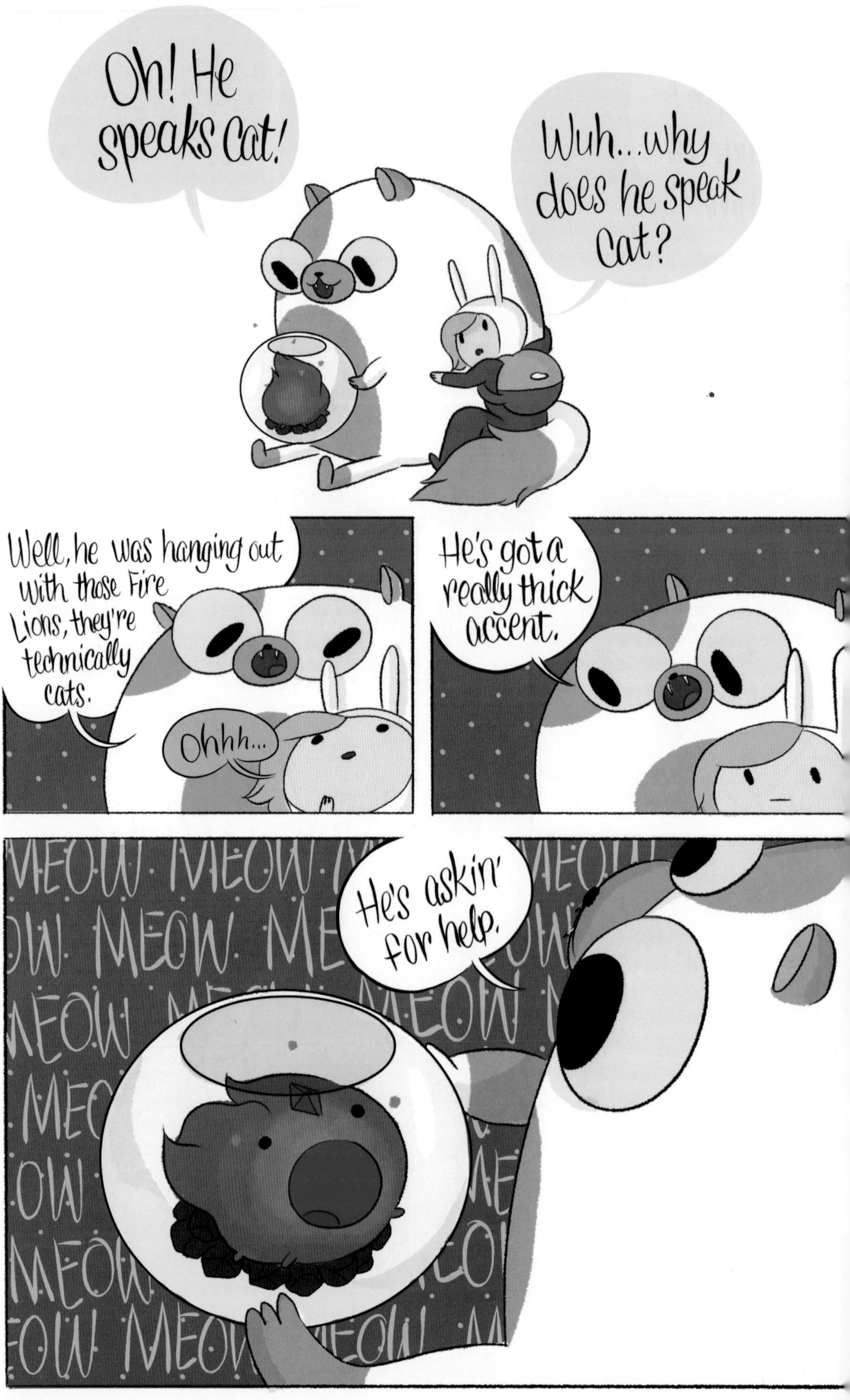
Oh! He speaks Cat!
Wuh...why does he speak Cat?
Well, he was hanging out with those Fire Lions, they're technically cats.
Ohhh...
He's got a really thick accent.
He's askin' for help.
MEOW MEOW MEOW

He says he needs
to find his Lion Pride so he
can protect his family's
babies from the rain
and the Ice Queen 'til
monsoon season is over...

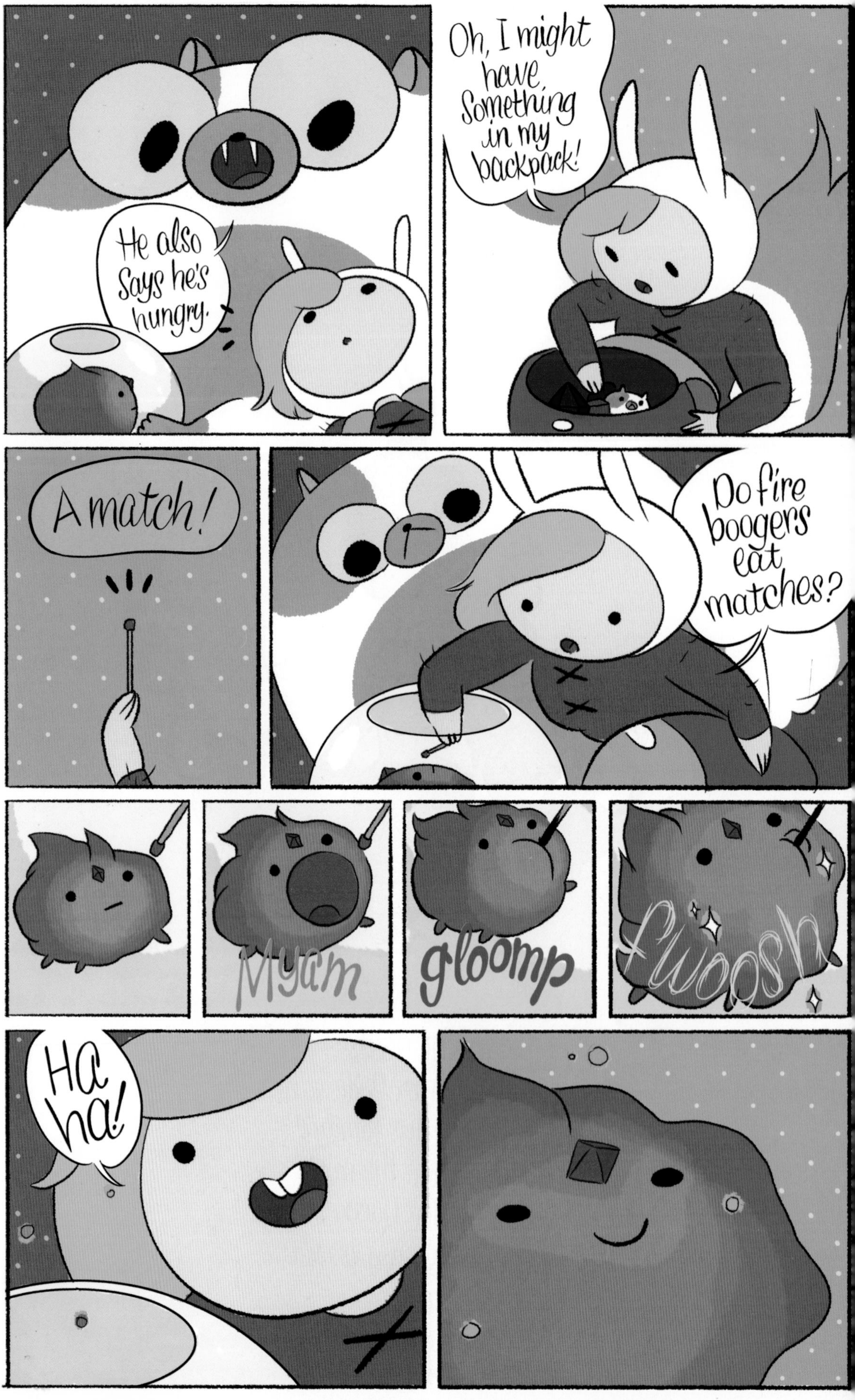
He also Says he's hungry.
Oh, I might have Something in my backpack!
A match!
Do fire boogers eat matches?
Myam
gloomp
fwoosh
Ha ha!

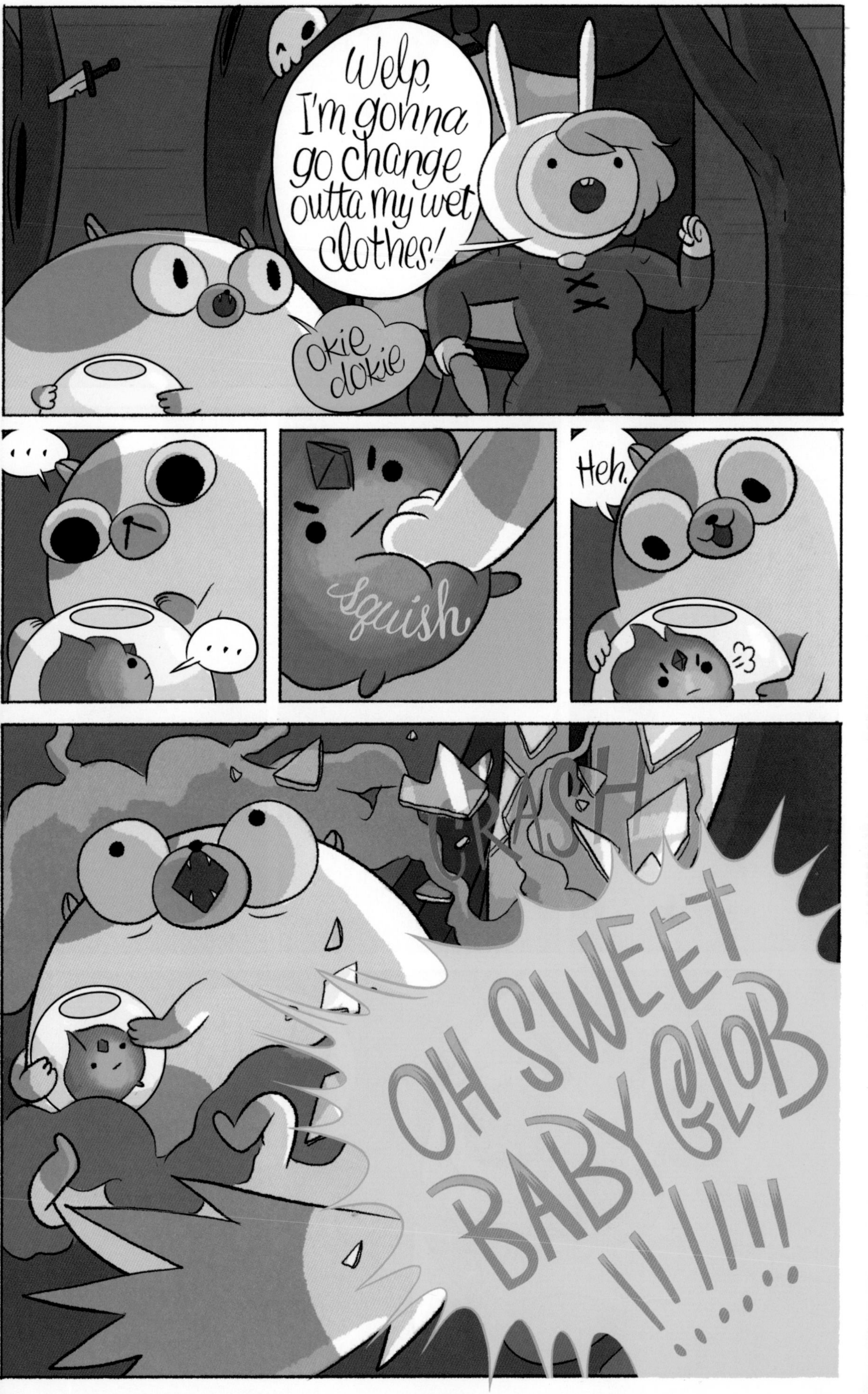
Welp, I'm gonna go change outta my wet clothes!
Okie dokie
...
...
Squish
Heh.
CRASH
OH SWEET BABY GLOB !!!!!!

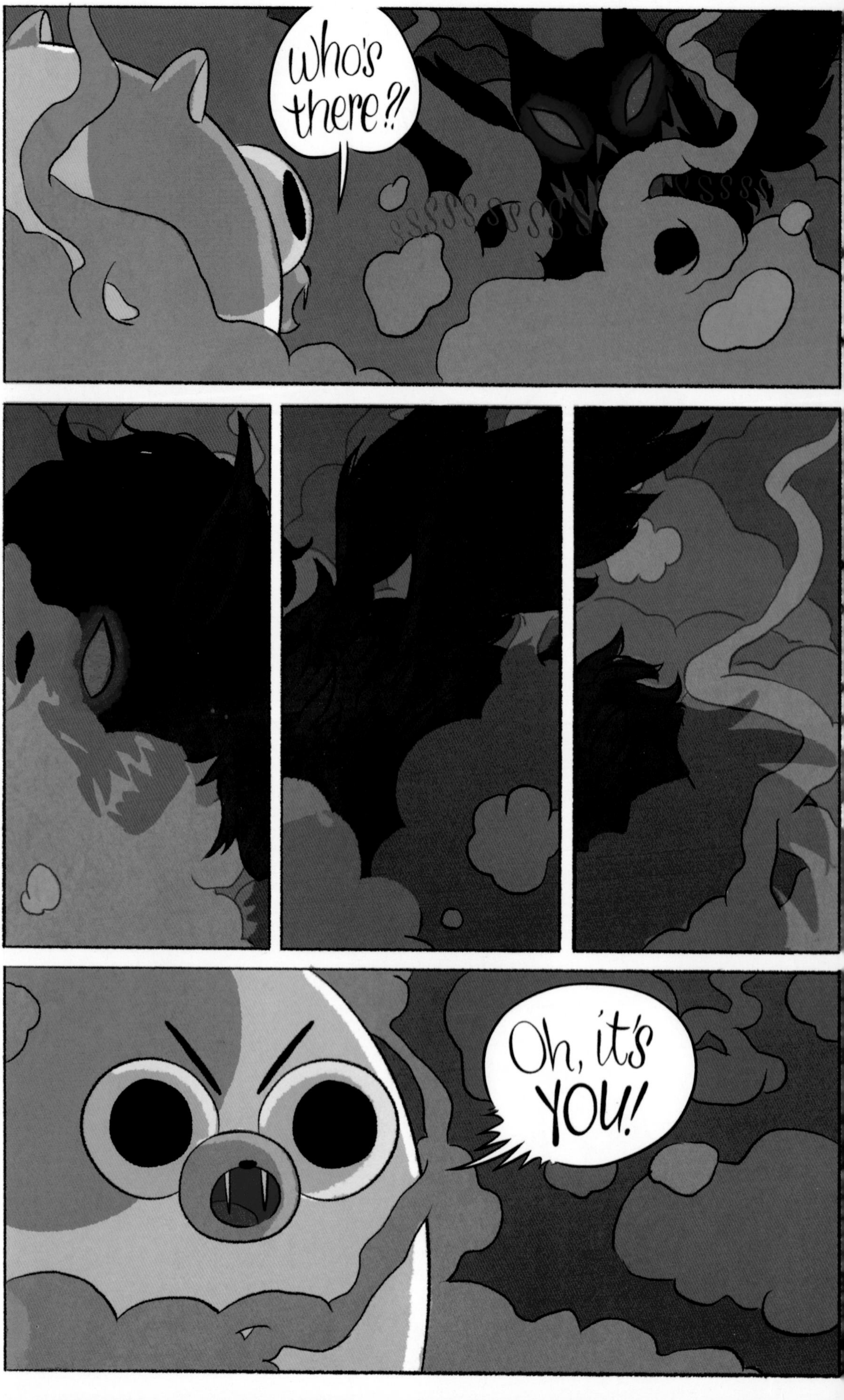
who's there?!
Oh, it's YOU!

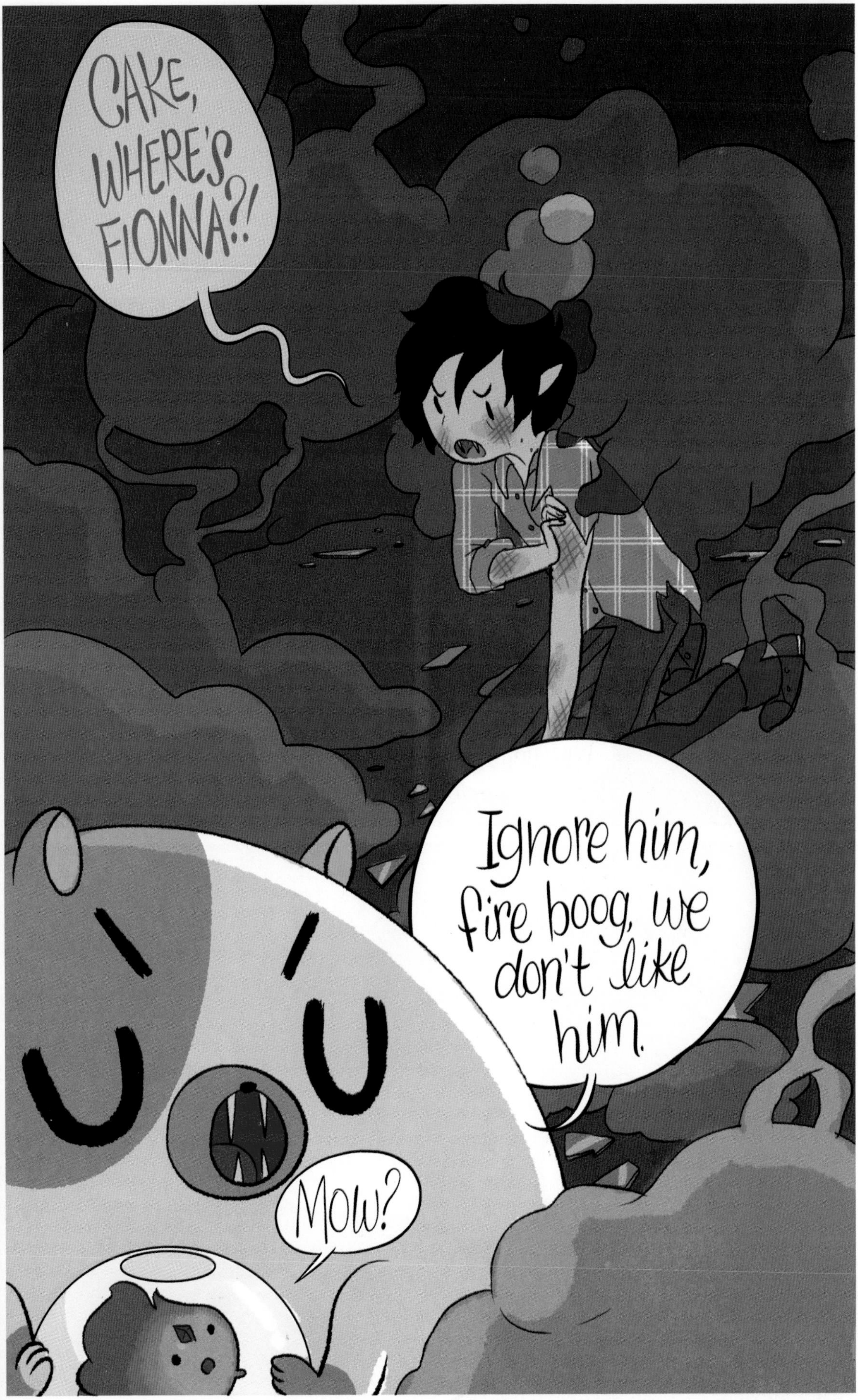
CAKE, WHERE'S FIONNA?!
Ignore him, fire boog, we don't like him.
Mow?

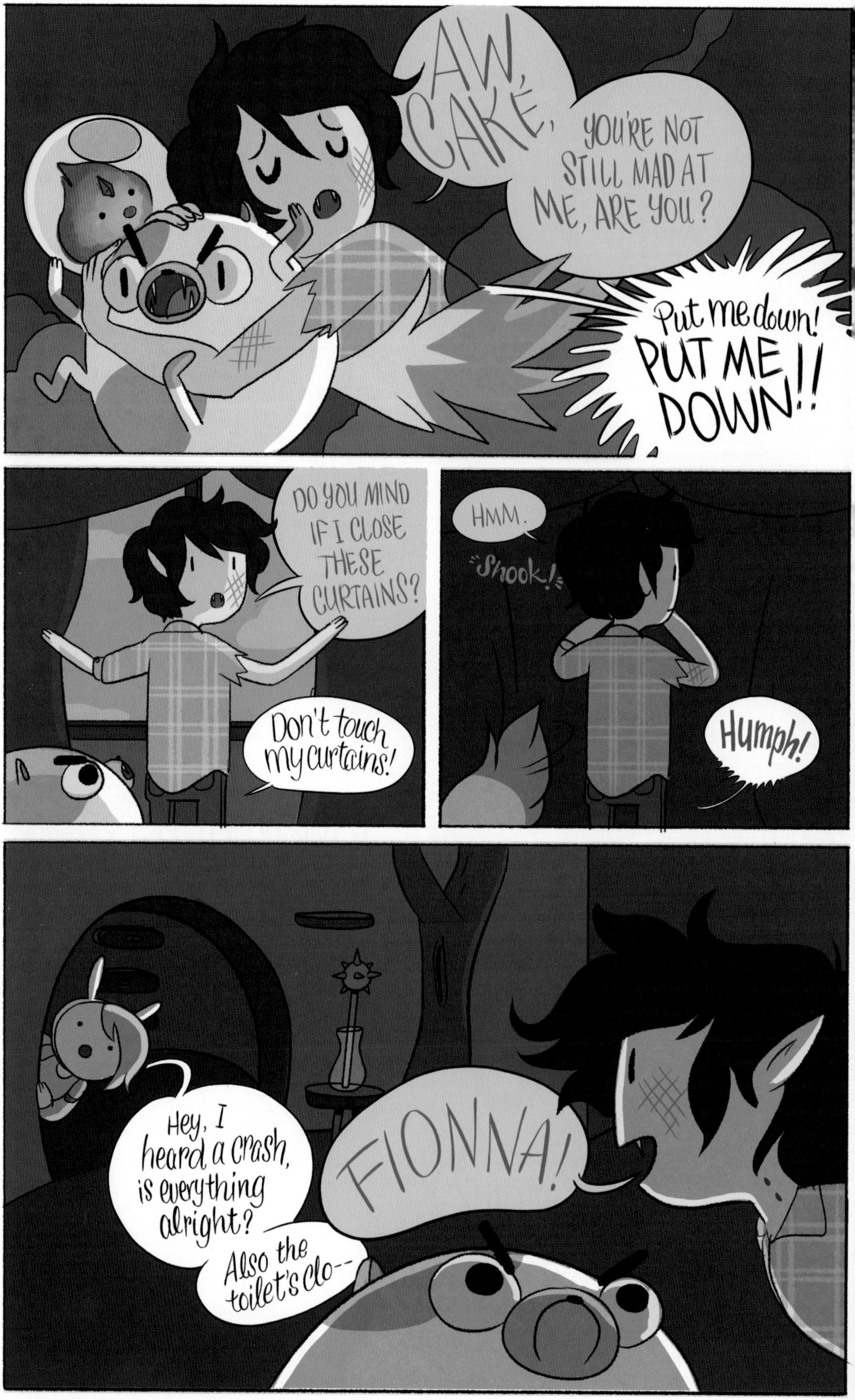
AW, CAKE,
YOU'RE NOT STILL MAD AT ME, ARE YOU?
Put me down! PUT ME DOWN!!
DO YOU MIND IF I CLOSE THESE CURTAINS?
Don't touch my curtains!
HMM.
Shook!
Humph!
Hey, I heard a crash, is everything alright?
Also the toilet's clo--
FIONNA!

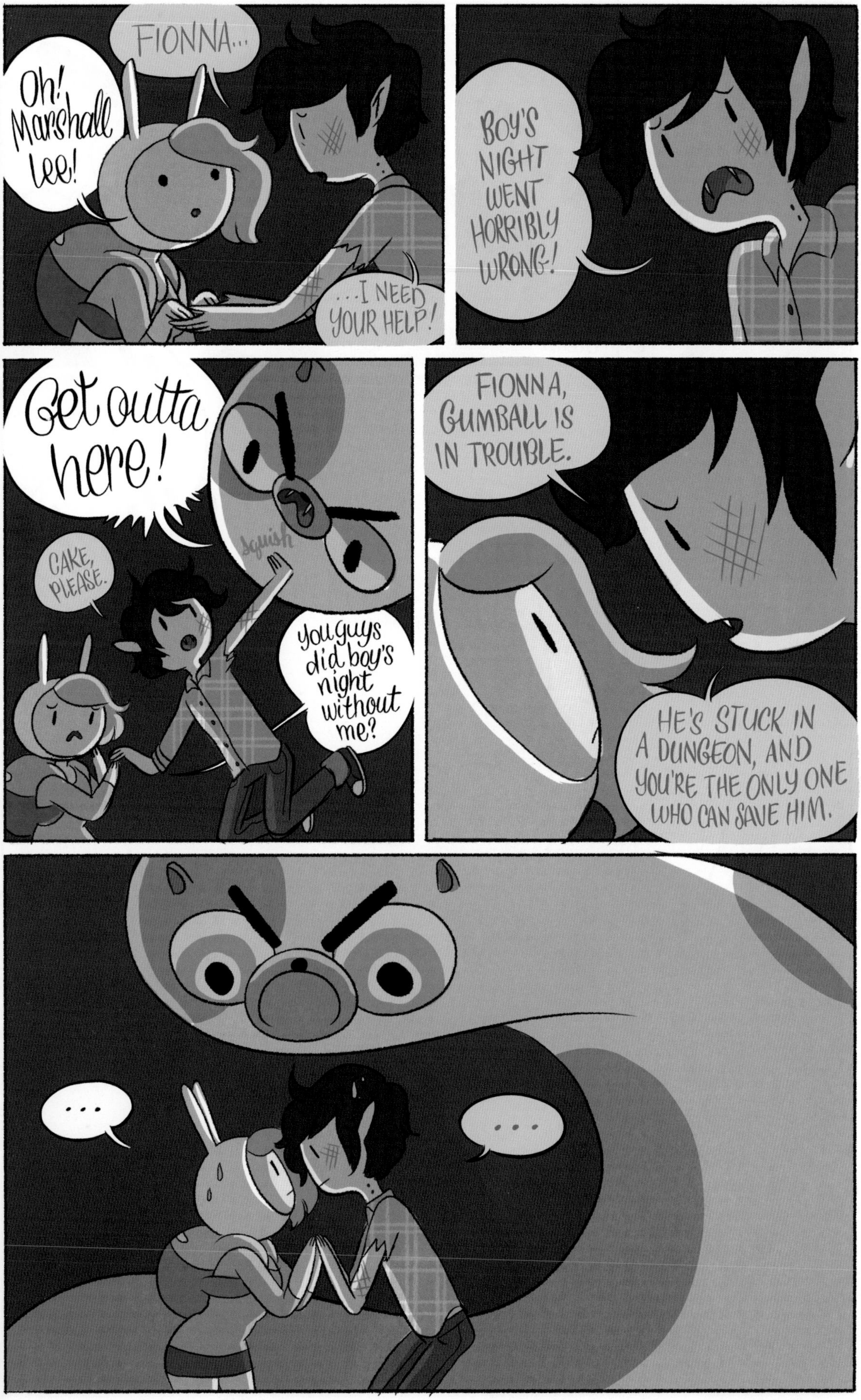
FIONNA...
Oh! Marshall Lee!
...I NEED YOUR HELP!
BOY'S NIGHT WENT HORRIBLY WRONG!
Get outta here!
Squish
CAKE, PLEASE.
You guys did boy's night without me?
FIONNA, GUMBALL IS IN TROUBLE.
HE'S STUCK IN A DUNGEON, AND YOU'RE THE ONLY ONE WHO CAN SAVE HIM.
...
...

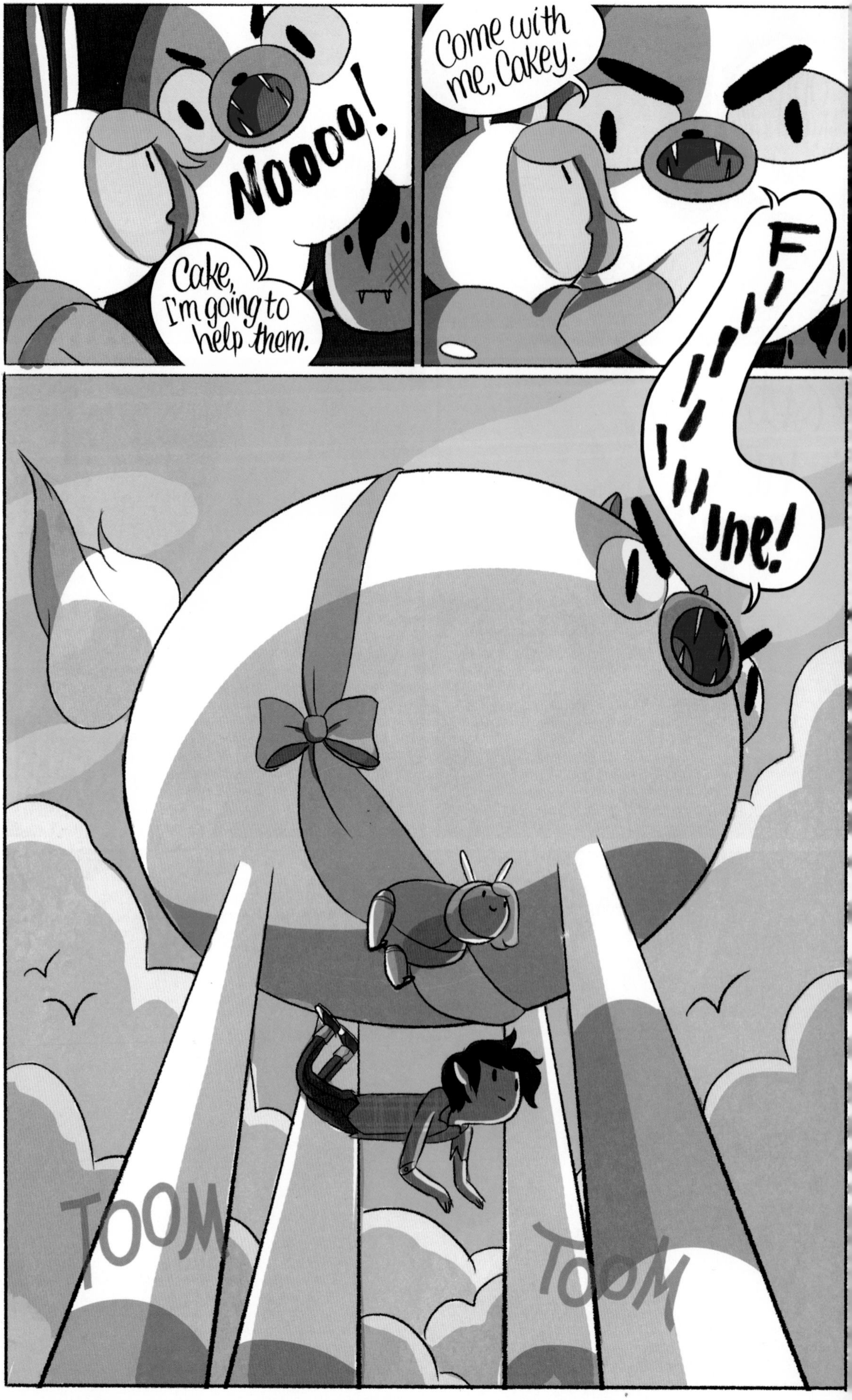
NOOOO!
Cake, I'm going to help them.
Come with me, Cakey.
F------ine!
TOOM
TOOM

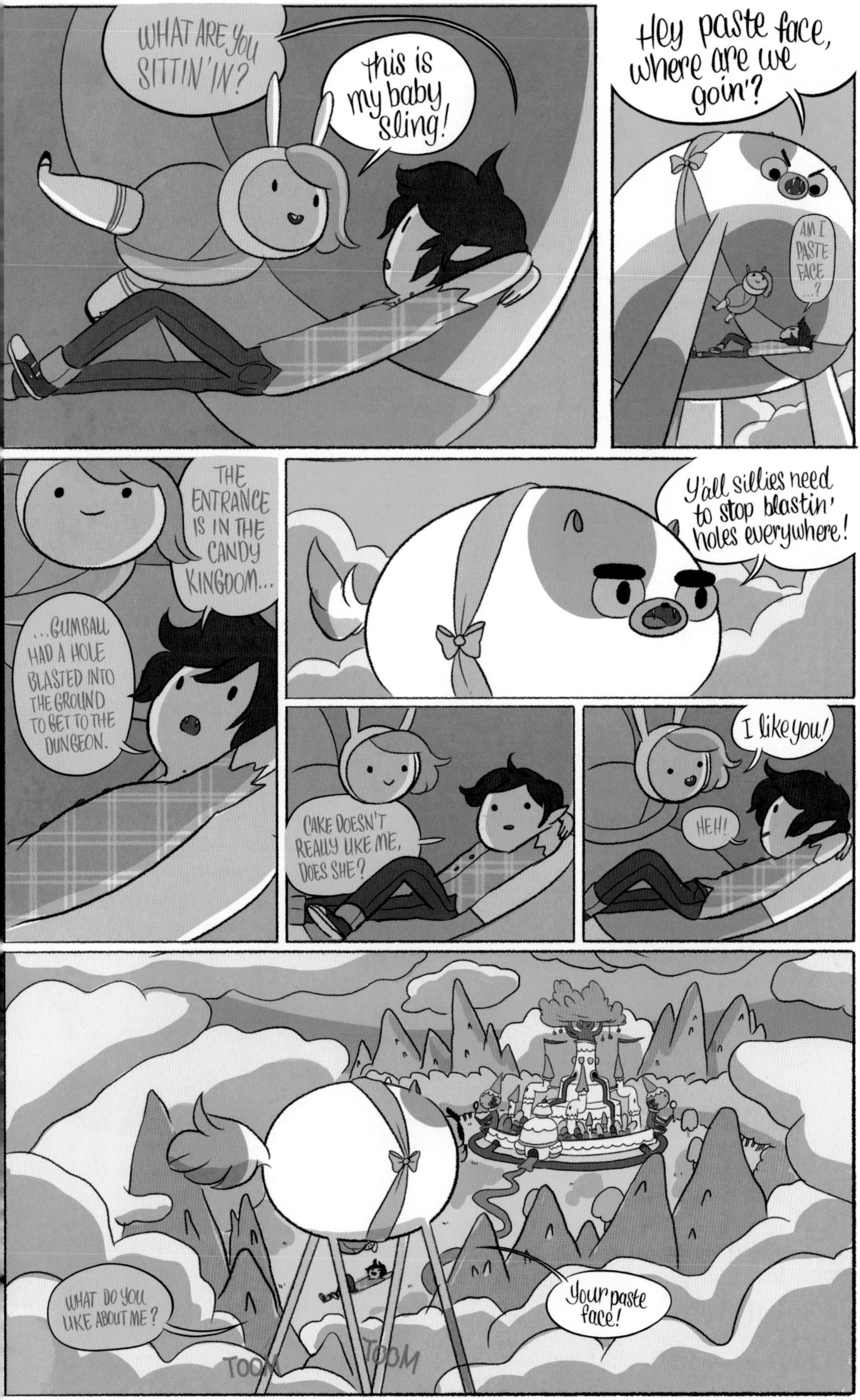
WHAT ARE YOU SITTIN' IN?
this is my baby sling!
Hey paste face, where are we goin'?
AM I PASTE FACE ...?
THE ENTRANCE IS IN THE CANDY KINGDOM...
...GUMBALL HAD A HOLE BLASTED INTO THE GROUND TO GET TO THE DUNGEON.
Y'all sillies need to stop blastin' holes everywhere!
CAKE DOESN'T REALLY LIKE ME, DOES SHE?
I like you!
HEH!
WHAT DO YOU LIKE ABOUT ME?
Your paste face!
TOOM
TOOM

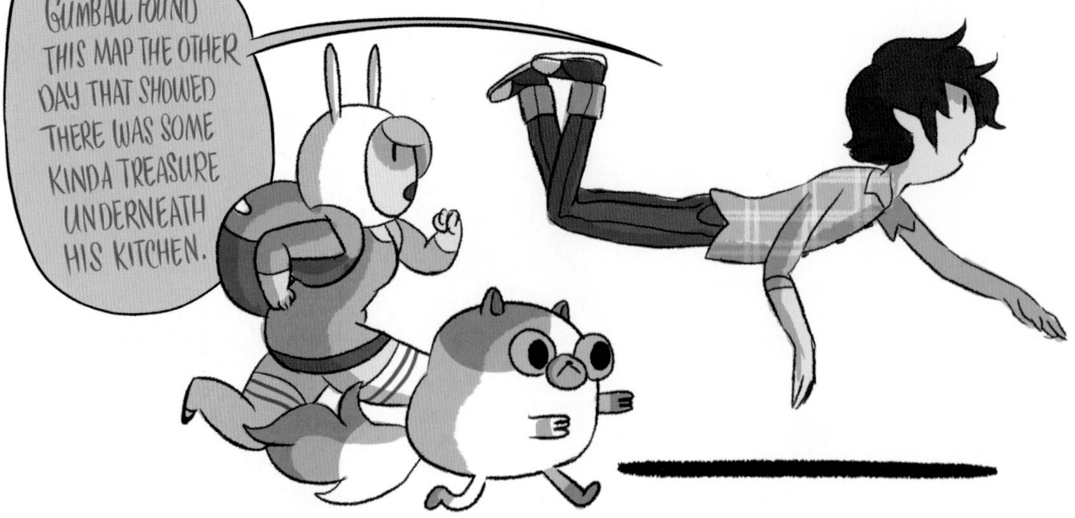
GUMBALL FOUND THIS MAP THE OTHER DAY THAT SHOWED THERE WAS SOME KINDA TREASURE UNDERNEATH HIS KITCHEN.

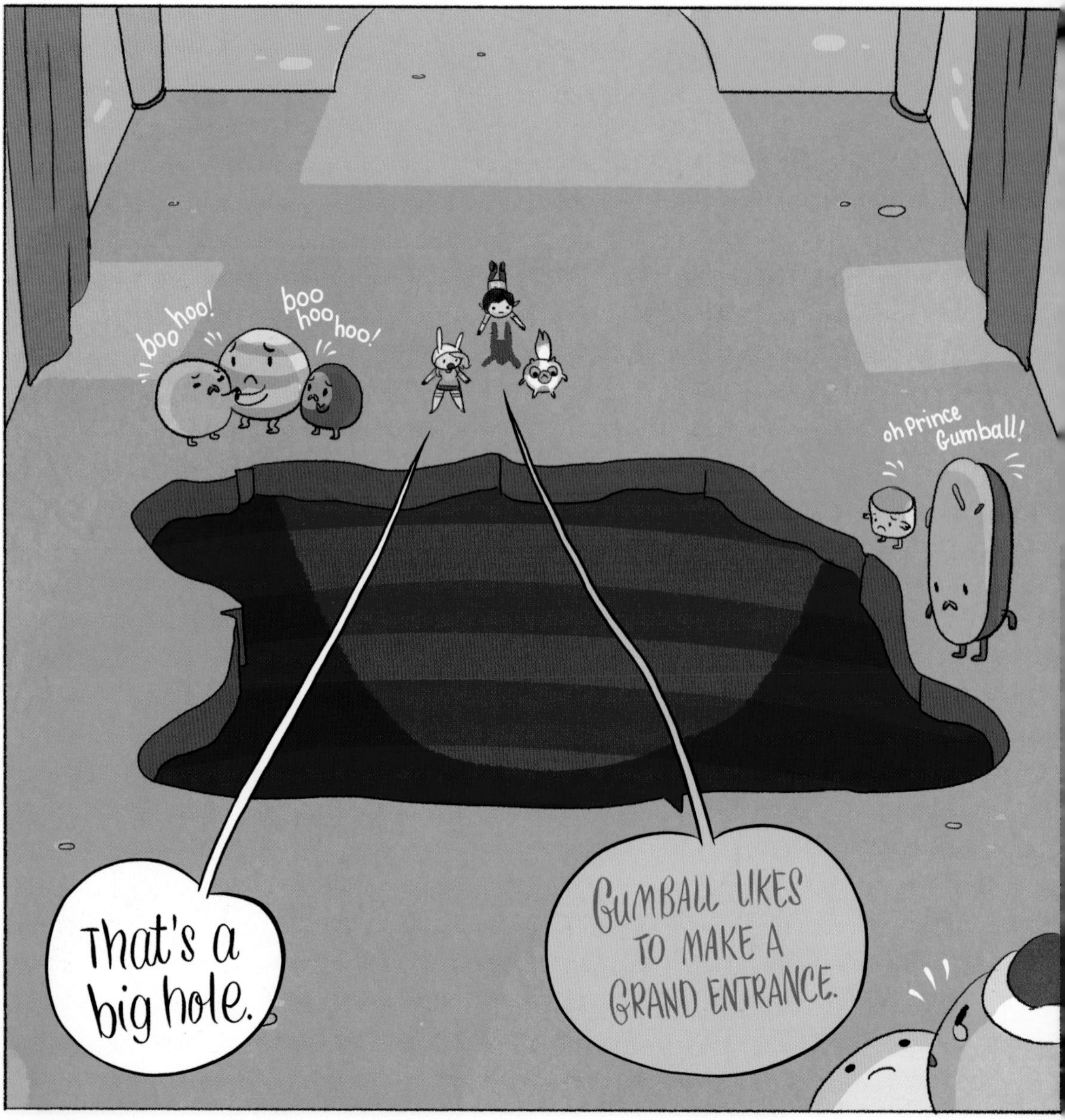
boo hoo!
boo hoo hoo!
oh Prince Gumball!
That's a big hole.
GUMBALL LIKES TO MAKE A GRAND ENTRANCE.

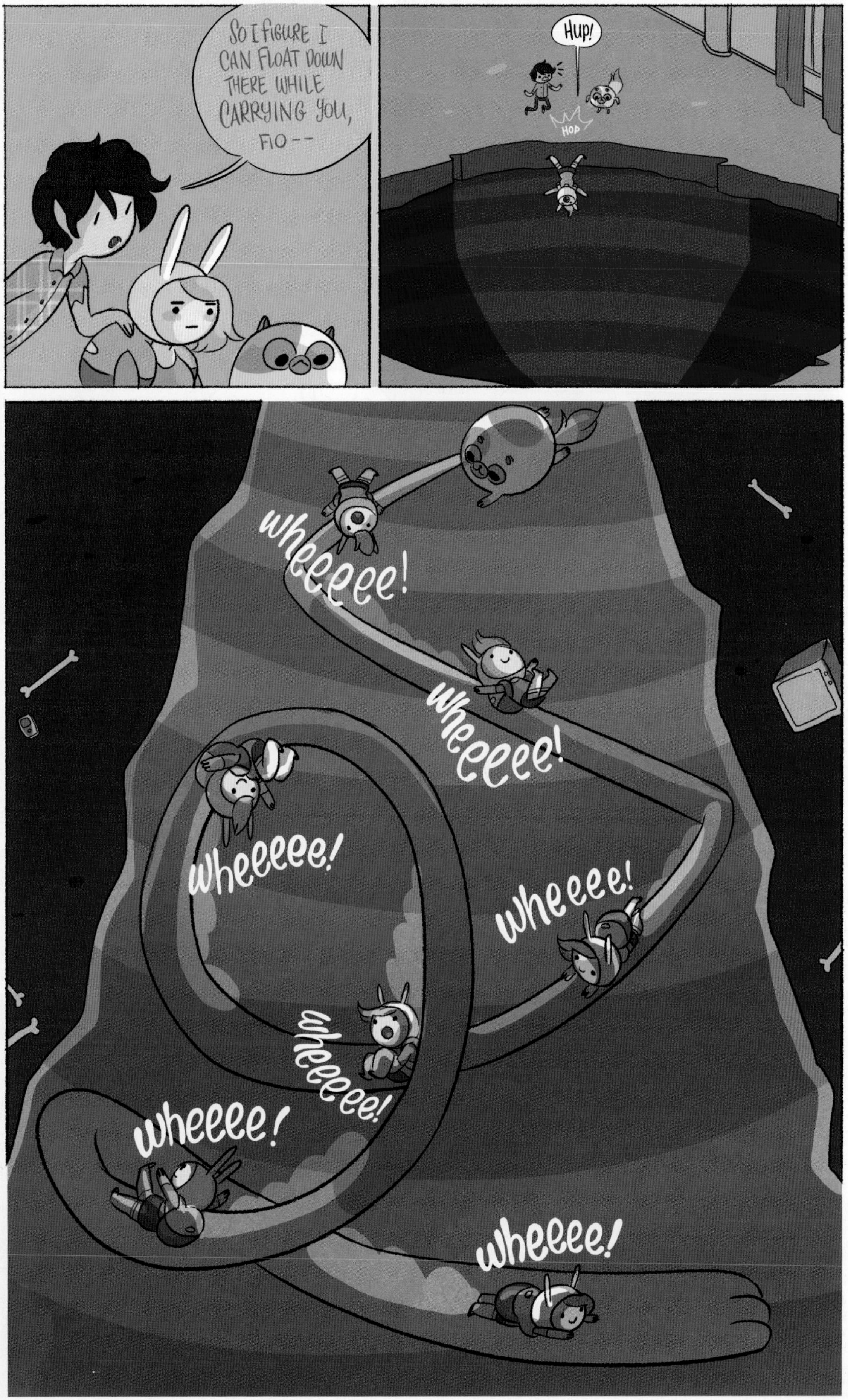

SO I FIGURE I CAN FLOAT DOWN THERE WHILE CARRYING YOU, FIO--
Hup!
HOP
wheeeee!
wheeeee!
wheeeee!
wheeee!
wheeeee!
wheeee!
wheeee!

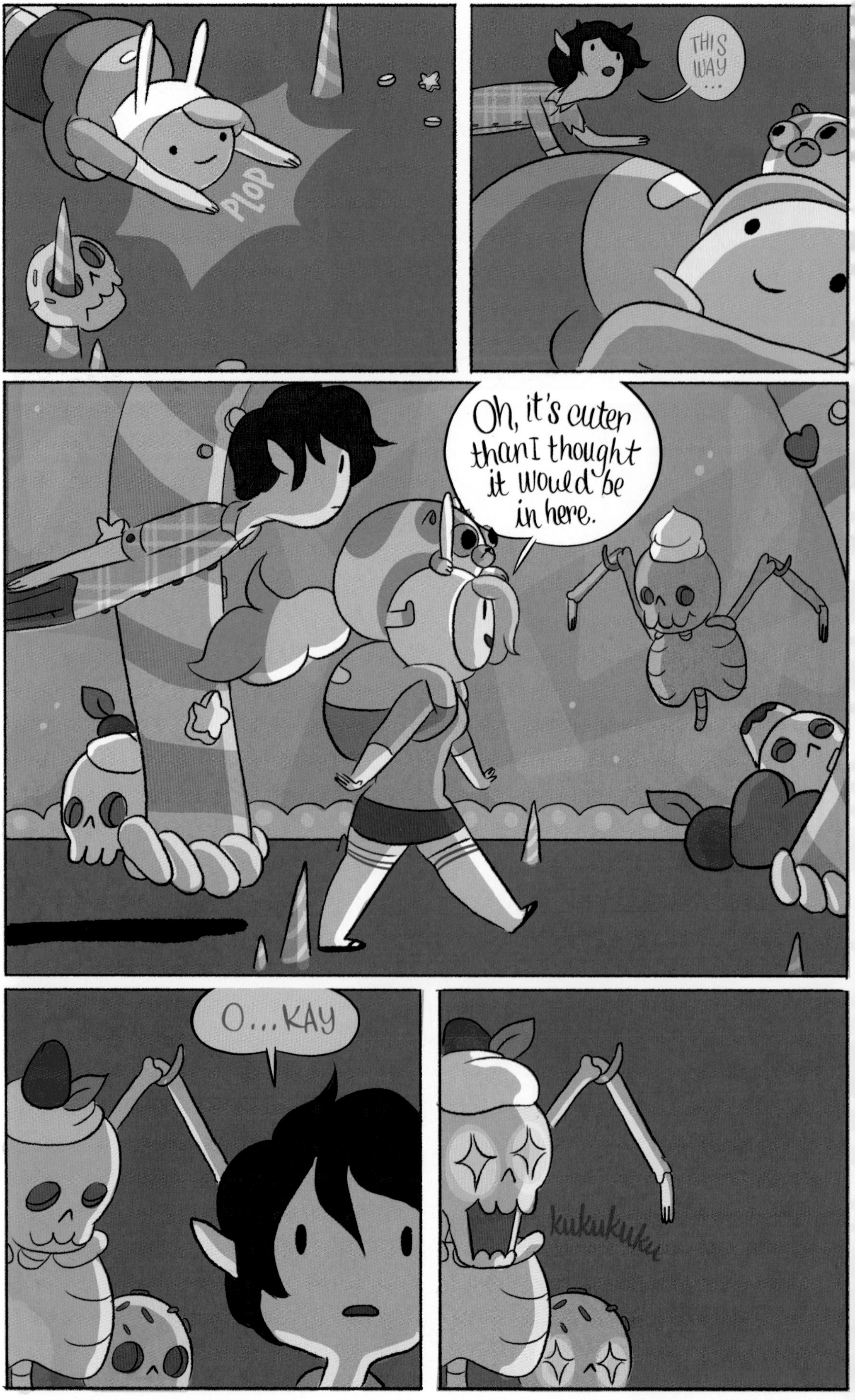
PLOP
THIS WAY...
Oh, it's cuter than I thought it would be in here.
O...KAY
kukukuku

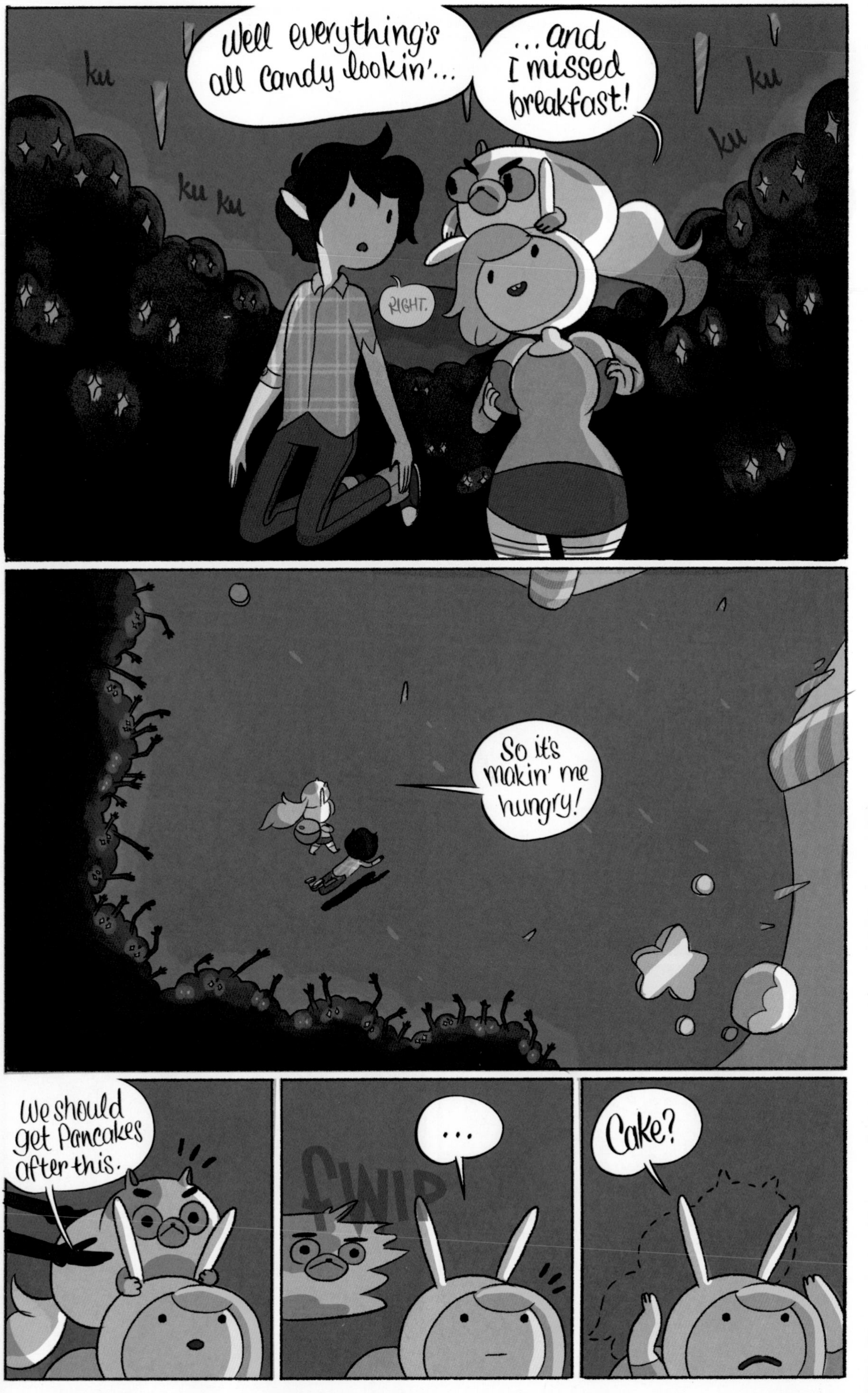
KU
Well everything's all candy lookin'...
...and I missed breakfast!
KU
KU
KU KU
RIGHT.
So it's makin' me hungry!
We should get pancakes after this.
...
FWIP
Cake?

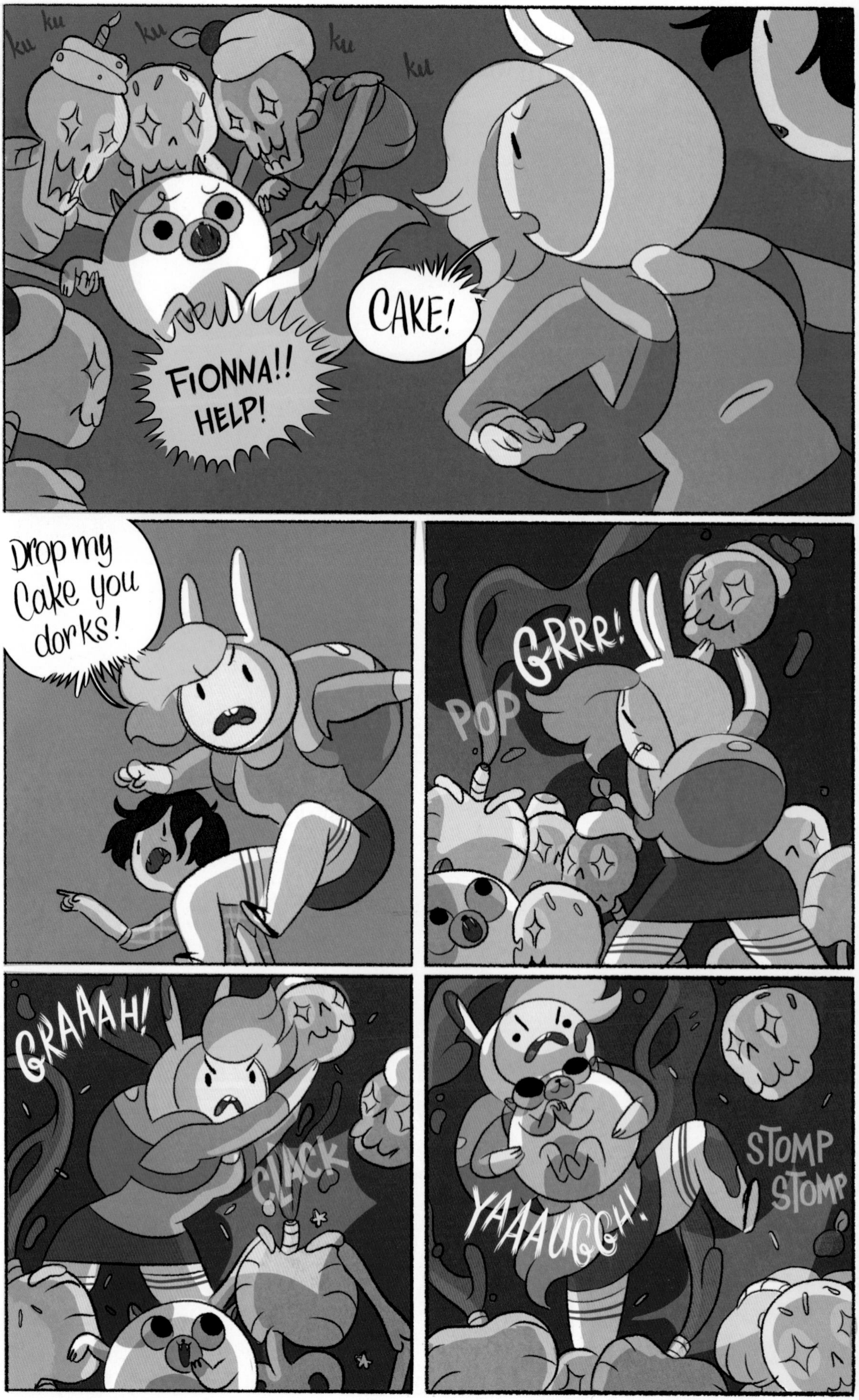
ku ku ku ku ku
FIONNA!! HELP!
CAKE!
Drop my Cake you dorks!
GRRR!
POP
GRAAAH!
CLACK
YAAAUGGH!
STOMP STOMP

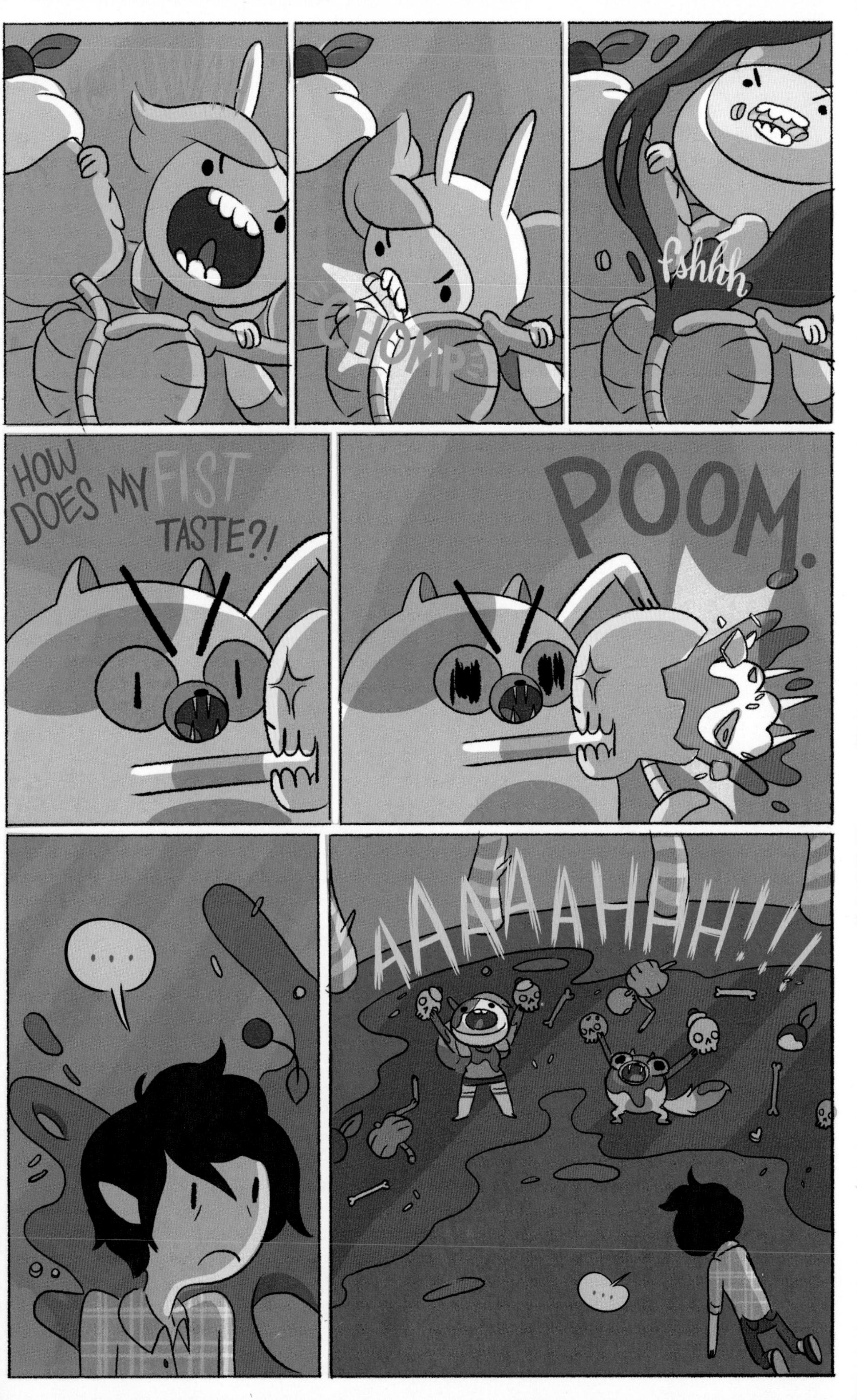
fshhh
HOW DOES MY FIST TASTE?!
POOM.
...
AAAAAAHHH!!!
...

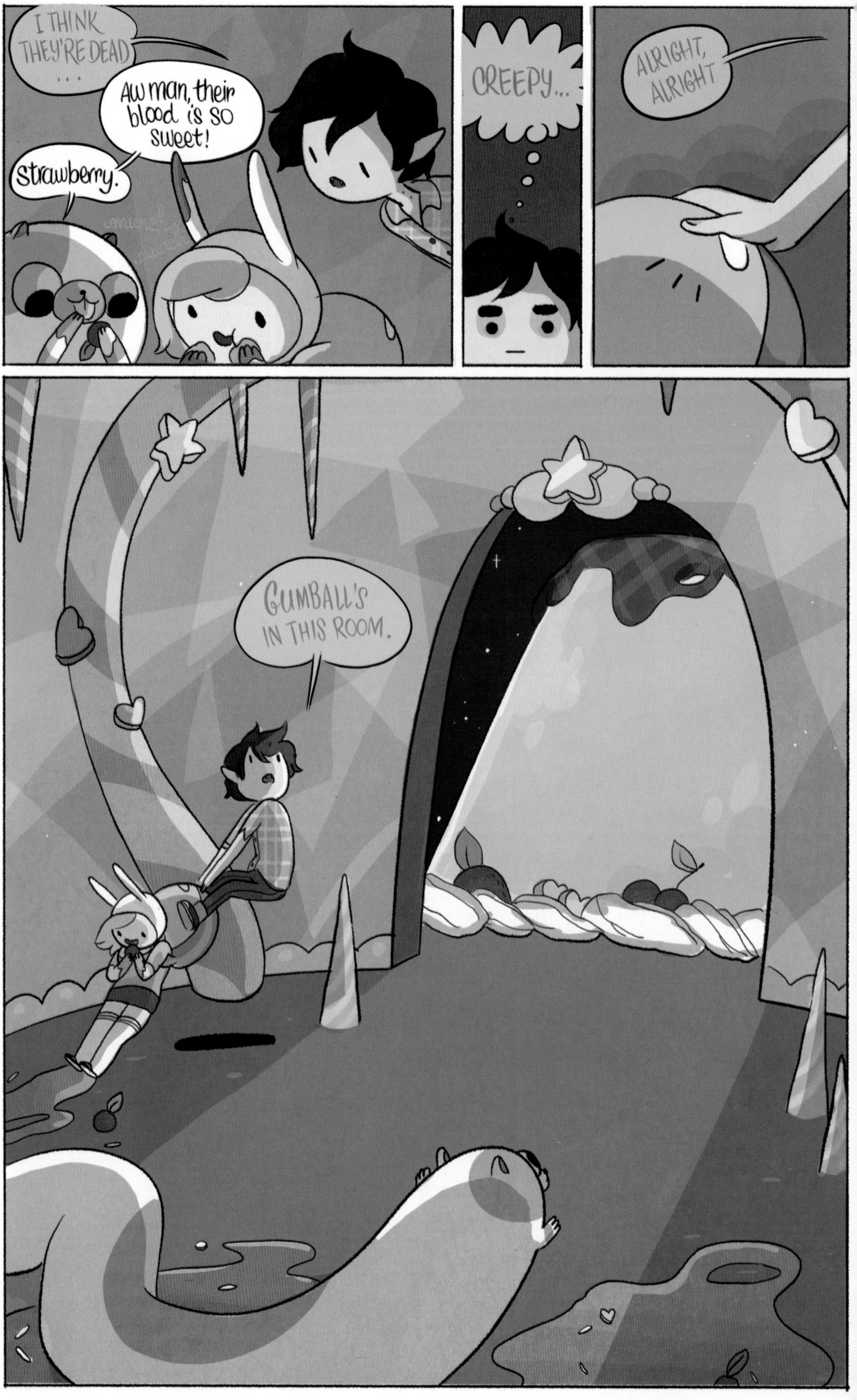
I THINK THEY'RE DEAD . . .
Aw man, their blood is so sweet!
Strawberry.
CREEPY...
ALRIGHT, ALRIGHT
GUMBALL'S IN THIS ROOM.

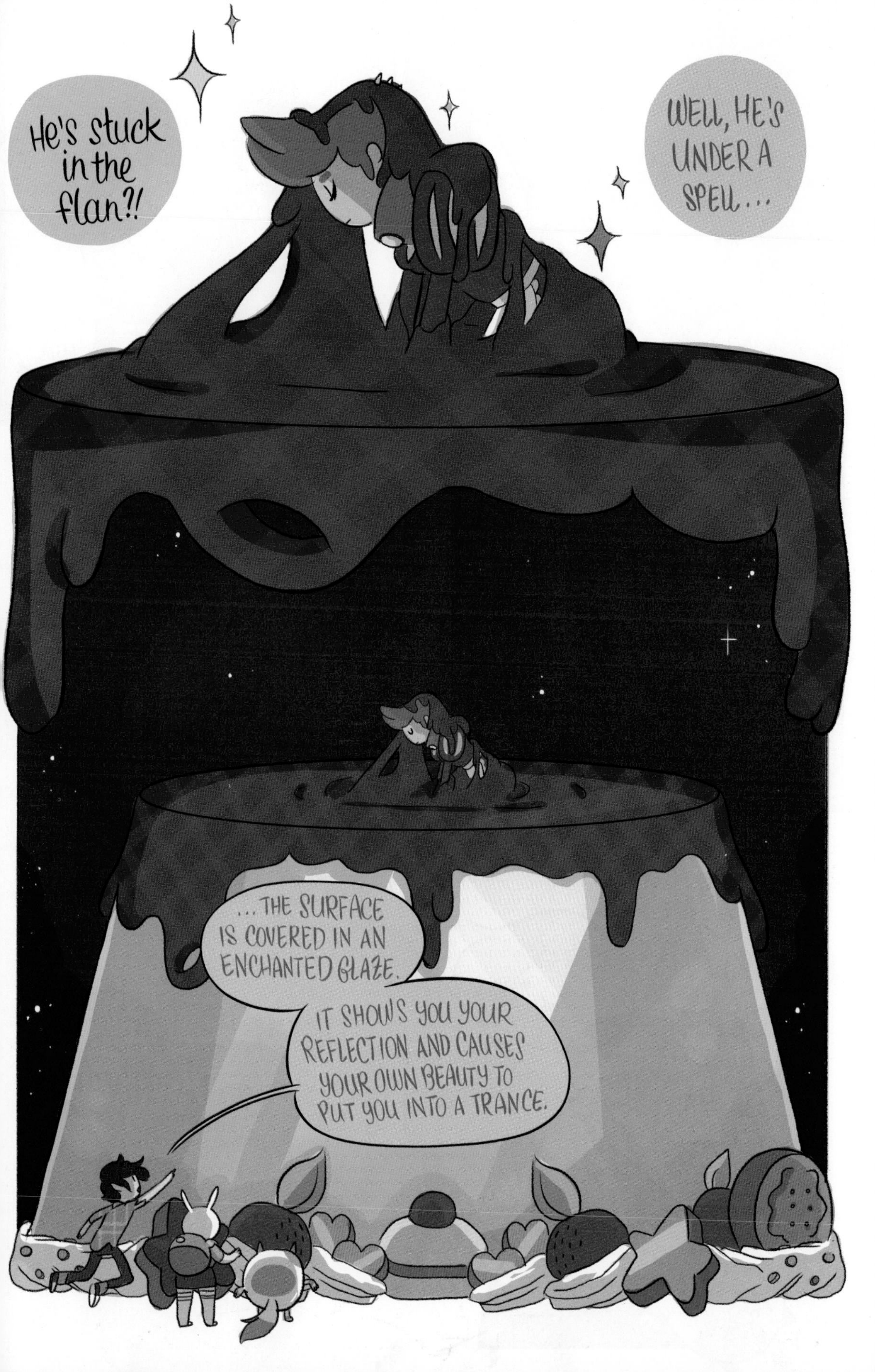
He's stuck in the flan?!
WELL, HE'S UNDER A SPELL...
...THE SURFACE IS COVERED IN AN ENCHANTED GLAZE.
IT SHOWS YOU YOUR REFLECTION AND CAUSES YOUR OWN BEAUTY TO PUT YOU INTO A TRANCE.

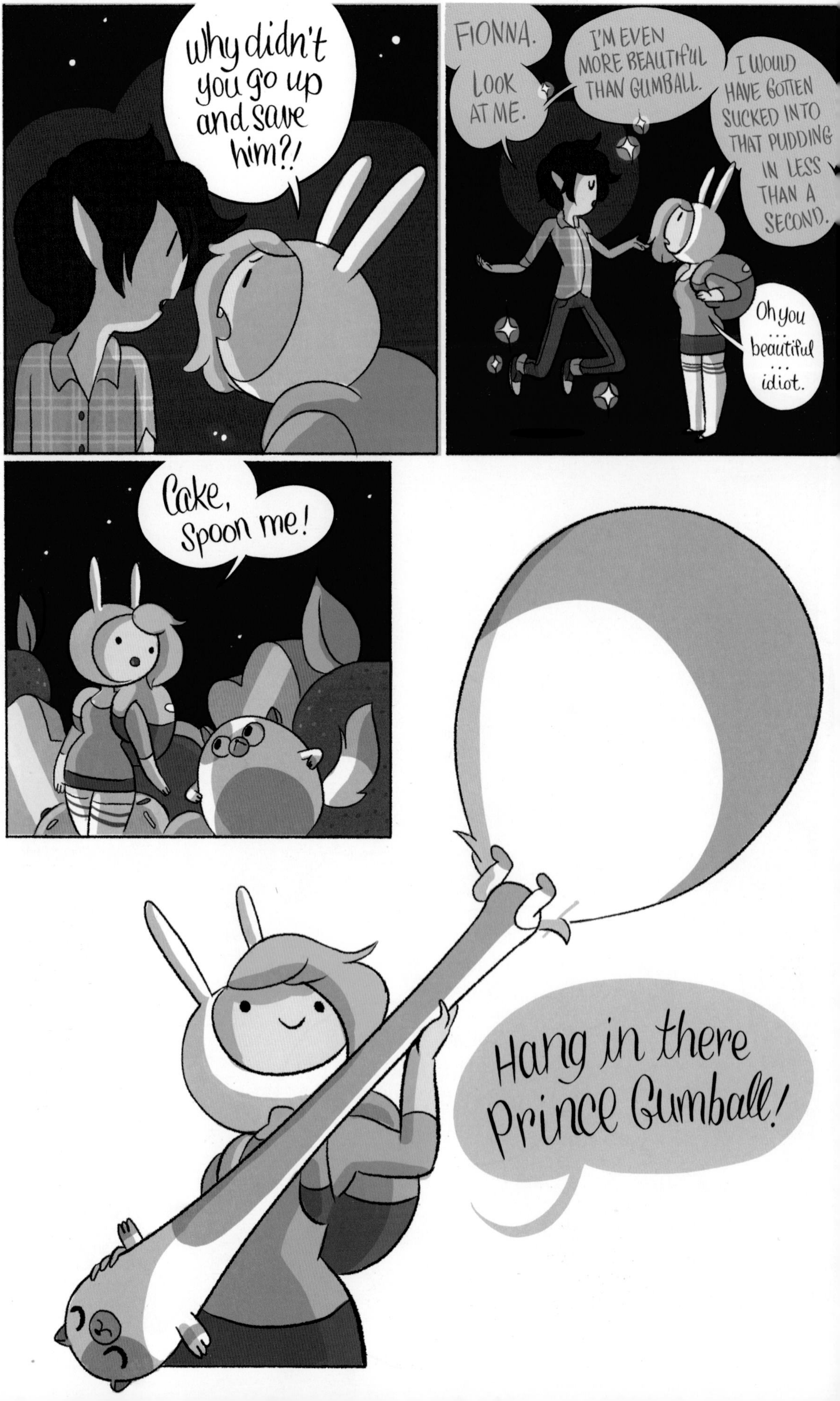
why didn't you go up and save him?!
FIONNA.
LOOK AT ME.
I'M EVEN MORE BEAUTIFUL THAN GUMBALL.
I WOULD HAVE GOTTEN SUCKED INTO THAT PUDDING IN LESS THAN A SECOND.
Oh you ... beautiful ... idiot.
Cake, Spoon me!
Hang in there Prince Gumball!

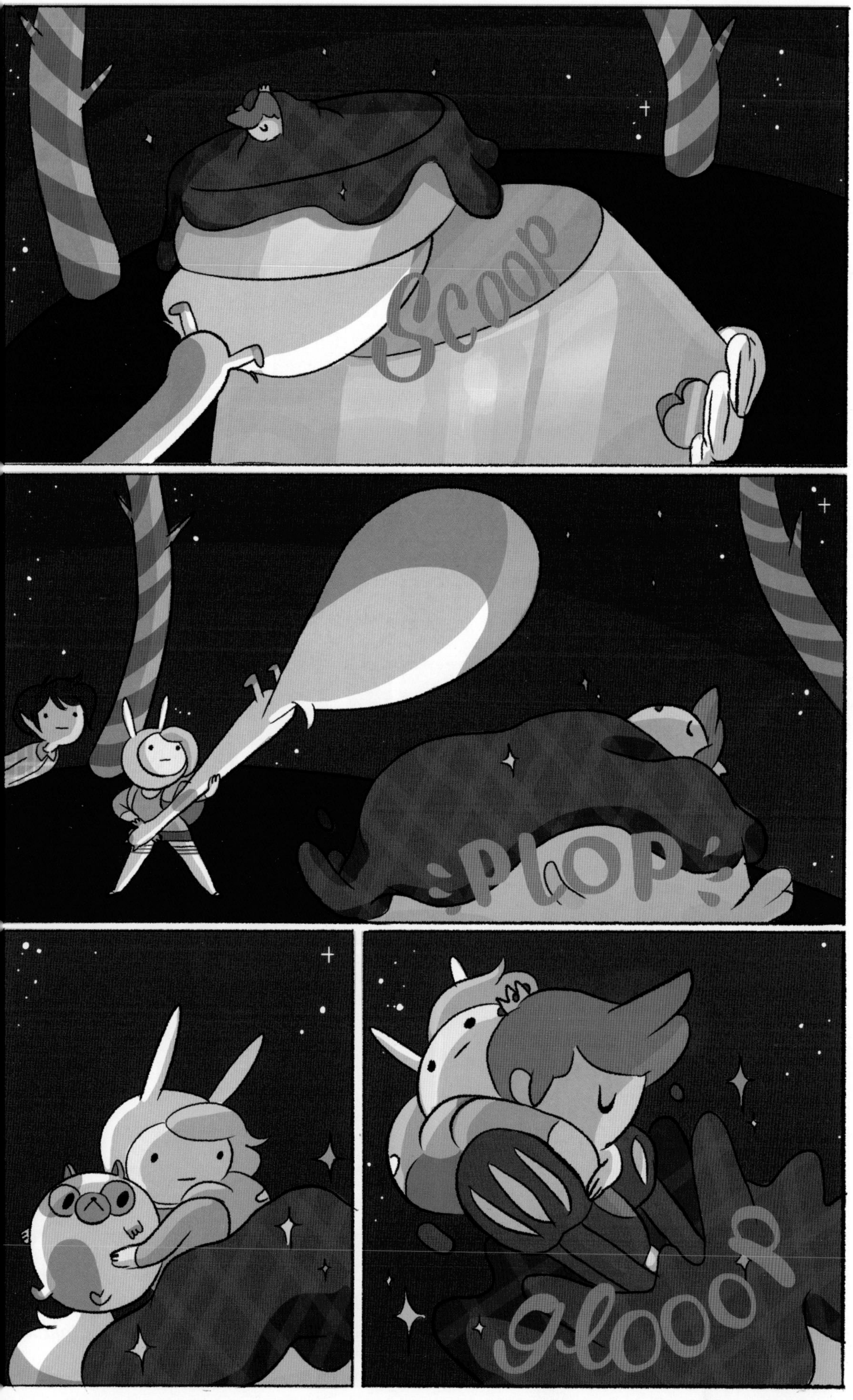
SCOOP
PLOP
GLOOOP

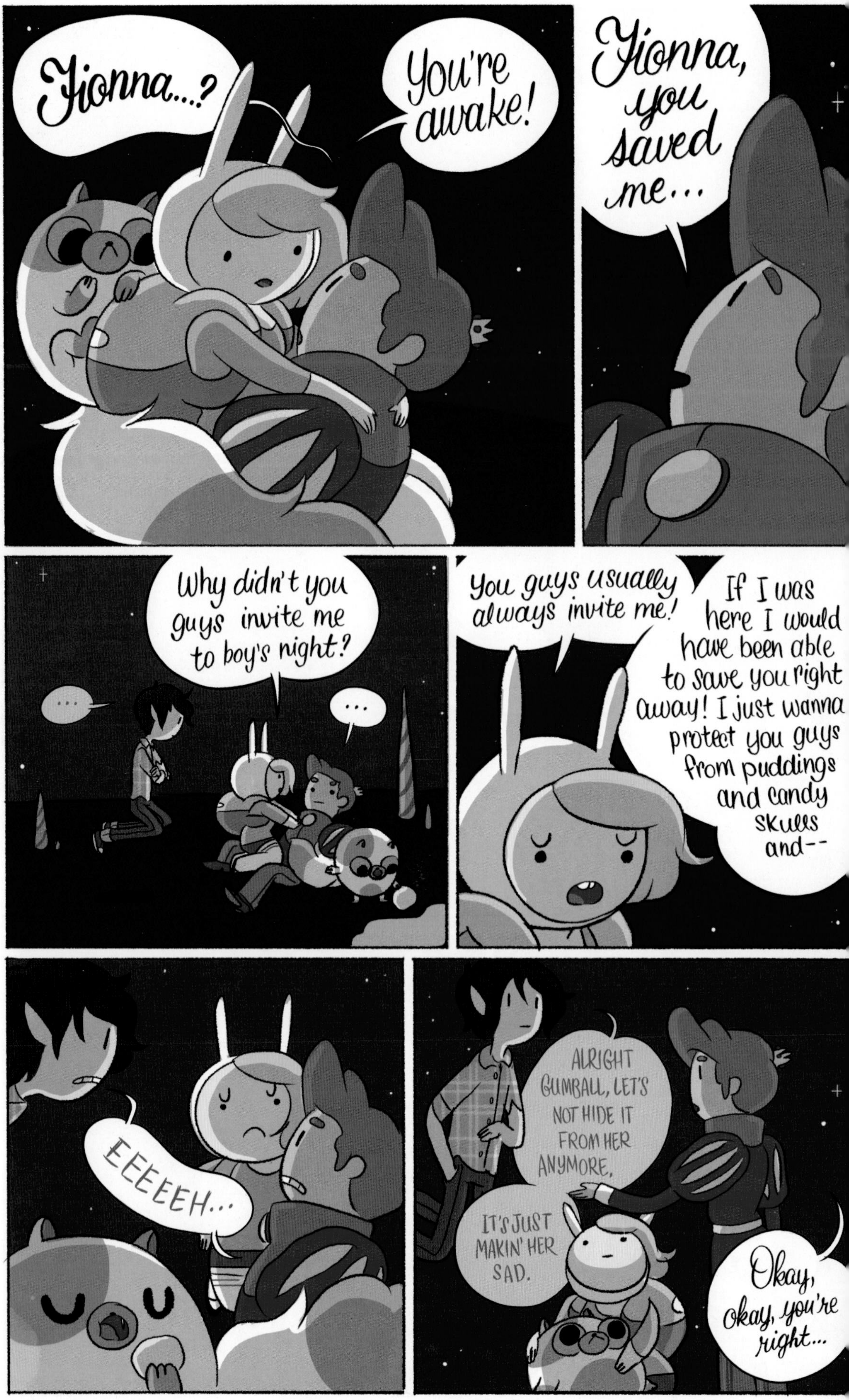
Fionna...?
You're awake!
Fionna, you saved me...
Why didn't you guys invite me to boy's night?
...
...
You guys usually always invite me!
If I was here I would have been able to save you right away! I just wanna protect you guys from puddings and candy skulls and--
EEEEEH...
ALRIGHT GUMBALL, LET'S NOT HIDE IT FROM HER ANYMORE.
IT'S JUST MAKIN' HER SAD.
Okay, okay, you're right...

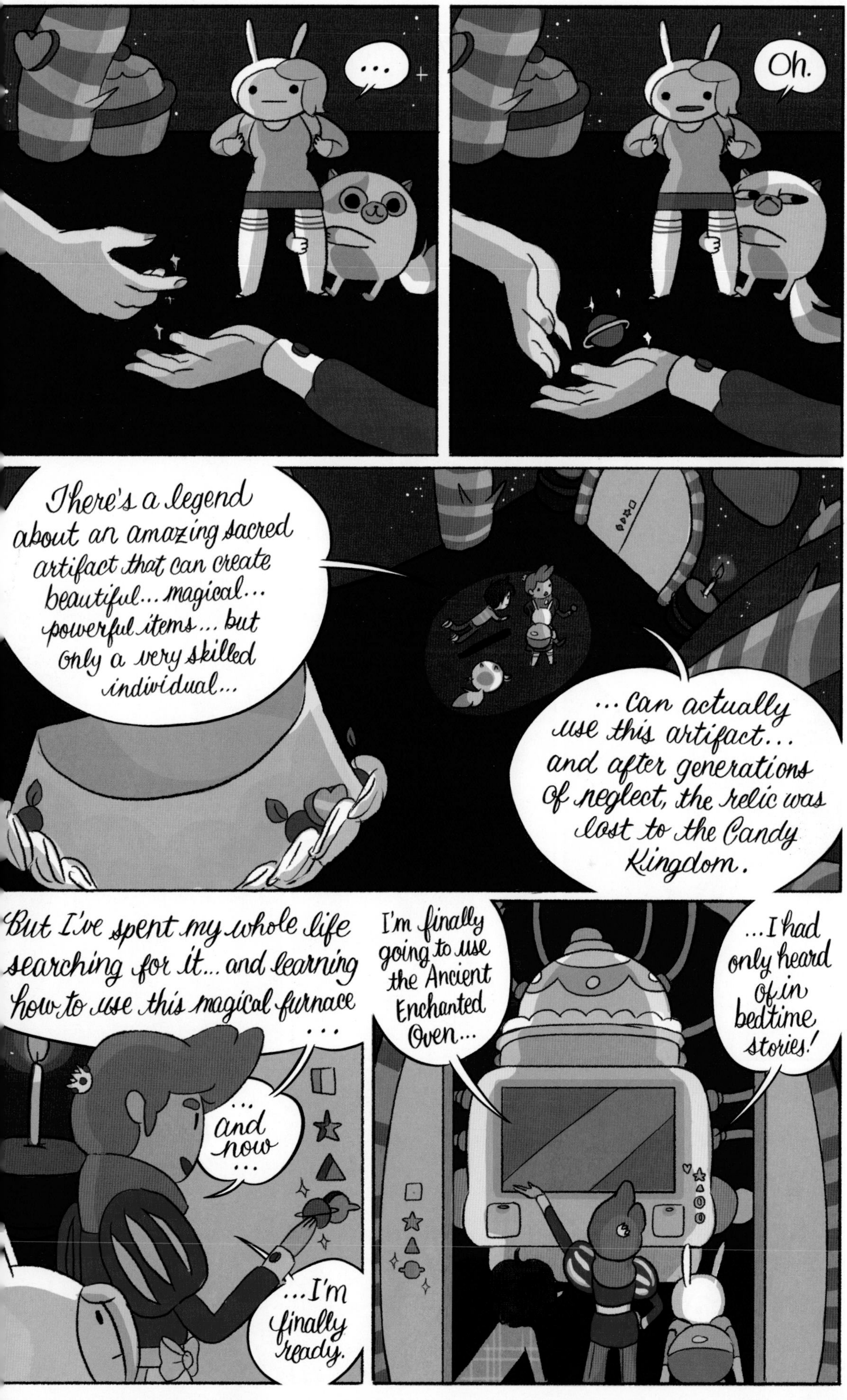
...
Oh.
There's a legend about an amazing sacred artifact that can create beautiful... magical... powerful items... but only a very skilled individual...
...can actually use this artifact... and after generations of neglect, the relic was lost to the Candy Kingdom.
But I've spent my whole life searching for it... and learning how to use this magical furnace...
...and now...
...I'm finally ready.
I'm finally going to use the Ancient Enchanted Oven...
...I had only heard of in bedtime stories!

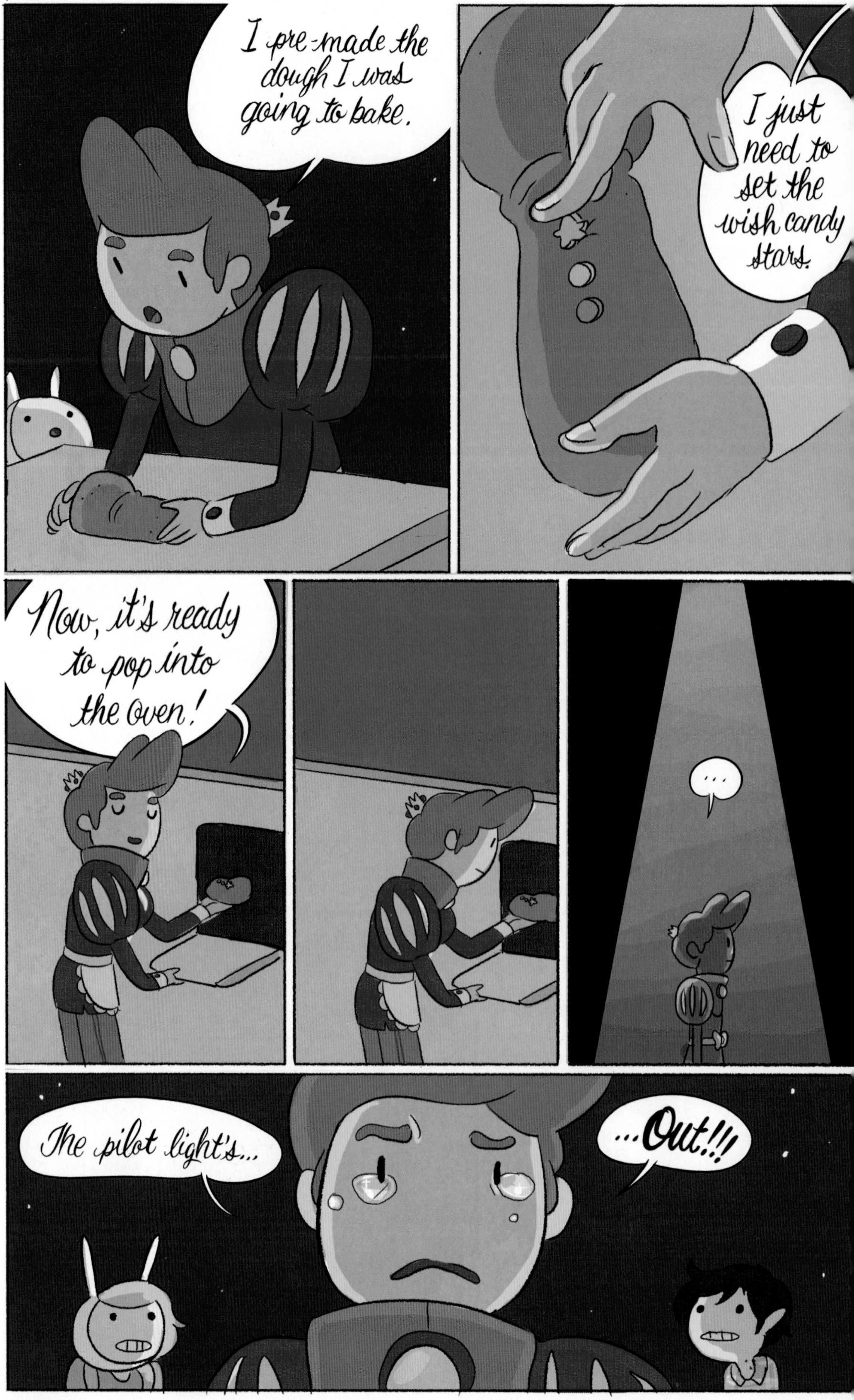
I pre-made the dough I was going to bake.
I just need to set the wish candy stars.
Now, it's ready to pop into the Oven!
...
The pilot light's...
...Out!!!

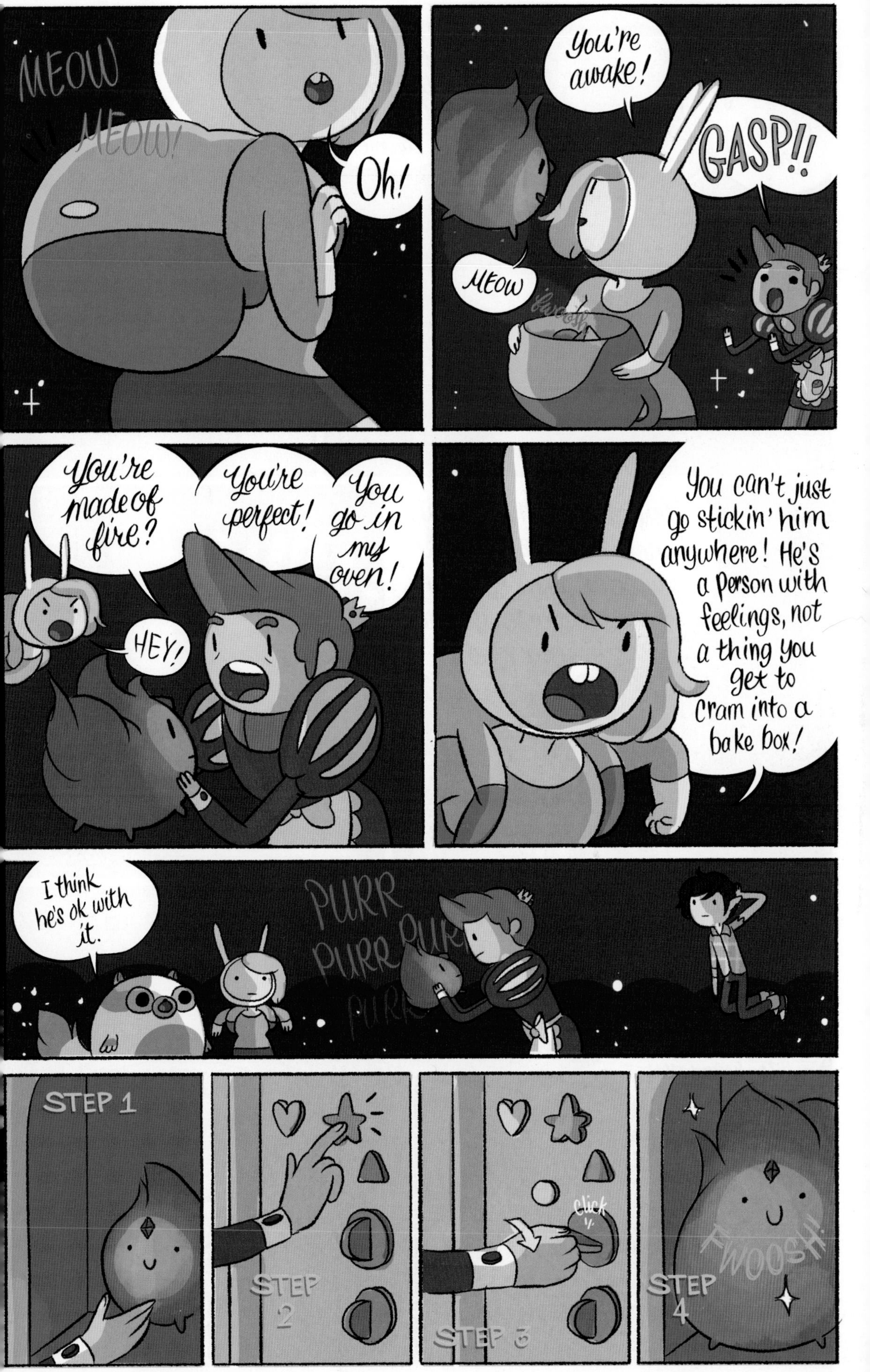
MEOW
MEOW!
Oh!
You're awake!
GASP!!
MEOW
You're made of fire?
You're perfect!
You go in my oven!
HEY!
You can't just go stickin' him anywhere! He's a person with feelings, not a thing you get to cram into a bake box!
I think he's ok with it.
PURR
PURR PURR
PURR
STEP 1
STEP 2
click
STEP 3
STEP 4
FWOOSH!

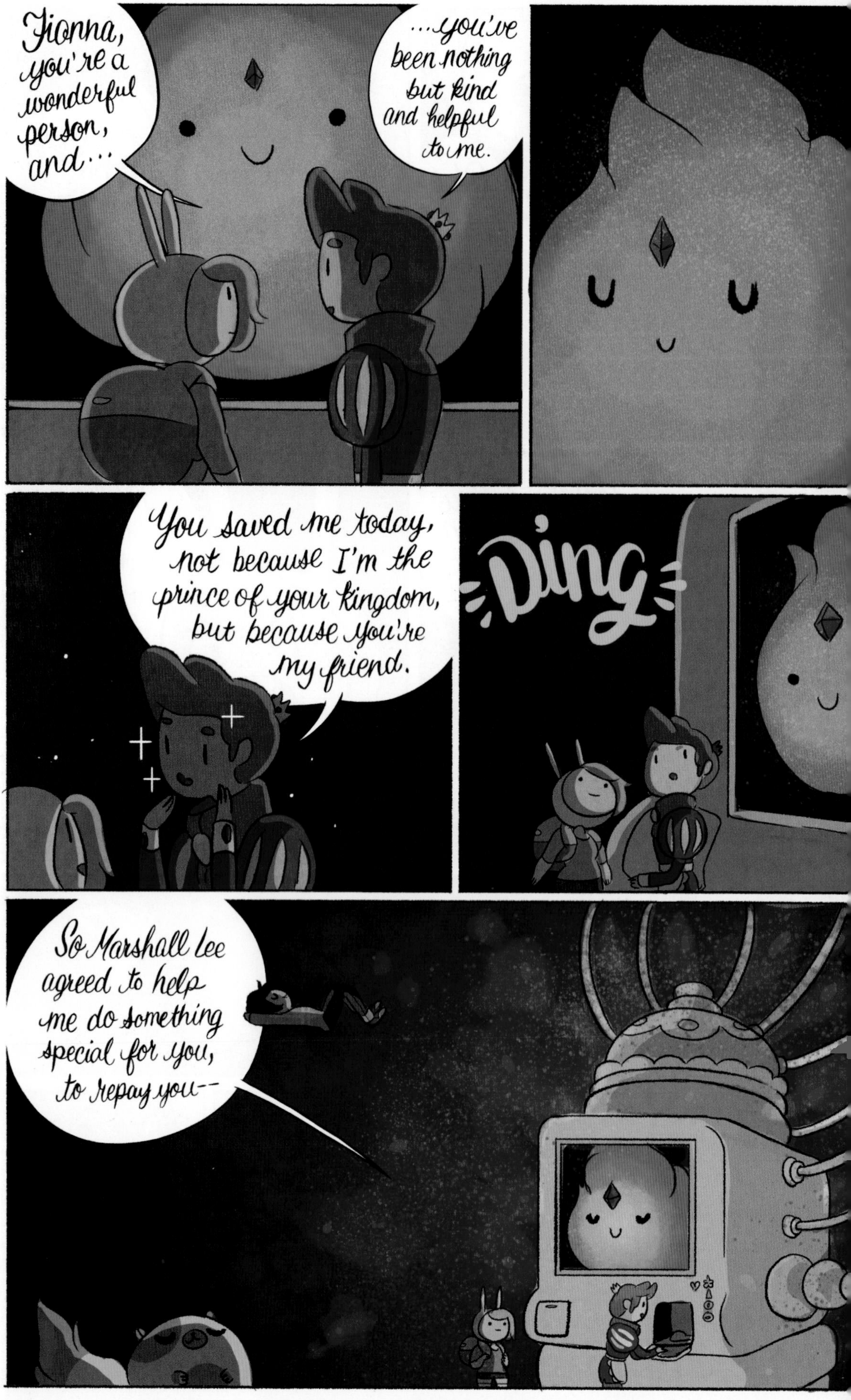
Fionna, you're a wonderful person, and...
...you've been nothing but kind and helpful to me.
You saved me today, not because I'm the prince of your kingdom, but because you're my friend.
Ding
So Marshall Lee agreed to help me do something special for you, to repay you--

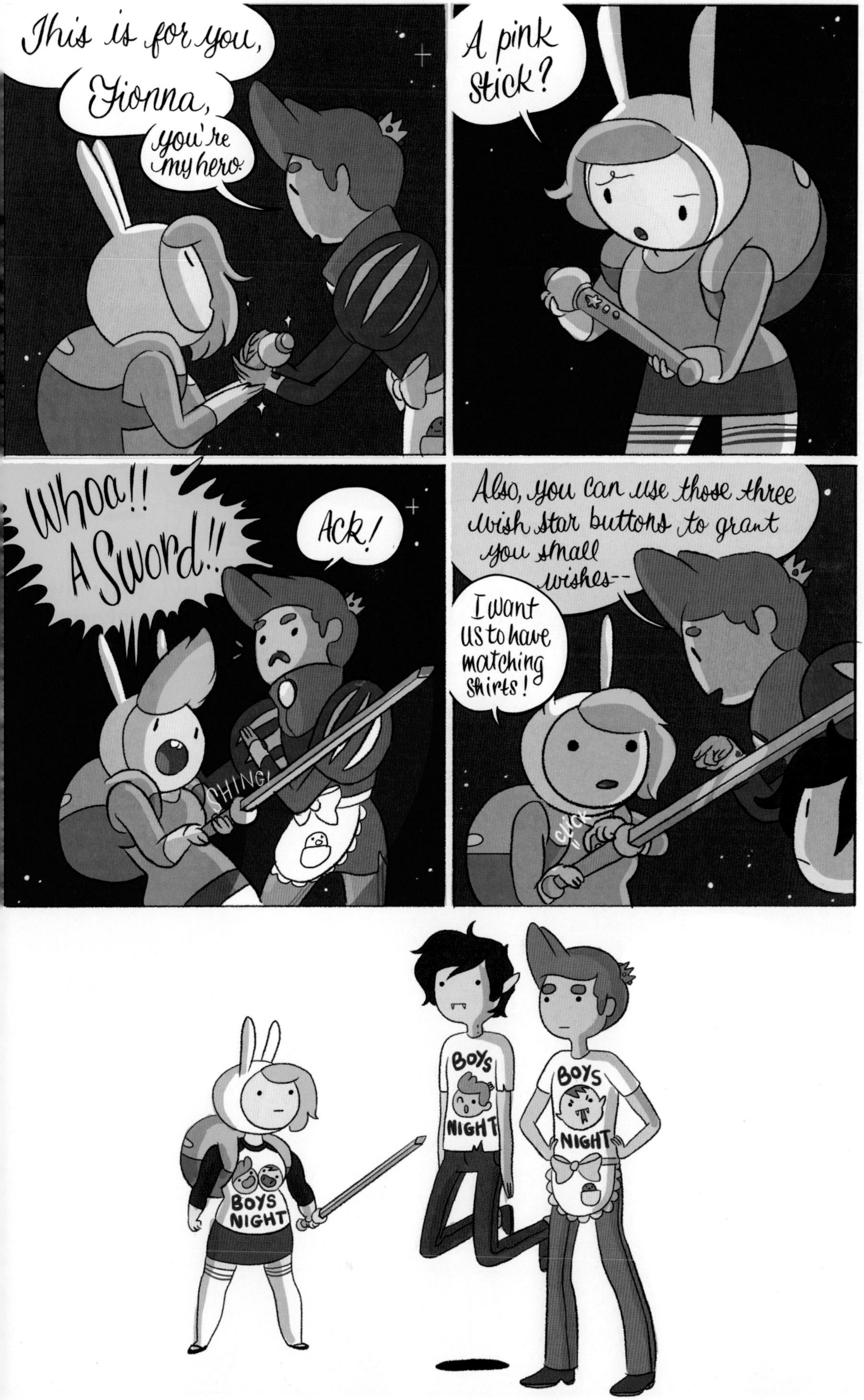
This is for you,
Fionna,
you're my hero.
A pink stick?
Whoa!! A Sword!!
ACK!
SHING!
Also, you can use those three wish star buttons to grant you small wishes--
I want us to have matching shirts!
CLICK
BOYS NIGHT
BOYS NIGHT
BOYS NIGHT

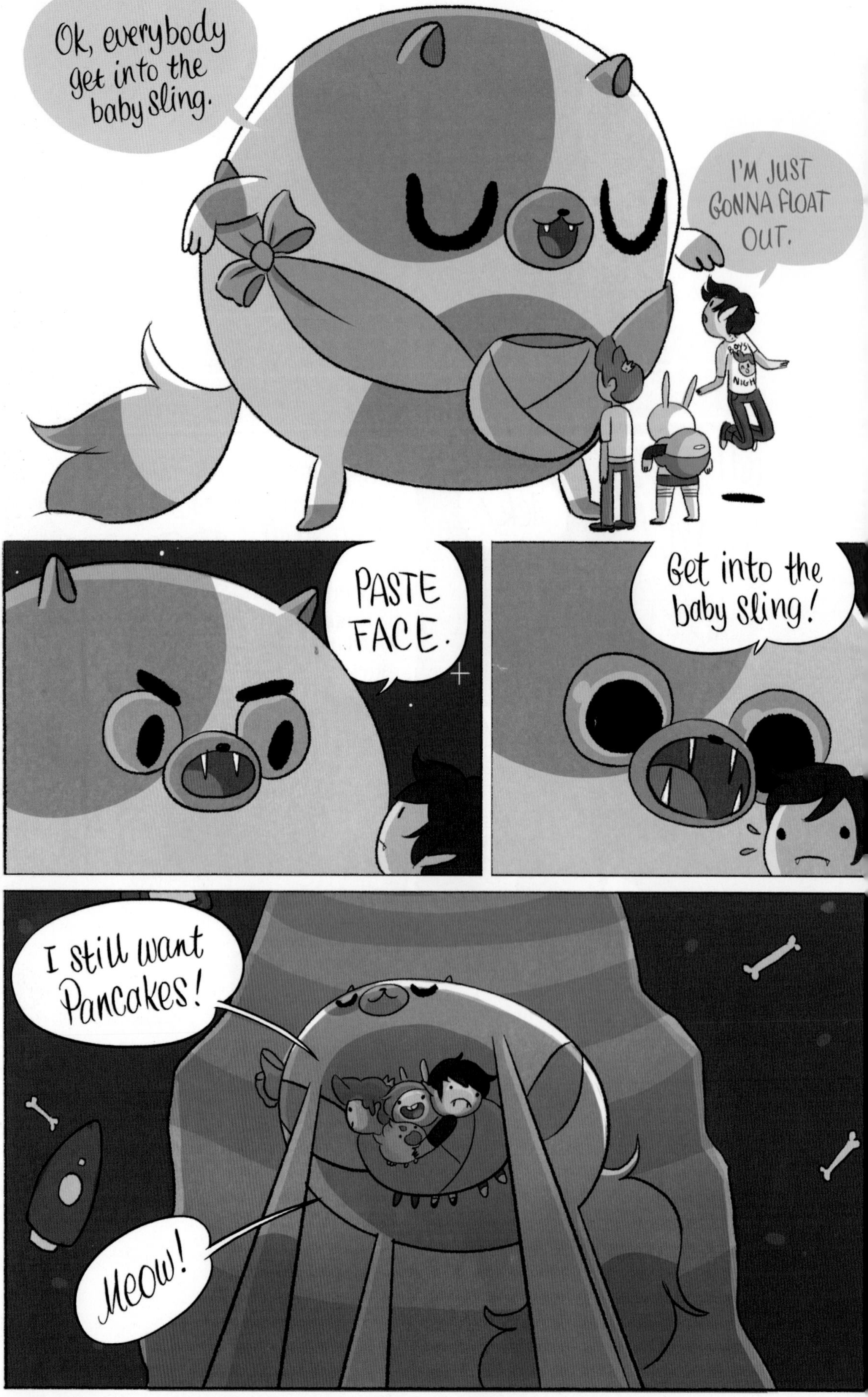
Ok, everybody get into the baby Sling.
I'M JUST GONNA FLOAT OUT.
PASTE FACE.
Get into the baby Sling!
I still want Pancakes!
Meow!

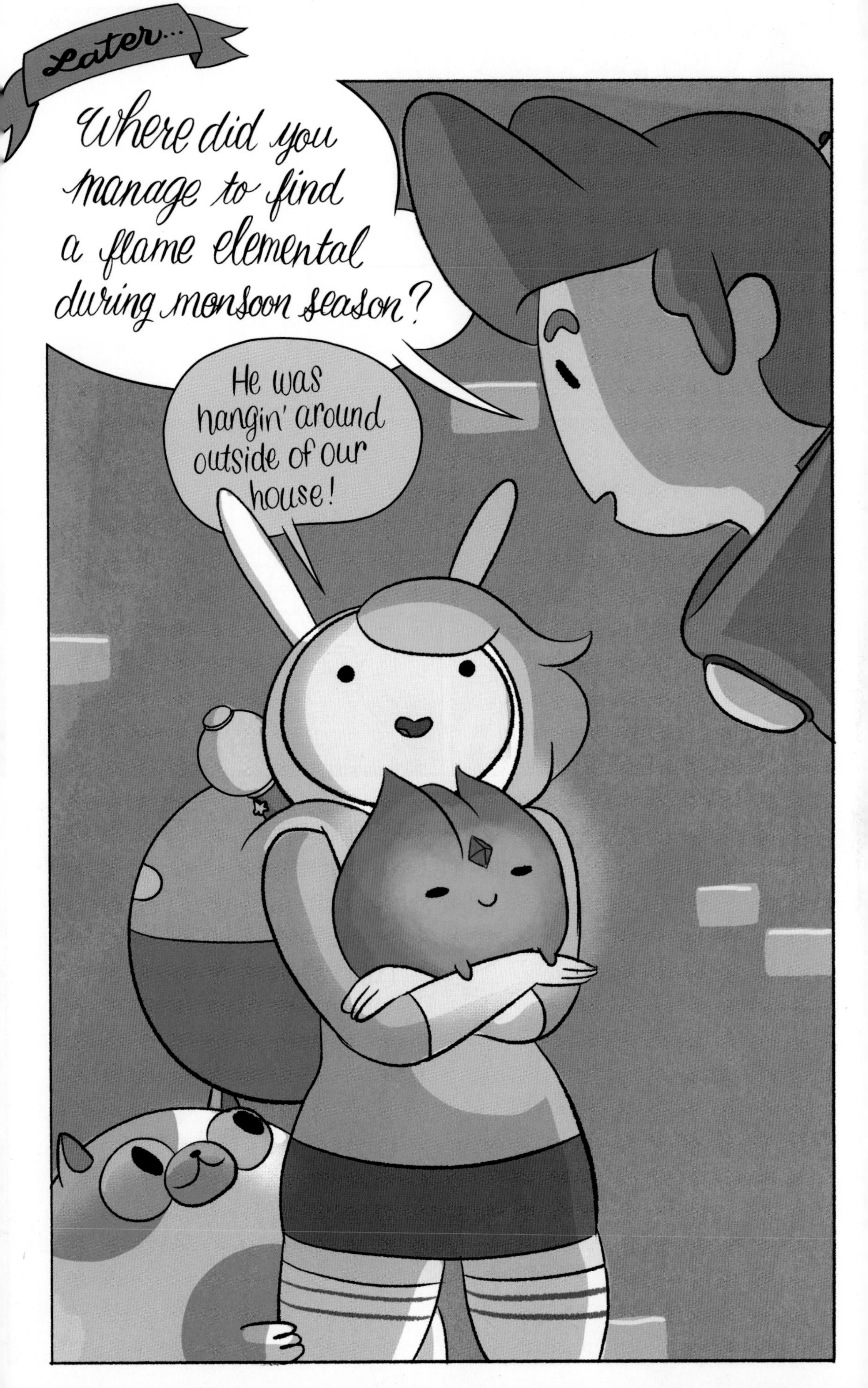
Later...
Where did you manage to find a flame elemental during monsoon season?
He was hangin' around outside of our house!

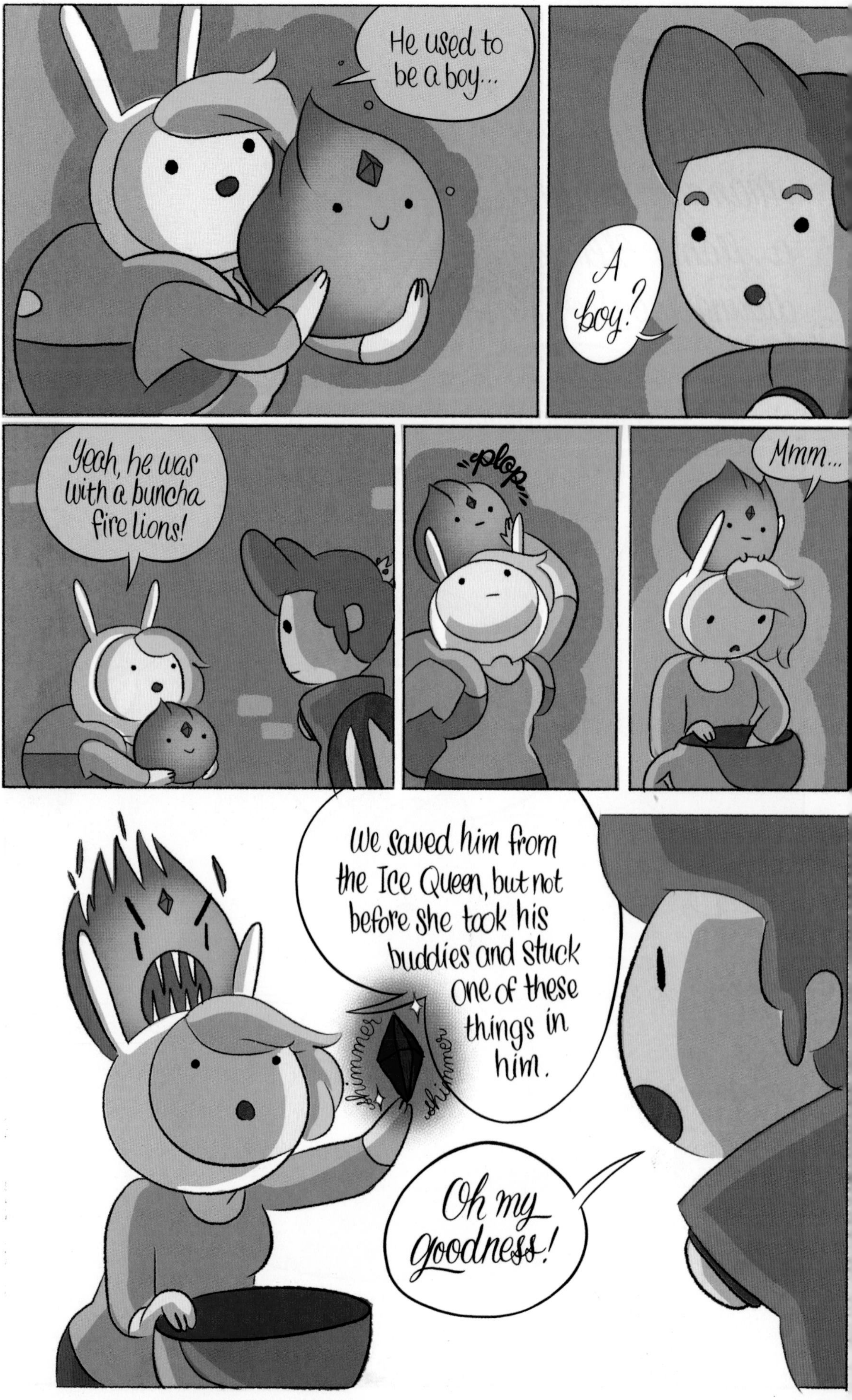
He used to be a boy...
A boy?
Yeah, he was with a buncha fire lions!
plop
Mmm...
We saved him from the Ice Queen, but not before she took his buddies and stuck one of these things in him.
shimmer
shimmer
Oh my goodness!

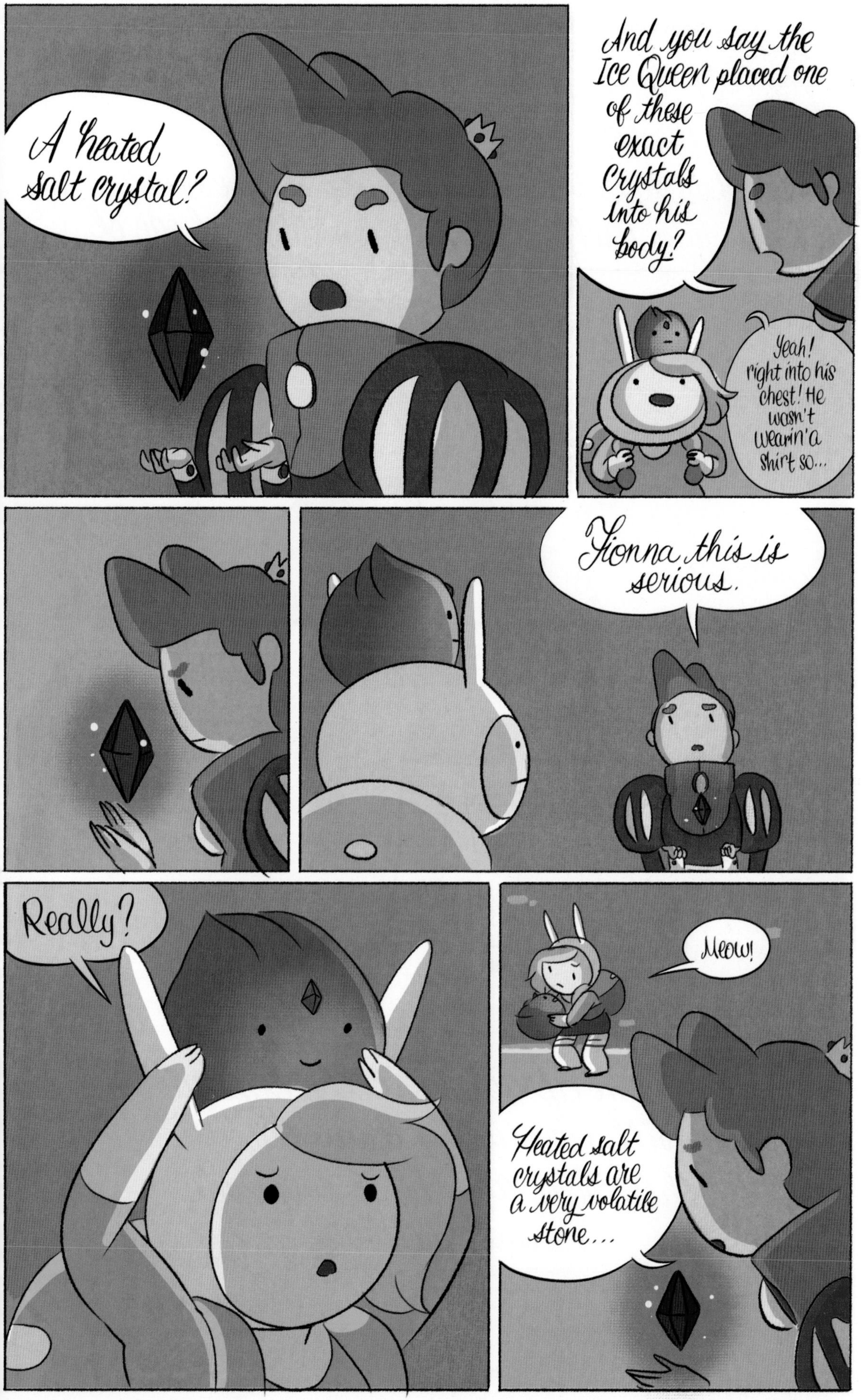
A heated salt crystal?
And you say the Ice Queen placed one of these exact Crystals into his body?
Yeah! right into his chest! He wasn't wearin'a shirt so...
Fionna, this is serious.
Really?
Meow!
Heated salt crystals are a very volatile stone...

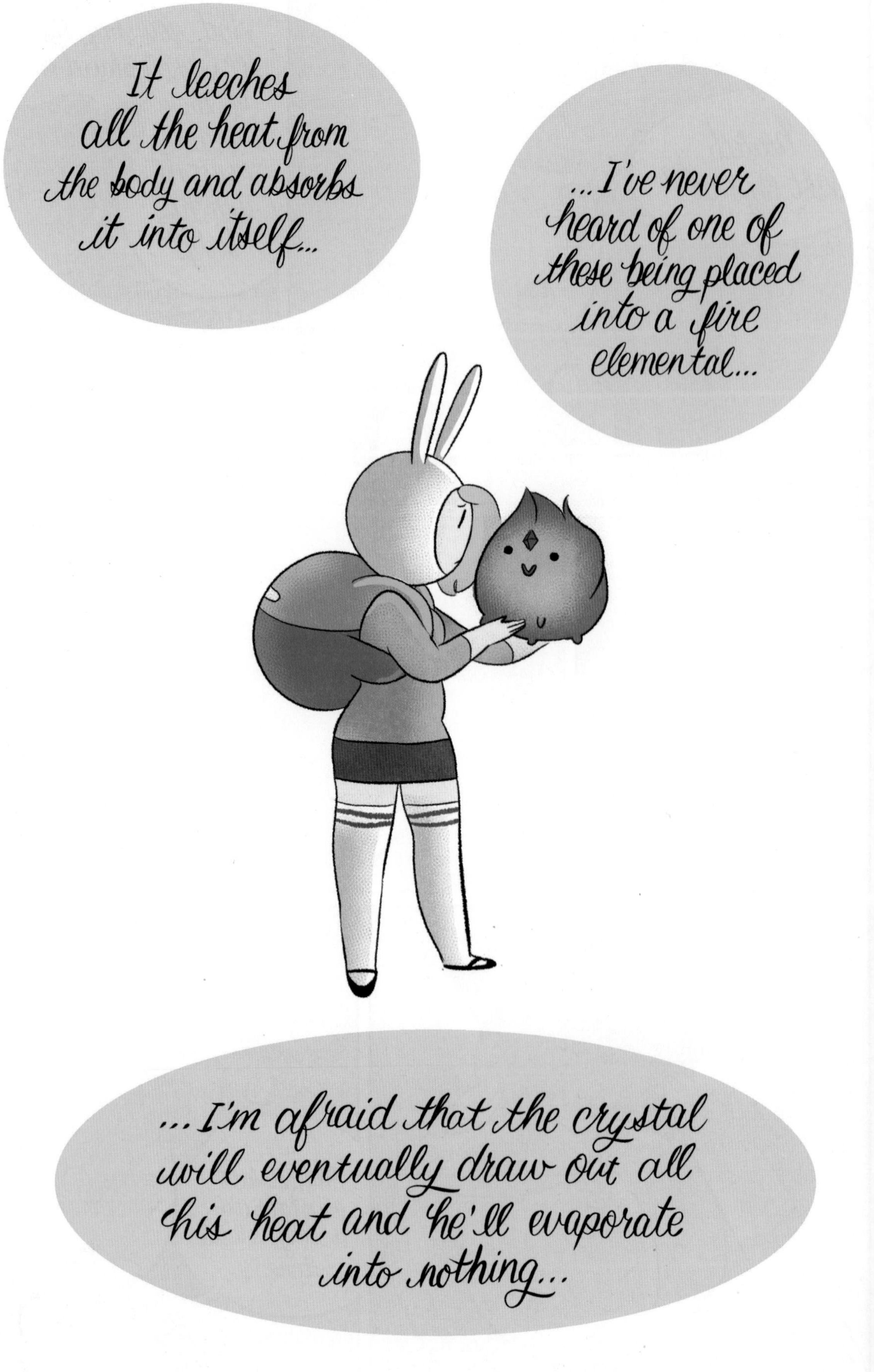
It leeches all the heat from the body and absorbs it into itself...
...I've never heard of one of these being placed into a fire elemental...
...I'm afraid that the crystal will eventually draw out all his heat and he'll evaporate into nothing...

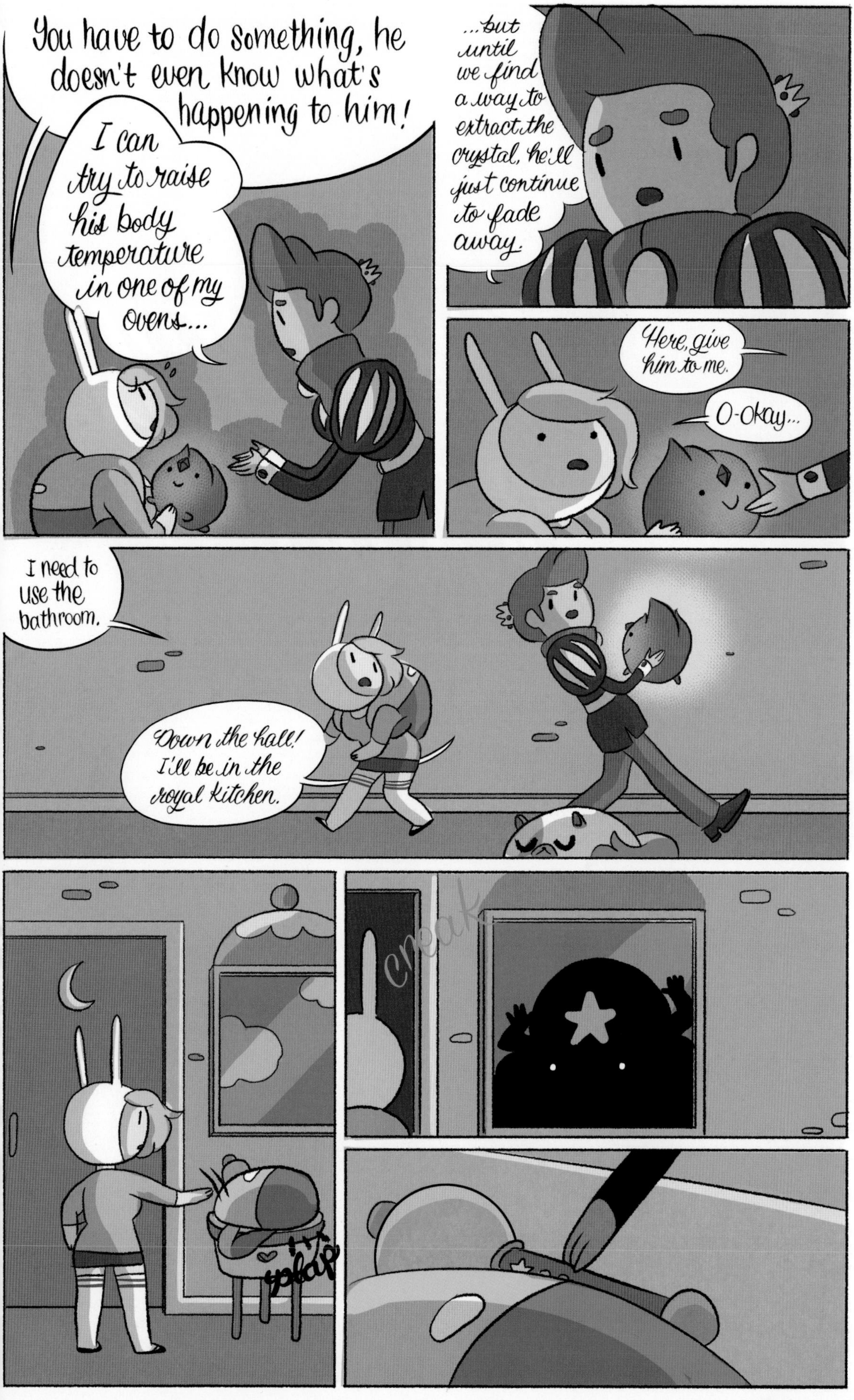
You have to do something, he doesn't even know what's happening to him!
I can try to raise his body temperature in one of my ovens...
...but until we find a way to extract the crystal, he'll just continue to fade away.
Here, give him to me.
O-okay...
I need to use the bathroom.
Down the hall! I'll be in the royal kitchen.
creak
splap

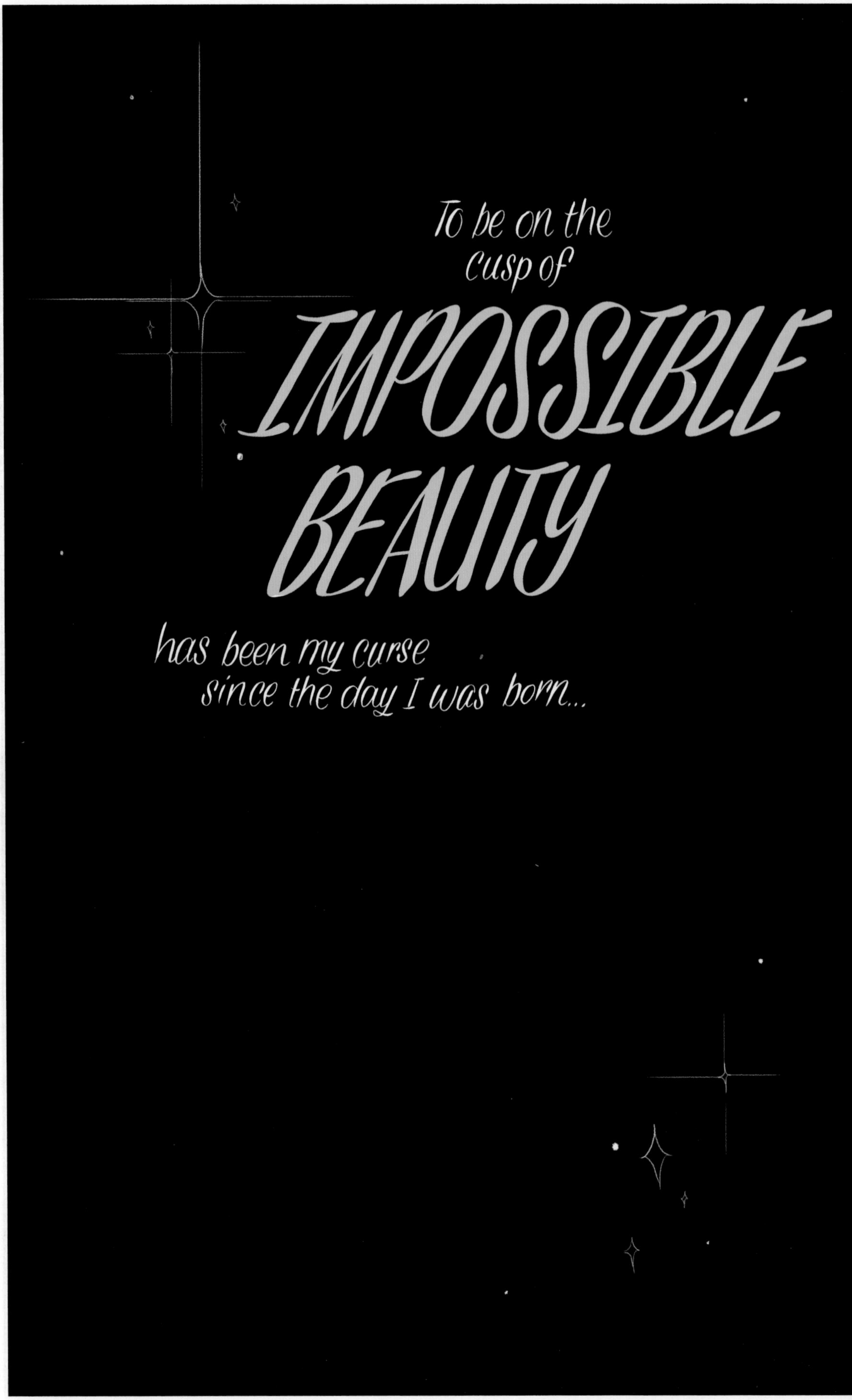
To be on the cusp of
IMPOSSIBLE BEAUTY
has been my curse since the day I was born...

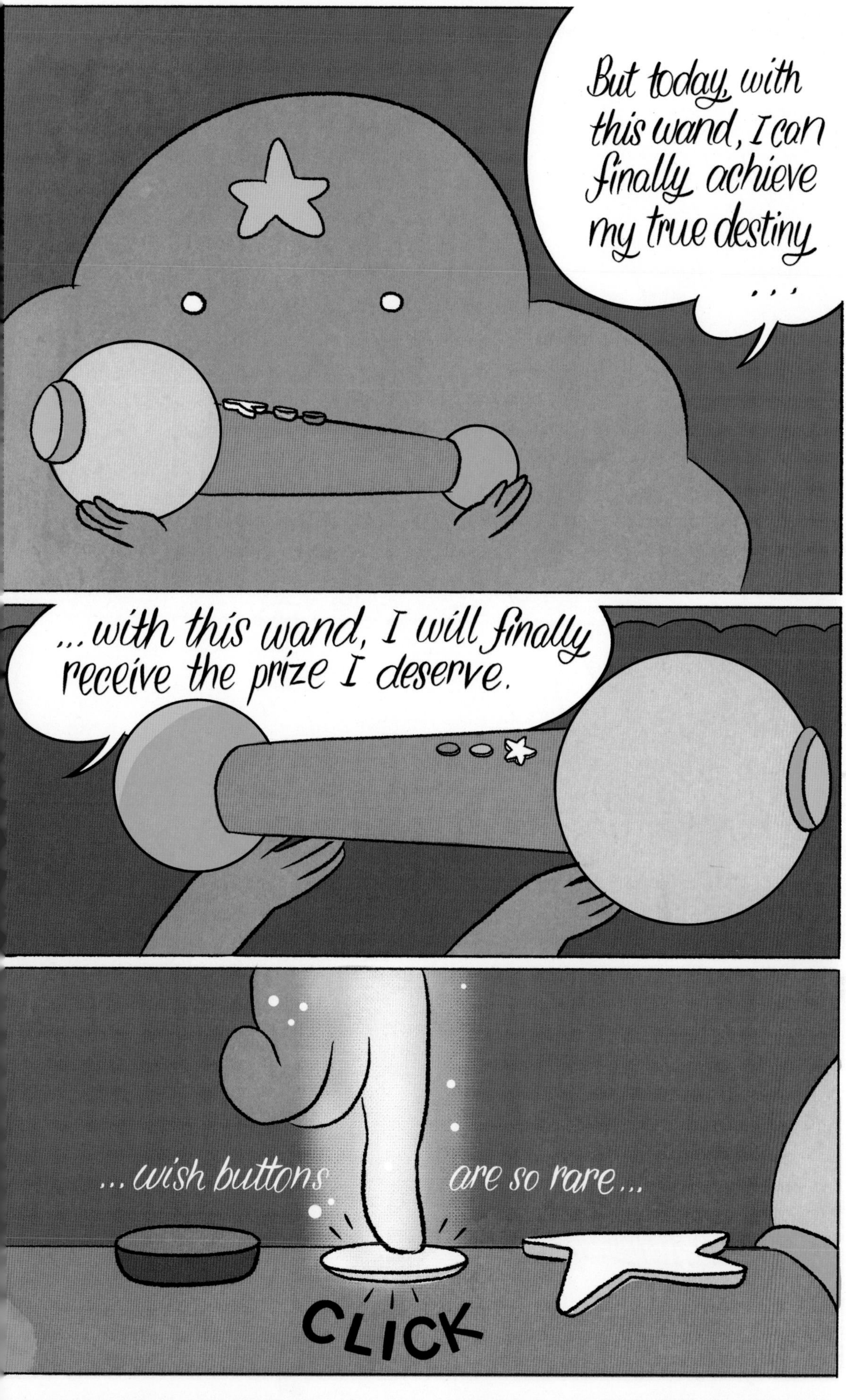
But today, with this wand, I can finally achieve my true destiny ...
... with this wand, I will finally receive the prize I deserve.
... wish buttons are so rare ...
CLICK

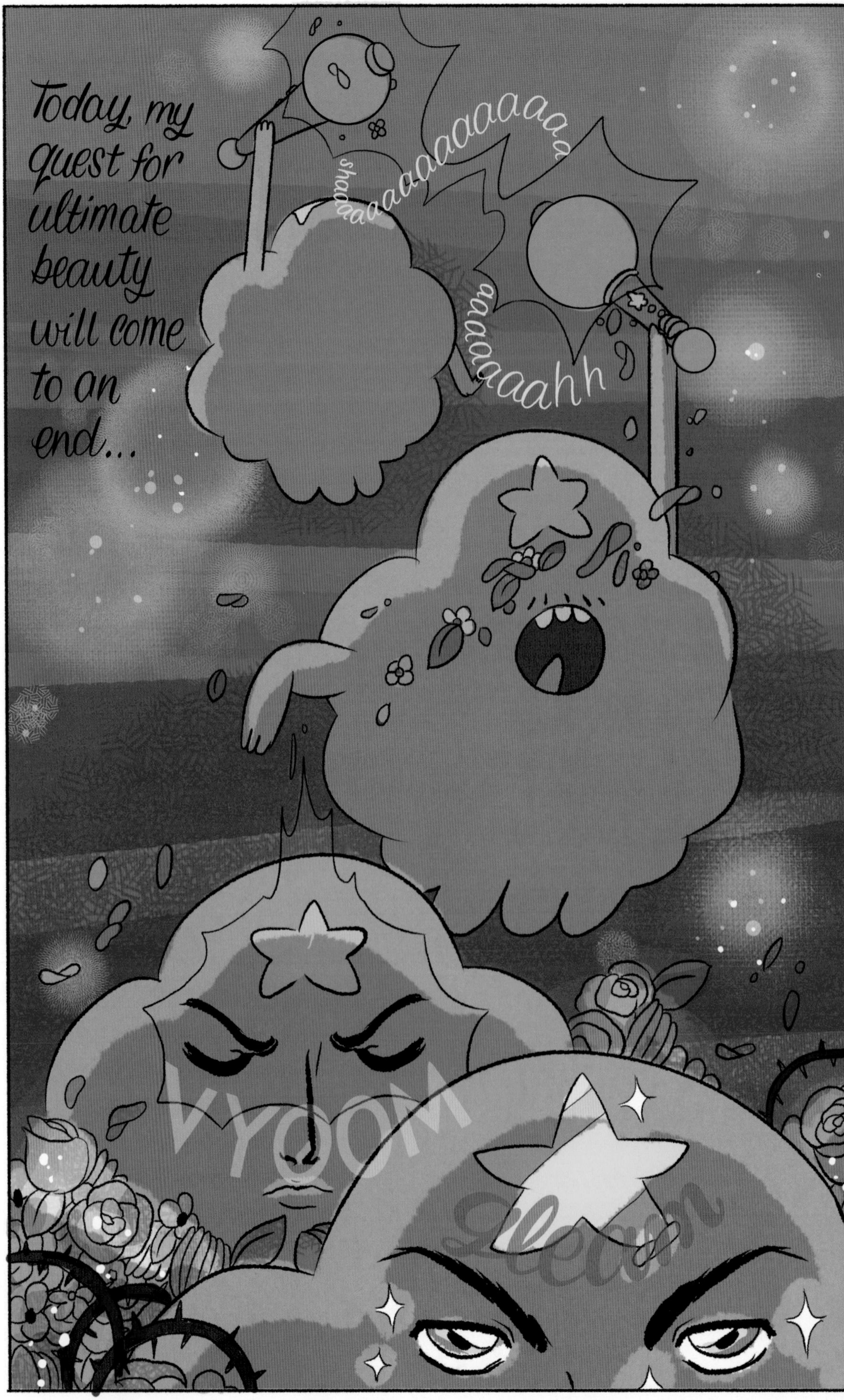
Today, my quest for ultimate beauty will come to an end...
shaaaaaaaaaaaaaaaaa
aaaaaaaahh
VYOOM
gleam

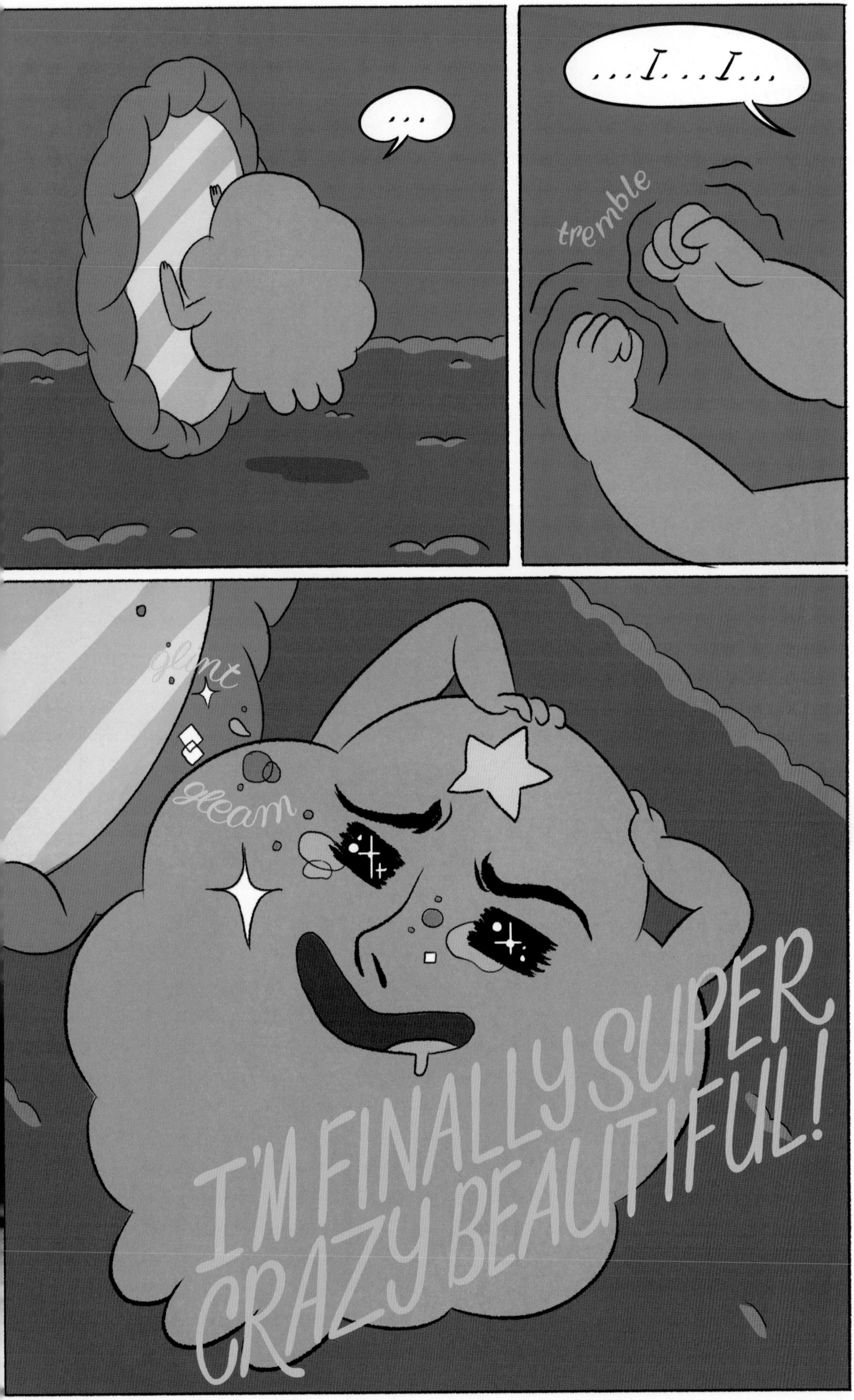
...
...I...I...
tremble
glint
gleam
I'M FINALLY SUPER CRAZY BEAUTIFUL!

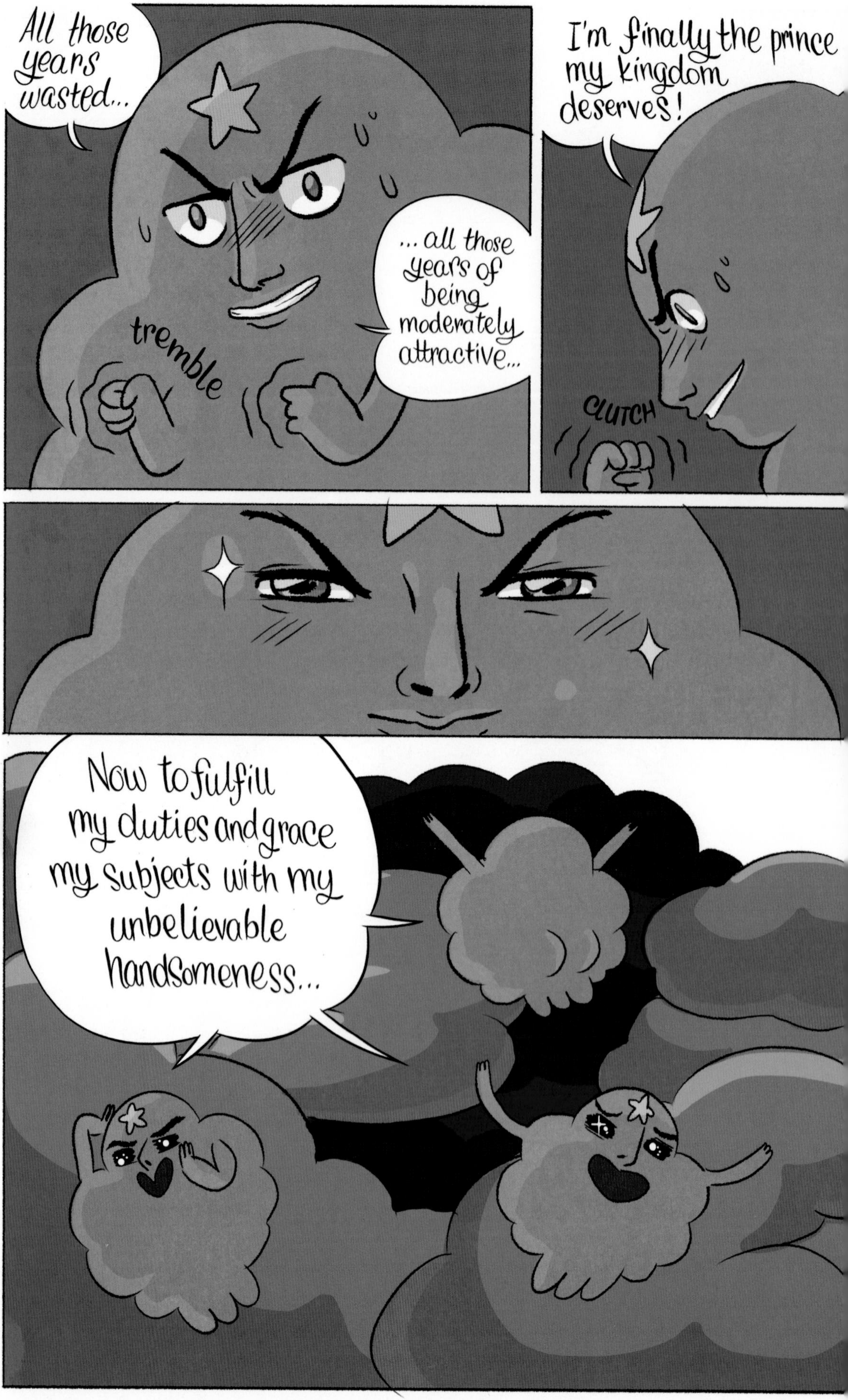
All those years wasted...
...all those years of being moderately attractive...
tremble
I'm finally the prince my kingdom deserves!
CLUTCH
Now to fulfill my duties and grace my subjects with my unbelievable handsomeness...

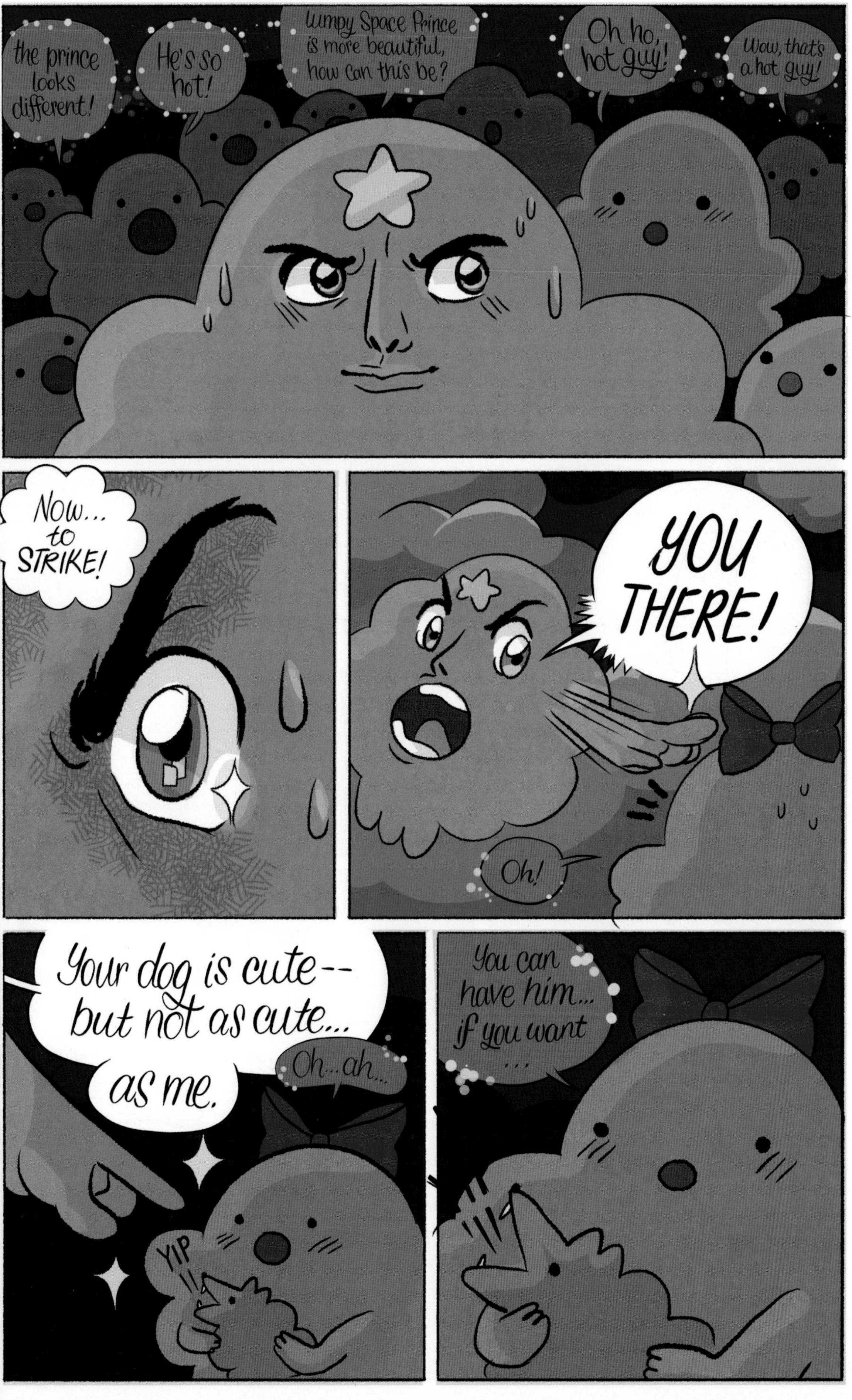

the prince looks different!
He's so hot!
Lumpy Space Prince is more beautiful, how can this be?
Oh ho, hot guy!
Wow, that's a hot guy!
Now... to STRIKE!
YOU THERE!
Oh!
Your dog is cute-- but not as cute...
as me.
Oh...ah...
YIP
You can have him... if you want . . .

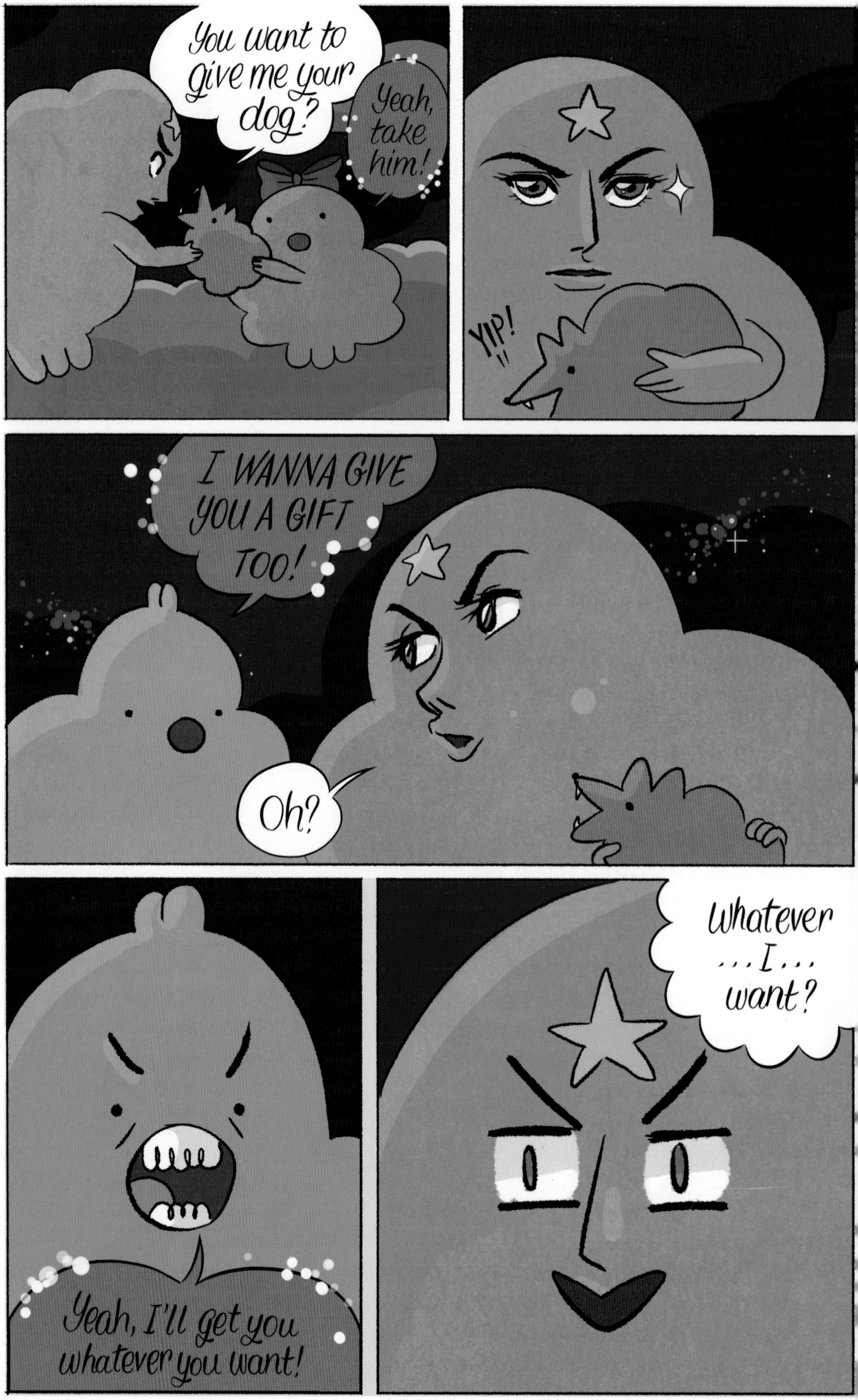
You want to give me your dog?
Yeah, take him!
YIP!
I WANNA GIVE YOU A GIFT TOO!
Oh?
Yeah, I'll get you whatever you want!
Whatever ...I... want?

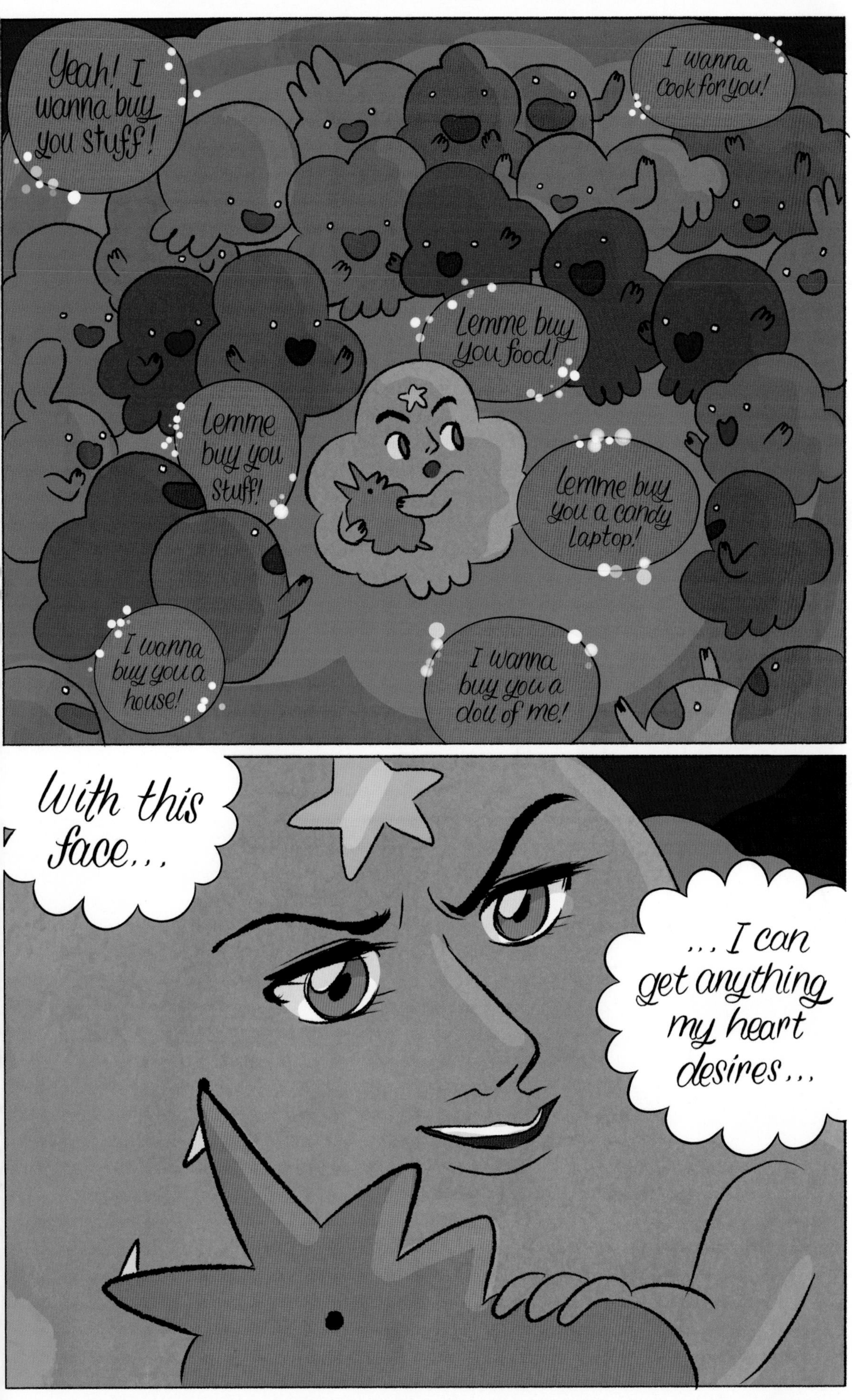
Yeah! I wanna buy you stuff!
I wanna cook for you!
Lemme buy you food!
Lemme buy you stuff!
Lemme buy you a candy laptop!
I wanna buy you a house!
I wanna buy you a doll of me!
With this face...
...I can get anything my heart desires...

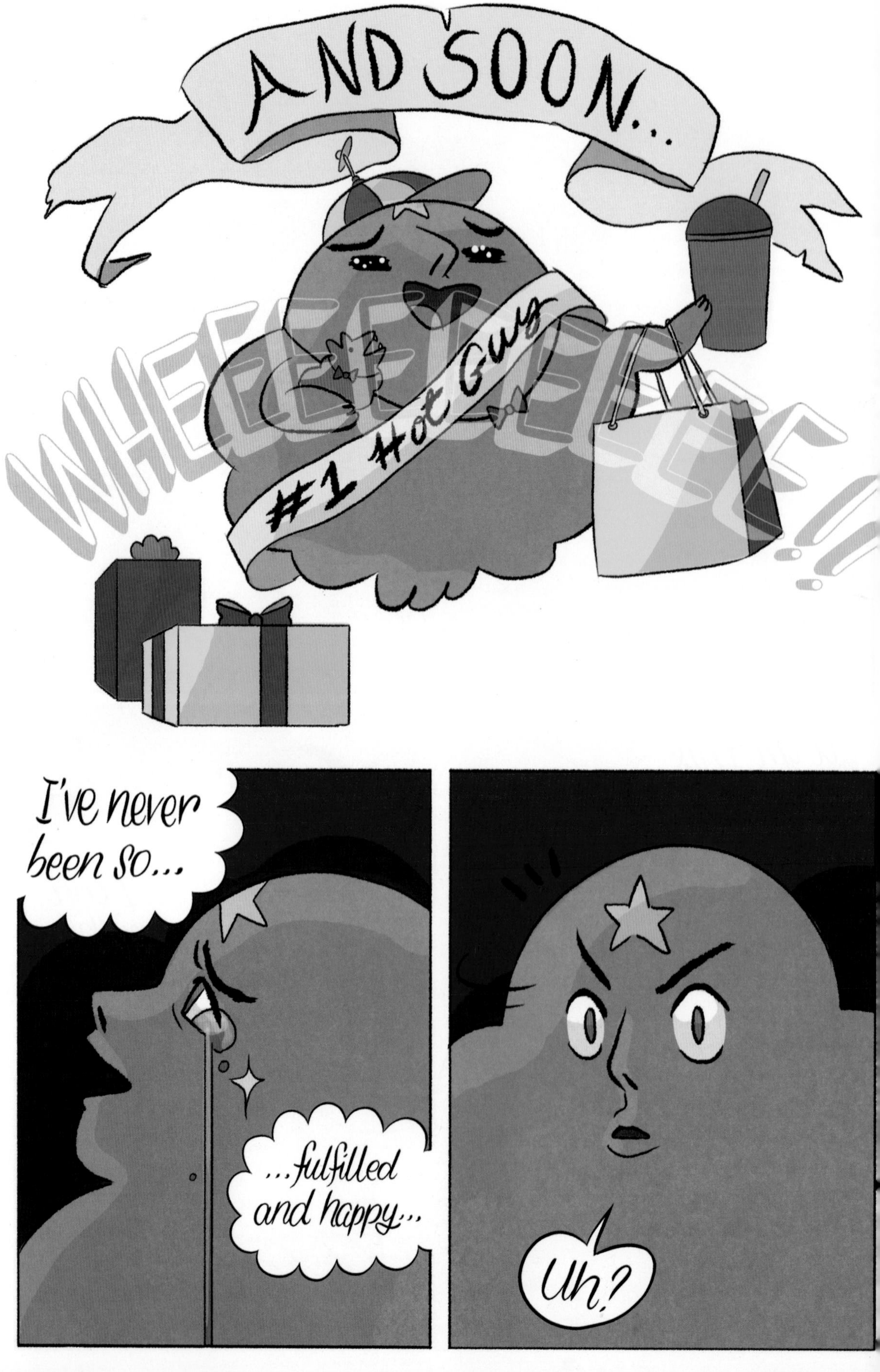

AND SOON...
#1 Hot Guy
WHEEEEEEEEE!!!
I've never been so...
...fulfilled and happy...
Uh?

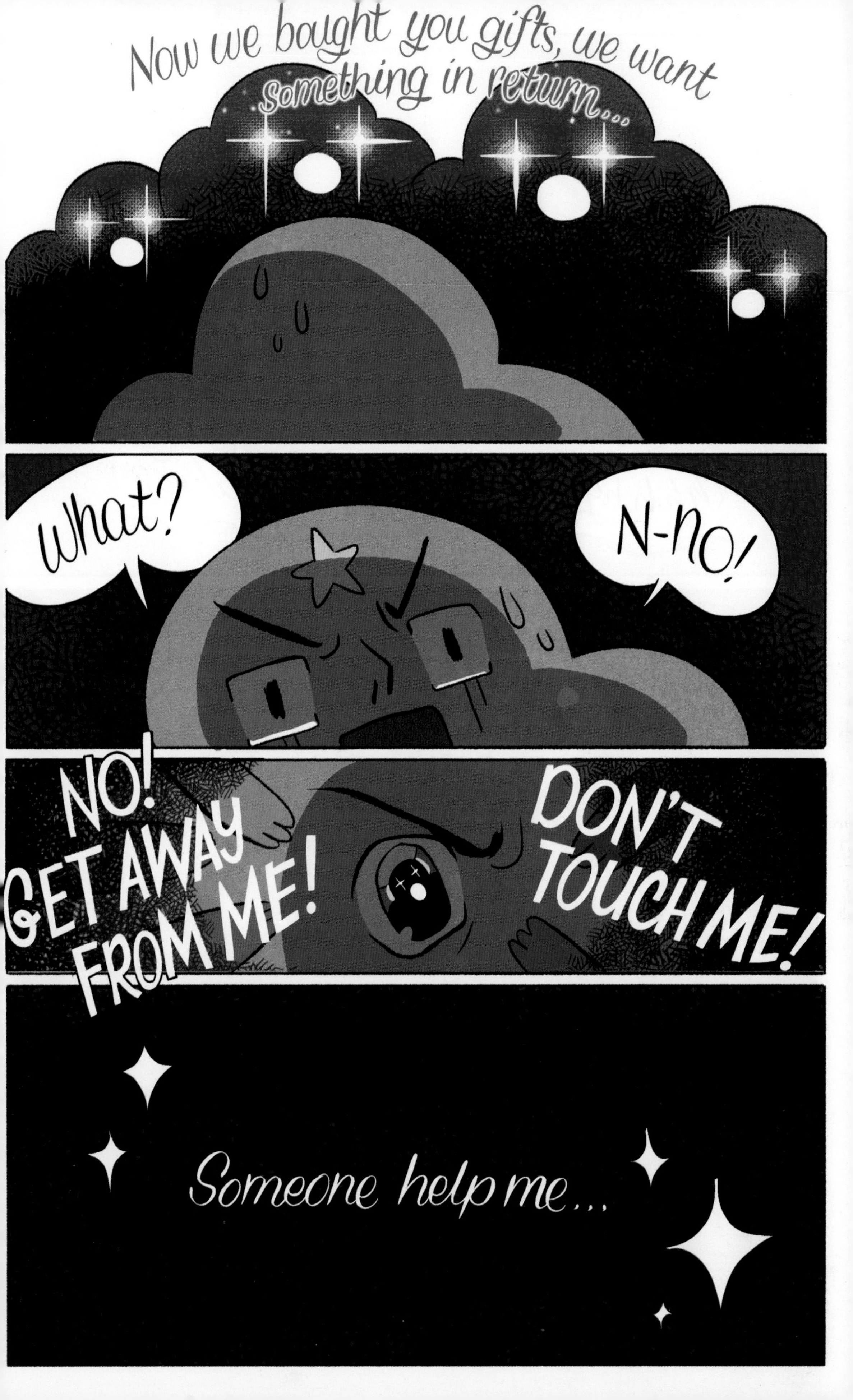
Now we bought you gifts, we want something in return...
What?
N-no!
NO! GET AWAY FROM ME!
DON'T TOUCH ME!
Someone help me...

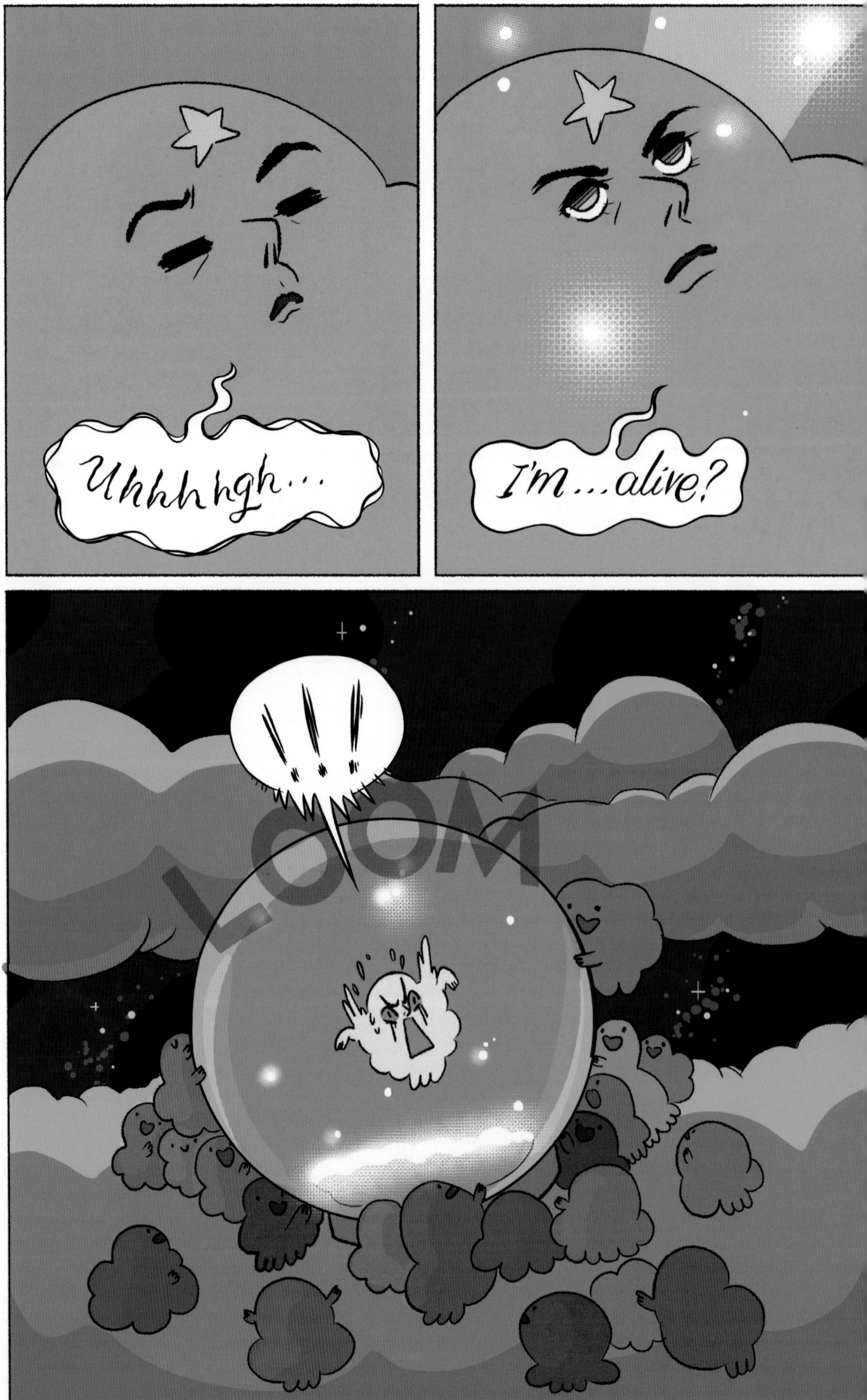
Uhhhhgh...
I'm...alive?
!!!
LOOM

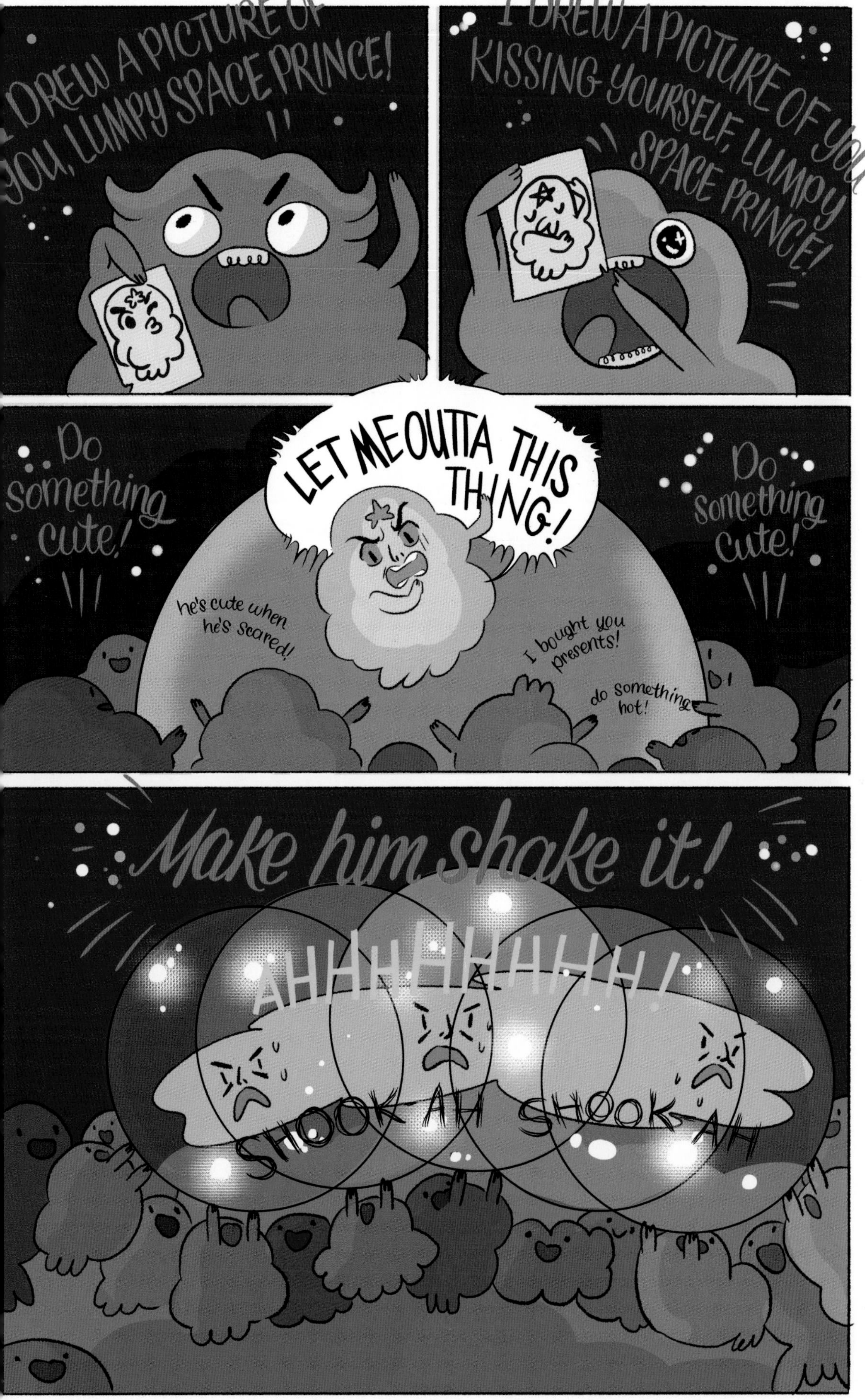
I DREW A PICTURE OF YOU, LUMPY SPACE PRINCE!
I DREW A PICTURE OF YOU KISSING YOURSELF, LUMPY SPACE PRINCE!
Do something cute!
LET ME OUTTA THIS THING!
Do something cute!
he's cute when he's scared!
I bought you presents!
do something hot!
Make him shake it!
AHHHHHHHHH!
SHOOK-AH SHOOK-AH

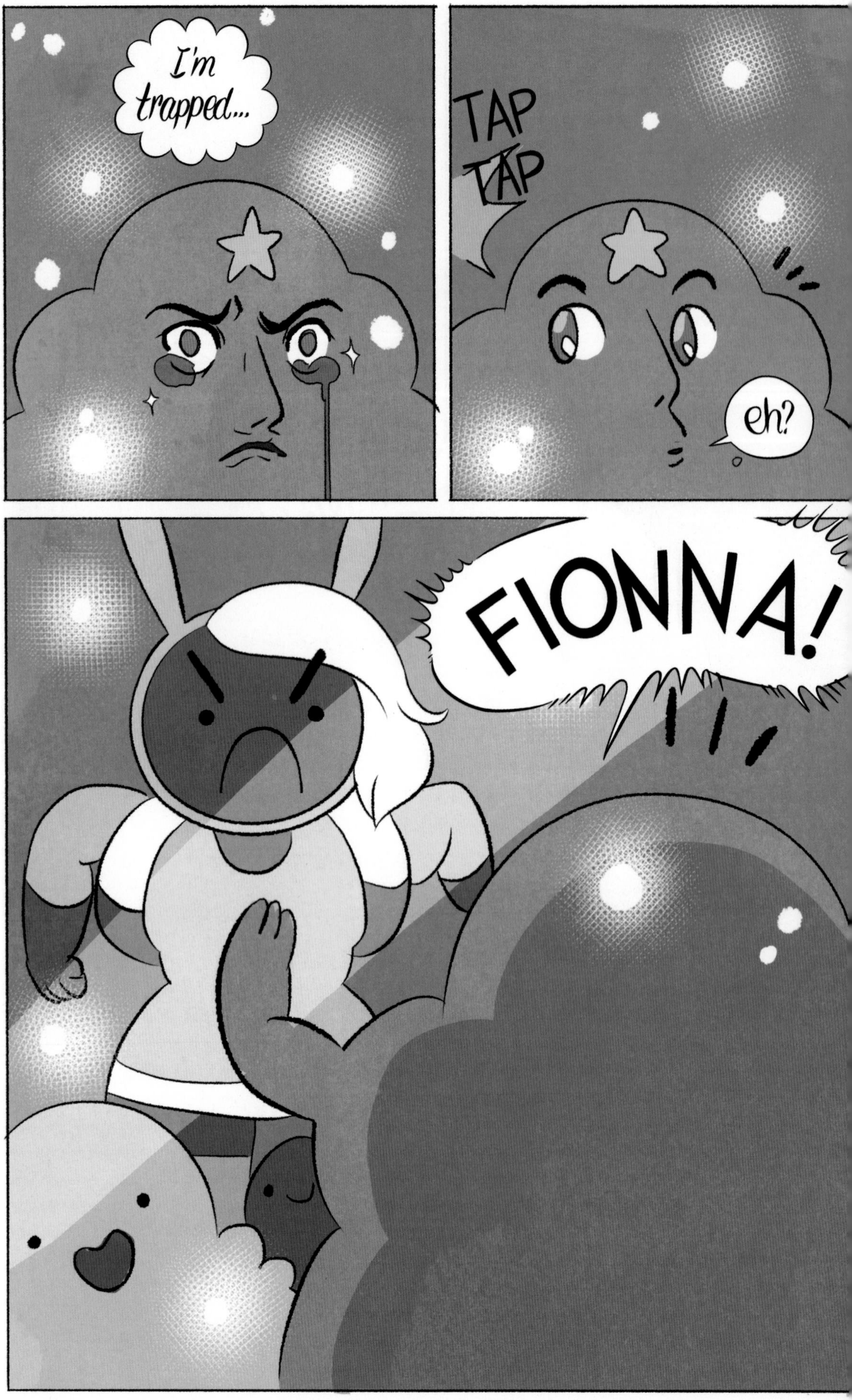
I'm trapped...
TAP
TAP
eh?
FIONNA!

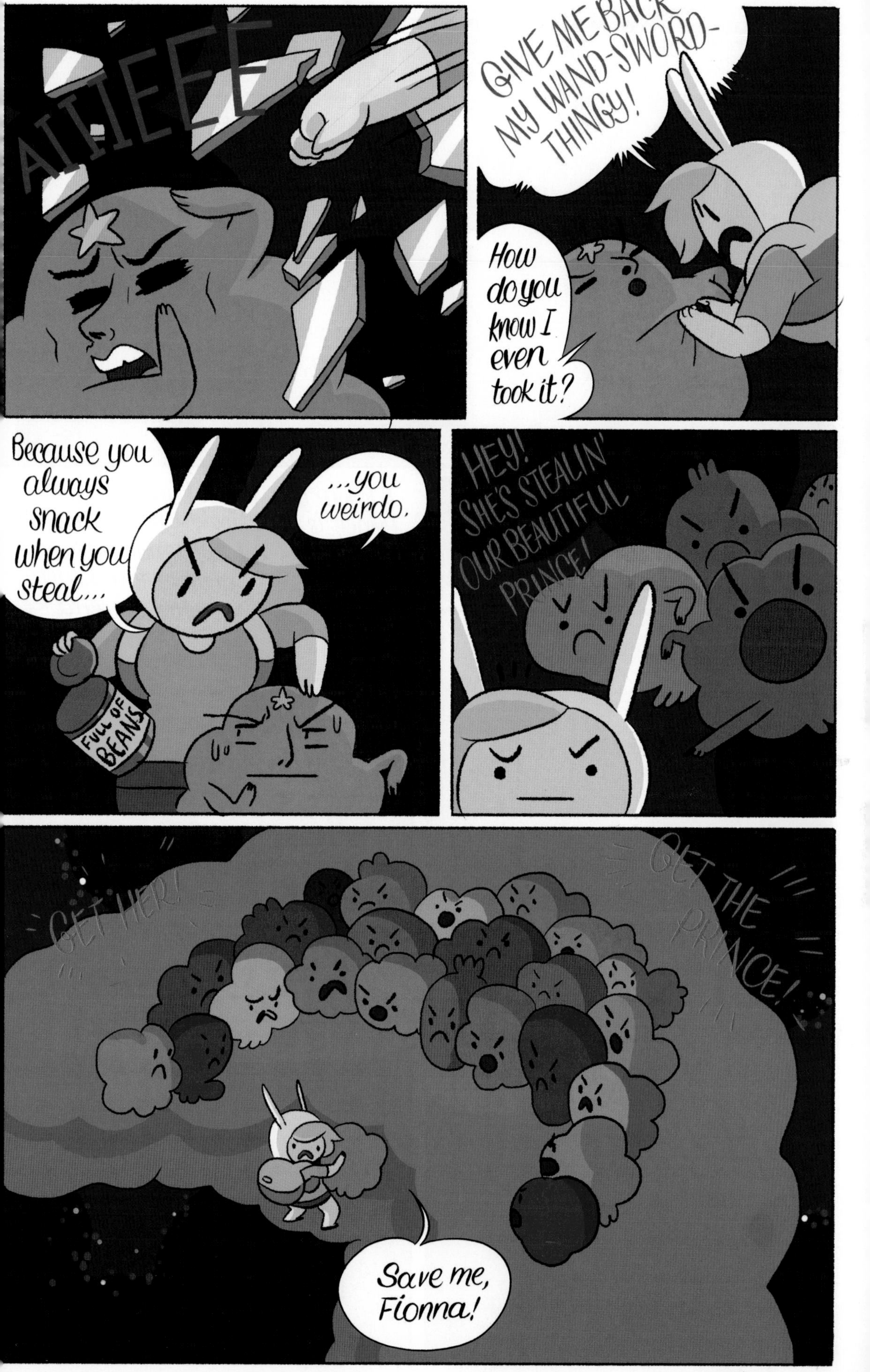
AIIIEEE
GIVE ME BACK MY WAND-SWORD-THINGY!
How do you know I even took it?
Because you always snack when you steal...
...you weirdo.
FULL OF BEANS
HEY! SHE'S STEALIN' OUR BEAUTIFUL PRINCE!
GET HER!
GET THE PRINCE!
Save me, Fionna!

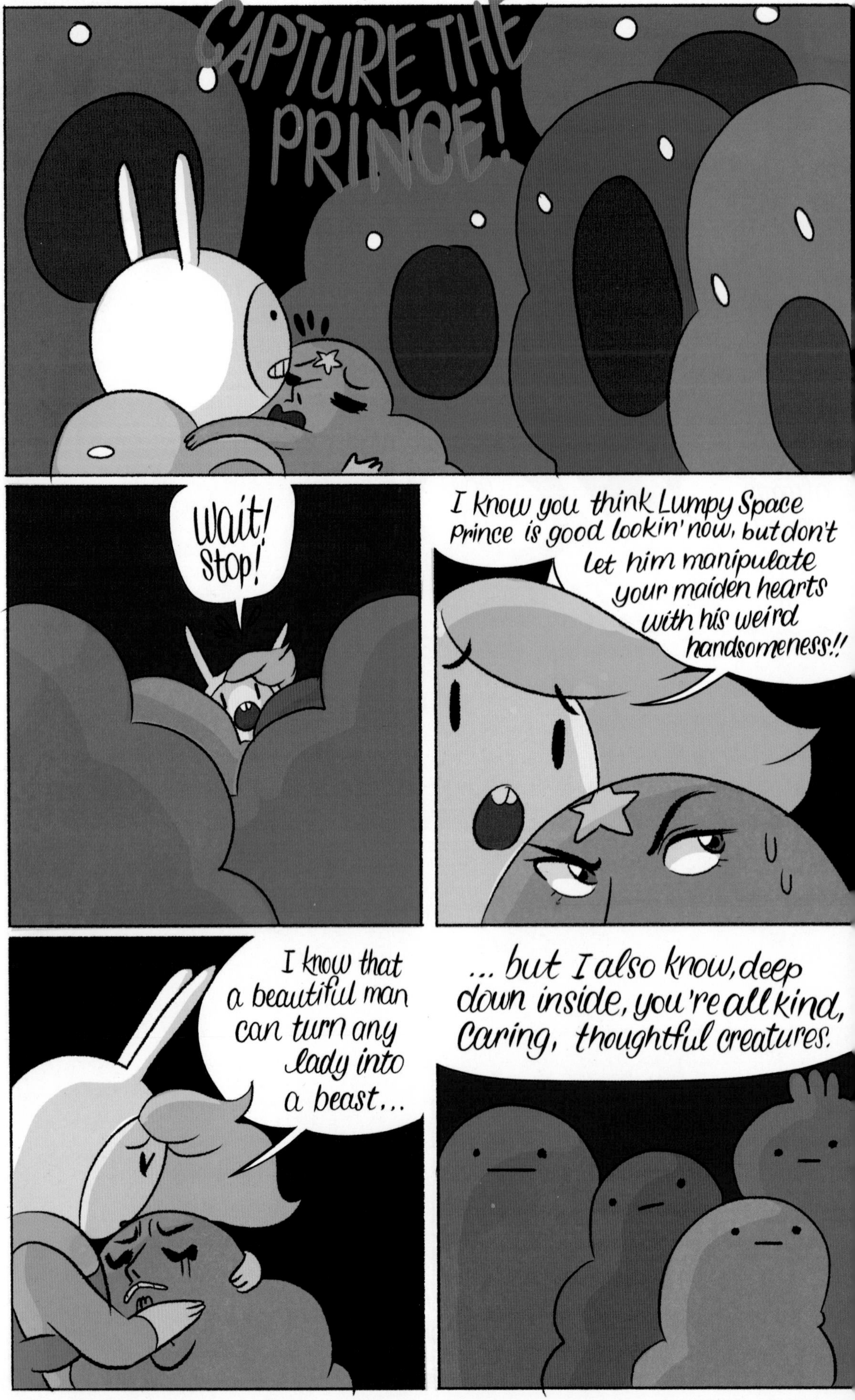
CAPTURE THE PRINCE!
Wait! Stop!
I know you think Lumpy Space Prince is good lookin' now, but don't let him manipulate your maiden hearts with his weird handsomeness!!
I know that a beautiful man can turn any lady into a beast...
... but I also know, deep down inside, you're all kind, Caring, thoughtful creatures.

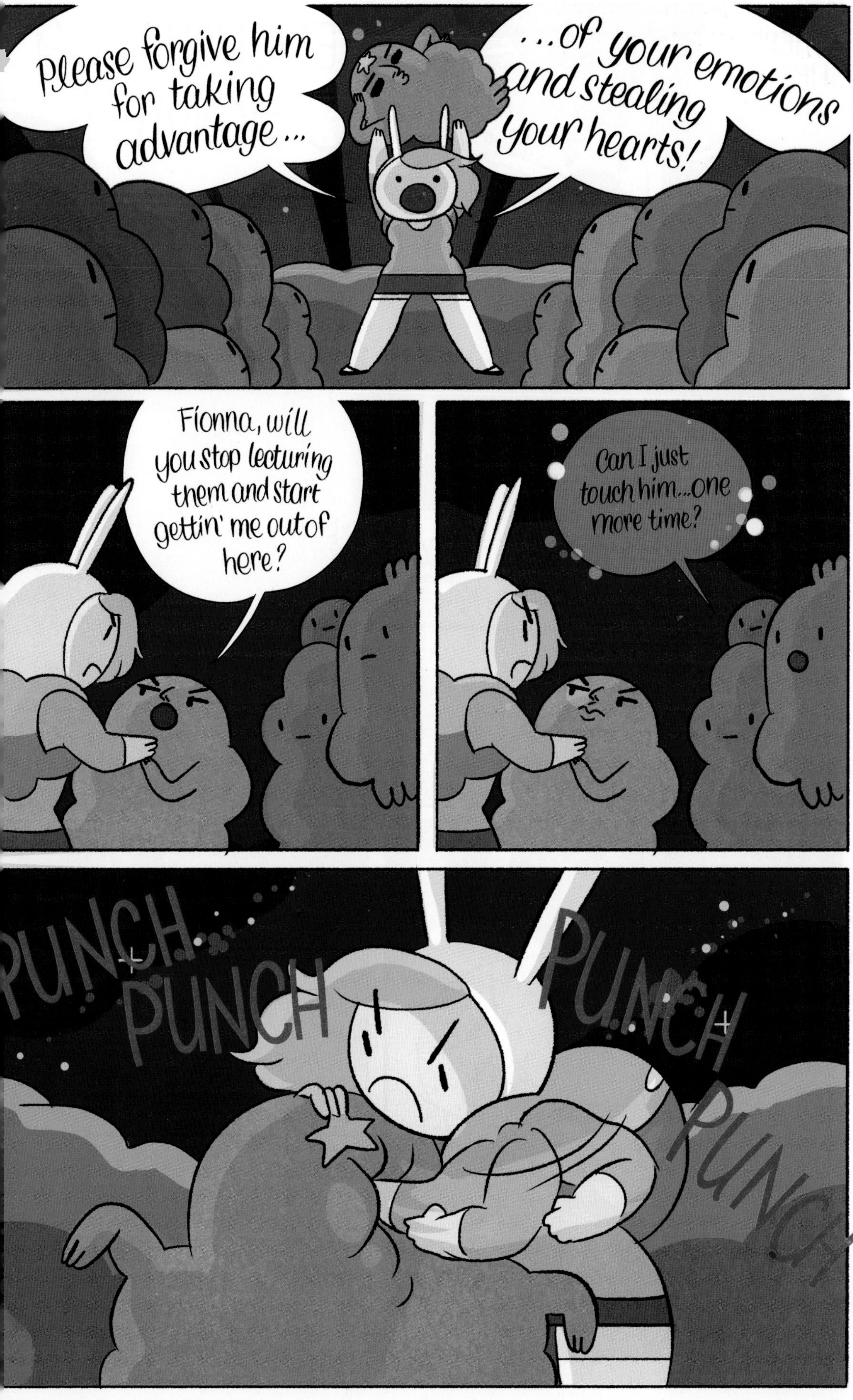
Please forgive him for taking advantage...
...of your emotions and stealing your hearts!
Fionna, will you stop lecturing them and start gettin' me out of here?
Can I just touch him...one more time?
PUNCH
PUNCH
PUNCH
PUNCH

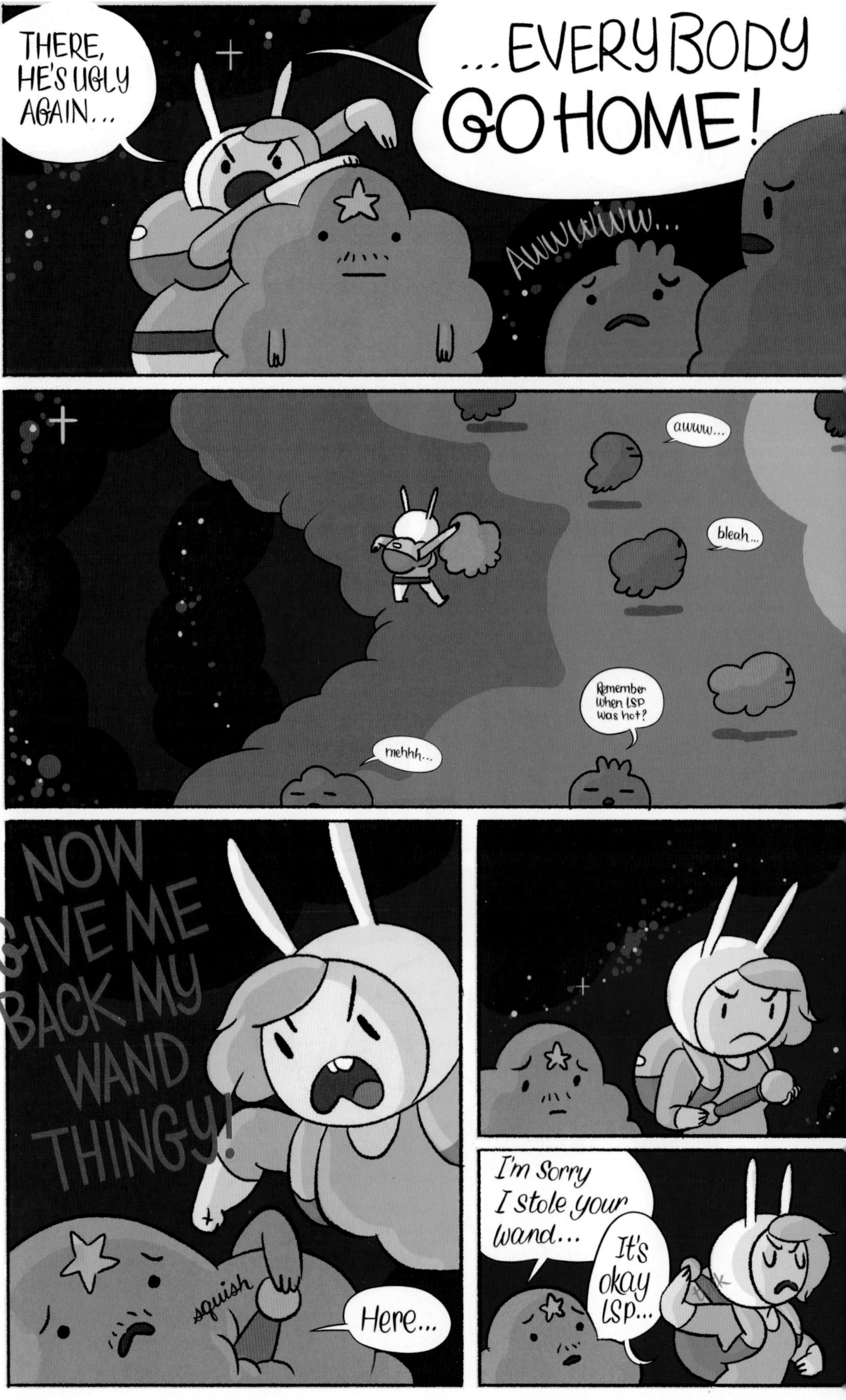
THERE, HE'S UGLY AGAIN...
...EVERYBODY GO HOME!
AWWWWW...
awww...
bleah...
Remember when LSP was hot?
mehhh...
NOW GIVE ME BACK MY WAND THINGY!
squish
Here...
I'm sorry I stole your wand...
It's okay LSP...

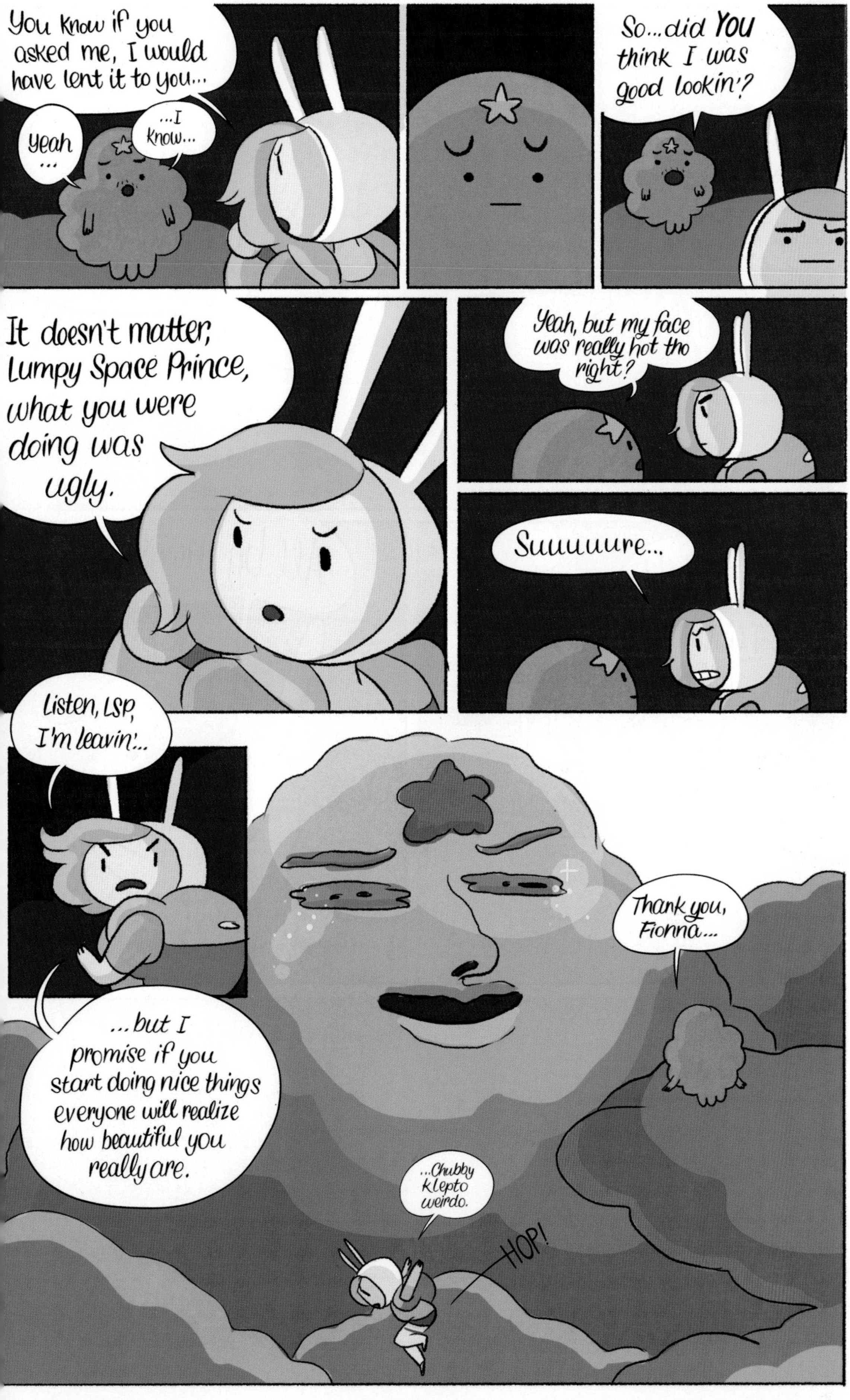
You know if you asked me, I would have lent it to you...
Yeah...
...I know...
So...did YOU think I was good lookin'?
It doesn't matter, Lumpy Space Prince, what you were doing was ugly.
Yeah, but my face was really hot tho right?
Suuuuure...
Listen, LSP, I'm leavin'...
...but I promise if you start doing nice things everyone will realize how beautiful you really are.
Thank you, Fionna...
...Chubby klepto weirdo.
HOP!

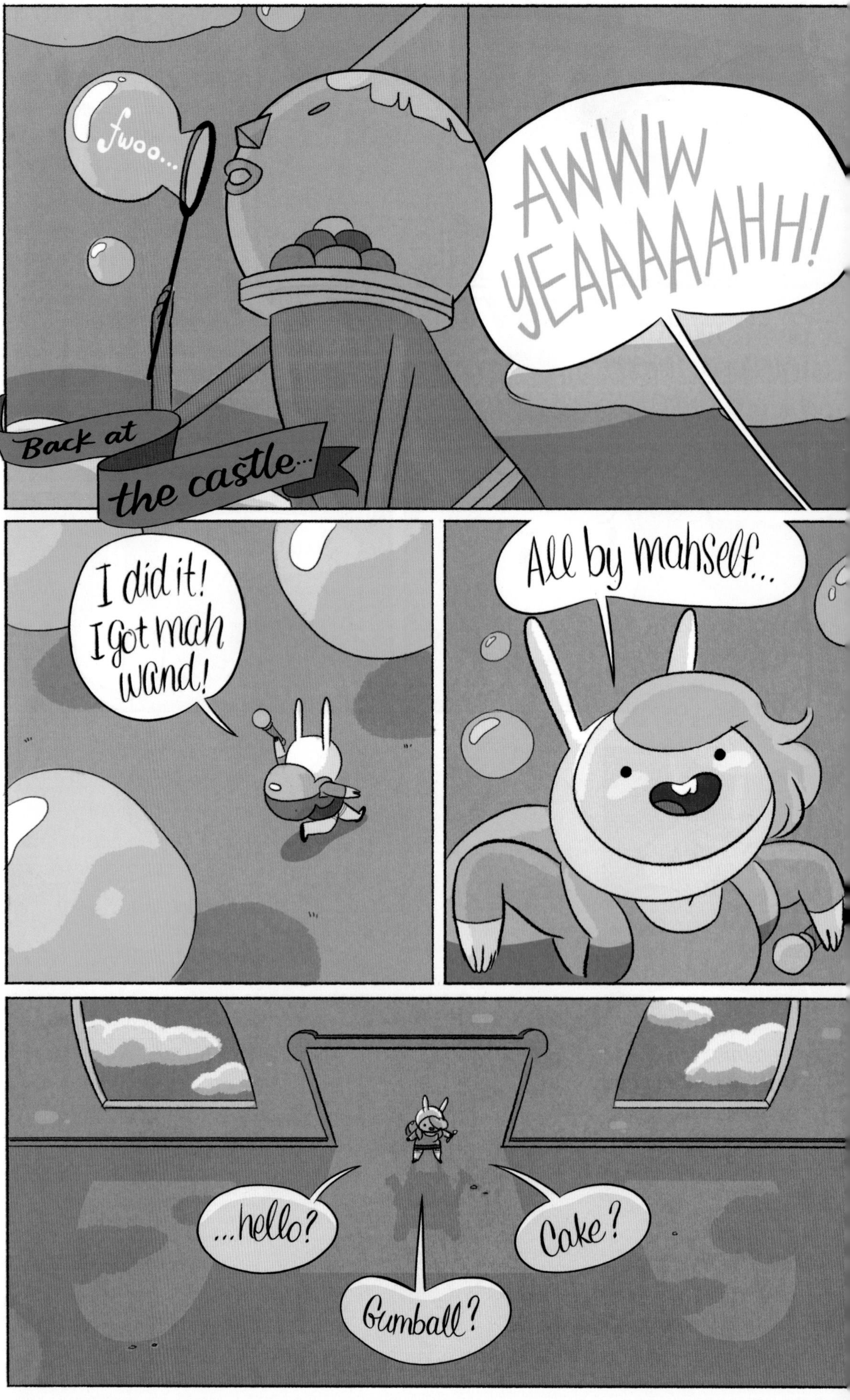
fwoo...
AWWW YEAAAAAHH!
Back at the castle...
I did it! I got mah wand!
All by mahself...
...hello?
Gumball?
Cake?

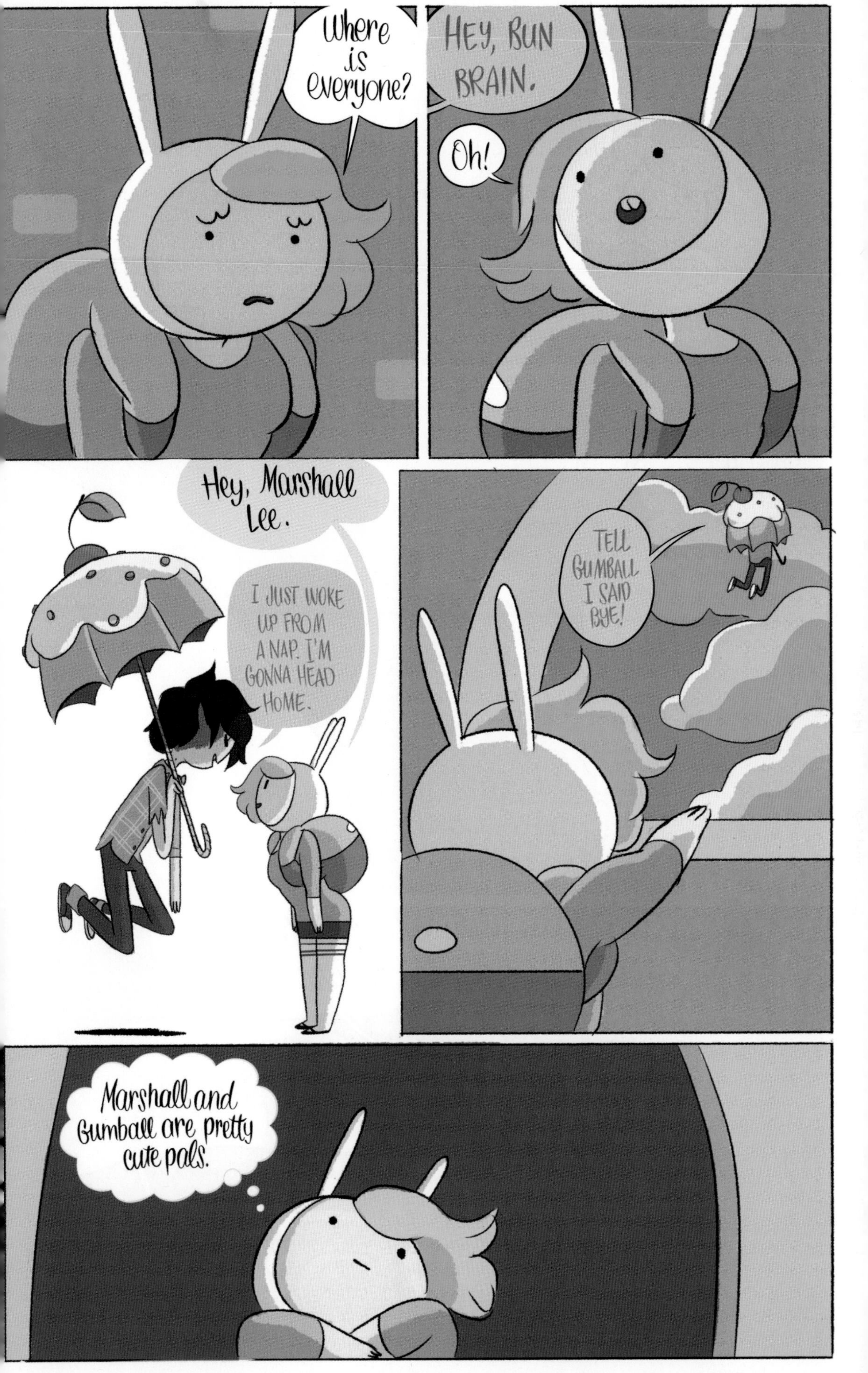
Where is everyone?
HEY, BUN BRAIN.
Oh!
Hey, Marshall Lee.
I JUST WOKE UP FROM A NAP. I'M GONNA HEAD HOME.
TELL GUMBALL I SAID BYE!
Marshall and Gumball are pretty cute pals.

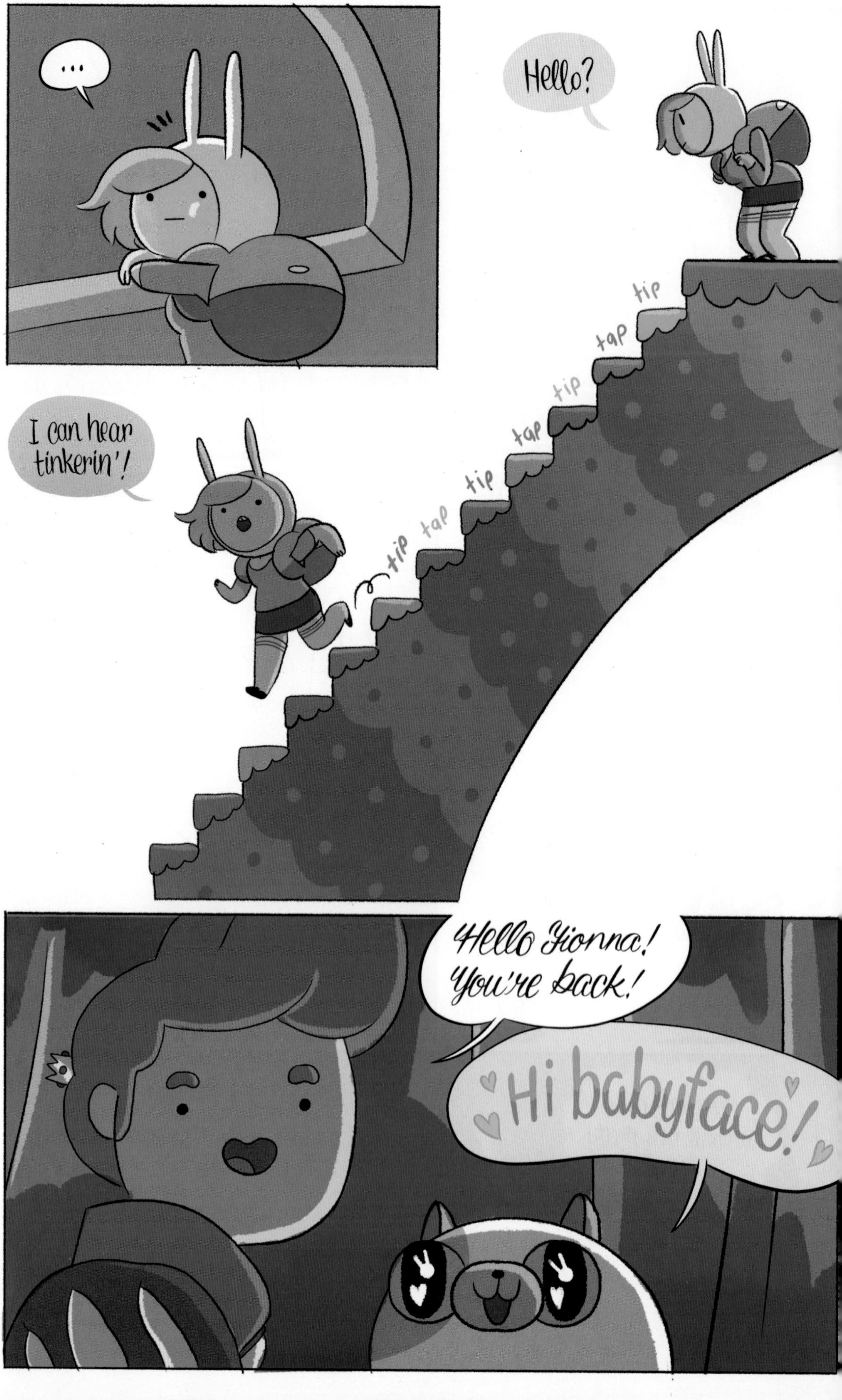
...
Hello?
tip
tap
tip
tap
tip
tap
tip
I can hear tinkerin'!
Hello Fionna! You're back!
Hi babyface!

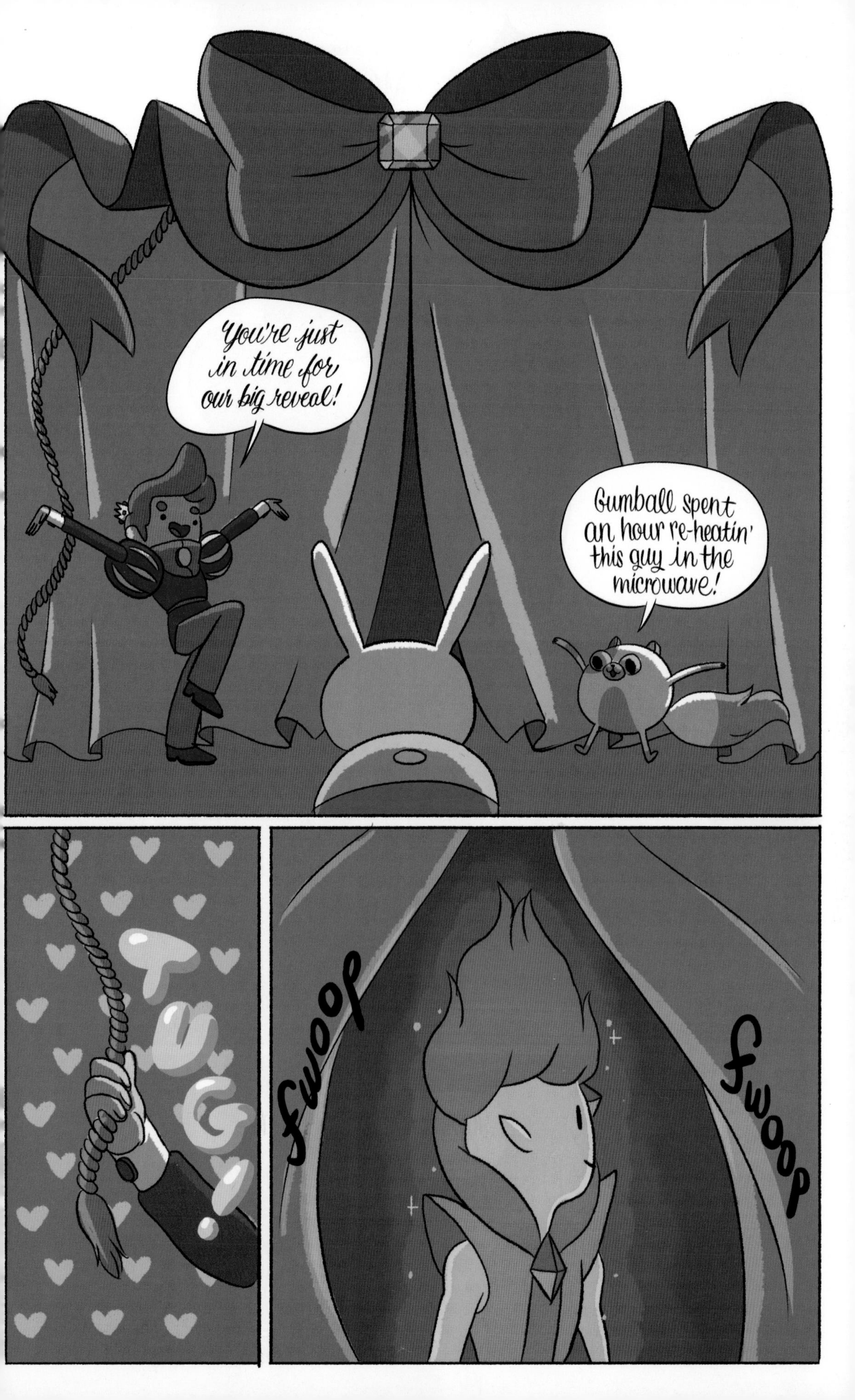
You're just in time for our big reveal!
Gumball spent an hour re-heatin' this guy in the microwave!
TUG
fwoop
fwoop

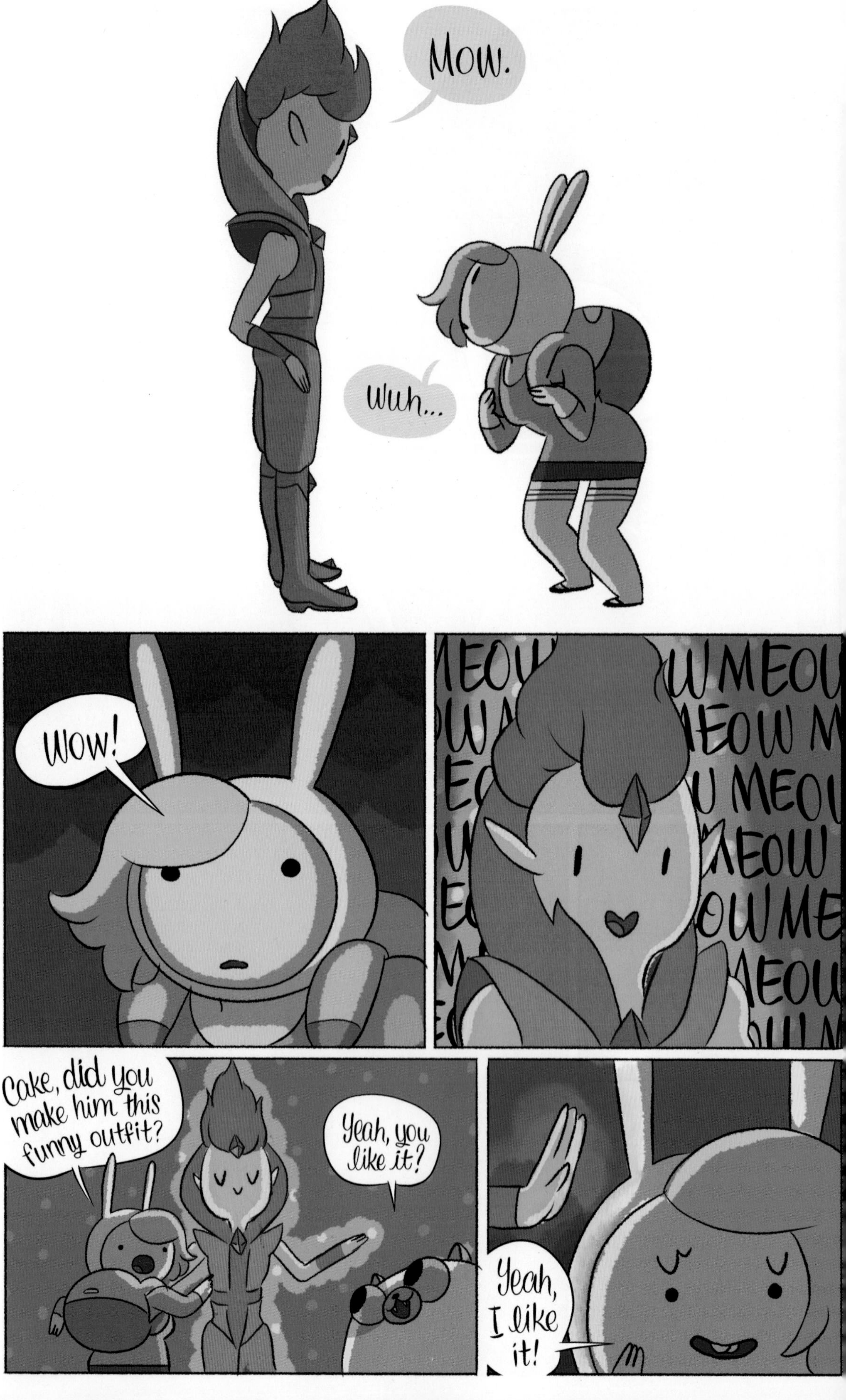
Mow.
Wuh...
Wow!
MEOW MEOW MEOW MEOW
Cake, did you make him this funny outfit?
Yeah, you like it?
Yeah, I like it!

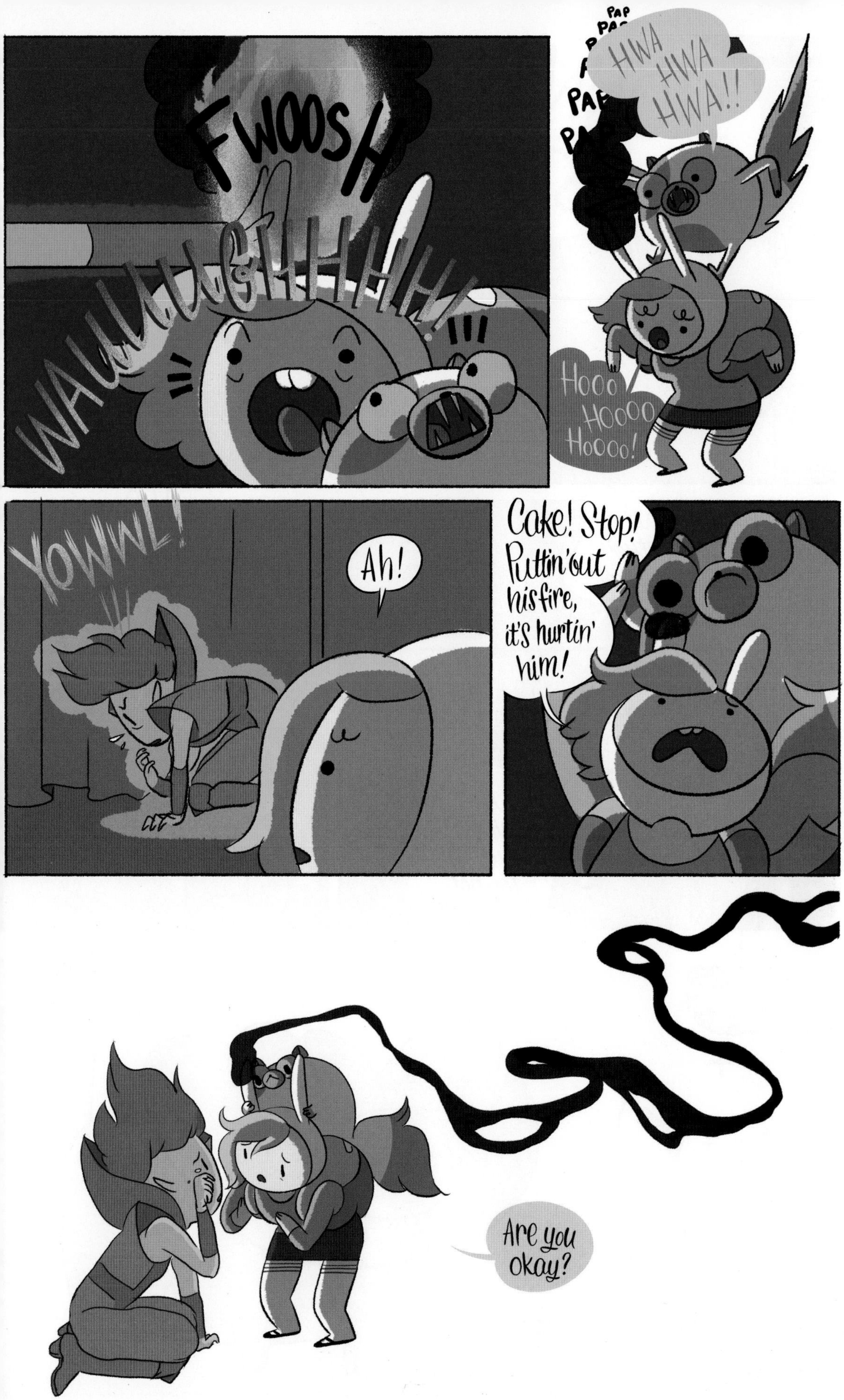
FWOOSH
WAUUUUGHHHHH!
PAP PAP PAP PAP PAP PAP
HWA HWA HWA!!
Hooo Hoooo Hoooo!
YOWWL!
Ah!
Cake! Stop! Puttin'out his fire, it's hurtin' him!
Are you okay?

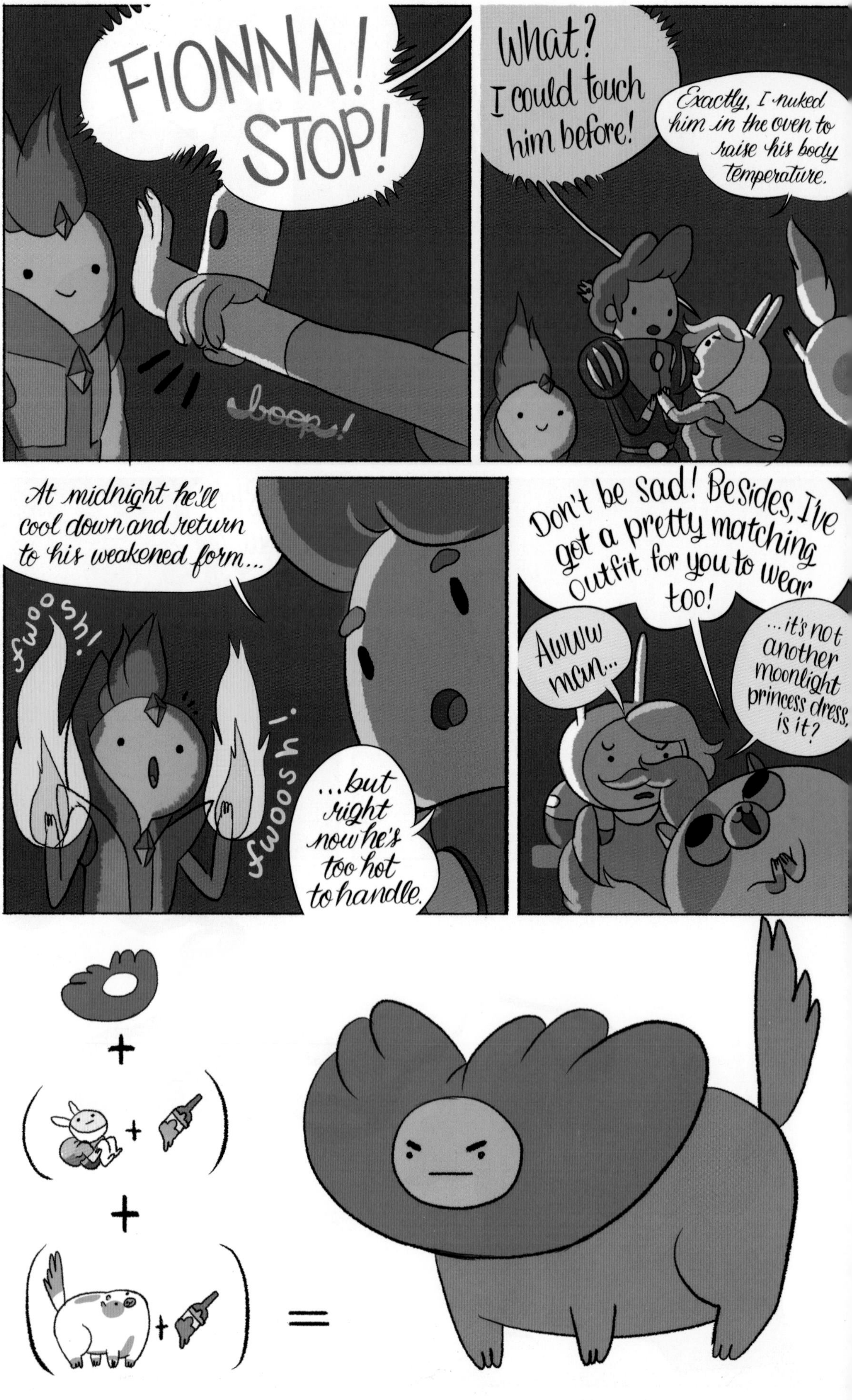
FIONNA! STOP!
boop!
What? I could touch him before!
Exactly, I nuked him in the oven to raise his body temperature.
At midnight he'll cool down and return to his weakened form...
fwoosh!
fwoosh!
...but right now he's too hot to handle.
Don't be sad! Besides, I've got a pretty matching outfit for you to wear too!
Awww man...
...it's not another moonlight princess dress, is it?

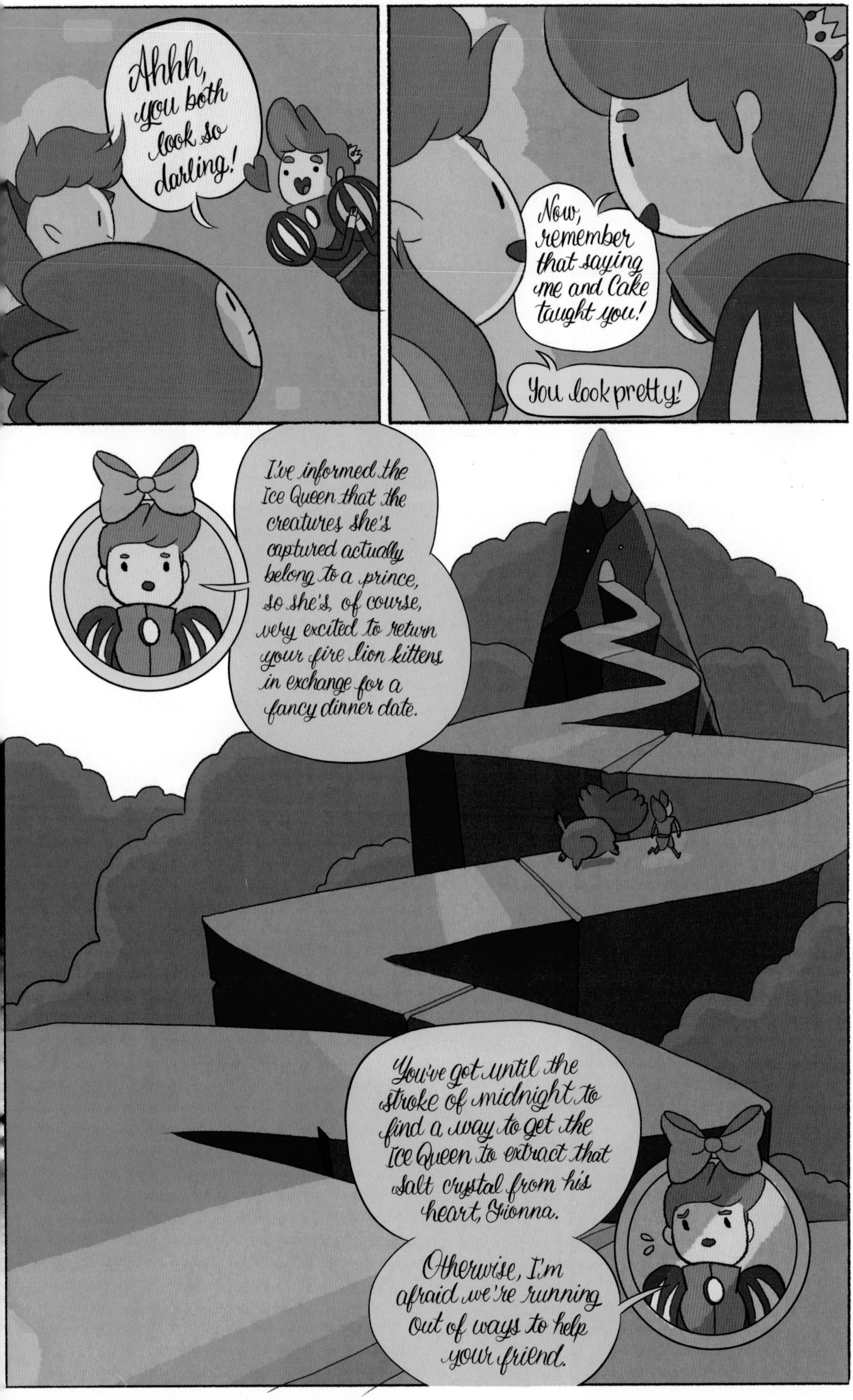
Ahhh, you both look so darling!
Now, remember that saying me and Cake taught you!
You look pretty!
I've informed the Ice Queen that the creatures she's captured actually belong to a prince, so she's, of course, very excited to return your fire lion kittens in exchange for a fancy dinner date.
You've got until the stroke of midnight to find a way to get the Ice Queen to extract that salt crystal from his heart, Fionna.
Otherwise, I'm afraid we're running out of ways to help your friend.

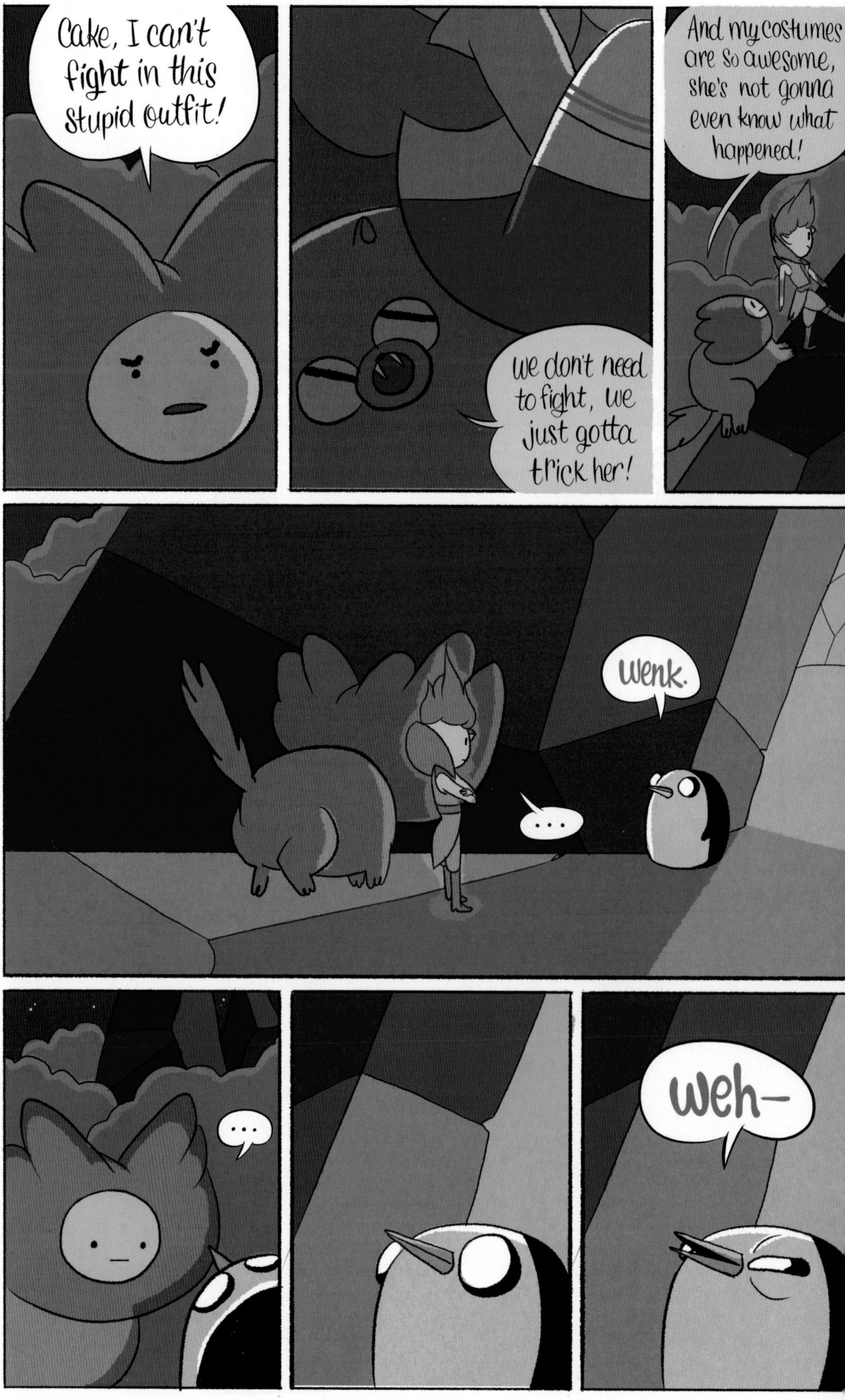
Cake, I can't fight in this stupid outfit!
We don't need to fight, we just gotta trick her!
And my costumes are so awesome, she's not gonna even know what happened!
Wenk.
...
...
Weh-

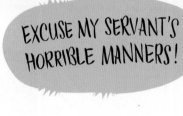

EXCUSE MY SERVANT'S HORRIBLE MANNERS!

I'M SO GLAD YOU COULD MAKE IT, FLAME PRINCE.

I'M SO SORRY ABOUT OUR HORRIBLE MISUNDERSTANDING EARLIER TODAY.

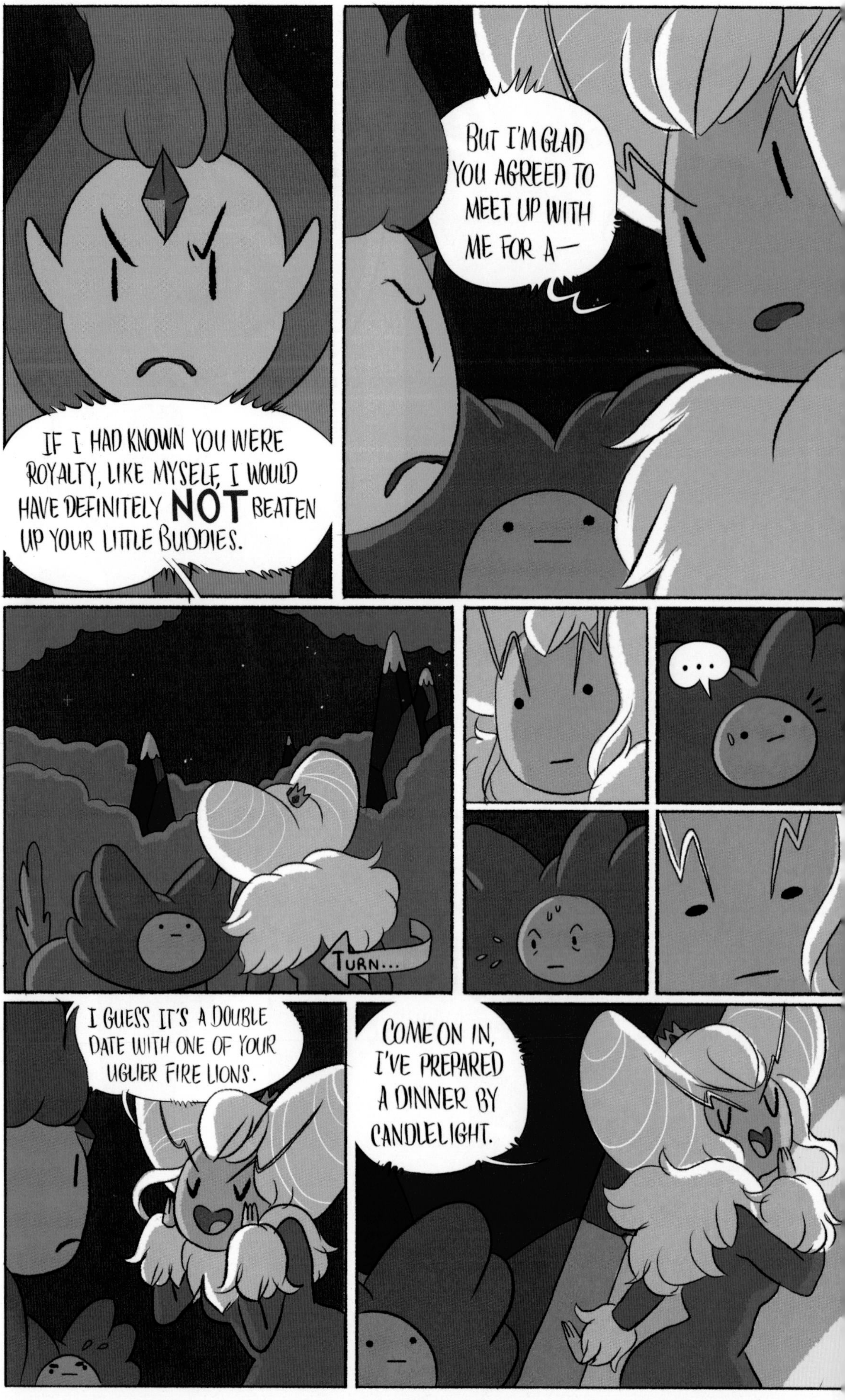
IF I HAD KNOWN YOU WERE ROYALTY, LIKE MYSELF, I WOULD HAVE DEFINITELY NOT BEATEN UP YOUR LITTLE BUDDIES.
BUT I'M GLAD YOU AGREED TO MEET UP WITH ME FOR A—
TURN...
...
I GUESS IT'S A DOUBLE DATE WITH ONE OF YOUR UGLIER FIRE LIONS.
COME ON IN, I'VE PREPARED A DINNER BY CANDLELIGHT.

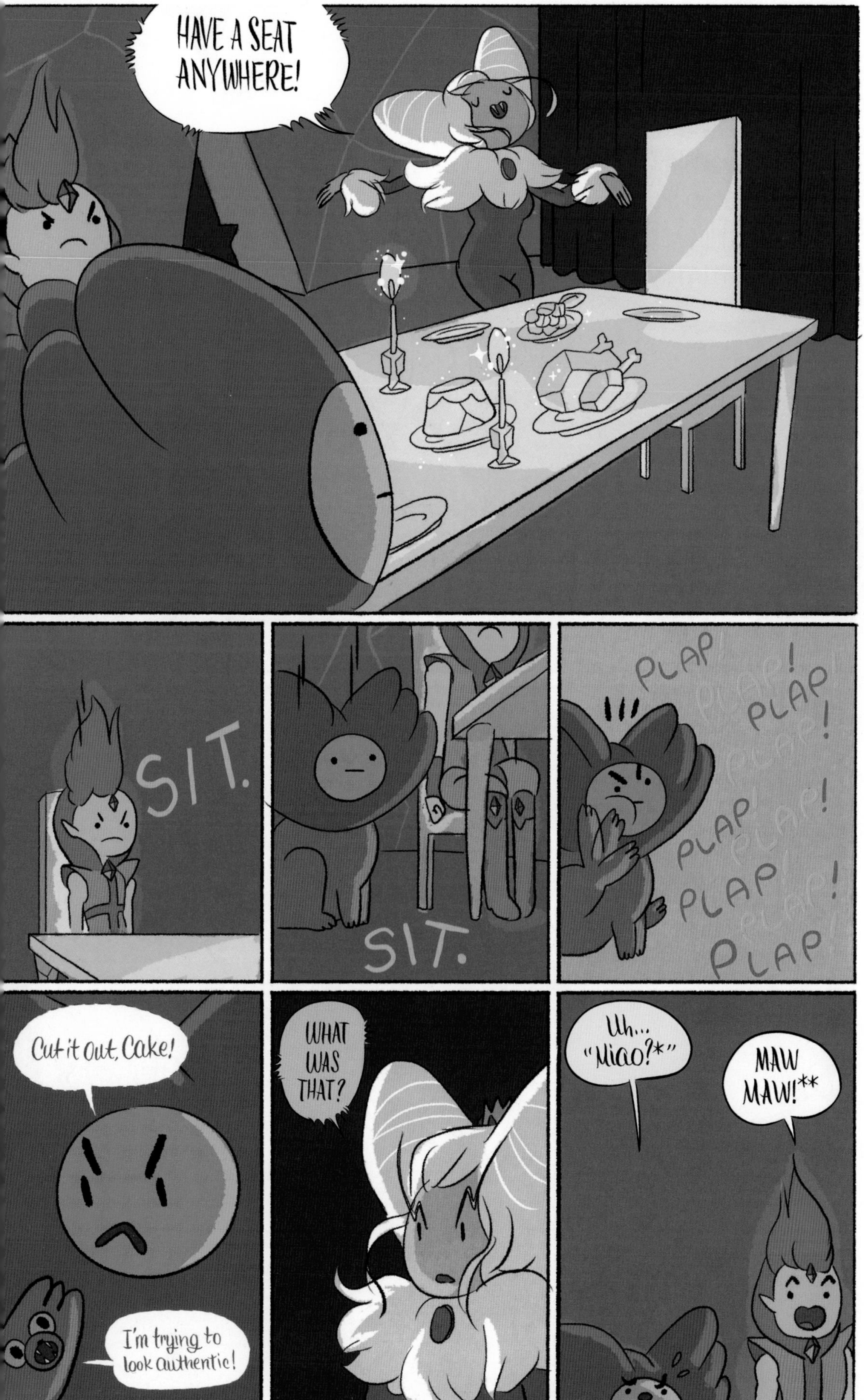

HAVE A SEAT ANYWHERE!
SIT.
SIT.
PLAP! PLAP! PLAP! PLAP! PLAP! PLAP! PLAP! PLAP! PLAP! PLAP! PLAP!
Cut it out, Cake!
I'm trying to look authentic!
WHAT WAS THAT?
Uh... "Miao?*"
MAW MAW!**

*poo
** HAW HAW!!

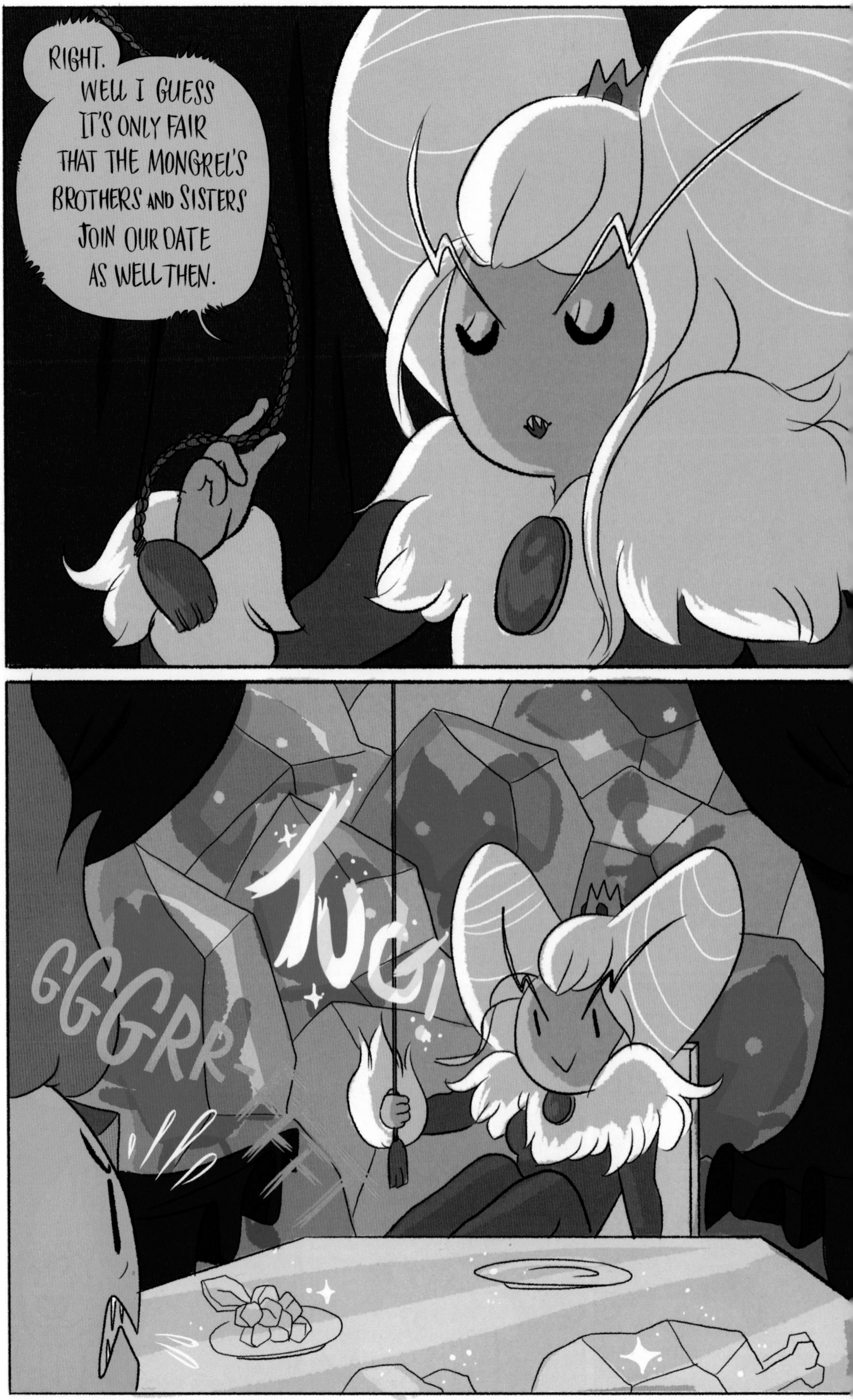
RIGHT. WELL I GUESS IT'S ONLY FAIR THAT THE MONGREL'S BROTHERS AND SISTERS JOIN OUR DATE AS WELL THEN.
TUG!
GGGRR

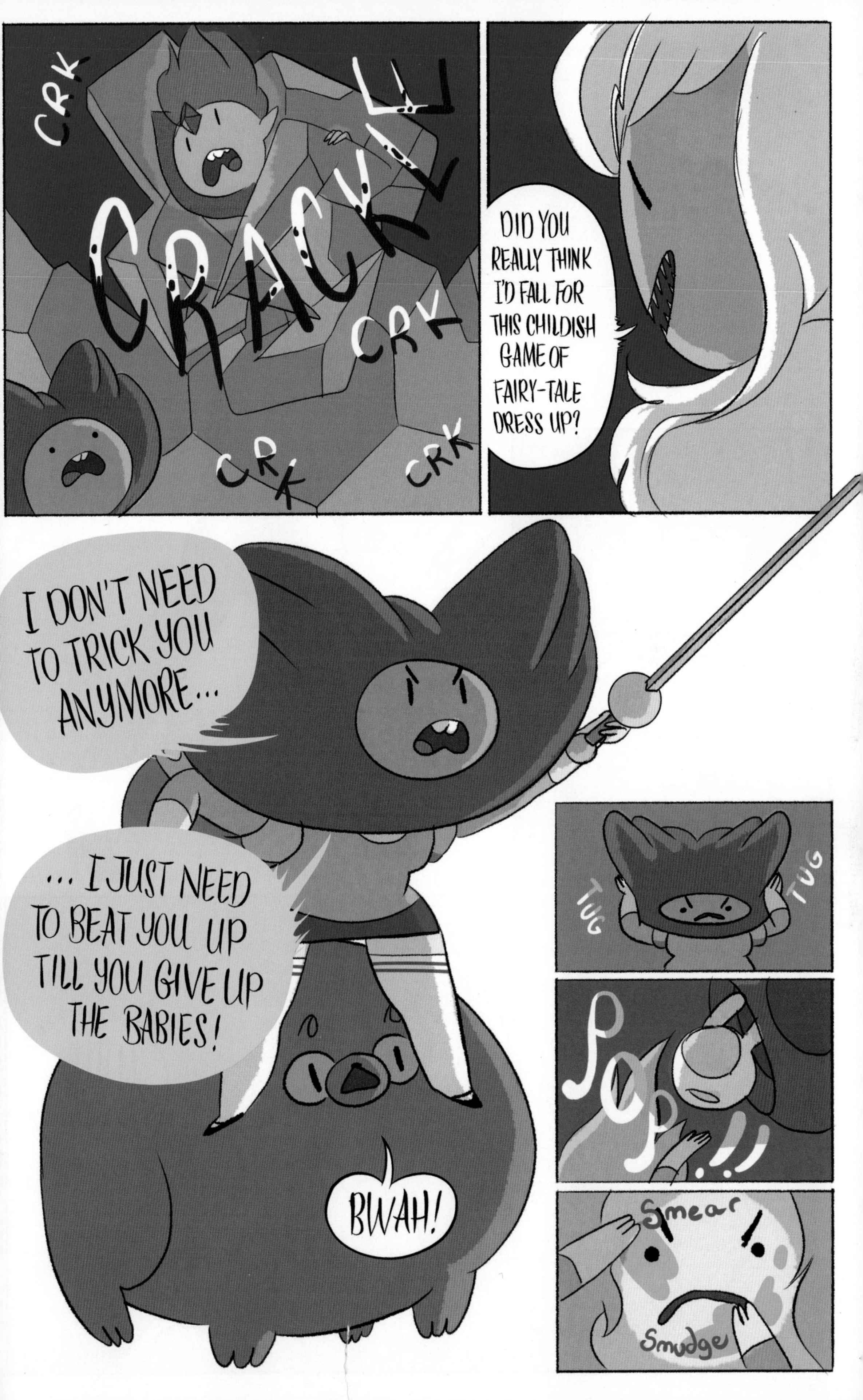
CRK
CRACKLE
CRK
CRK
CRK
DID YOU REALLY THINK I'D FALL FOR THIS CHILDISH GAME OF FAIRY-TALE DRESS UP?
I DON'T NEED TO TRICK YOU ANYMORE...
... I JUST NEED TO BEAT YOU UP TILL YOU GIVE UP THE BABIES!
BWAH!
TUG TUG
POP...!!
Smear
Smudge

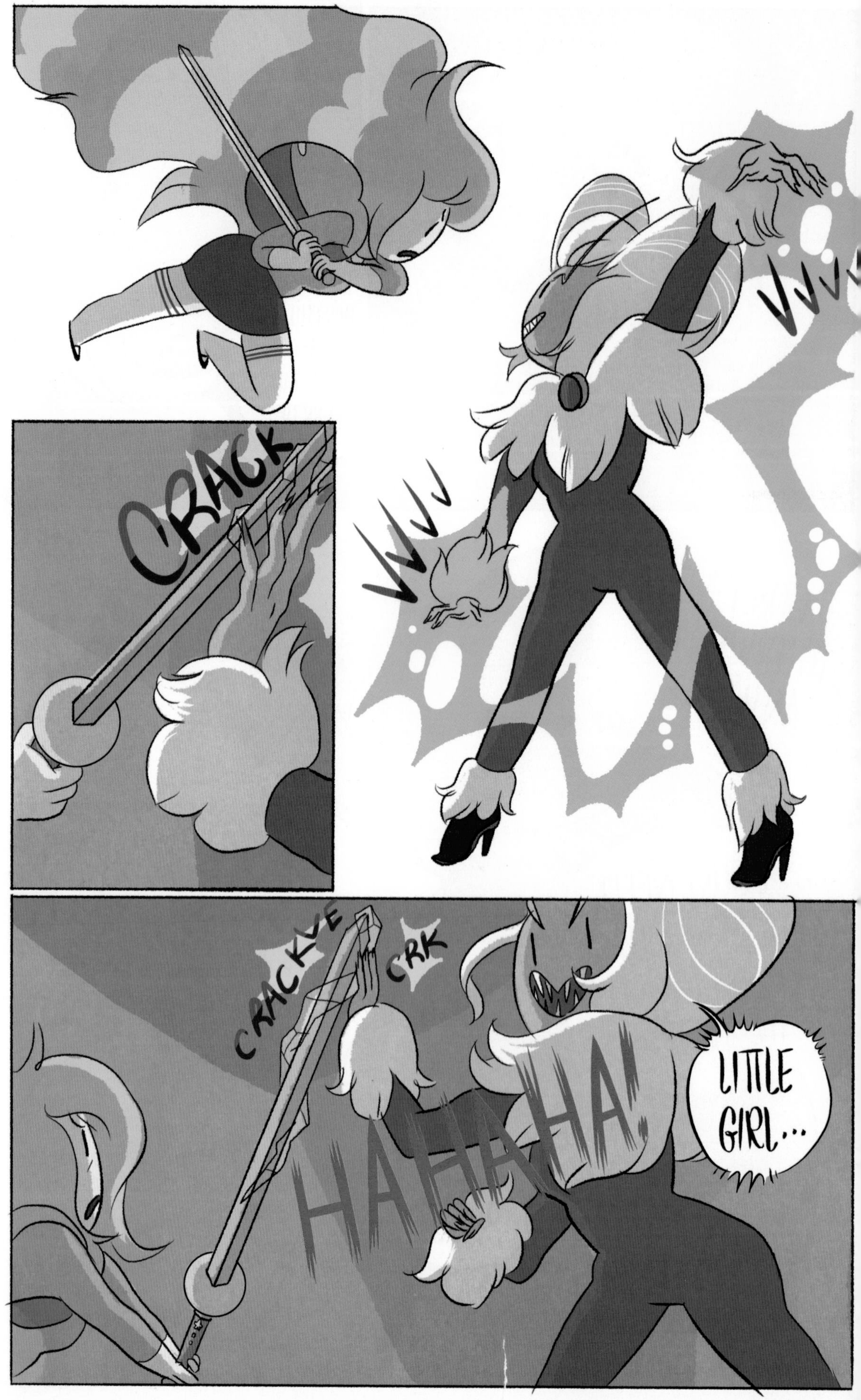
VVVV
VVVV
CRACK
CRACKLE
CRK
HAHAHA!
LITTLE GIRL...

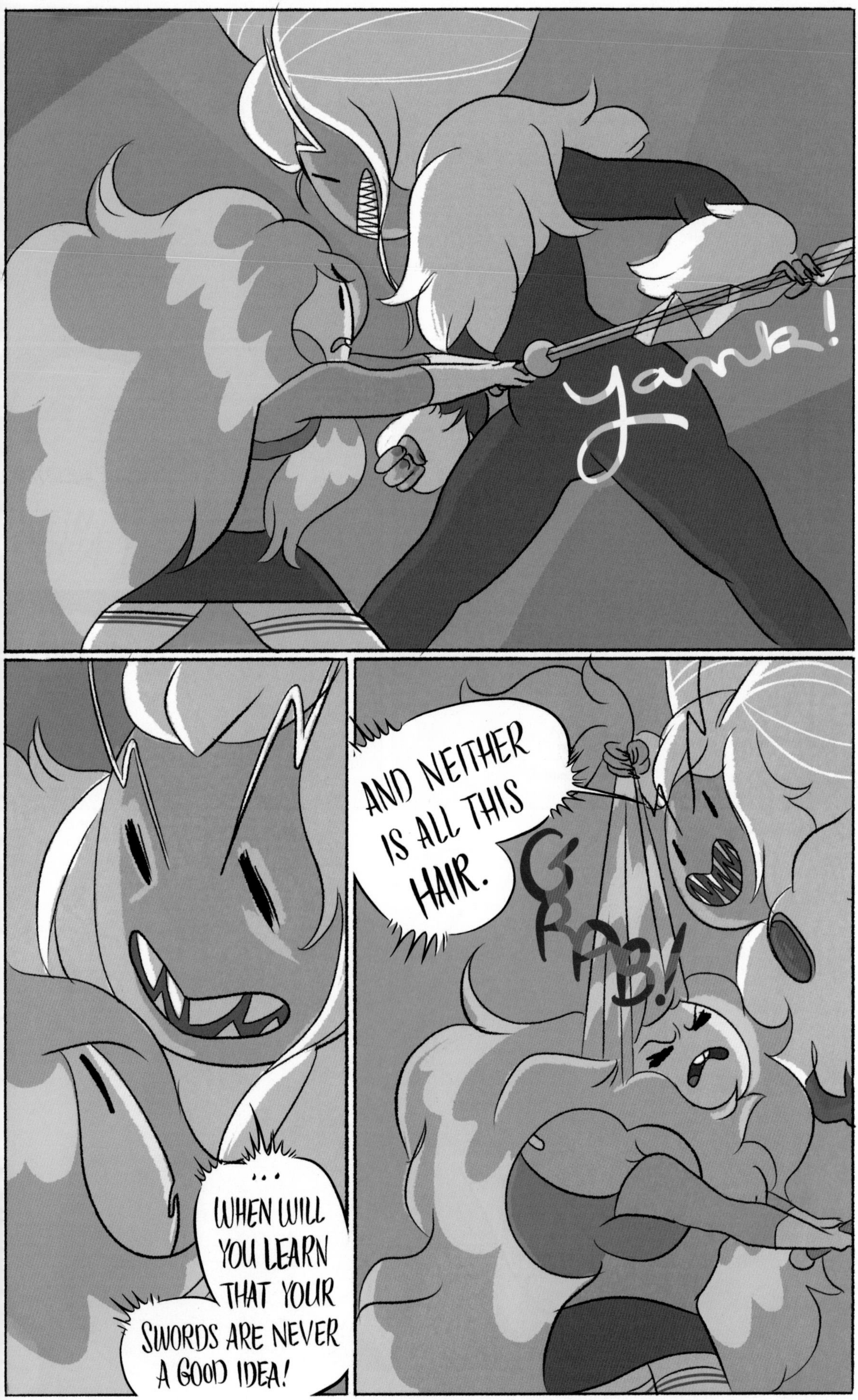
yank!
...WHEN WILL YOU LEARN THAT YOUR SWORDS ARE NEVER A GOOD IDEA!
AND NEITHER IS ALL THIS HAIR.
GRAB!

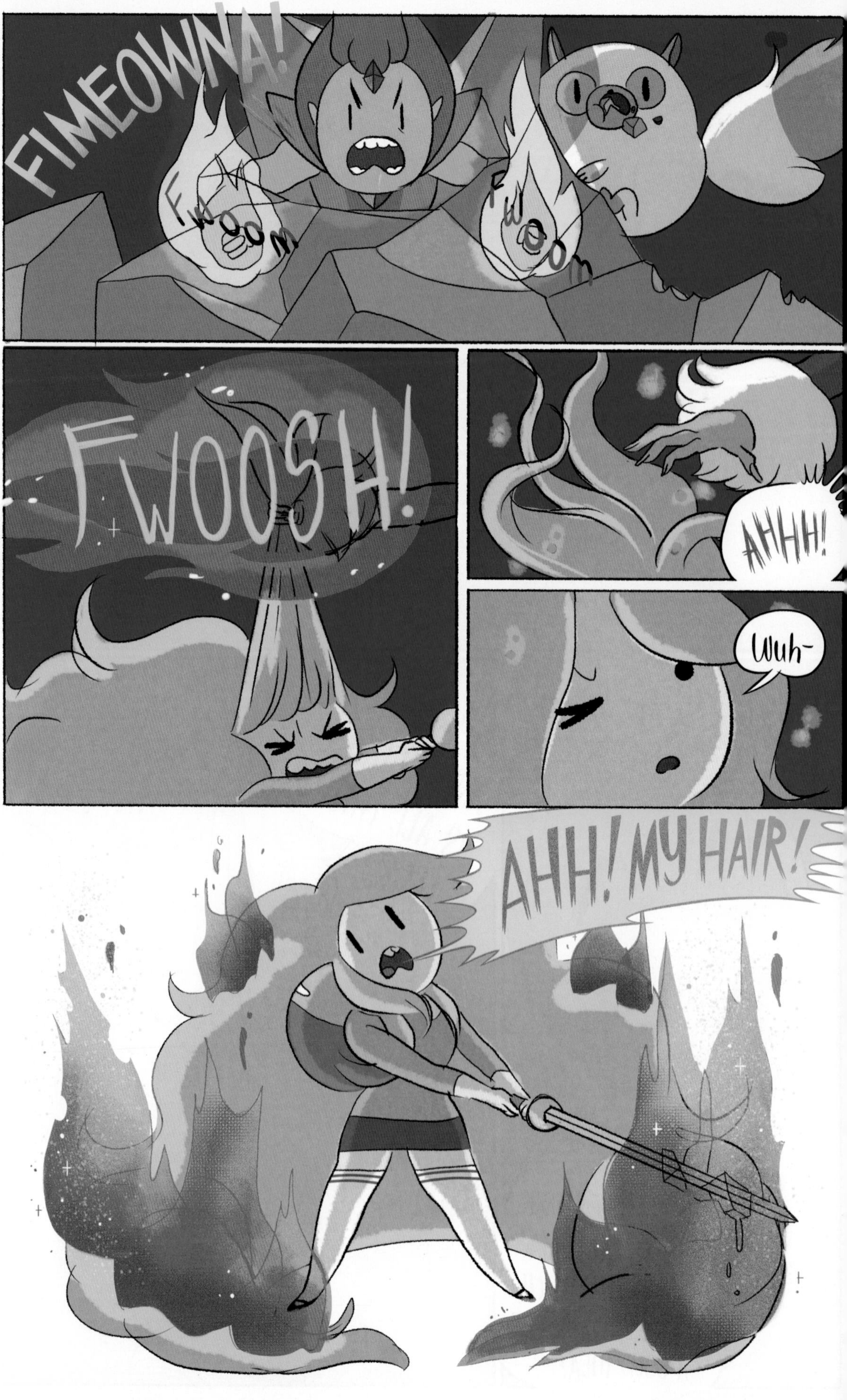

FIMEOWNA!
Fwoom
Fwoom
FWOOSH!
AHHH!
Wuh-
AHH! MY HAIR!

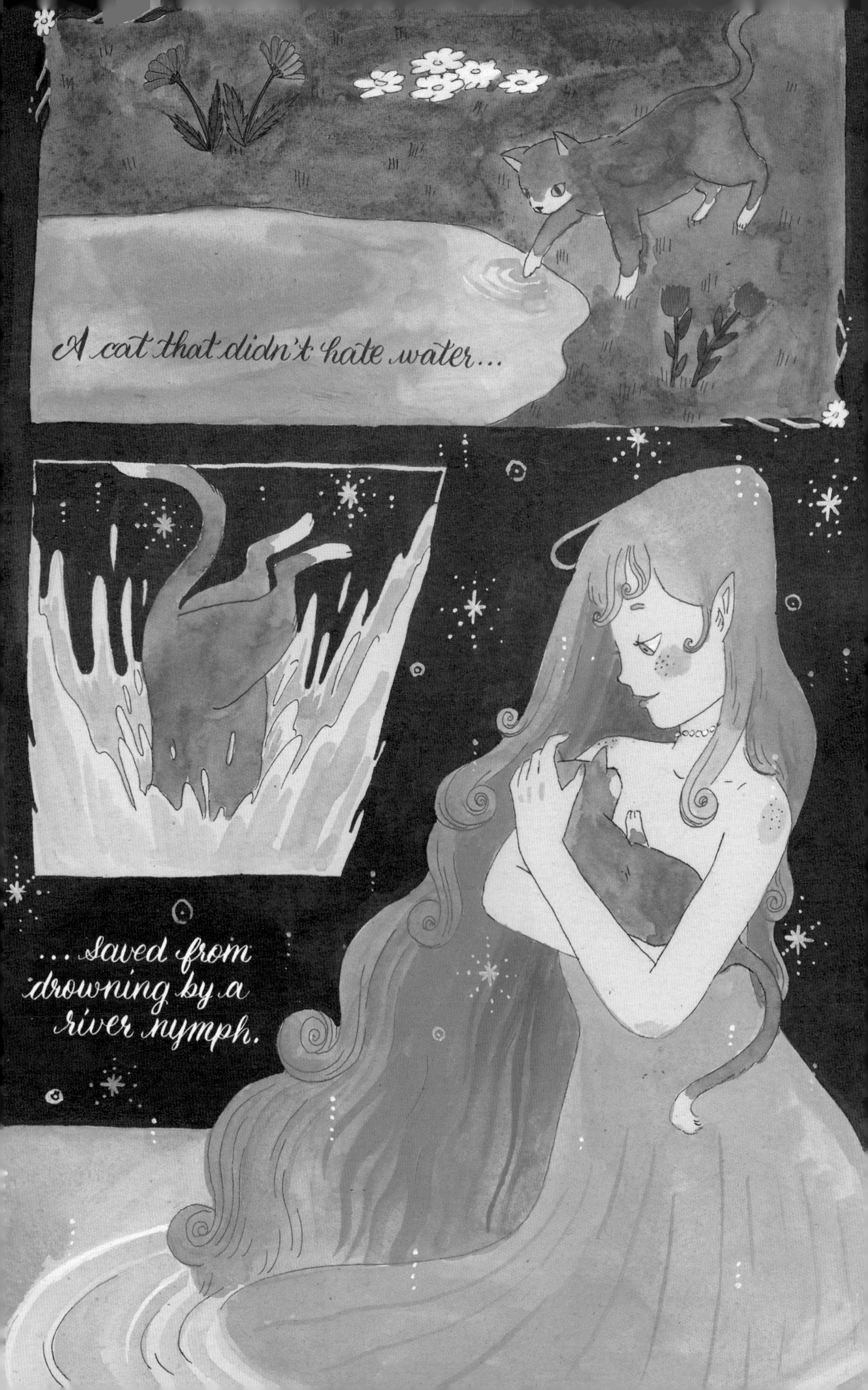
A cat that didn't hate water...
... saved from drowning by a river nymph.

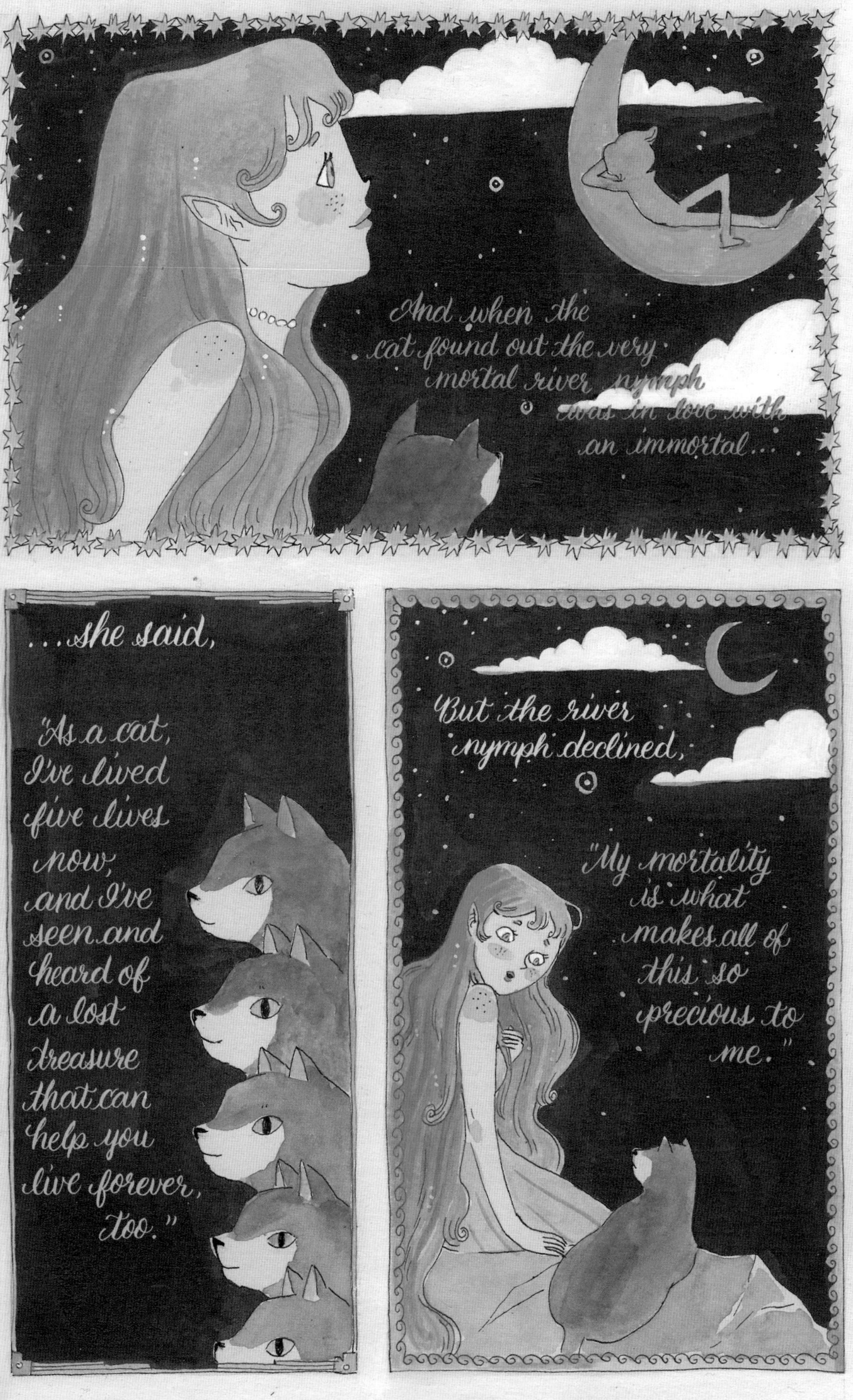
And when the cat found out the very mortal river nymph was in love with an immortal...
...she said,
"As a cat, I've lived five lives now, and I've seen and heard of a lost treasure that can help you live forever, too."
But the river nymph declined,
"My mortality is what makes all of this so precious to me."

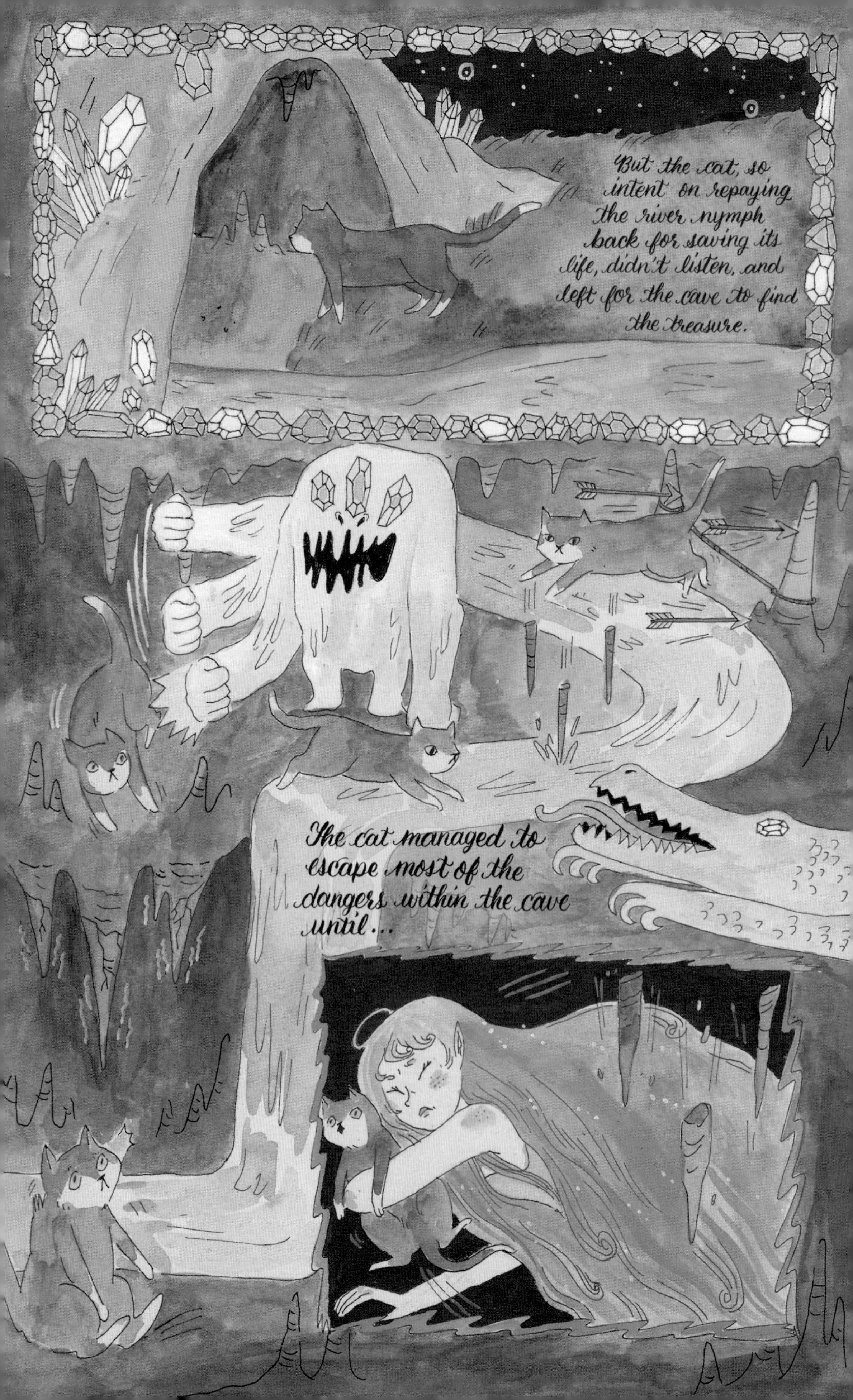
But the cat, so intent on repaying the river nymph back for saving its life, didn't listen, and left for the cave to find the treasure.
The cat managed to escape most of the dangers within the cave until...

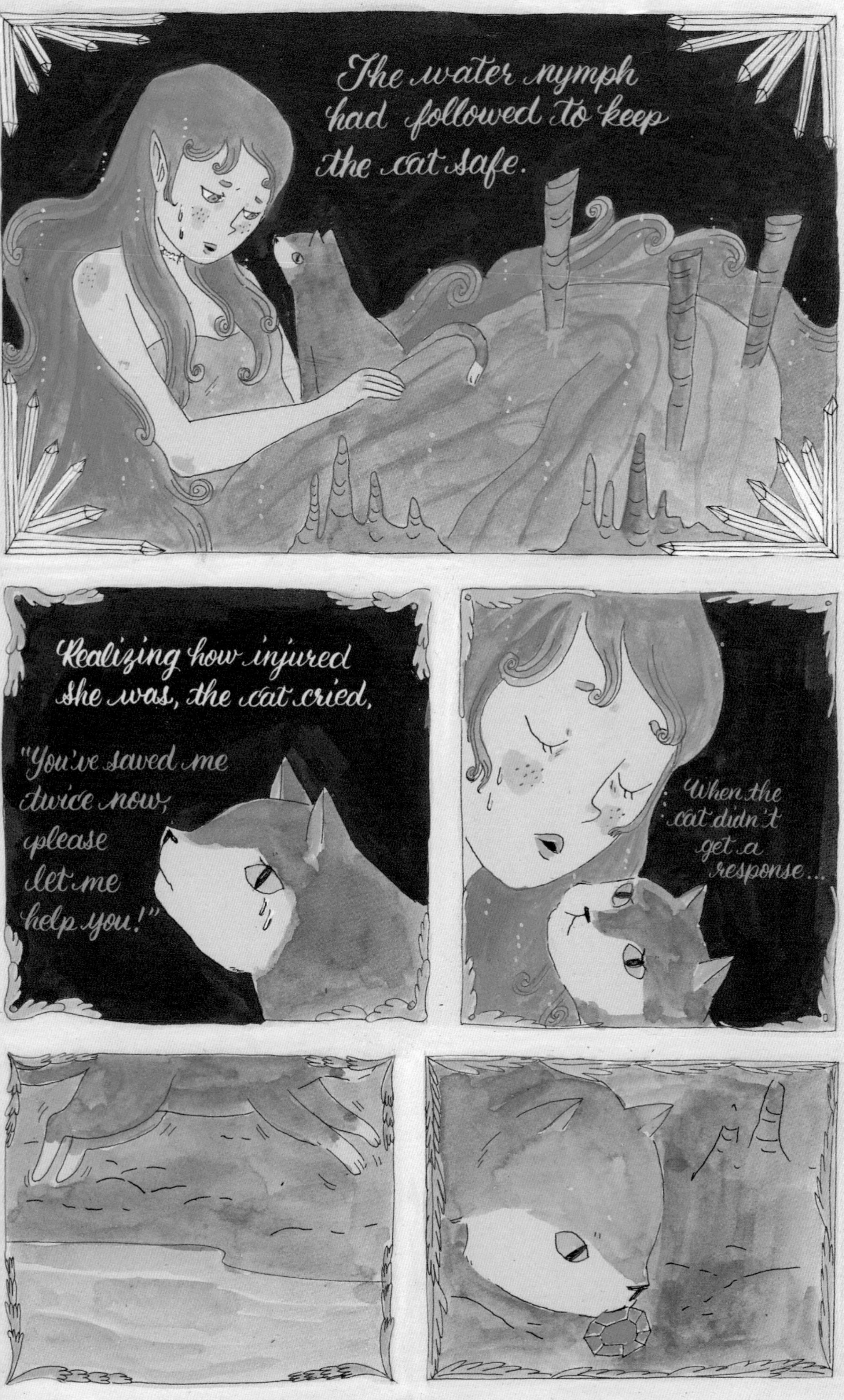
The water nymph had followed to keep the cat safe.
Realizing how injured she was, the cat cried,
"You've saved me twice now, please let me help you!"
When the cat didn't get a response...

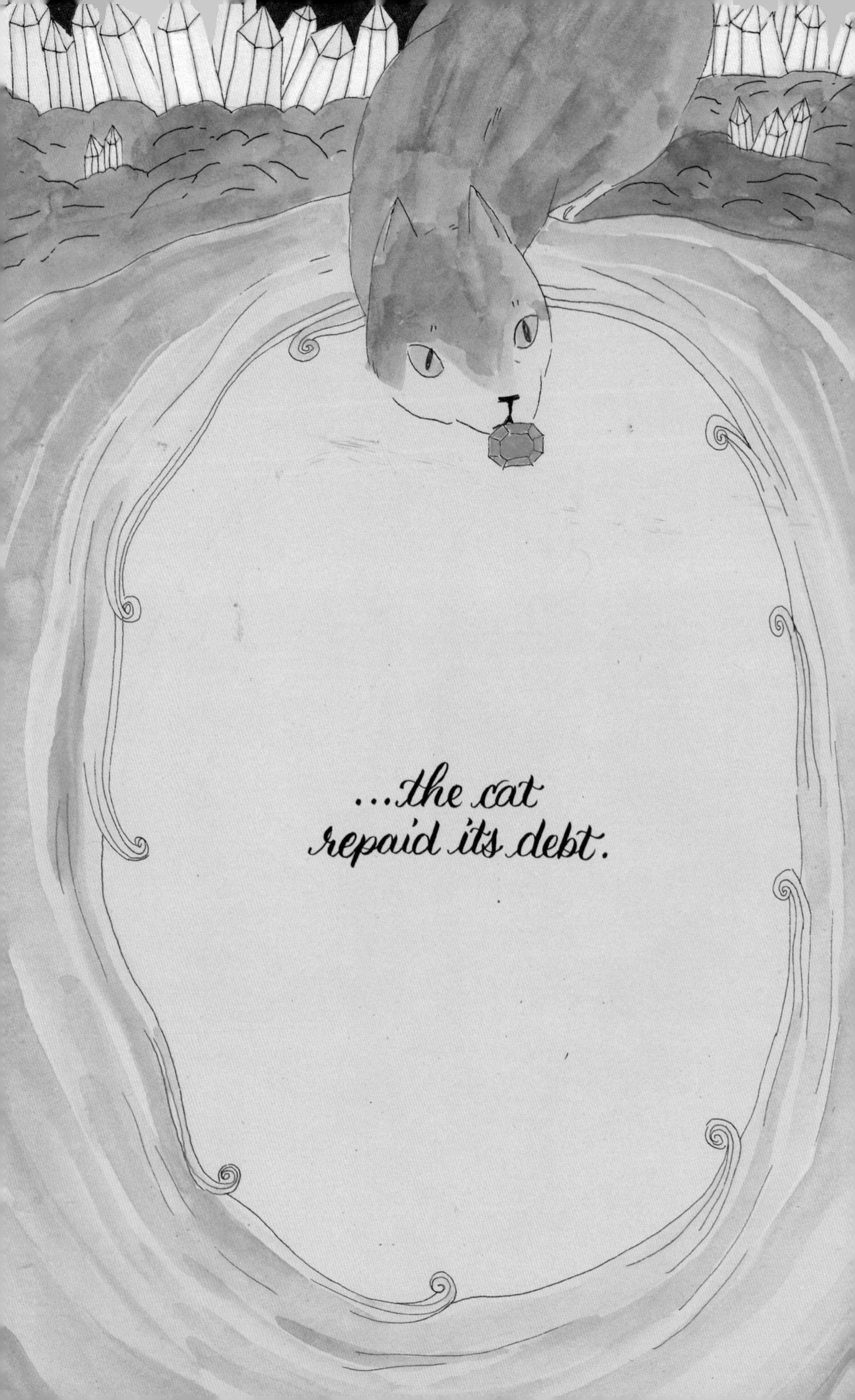
...the cat
repaid its debt.

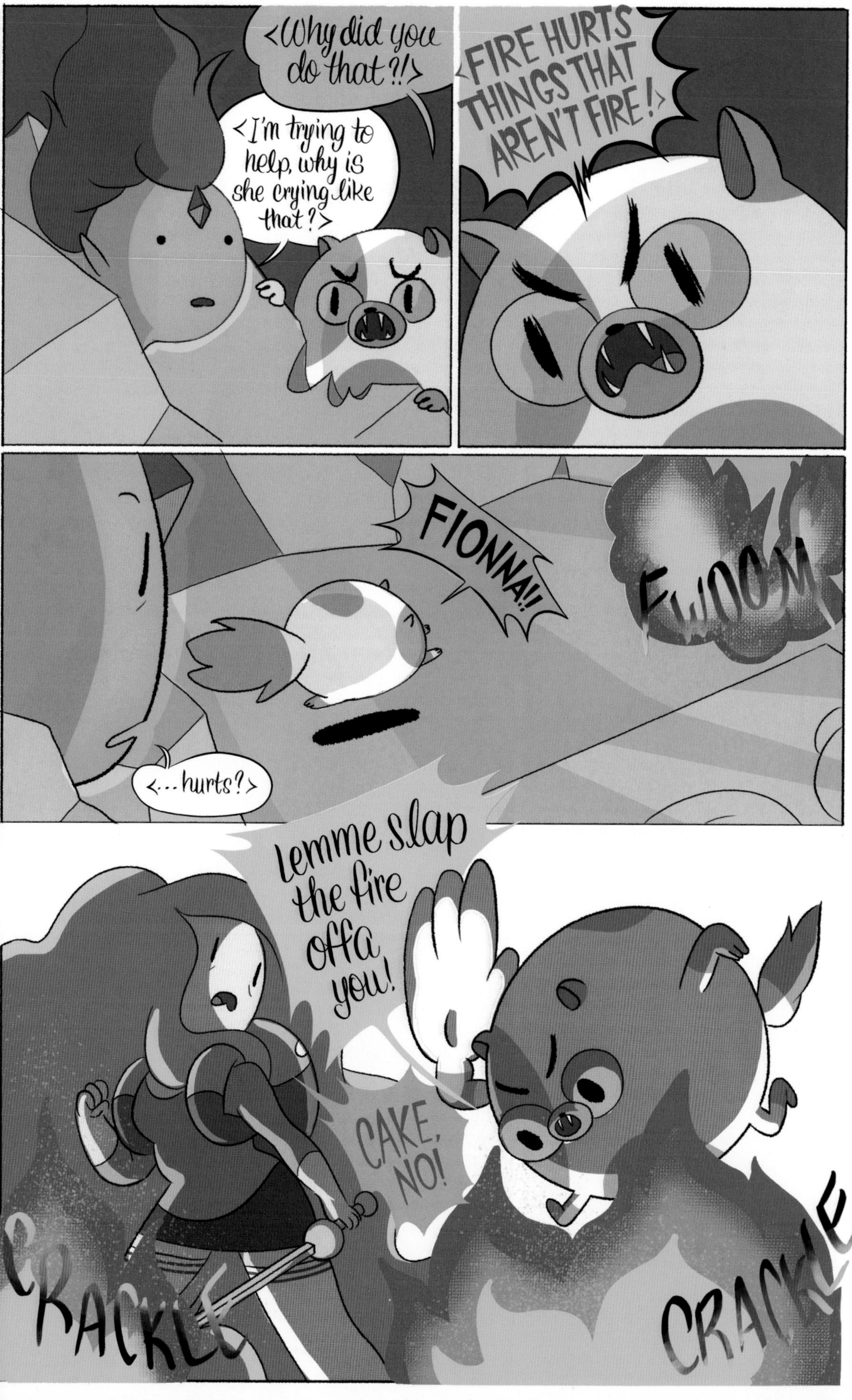
<Why did you do that?!>
<I'm trying to help, why is she crying like that?>
<FIRE HURTS THINGS THAT AREN'T FIRE!>
FIONNA!!
FWOOM
<...hurts?>
Lemme slap the fire offa you!
CAKE, NO!
CRACKLE
CRACKLE

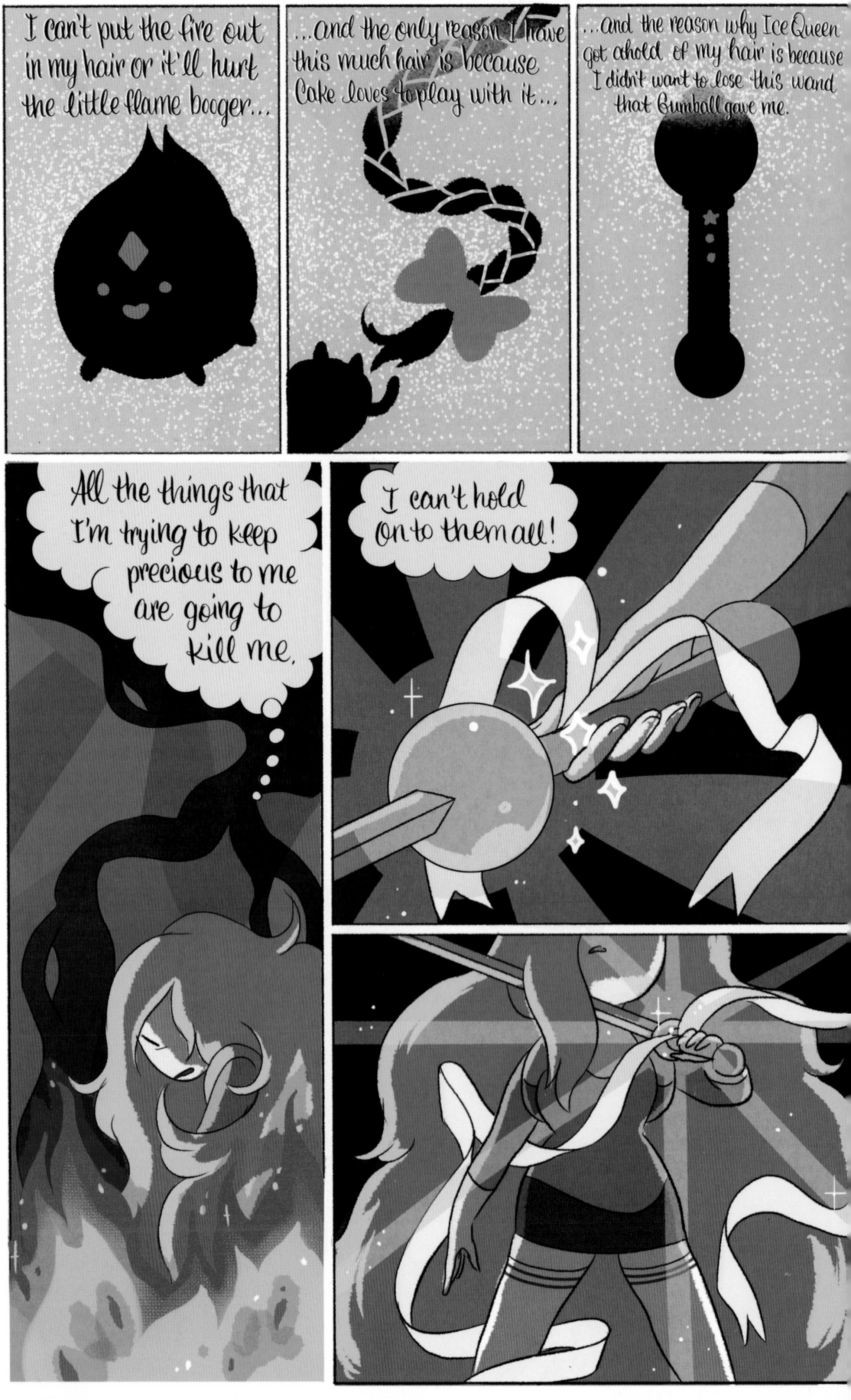
I can't put the fire out in my hair or it'll hurt the little flame booger...
...and the only reason I have this much hair is because Cake loves to play with it...
...and the reason why Ice Queen got ahold of my hair is because I didn't want to lose this wand that Gumball gave me.
All the things that I'm trying to keep precious to me are going to kill me.
I can't hold on to them all!

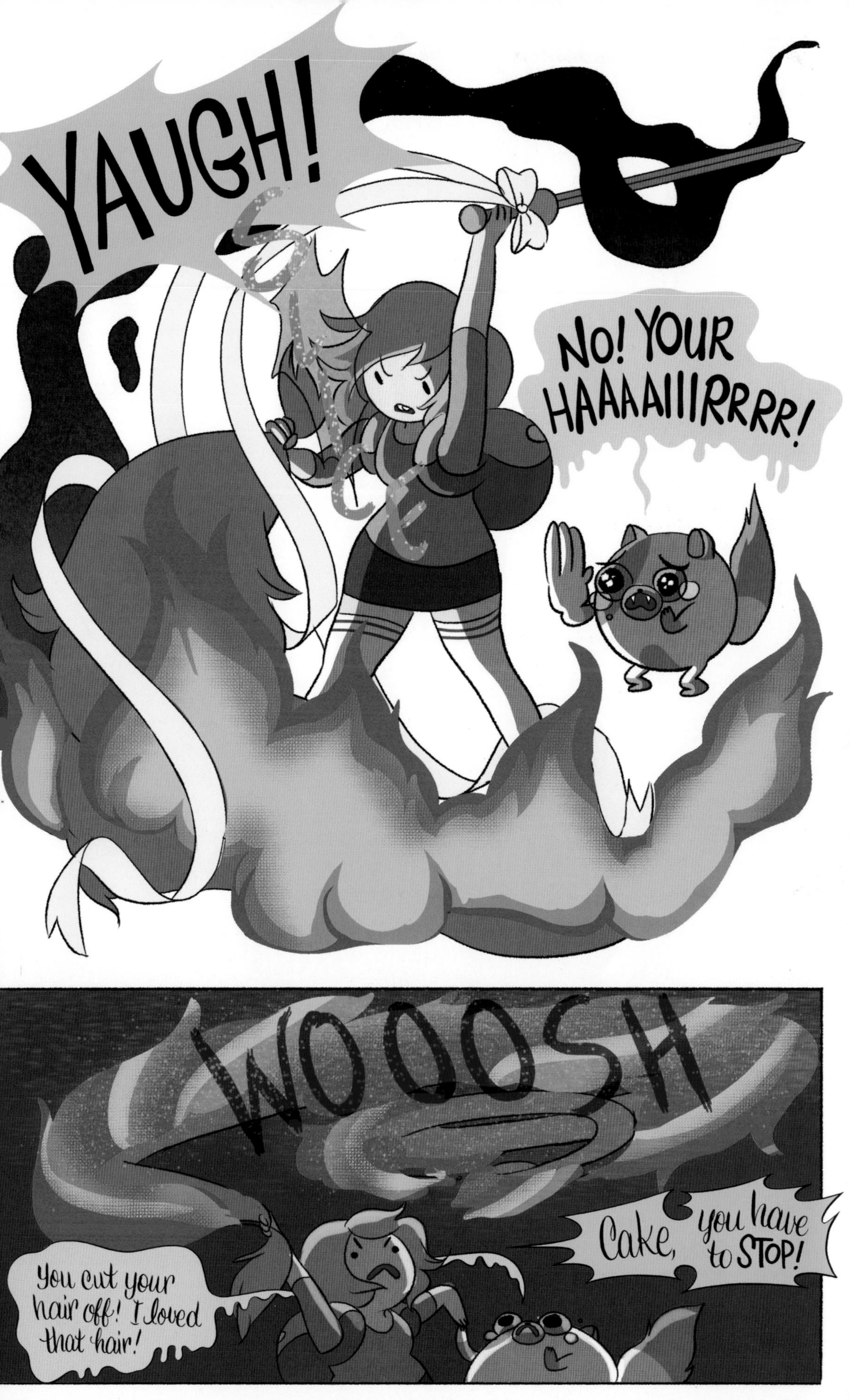
YAUGH!
No! YOUR HAAAAIIIRRRR!
WOOOSH
Cake, you have to STOP!
You cut your hair off! I loved that hair!

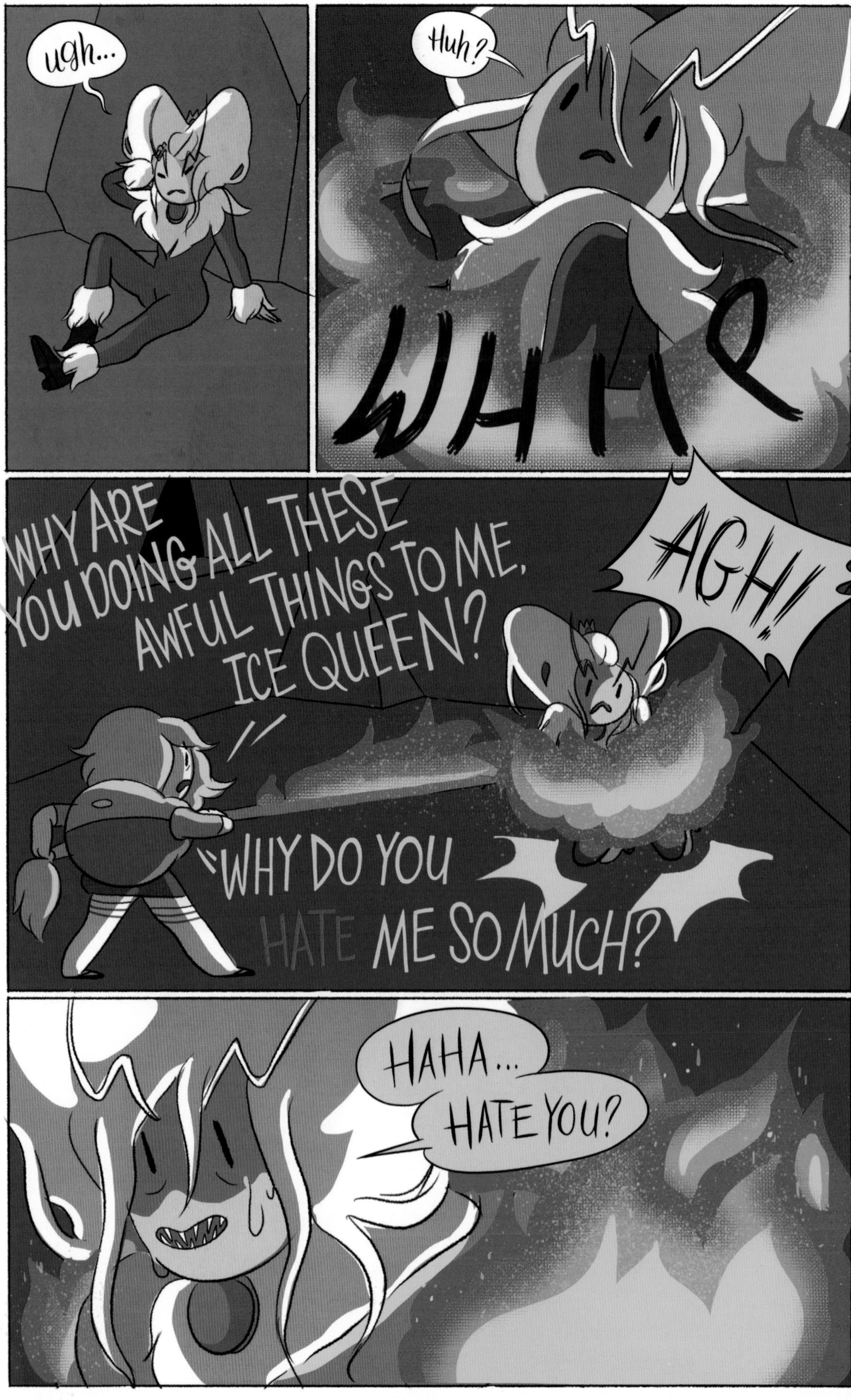
ugh...
Huh?
WHIP
WHY ARE YOU DOING ALL THESE AWFUL THINGS TO ME, ICE QUEEN?
AGH!
WHY DO YOU HATE ME SO MUCH?
HAHA...
HATE YOU?

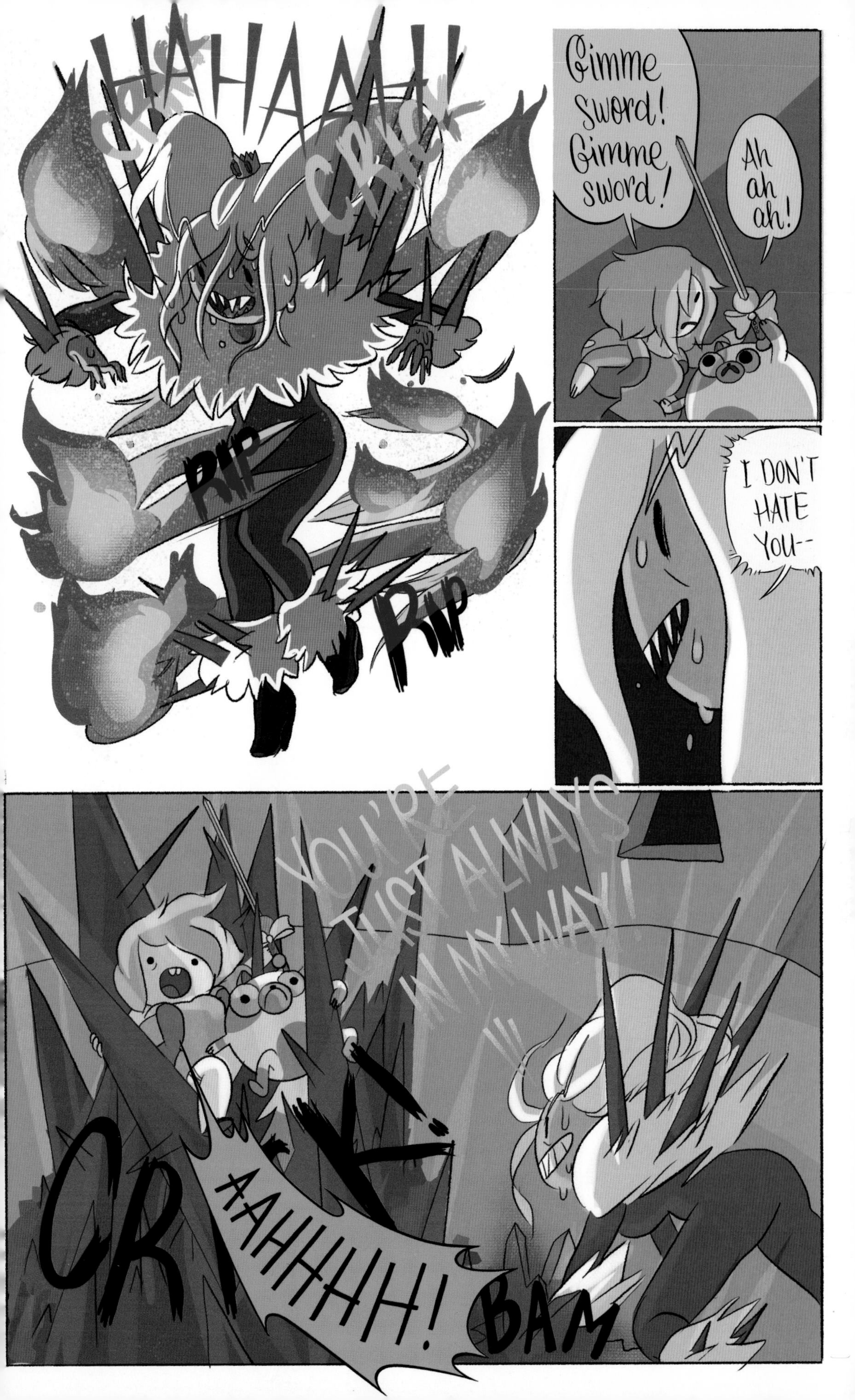
HAHAAAH!
CRICK
RIP
RIP
Gimme sword! Gimme sword!
Ah ah ah!
I DON'T HATE YOU--
YOU'RE JUST ALWAYS IN MY WAY!!!
CRIK!
AAHHHHH!
BAM

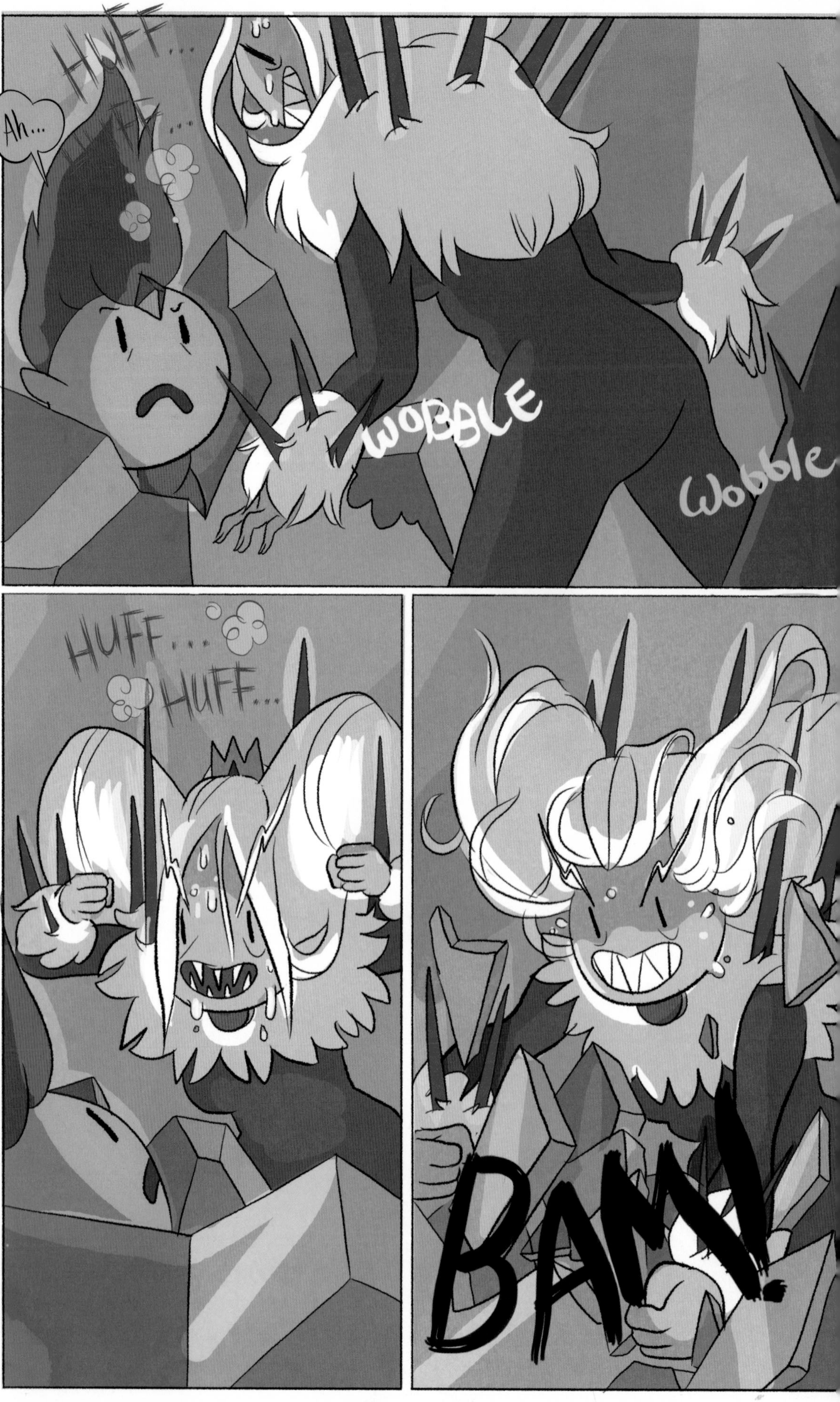

HUFF...
Ah...
HUFF...
WOBBLE
Wobble
HUFF...
HUFF...
BAM!

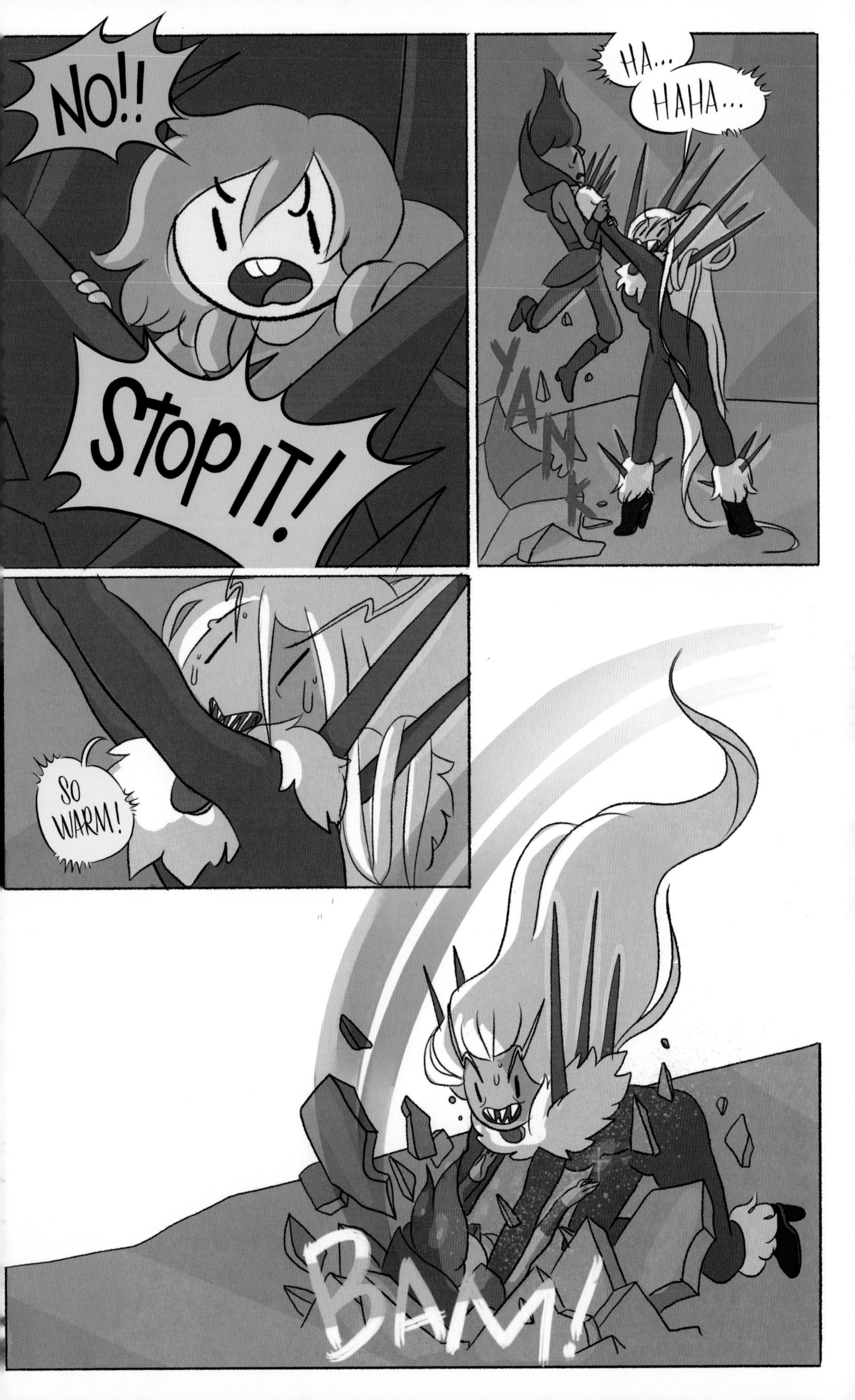
NO!!
STOP IT!
HA...
HAHA...
YANK
SO WARM!
BAM!

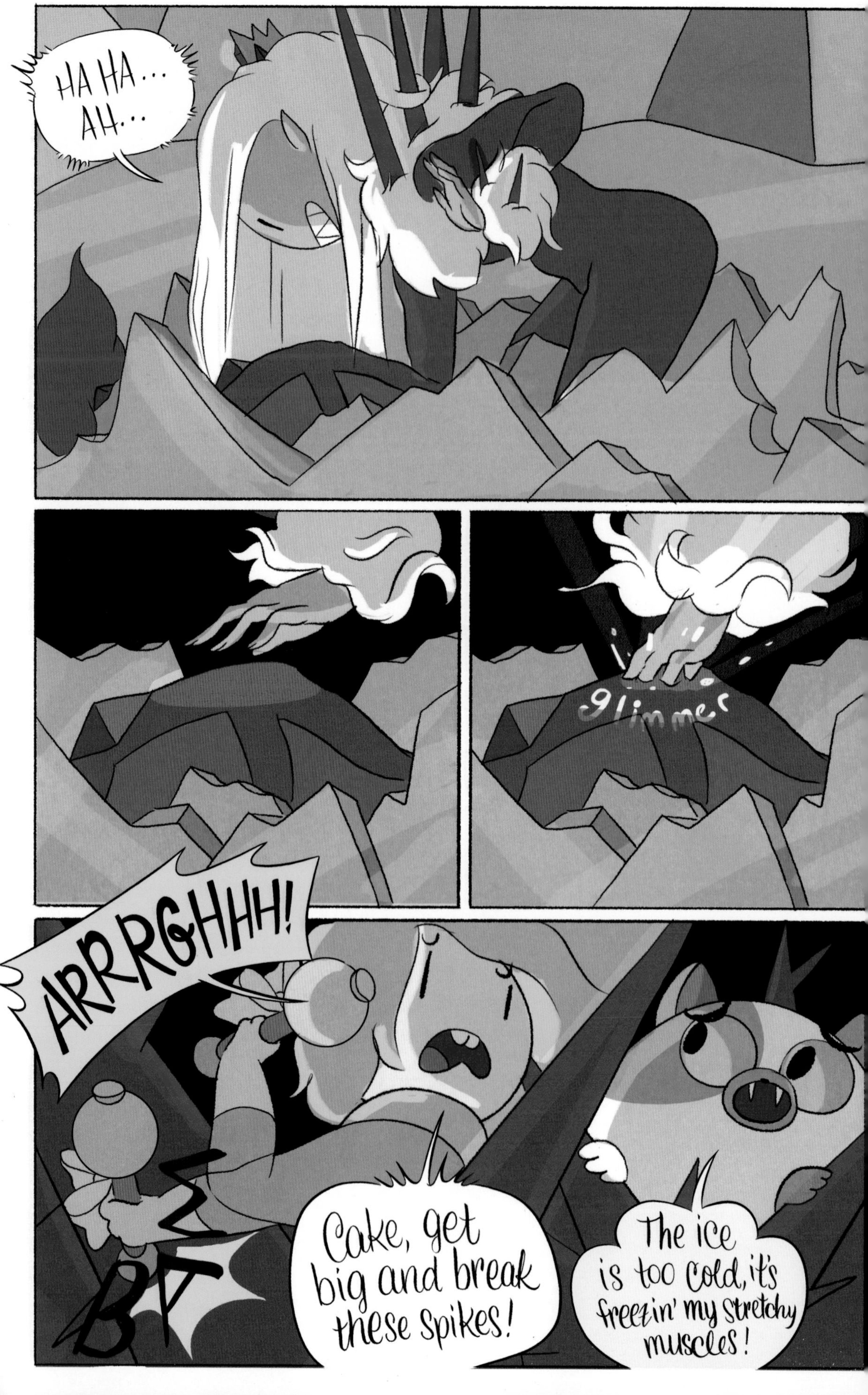
HA HA... AH...
glimmer
ARRRGHHH!
Cake, get big and break these spikes!
The ice is too cold, it's freezin' my stretchy muscles!
BAT

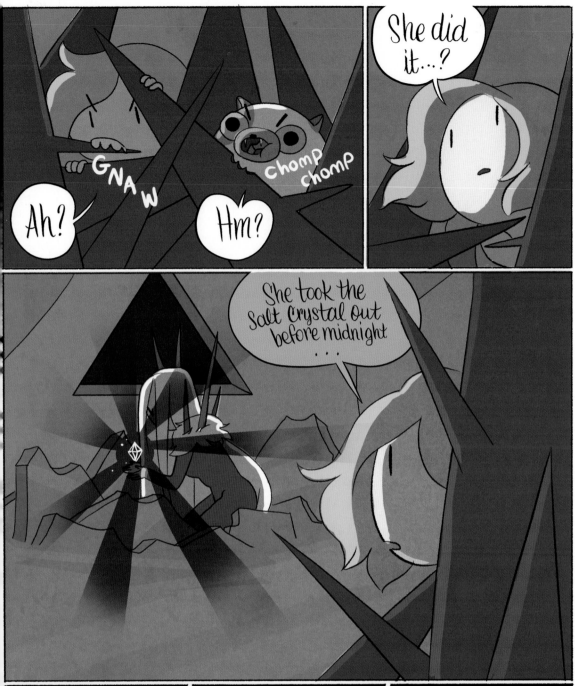

GNAW

Ah?

Hm?

chomp chomp

She did it...?

She took the salt crystal out before midnight...

I THOUGHT WHAT I NEEDED WAS THE LOVE OF A PRINCE...

... UNTIL I FOUND THESE FLAME ELEMENTALS.

BUT THIS CRYSTAL MANAGED TO HARNESS

EVEN MORE WARMTH THAN THE BOTH OF THOSE COMBINED.

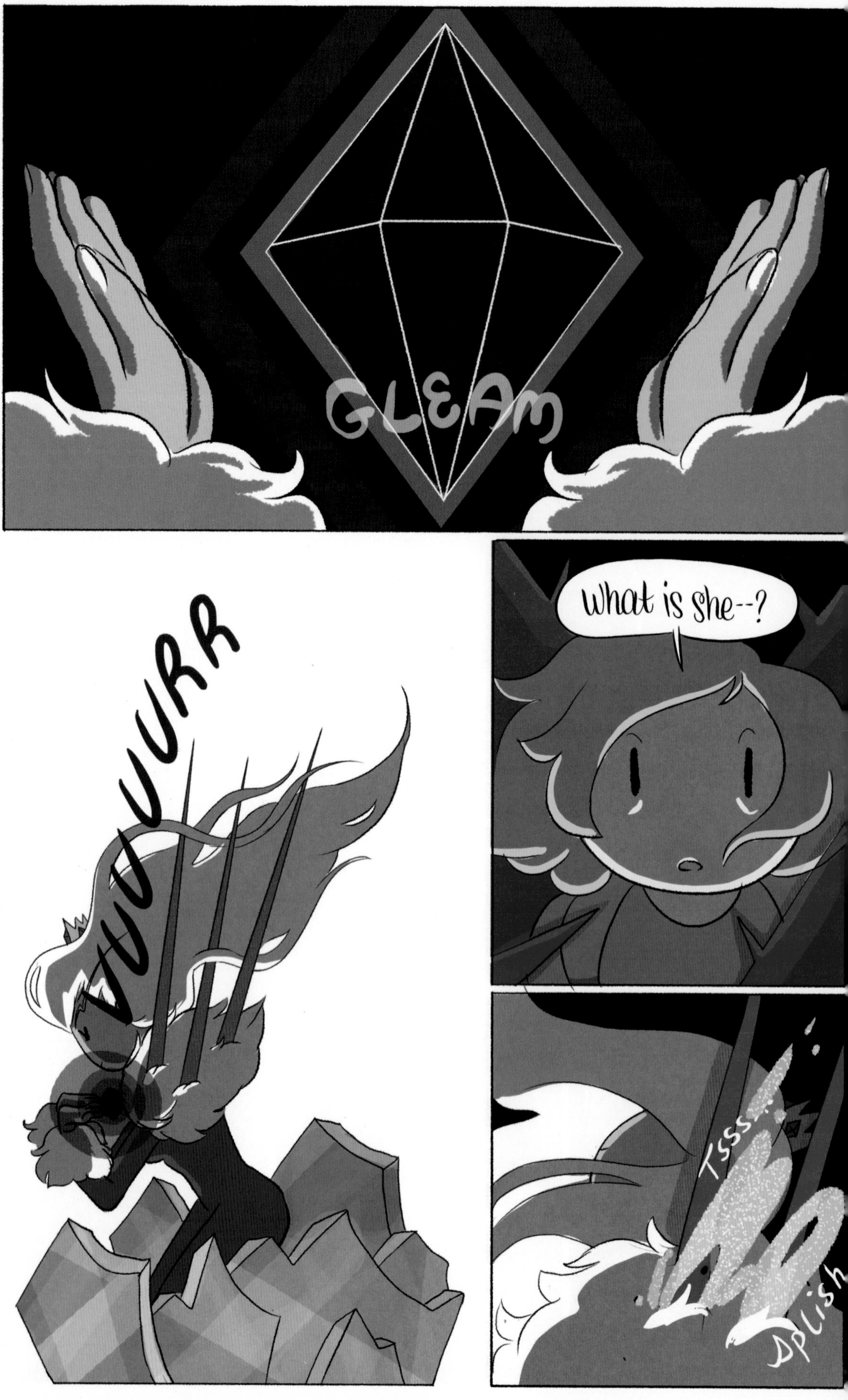
GLEAM
VVVVURR
What is she--?
Tsss...
splish

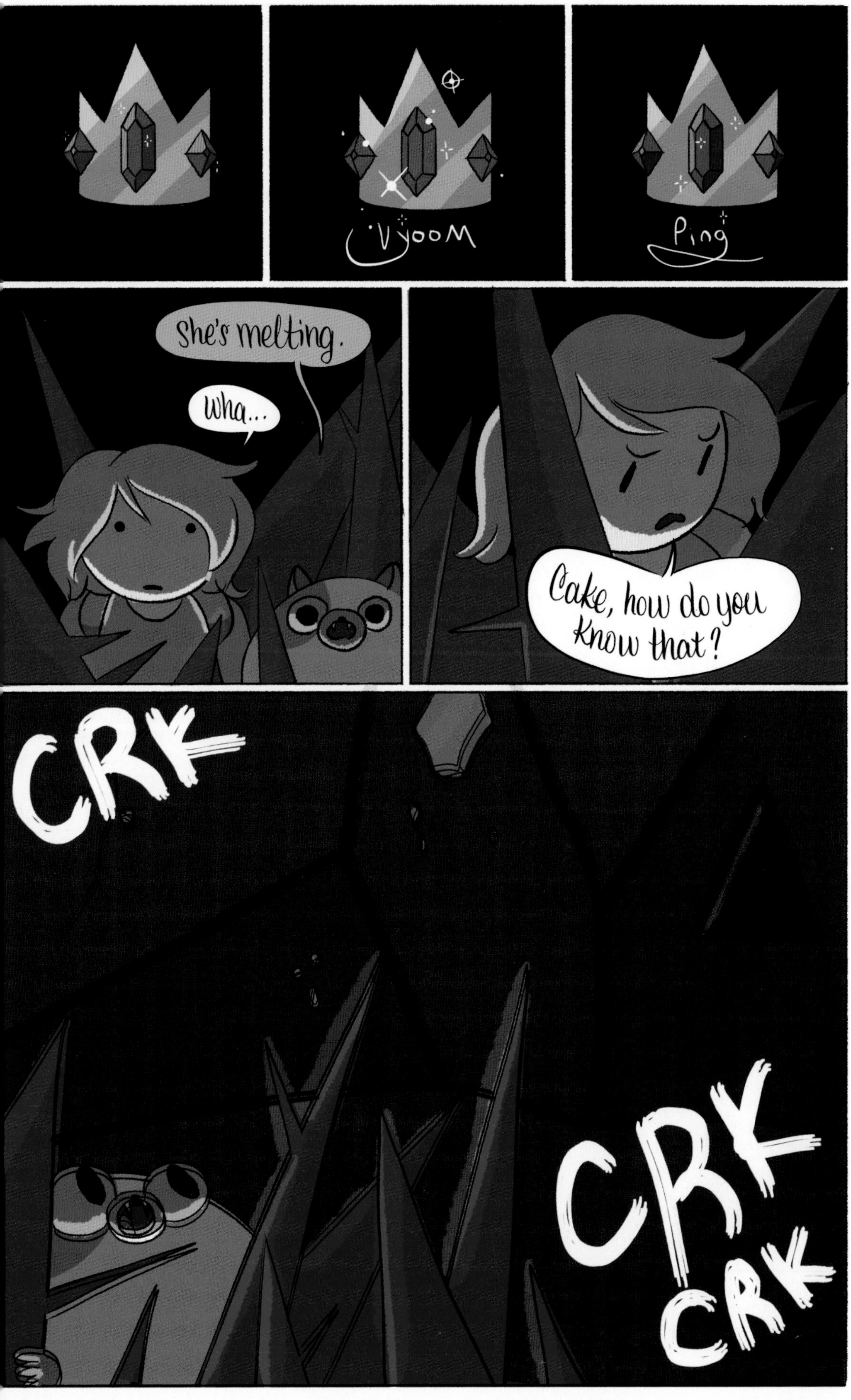
Vjoom
Ping
She's melting.
Wha...
Cake, how do you know that?
CRK
CRK
CRK

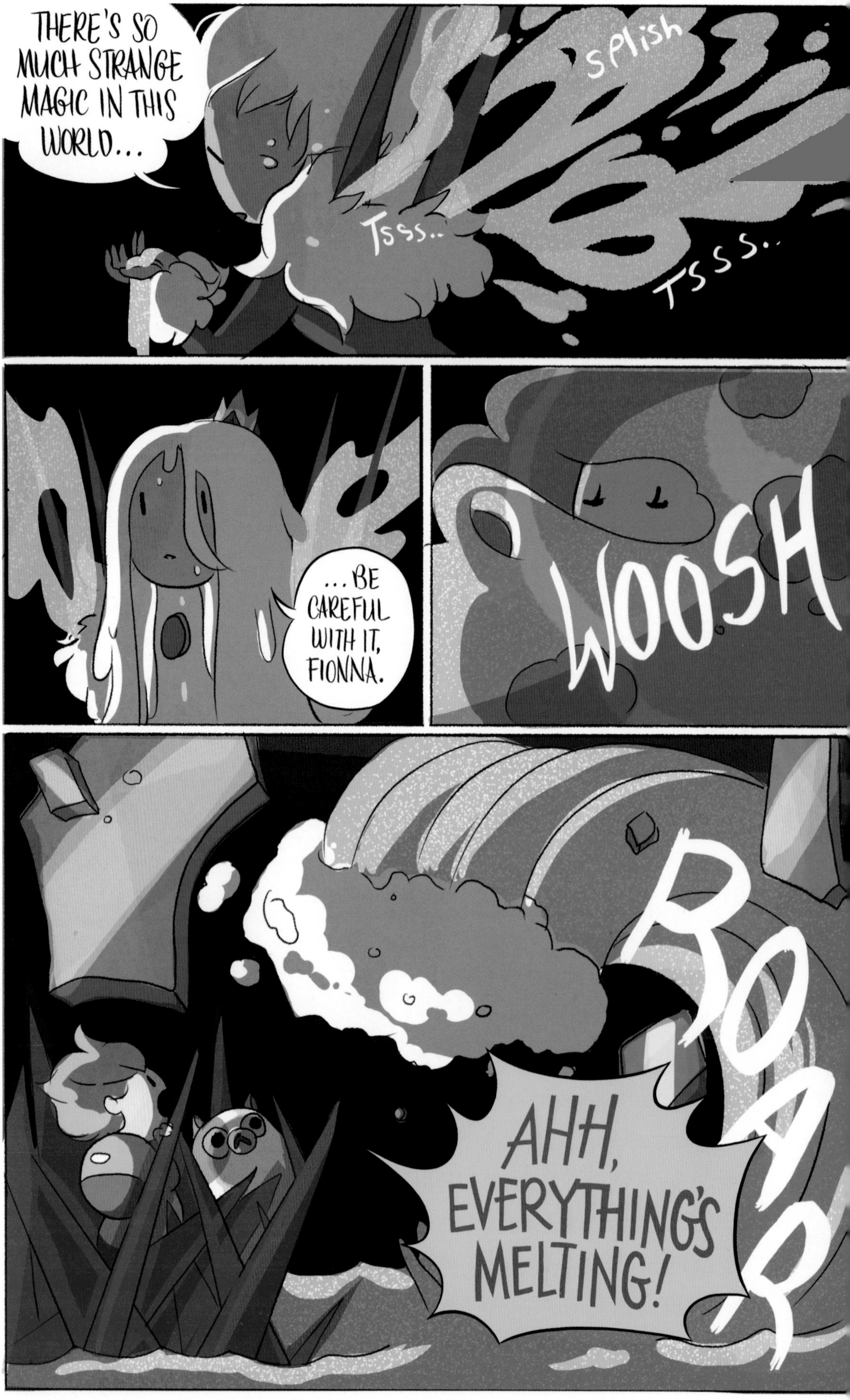
THERE'S SO MUCH STRANGE MAGIC IN THIS WORLD...
SPLISH
TSSS..
TSSS..
...BE CAREFUL WITH IT, FIONNA.
WOOSH
ROAR
AHH, EVERYTHING'S MELTING!

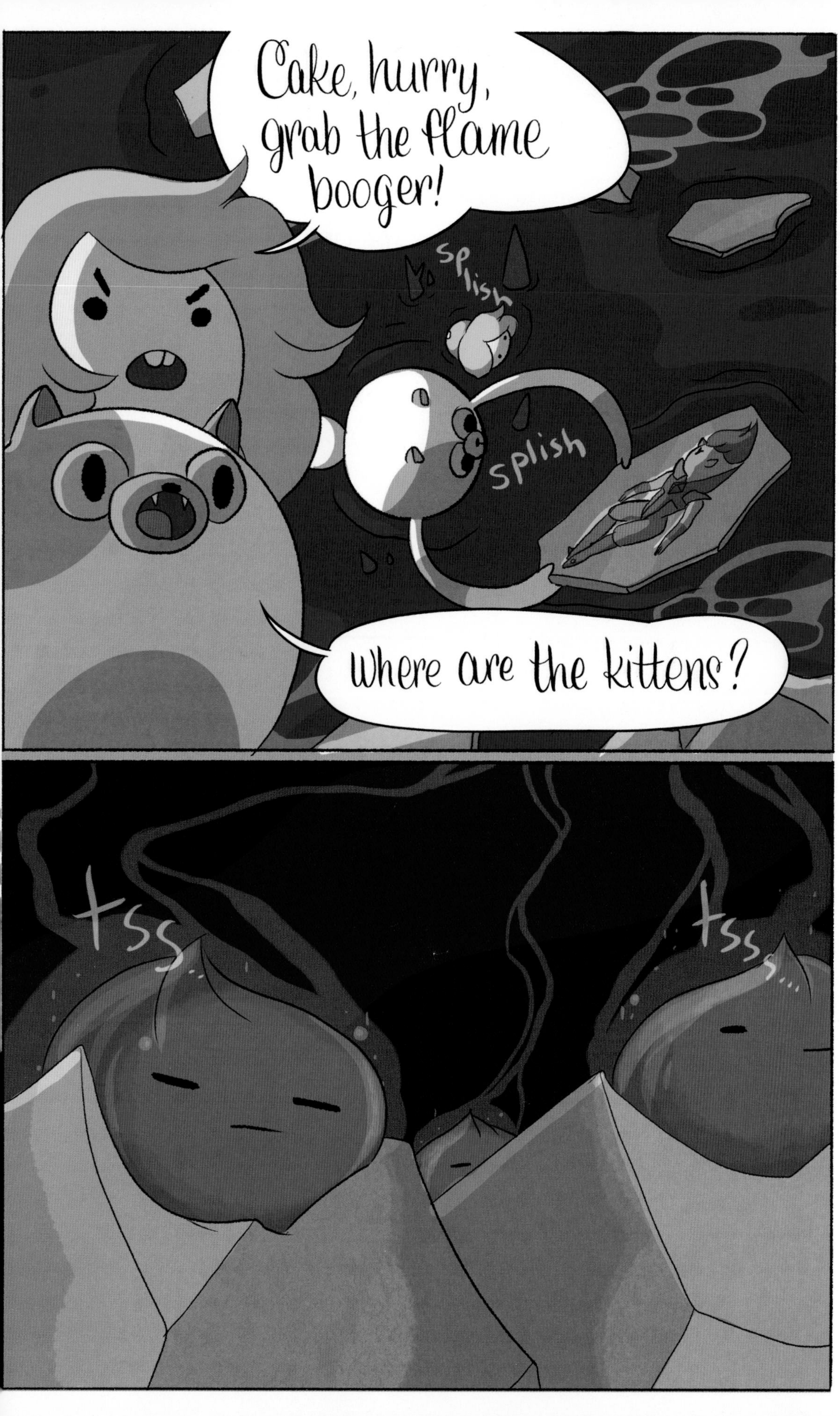
Cake, hurry, grab the flame booger!
splish
splish
Where are the kittens?
tss...
tss...

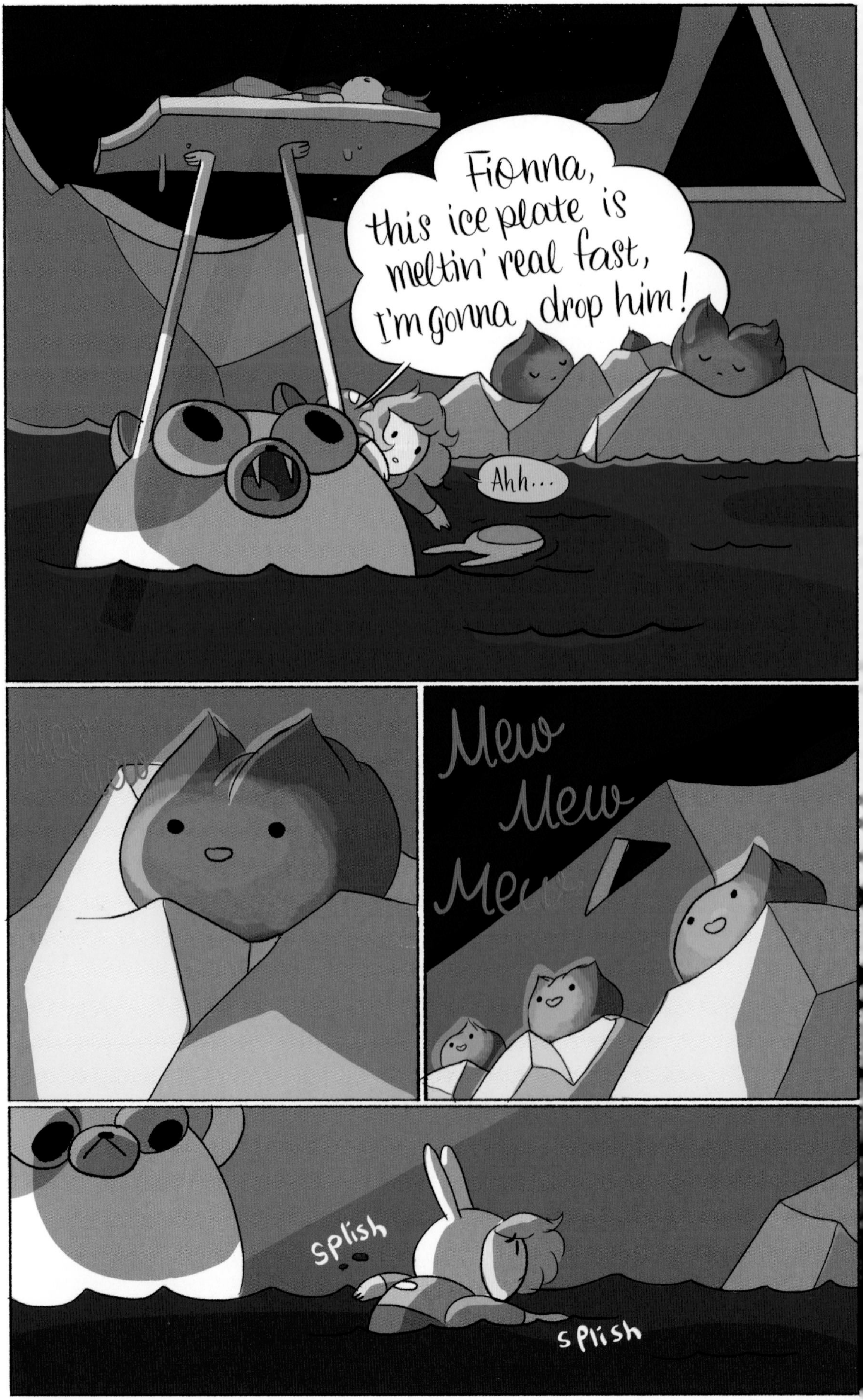
Fionna, this ice plate is meltin' real fast, I'm gonna drop him!
Ahh...
Mew
Mew
Mew
splish
splish

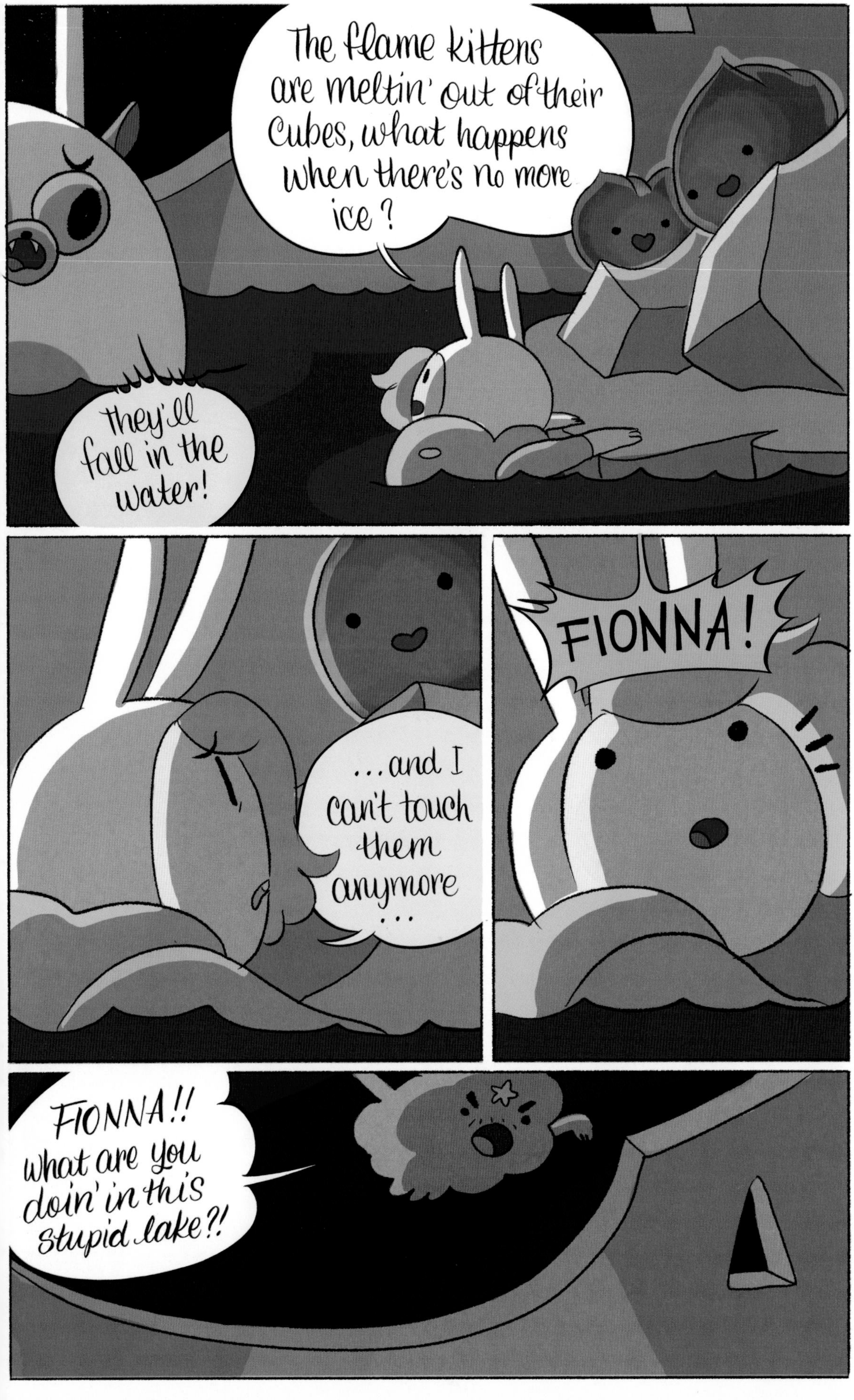
The flame kittens are meltin' out of their Cubes, what happens when there's no more ice?
they'll fall in the water!
...and I can't touch them anymore...
FIONNA!
FIONNA!! what are you doin' in this stupid lake?!

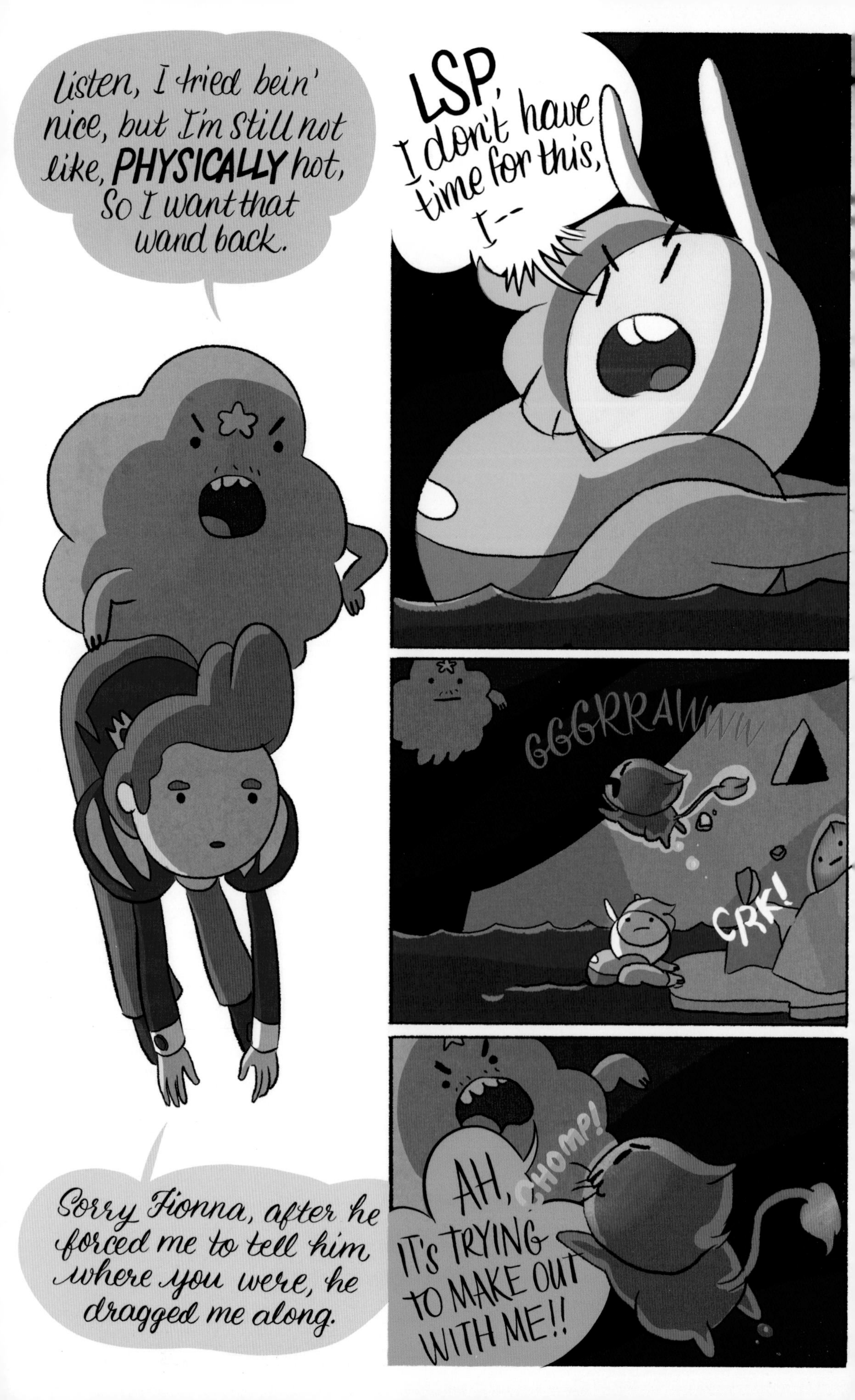
Listen, I tried bein' nice, but I'm still not like, PHYSICALLY hot, so I want that wand back.
Sorry Fionna, after he forced me to tell him where you were, he dragged me along.
LSP, I don't have time for this, I--
GGGRRAWWW
CRK!
AH, IT'S TRYING TO MAKE OUT WITH ME!!
CHOMP!

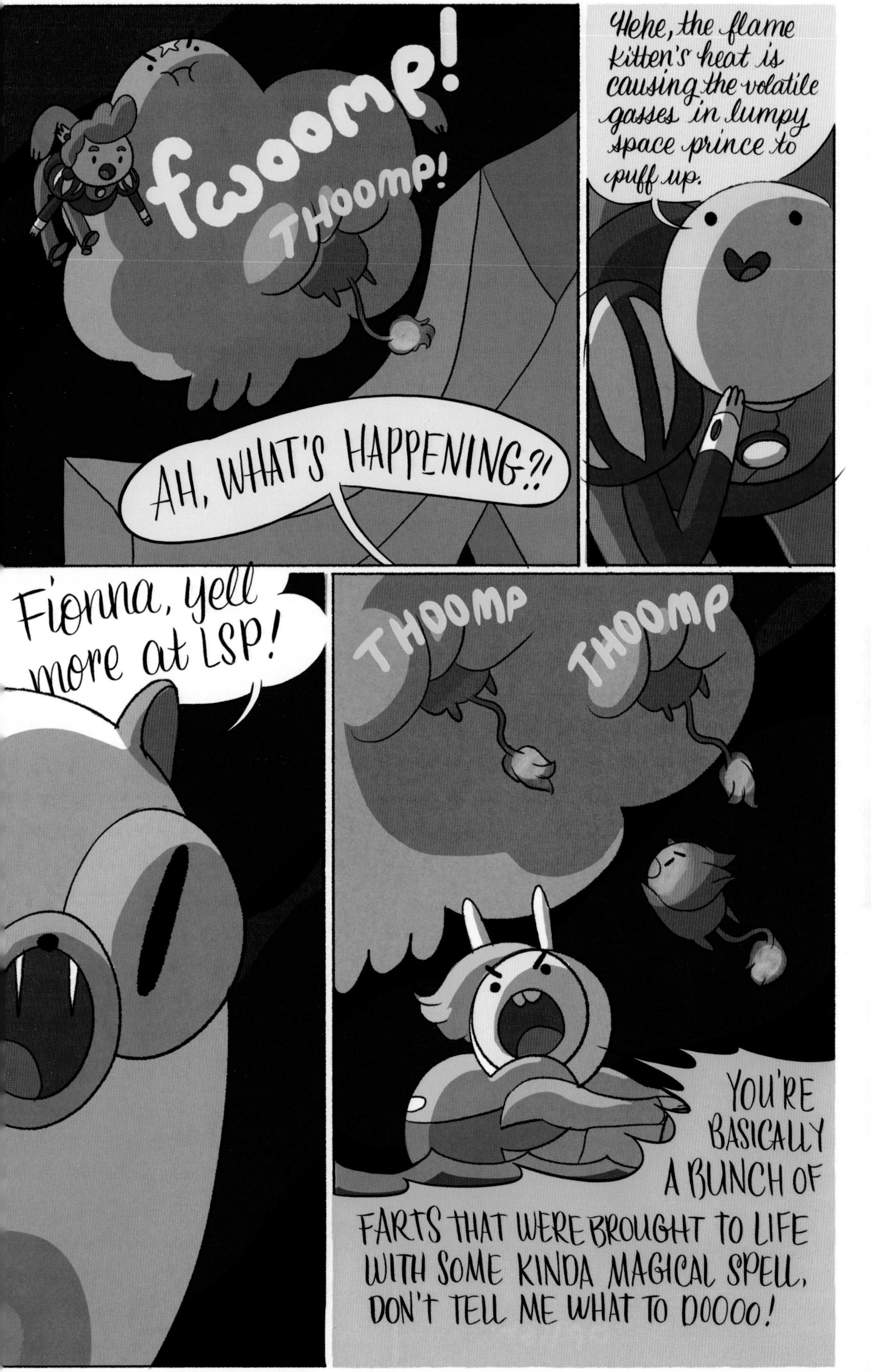
fwoomp!
THOOMP!
AH, WHAT'S HAPPENING?!
Hehe, the flame kitten's heat is causing the volatile gasses in lumpy space prince to puff up.
Fionna, yell more at LSP!
THOOMP
THOOMP
YOU'RE BASICALLY A BUNCH OF FARTS THAT WERE BROUGHT TO LIFE WITH SOME KINDA MAGICAL SPELL, DON'T TELL ME WHAT TO DOOOO!

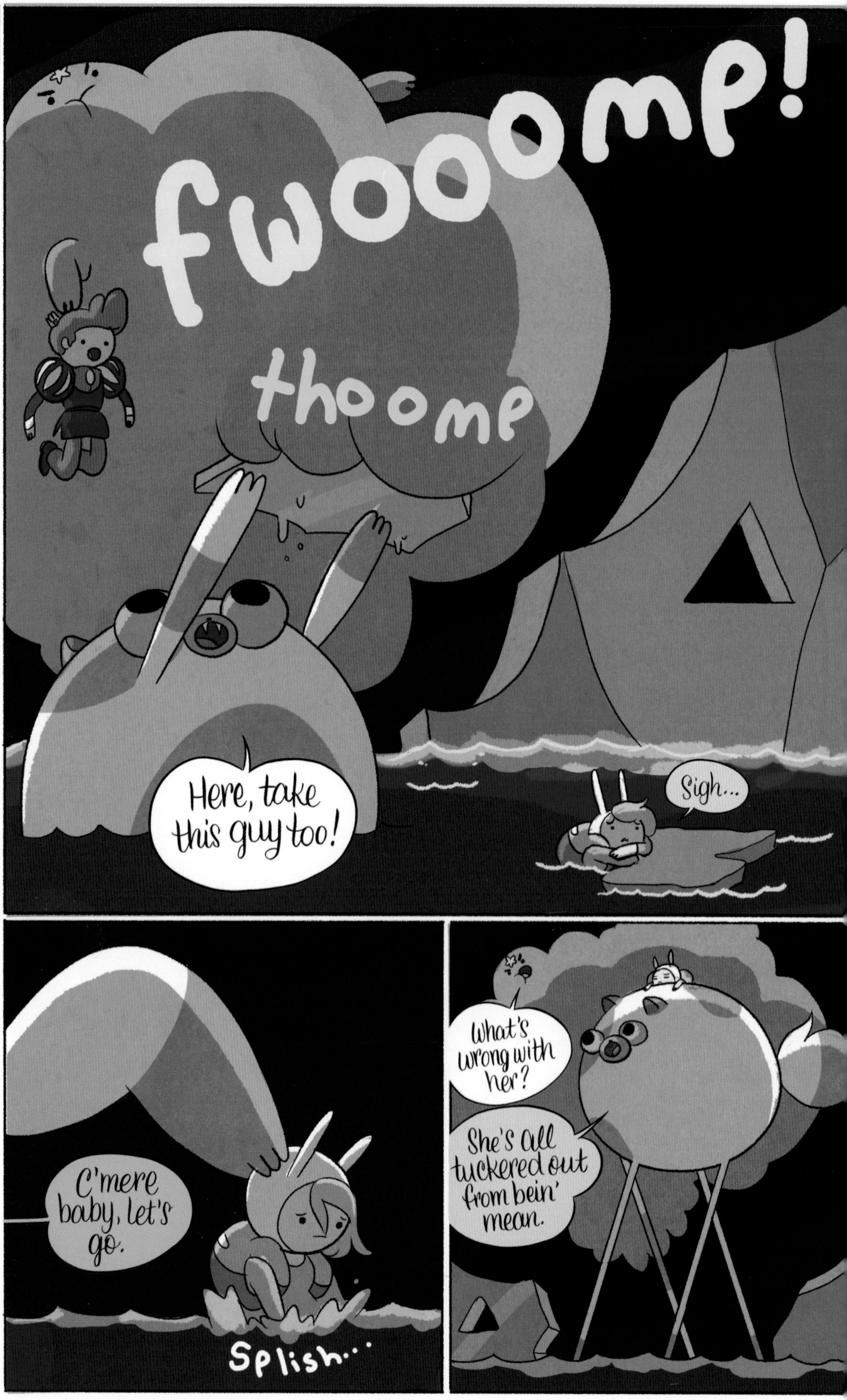
fwoooomp!
thoomp
Here, take this guy too!
Sigh...
C'mere baby, let's go.
Splish...
What's wrong with her?
She's all tuckered out from bein' mean.

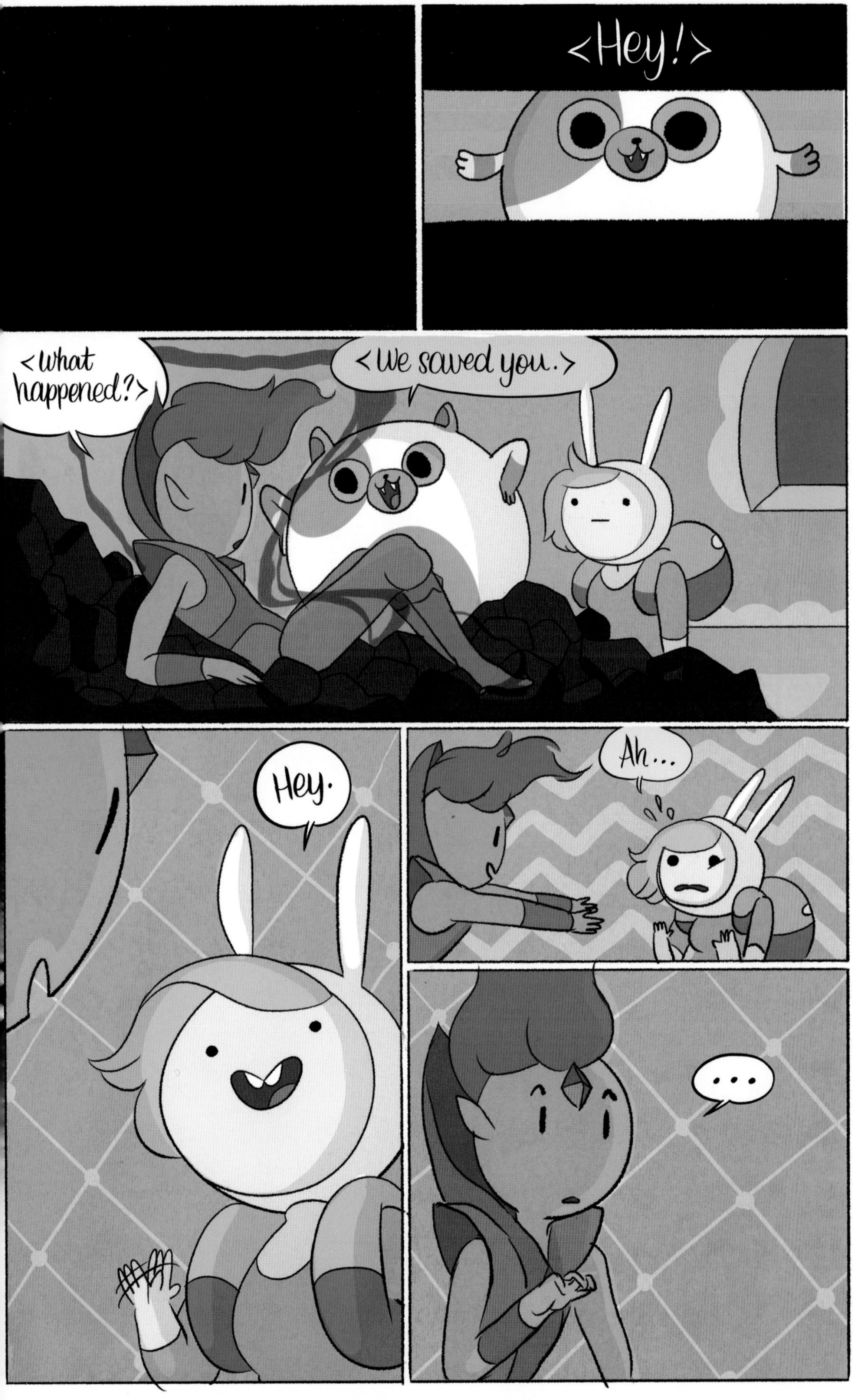
<Hey!>
<What happened?>
<We saved you.>
Hey.
Ah...
...

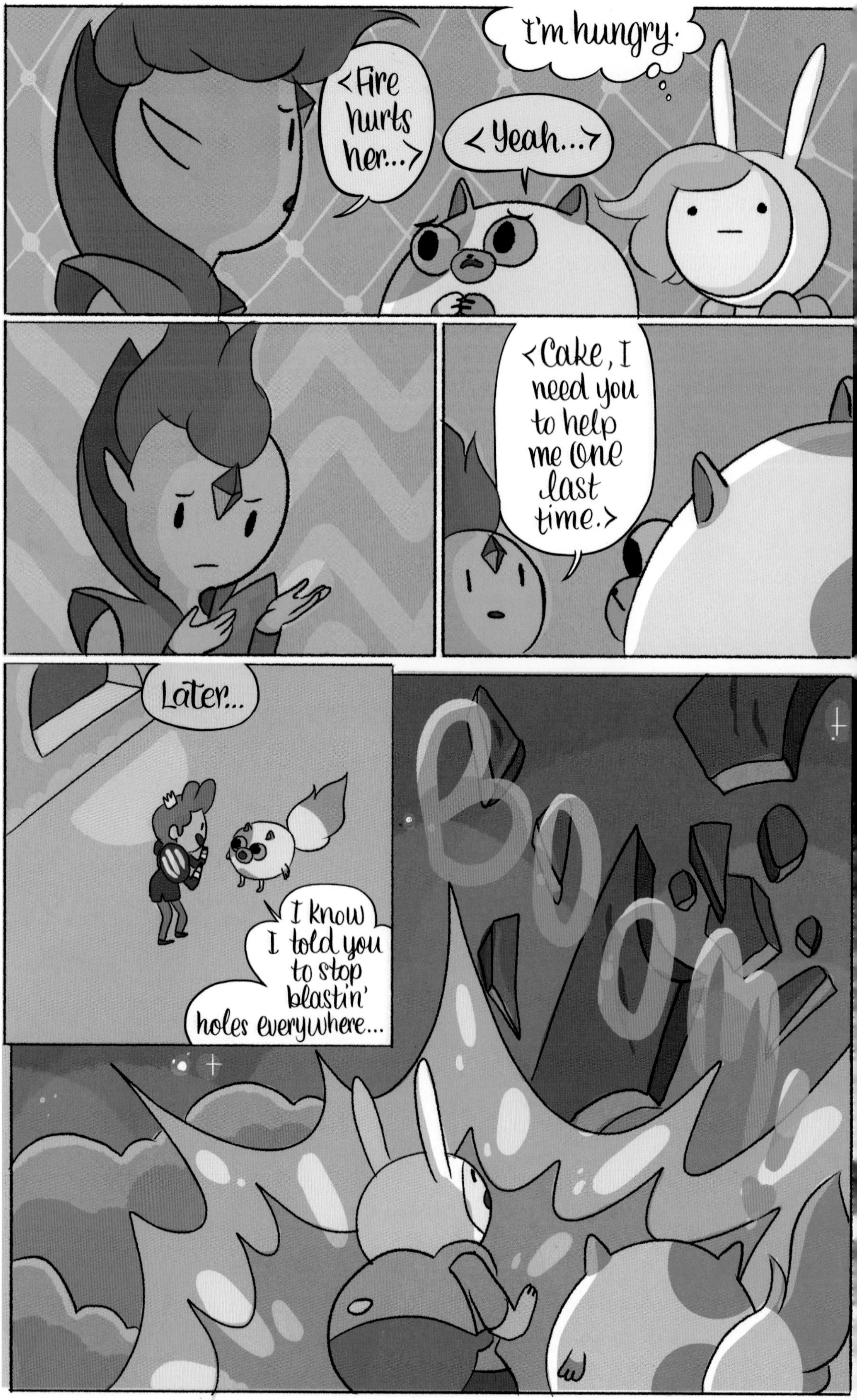

I'm hungry.
<Fire hurts her...>
<Yeah...>
<Cake, I need you to help me one last time.>
Later...
I know I told you to stop blastin' holes everywhere...
BOOM!

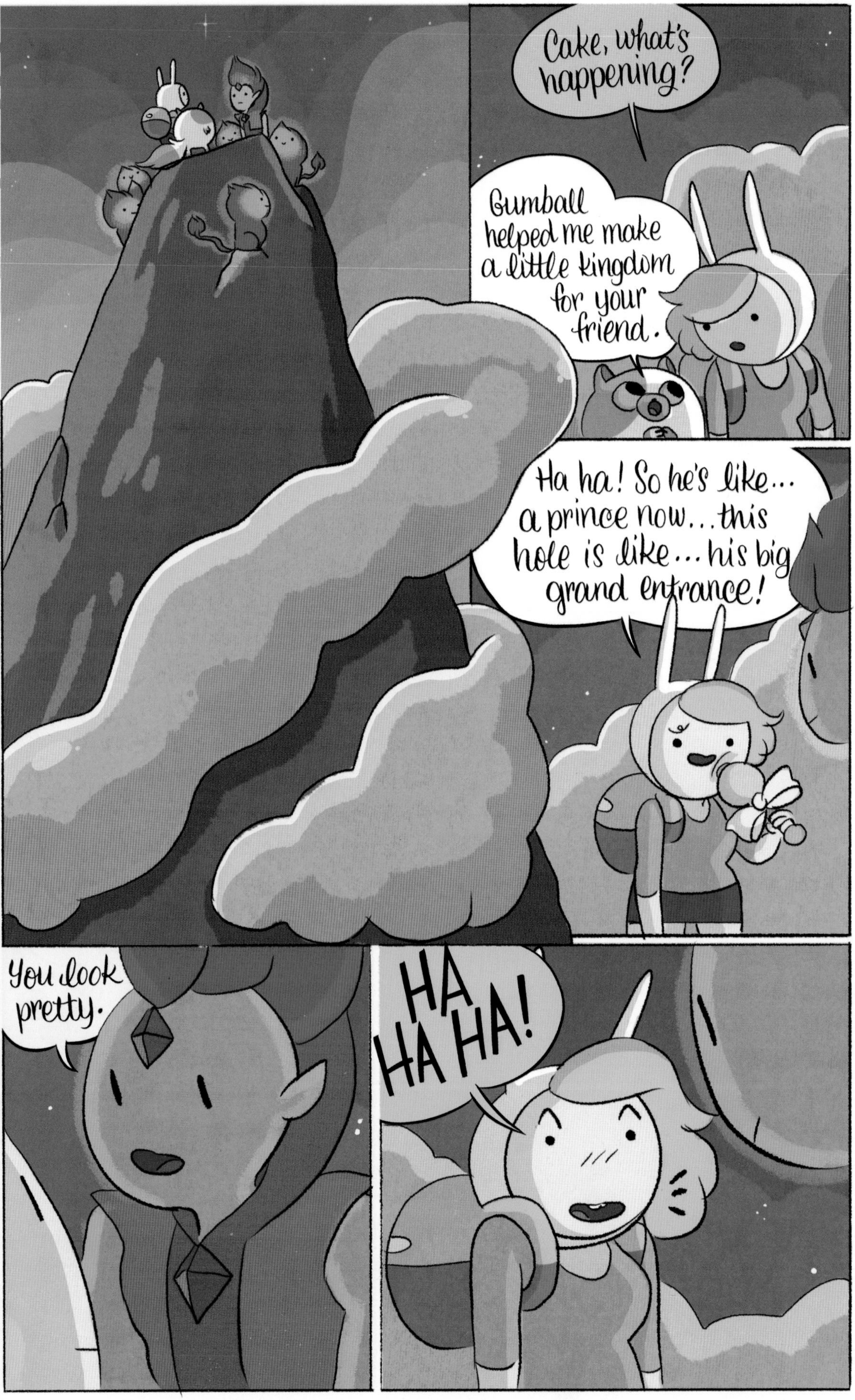
Cake, what's happening?
Gumball helped me make a little kingdom for your friend.
Ha ha! So he's like... a prince now... this hole is like... his big grand entrance!
You look pretty.
HA HA HA!

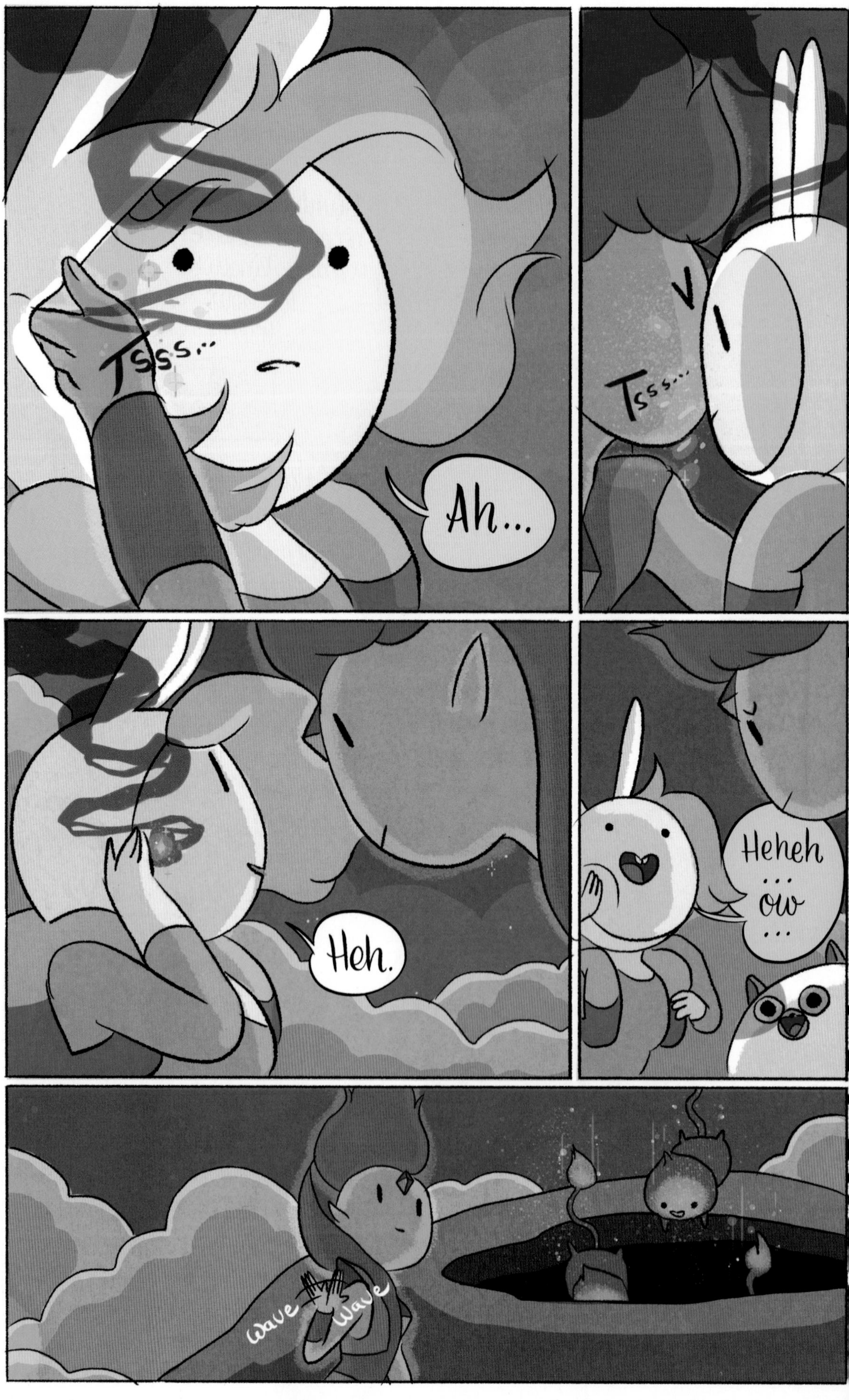

Tsss...
Ah...
Tsss...
Heh.
Heheh ... ow ...
wave wave

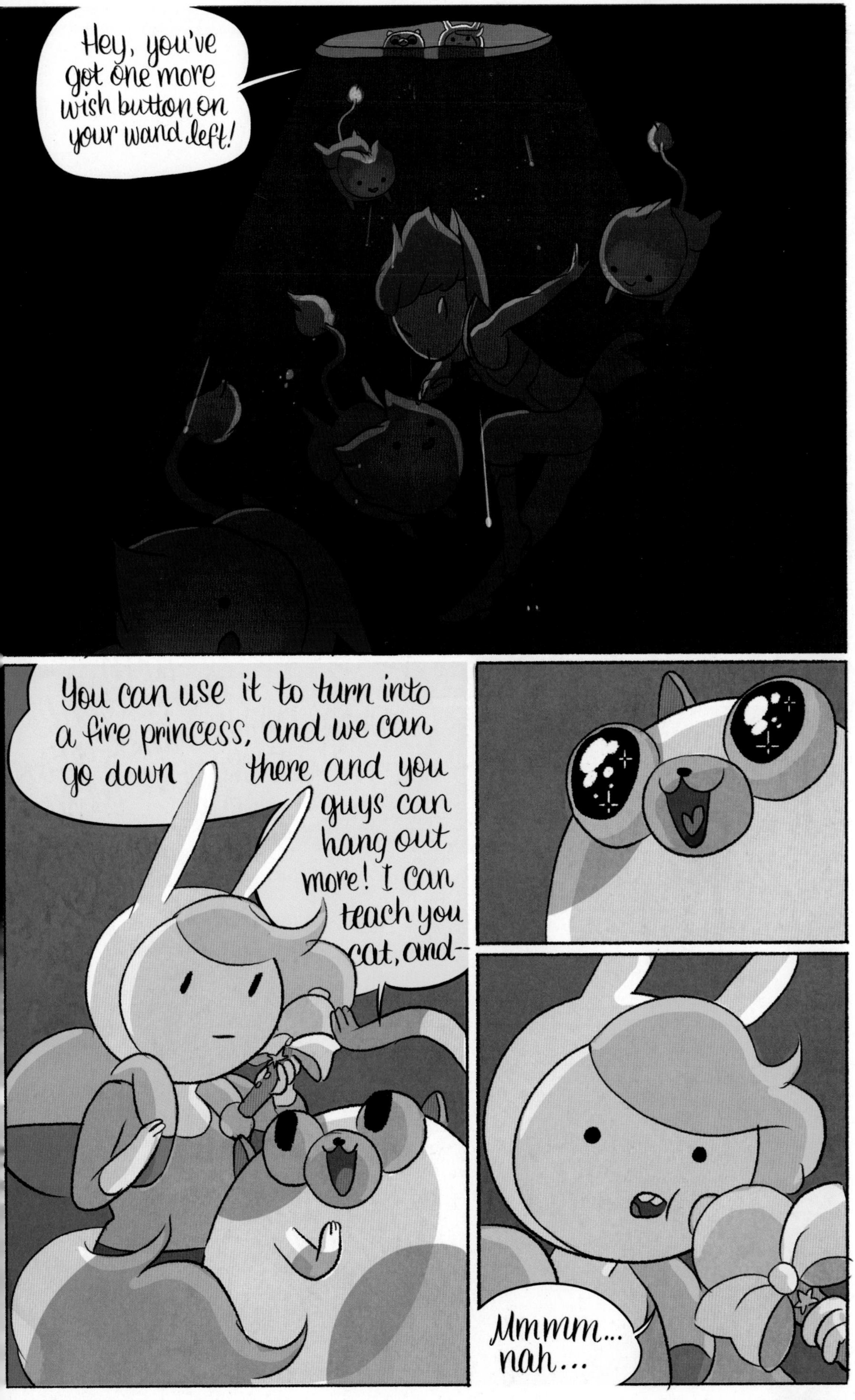
Hey, you've got one more wish button on your wand left!
You can use it to turn into a fire princess, and we can go down there and you guys can hang out more! I can teach you cat, and--
Mmmm... nah...

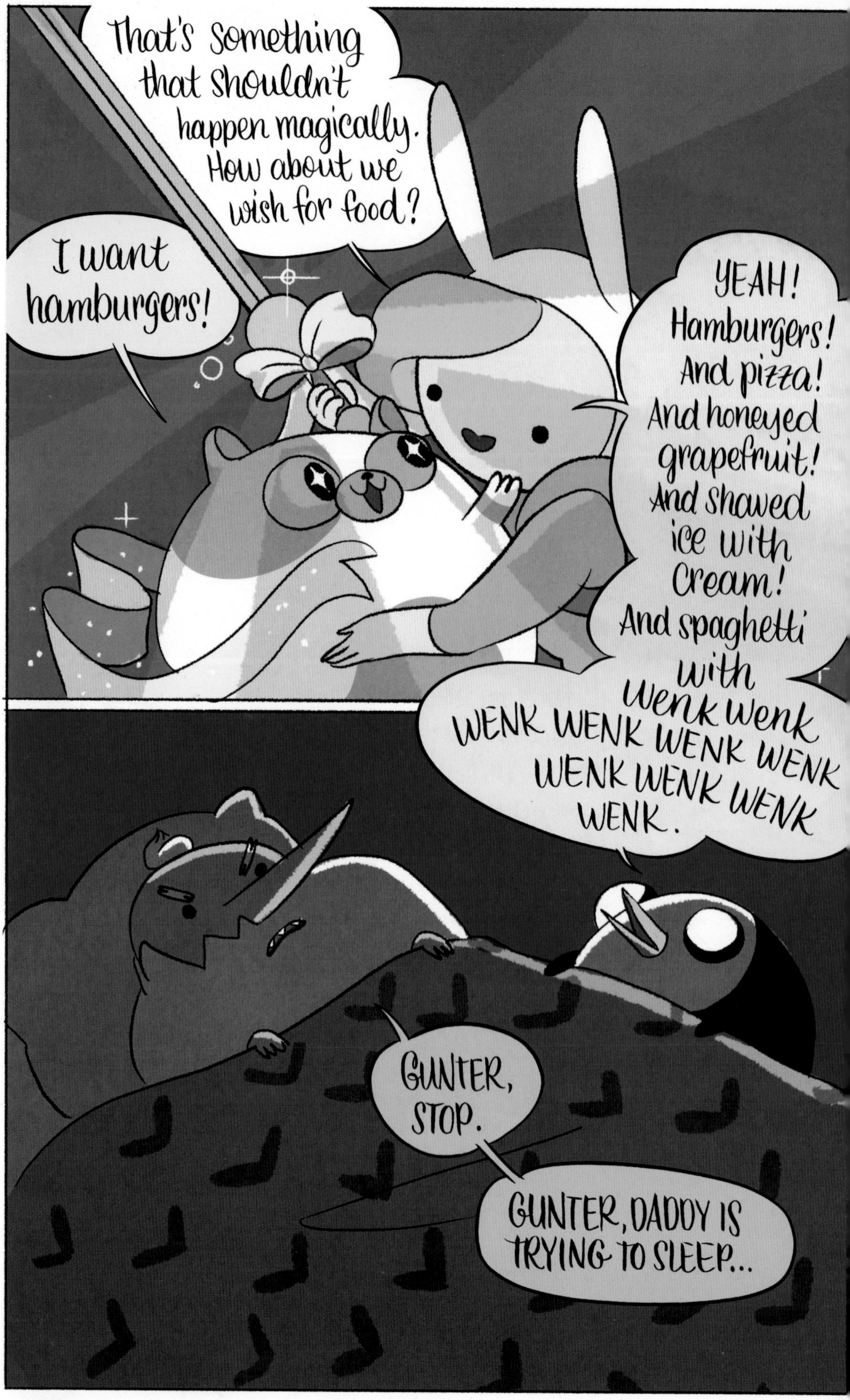
That's something that shouldn't happen magically. How about we wish for food?
I want hamburgers!
YEAH! Hamburgers! And pizza! And honeyed grapefruit! And shaved ice with cream! And spaghetti with wenk wenk WENK WENK WENK WENK WENK WENK WENK WENK.
GUNTER, STOP.
GUNTER, DADDY IS TRYING TO SLEEP...

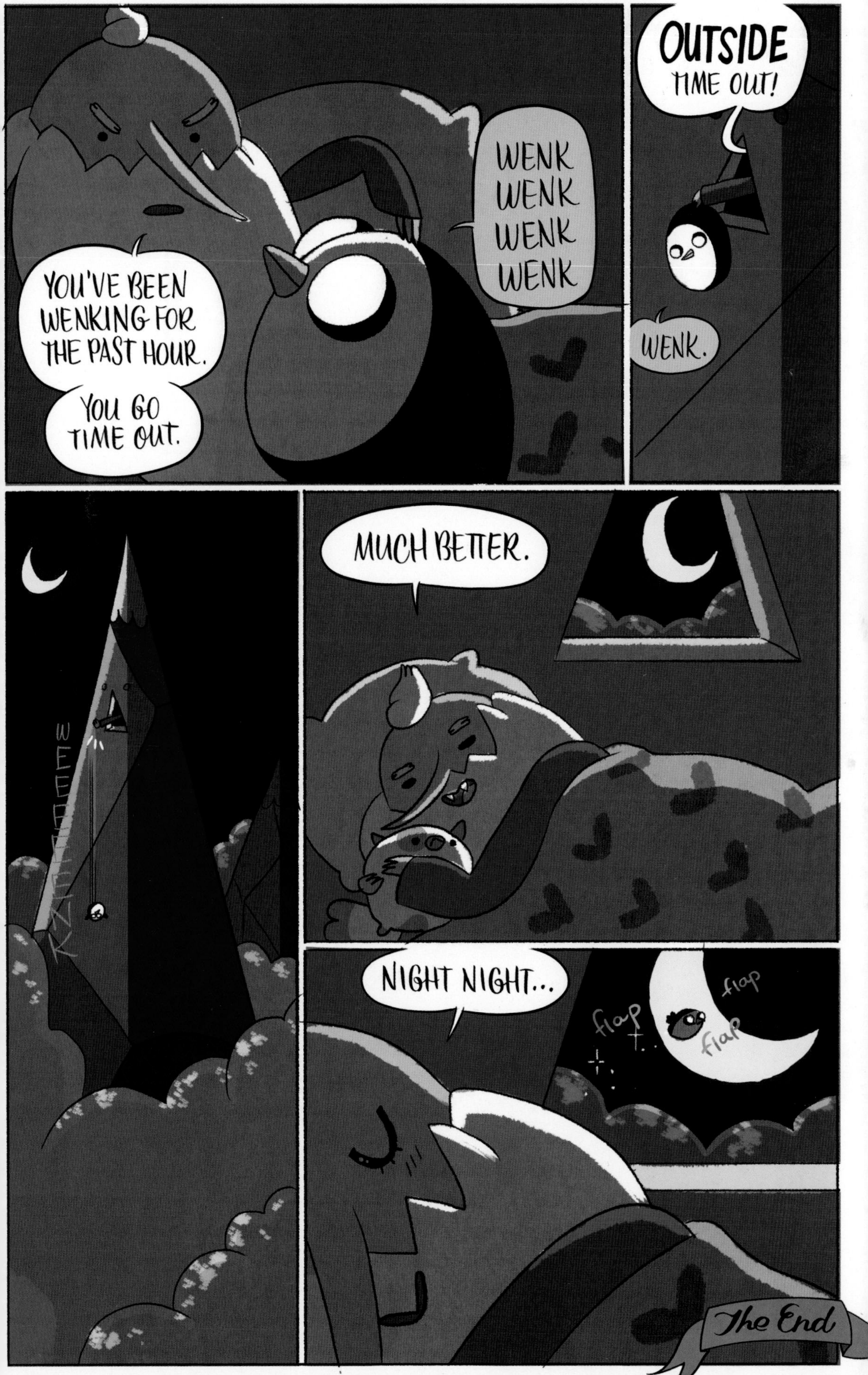
WENK
WENK
WENK
WENK
YOU'VE BEEN WENKING FOR THE PAST HOUR.
YOU GO TIME OUT.
OUTSIDE TIME OUT!
WENK.
WEEEEE
KZZZZ
MUCH BETTER.
NIGHT NIGHT...
flap
flap
flap
The End

Sweet Shorts

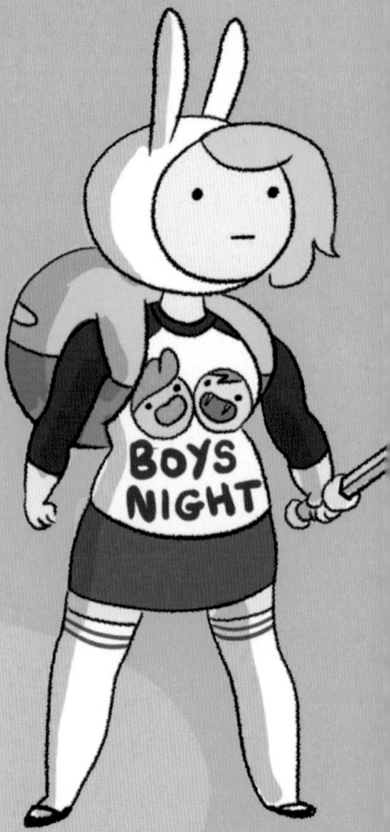
BOYS
NIGHT

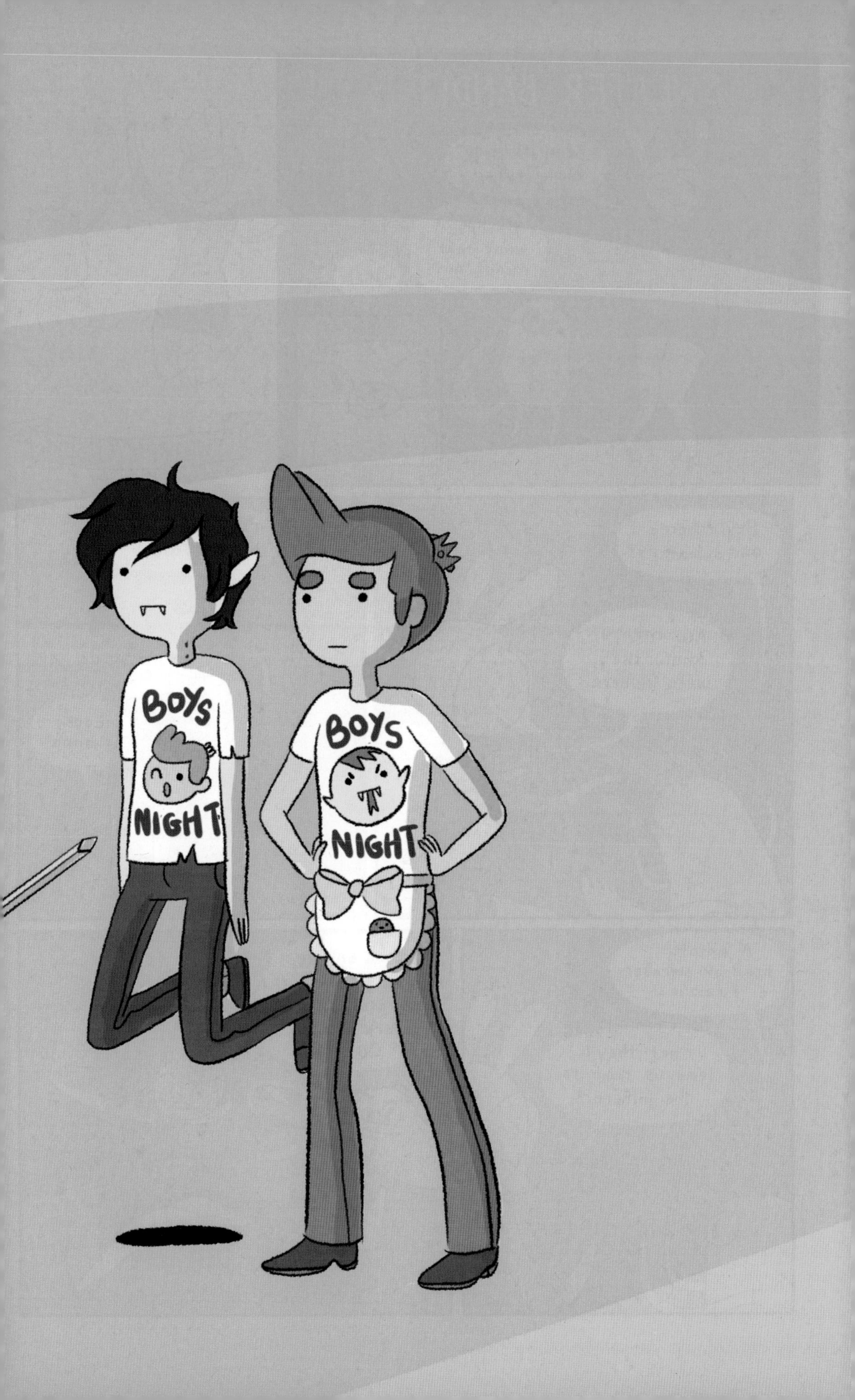
BOYS
NIGHT
BOYS
NIGHT

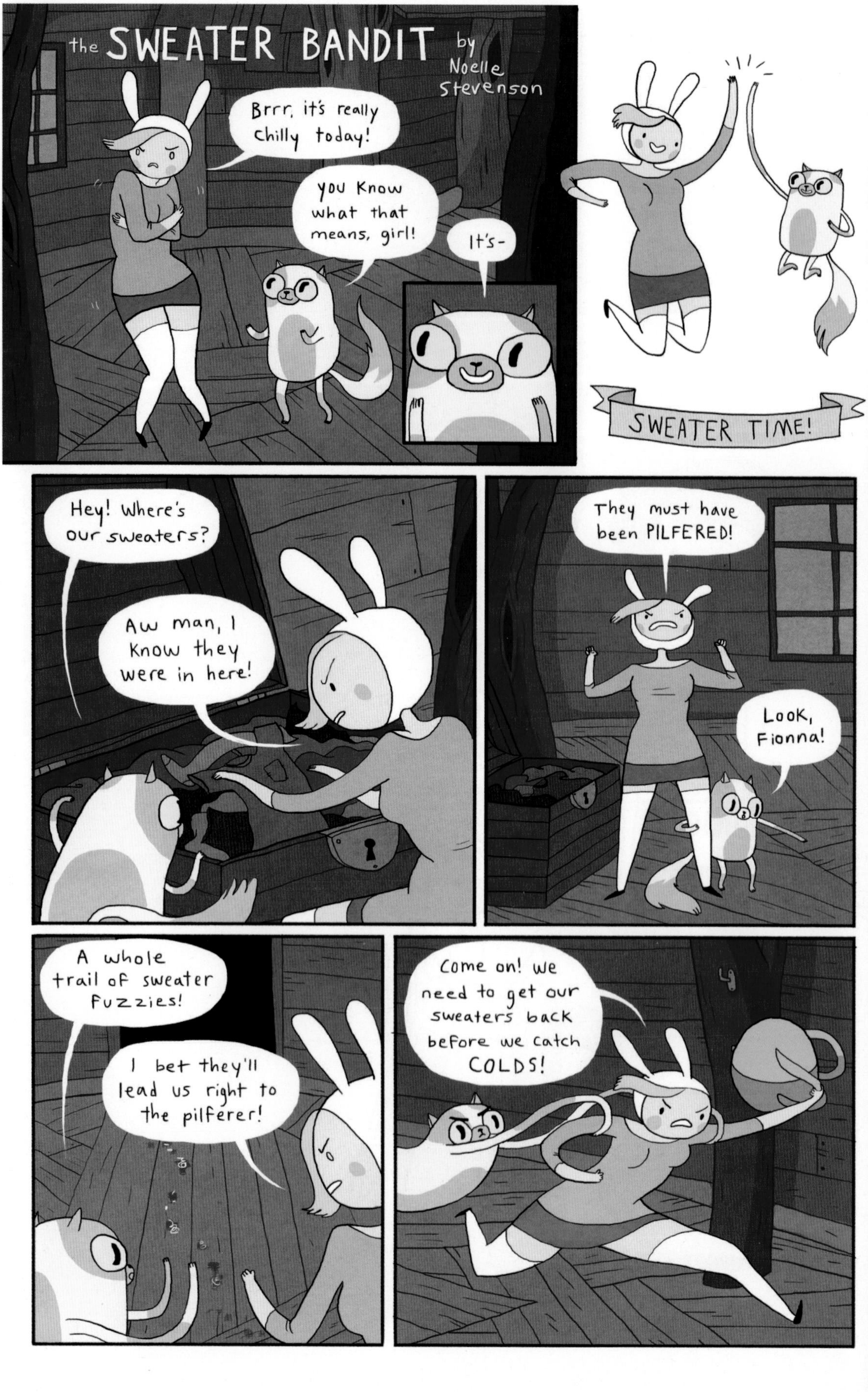
the SWEATER BANDIT by Noelle Stevenson
Brrr, it's really chilly today!
you know what that means, girl!
It's-
SWEATER TIME!
Hey! Where's our sweaters?
Aw man, I know they were in here!
They must have been PILFERED!
Look, Fionna!
A whole trail of sweater fuzzies!
I bet they'll lead us right to the pilferer!
Come on! We need to get our sweaters back before we catch COLDS!

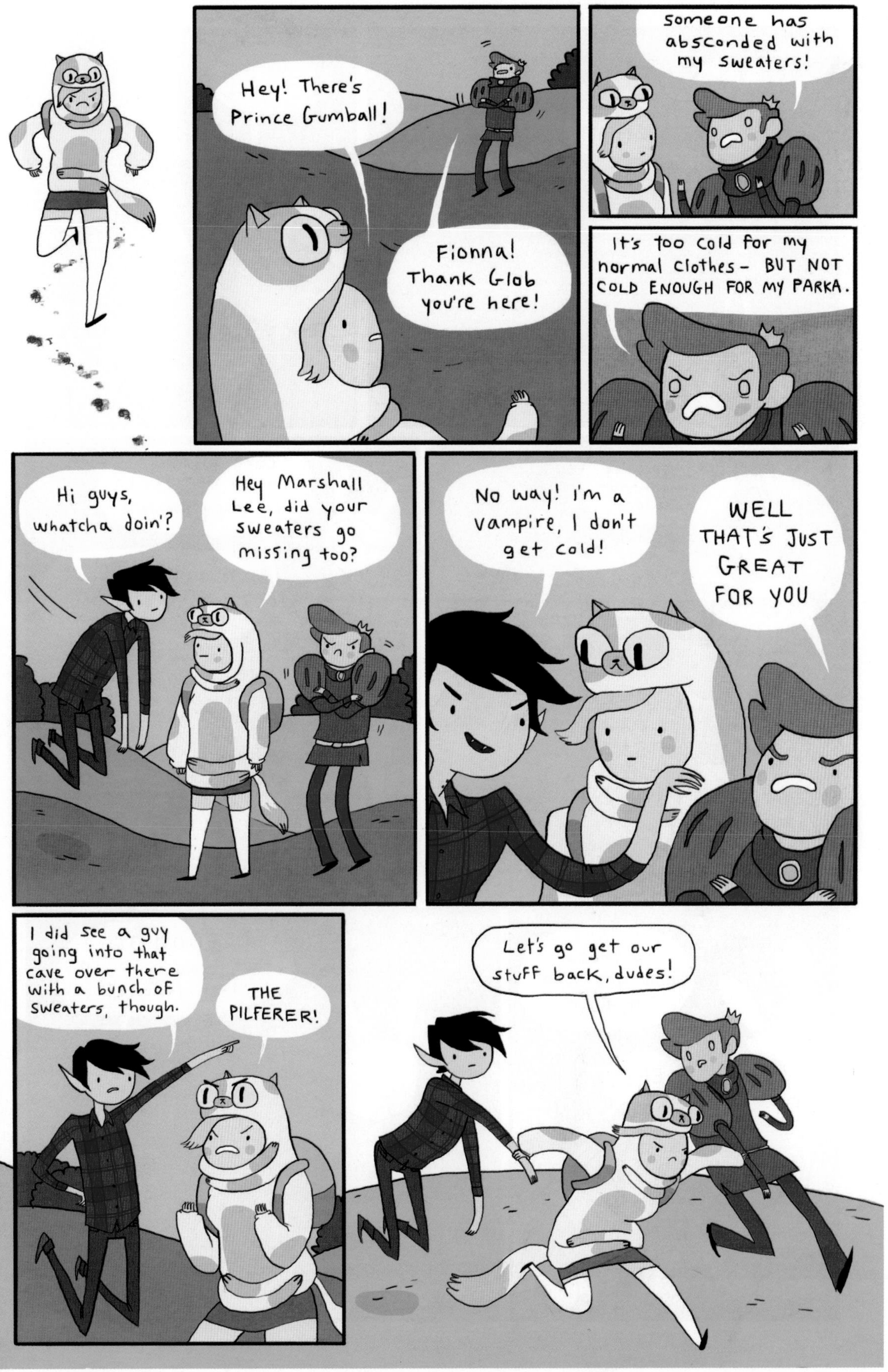
Hey! There's Prince Gumball!
Fionna! Thank Glob you're here!
Someone has absconded with my sweaters!
It's too cold for my normal clothes- BUT NOT COLD ENOUGH FOR MY PARKA.
Hi guys, whatcha doin'?
Hey Marshall Lee, did your sweaters go missing too?
No way! I'm a vampire, I don't get cold!
WELL THAT'S JUST GREAT FOR YOU
I did see a guy going into that cave over there with a bunch of sweaters, though.
THE PILFERER!
Let's go get our stuff back, dudes!

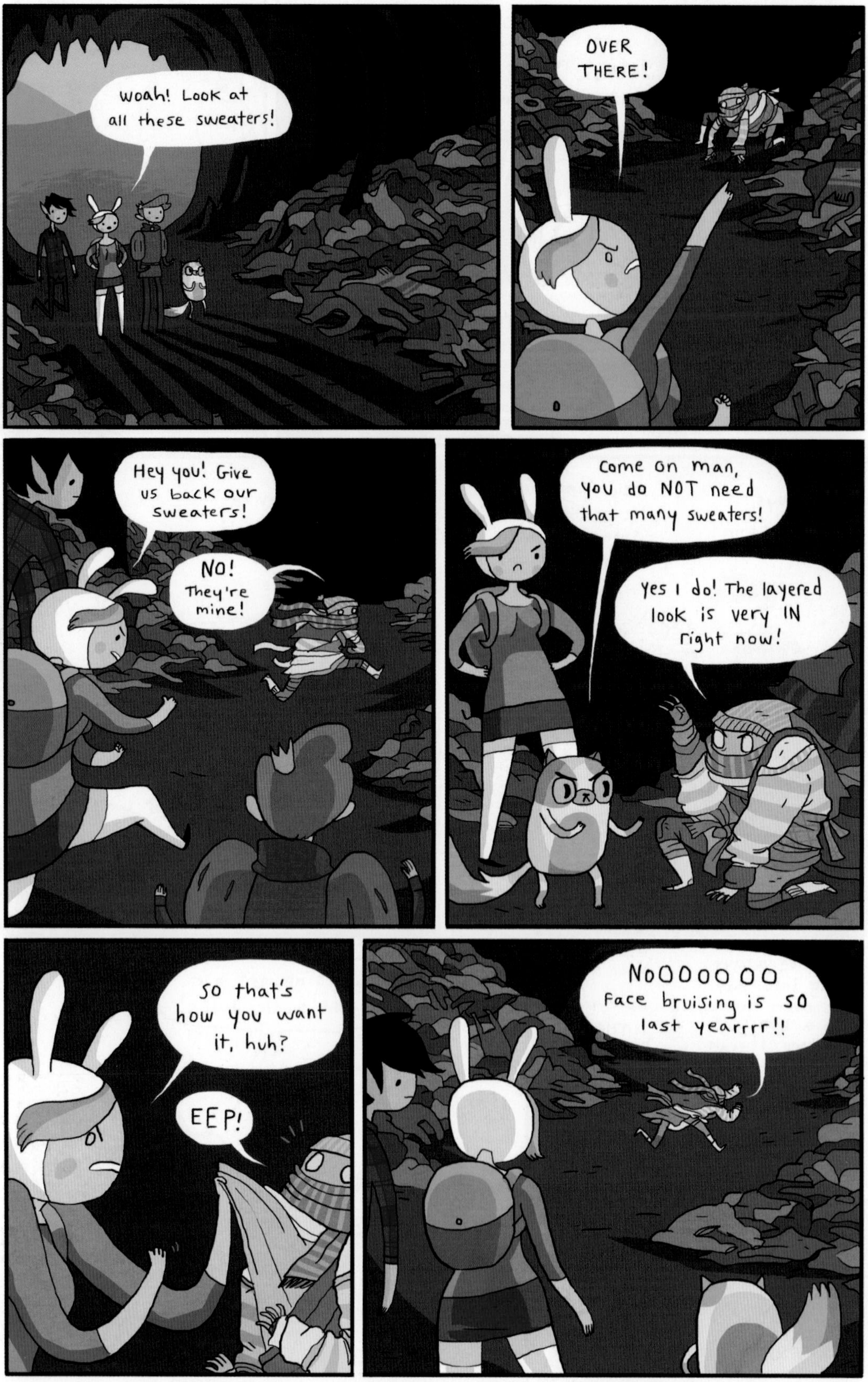
woah! Look at all these sweaters!
OVER THERE!
Hey you! Give us back our sweaters!
NO! They're mine!
Come on man, you do NOT need that many sweaters!
Yes I do! The layered look is very IN right now!
So that's how you want it, huh?
EEP!
NoOOOOOO Face bruising is SO last yearrrr!!

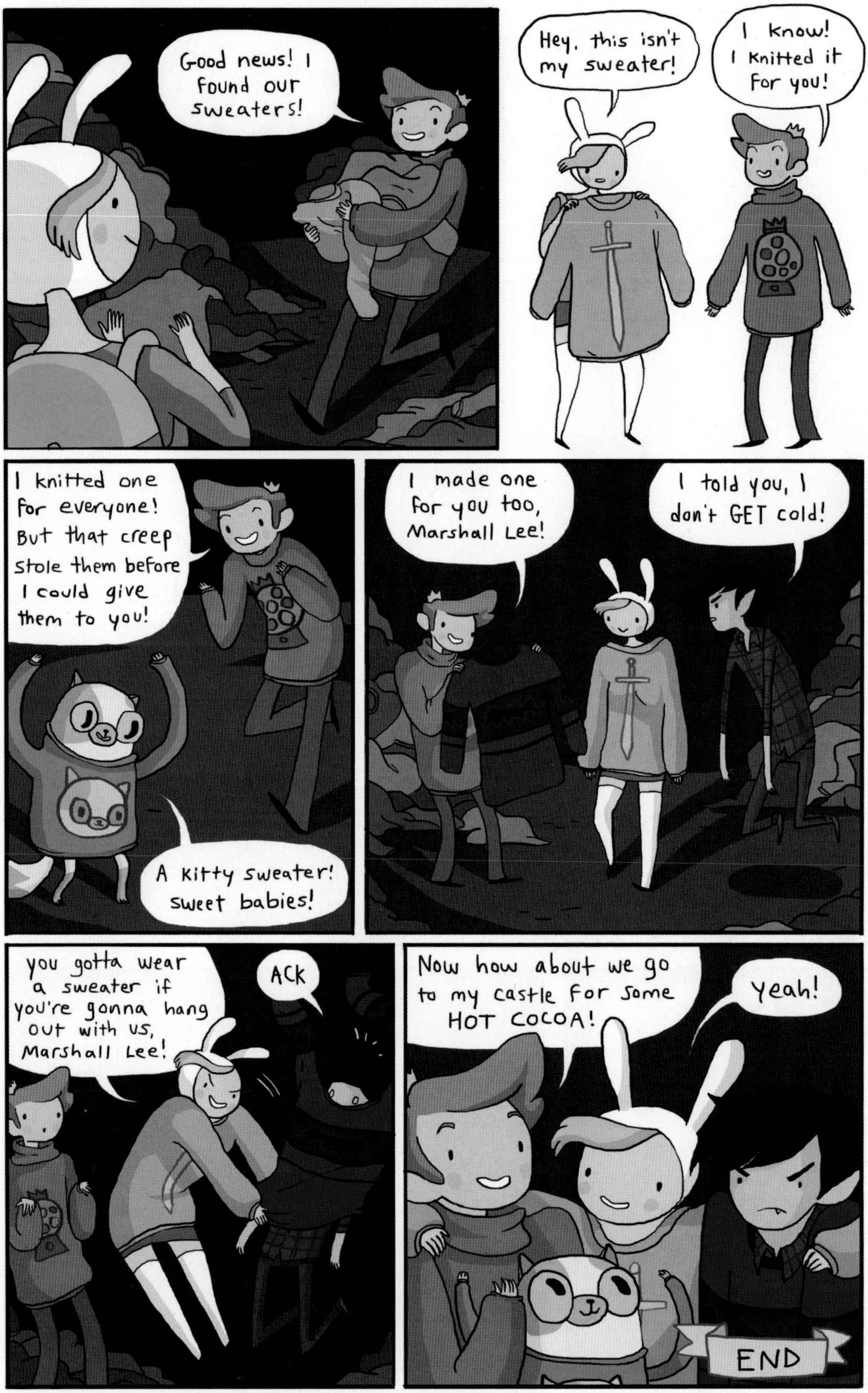
Good news! I found our sweaters!
Hey, this isn't my sweater!
I know! I knitted it for you!
I knitted one for everyone! But that creep stole them before I could give them to you!
A kitty sweater! sweet babies!
I made one for you too, Marshall Lee!
I told you, I don't GET cold!
you gotta wear a sweater if you're gonna hang out with us, Marshall Lee!
ACK
Now how about we go to my castle for some HOT COCOA!
Yeah!
END

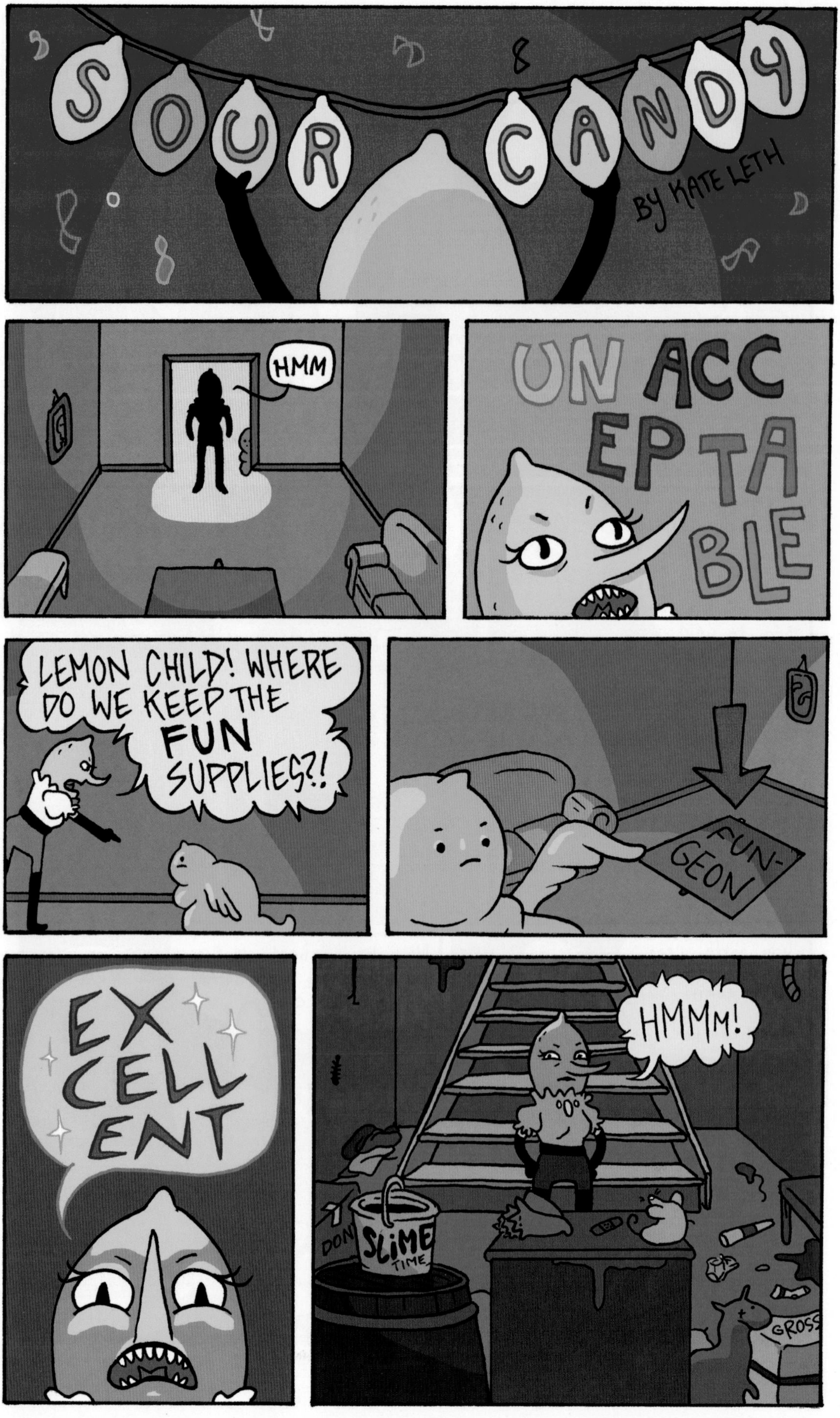
SOUR CANDY
BY KATE LETH
HMM
UN ACC EP TA BLE
LEMON CHILD! WHERE DO WE KEEP THE FUN SUPPLIES?!
FUN-GEON
EX CELL ENT
HMMM!
DON
SLIME TIME
GROSS

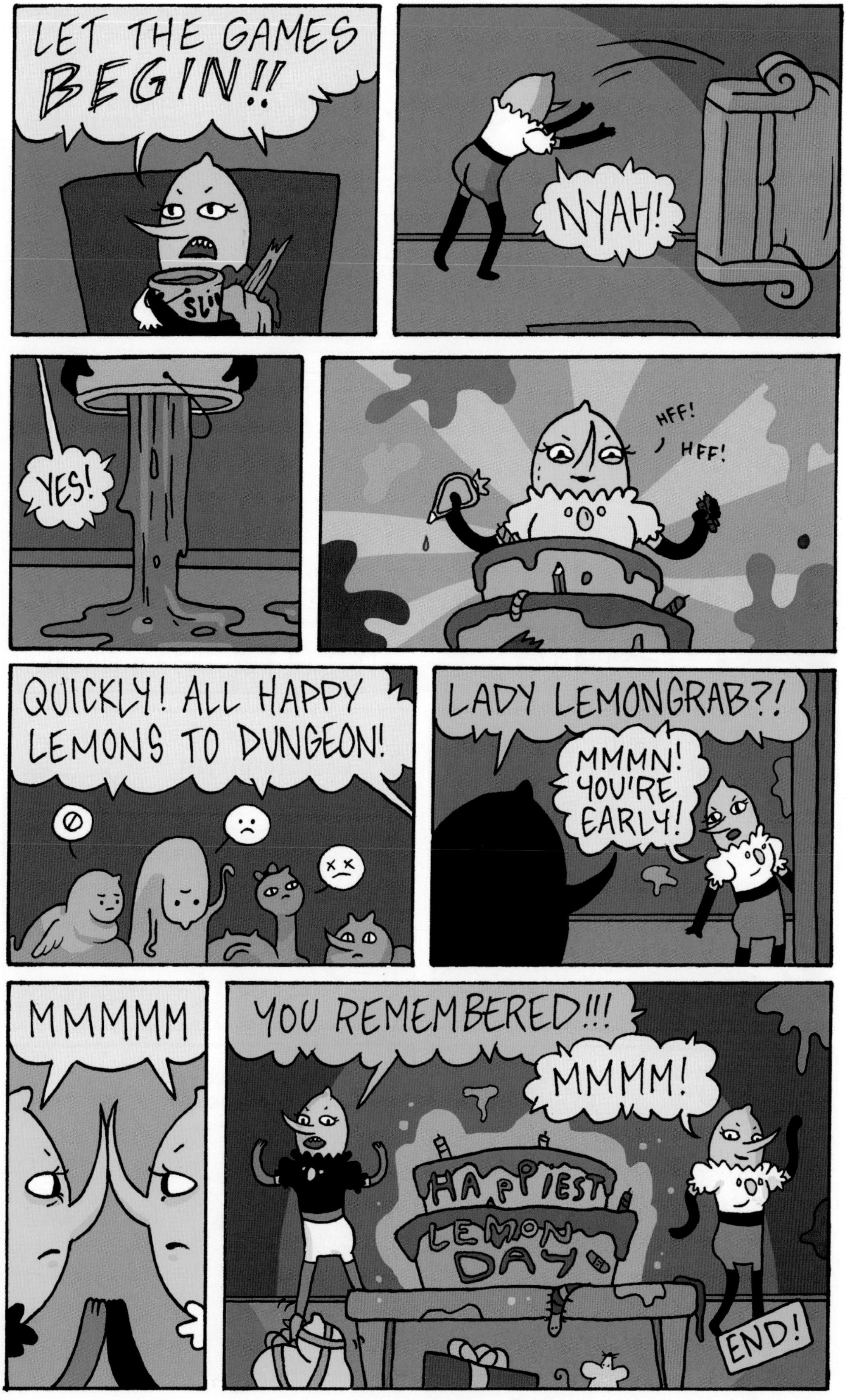
LET THE GAMES BEGIN!!
SL
NYAH!
YES!
HFF! HFF!
QUICKLY! ALL HAPPY LEMONS TO DUNGEON!
LADY LEMONGRAB?!
MMMN! YOU'RE EARLY!
MMMMM
YOU REMEMBERED!!!
MMMM!
HAPPIEST LEMON DAY
END!

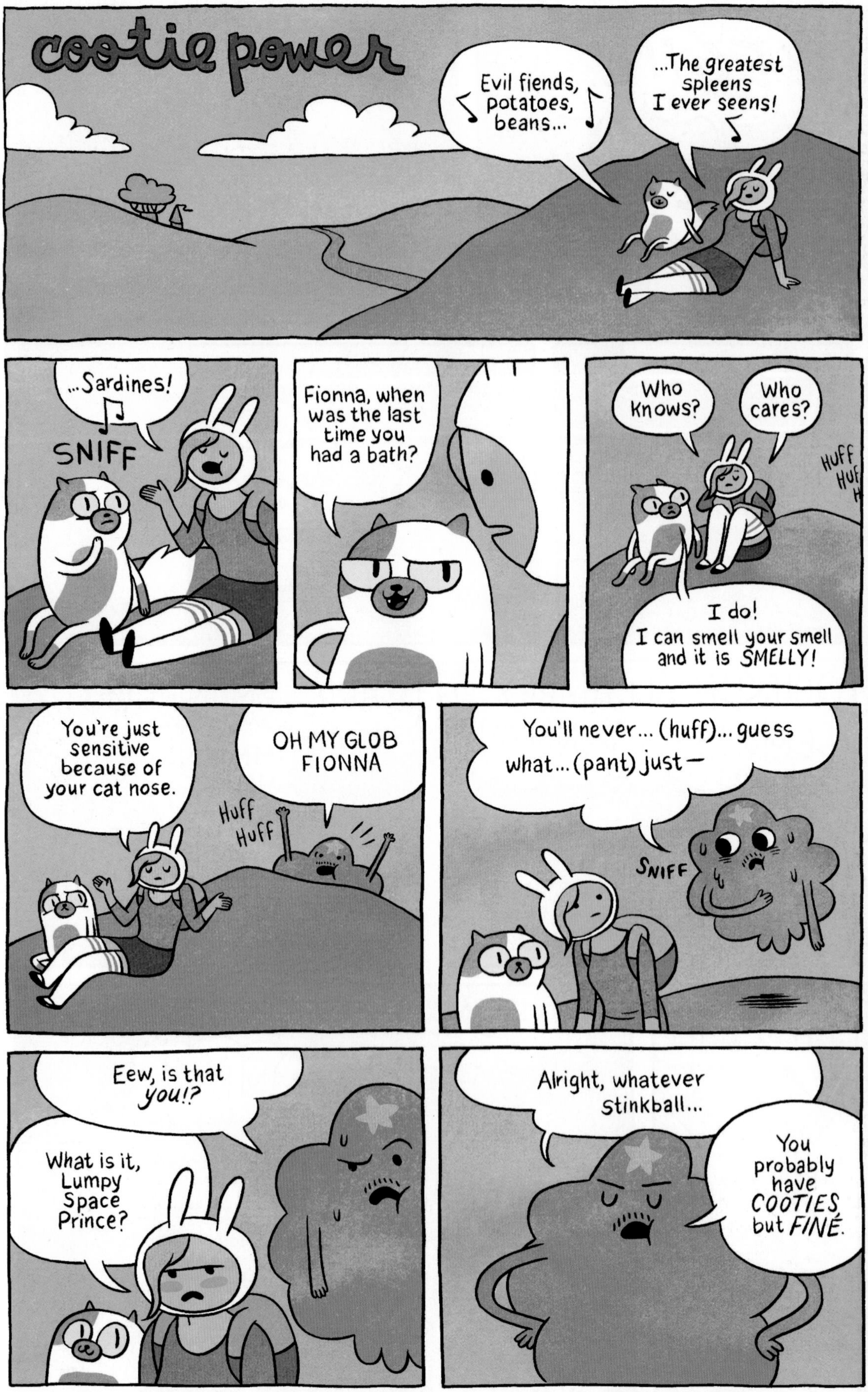
cootie power
Evil fiends, potatoes, beans...
...The greatest spleens I ever seens!
...Sardines!
SNIFF
Fionna, when was the last time you had a bath?
Who knows?
Who cares?
HUFF HUF
I do! I can smell your smell and it is SMELLY!
You're just sensitive because of your cat nose.
OH MY GLOB FIONNA
Huff Huff
You'll never... (huff)... guess what... (pant) just—
SNIFF
Eew, is that you!?
What is it, Lumpy Space Prince?
Alright, whatever stinkball...
You probably have COOTIES but FINÉ.

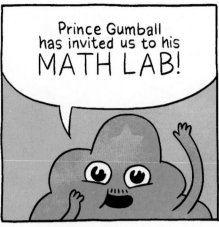

Prince Gumball has invited us to his MATH LAB!

And it's gonna be, like, TOTALLY GREAT.

Hm, I would like to see what Gumball is working on...

Sure you do.

He didn't even invite Bratwurst Prince, so it's like, EXCLUSIVE.

This is lumpin' awesome. Maybe I should wear this sweet hat I just bought.

Maybe YOU should take a BATH!

NAW.

It's not like this is a DATE.

GLOB, Cake!

Soon:

Hello, my friends!

Are you ready to tour my very special Math Lab?

I especially want to show YOU, Fionna!

Me?

ABSOLUTELY!

The safety of my experiments from monster attacks is paramount to...

Sniff

Fionna... Is that YOU?

Sniff Sniff

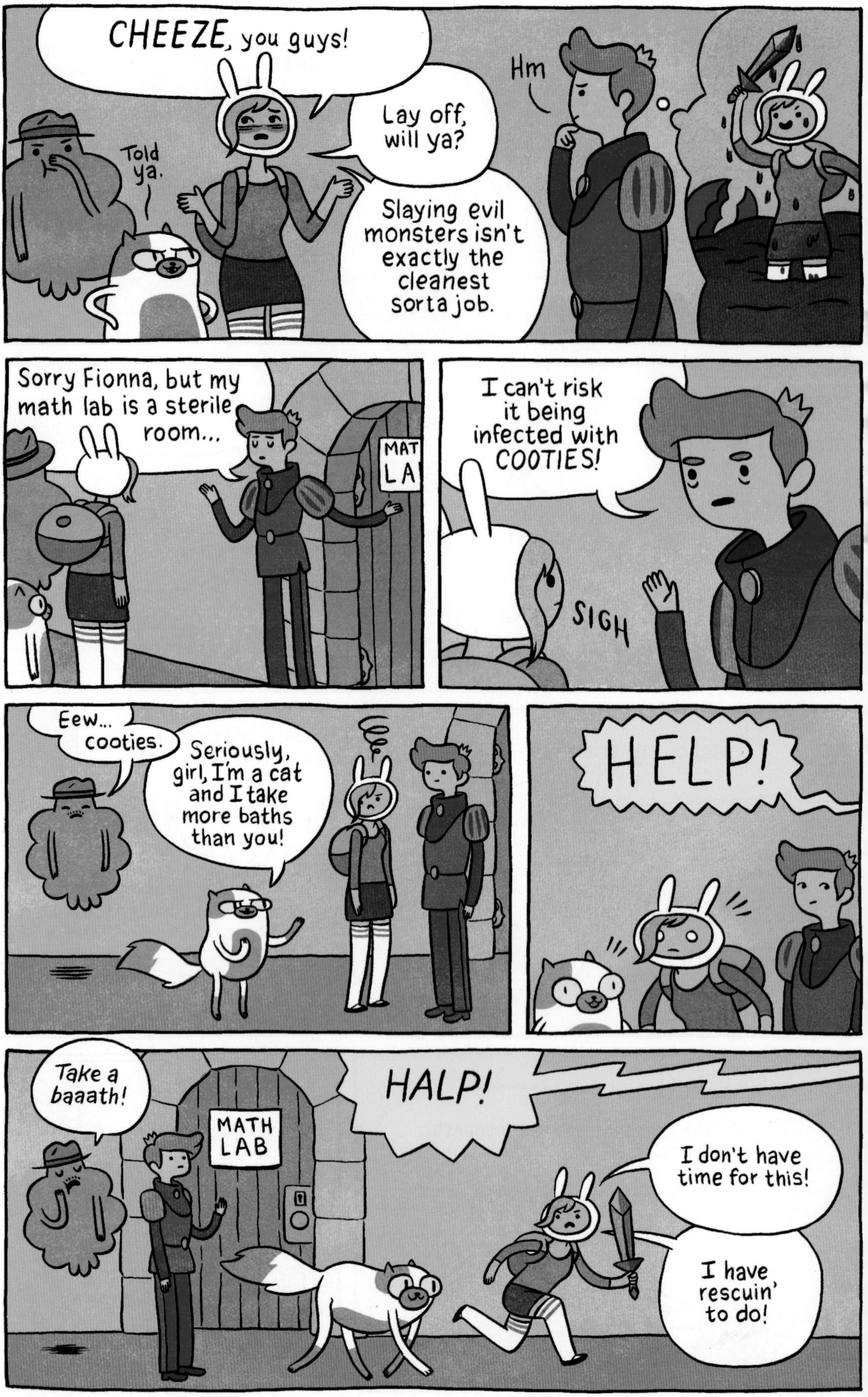
CHEEZE, you guys!
Told ya.
Lay off, will ya?
Slaying evil monsters isn't exactly the cleanest sorta job.
Hm
Sorry Fionna, but my math lab is a sterile room...
MAT LA
I can't risk it being infected with COOTIES!
SIGH
Eew... cooties.
Seriously, girl, I'm a cat and I take more baths than you!
HELP!
Take a baaath!
MATH LAB
HALP!
I don't have time for this!
I have rescuin' to do!

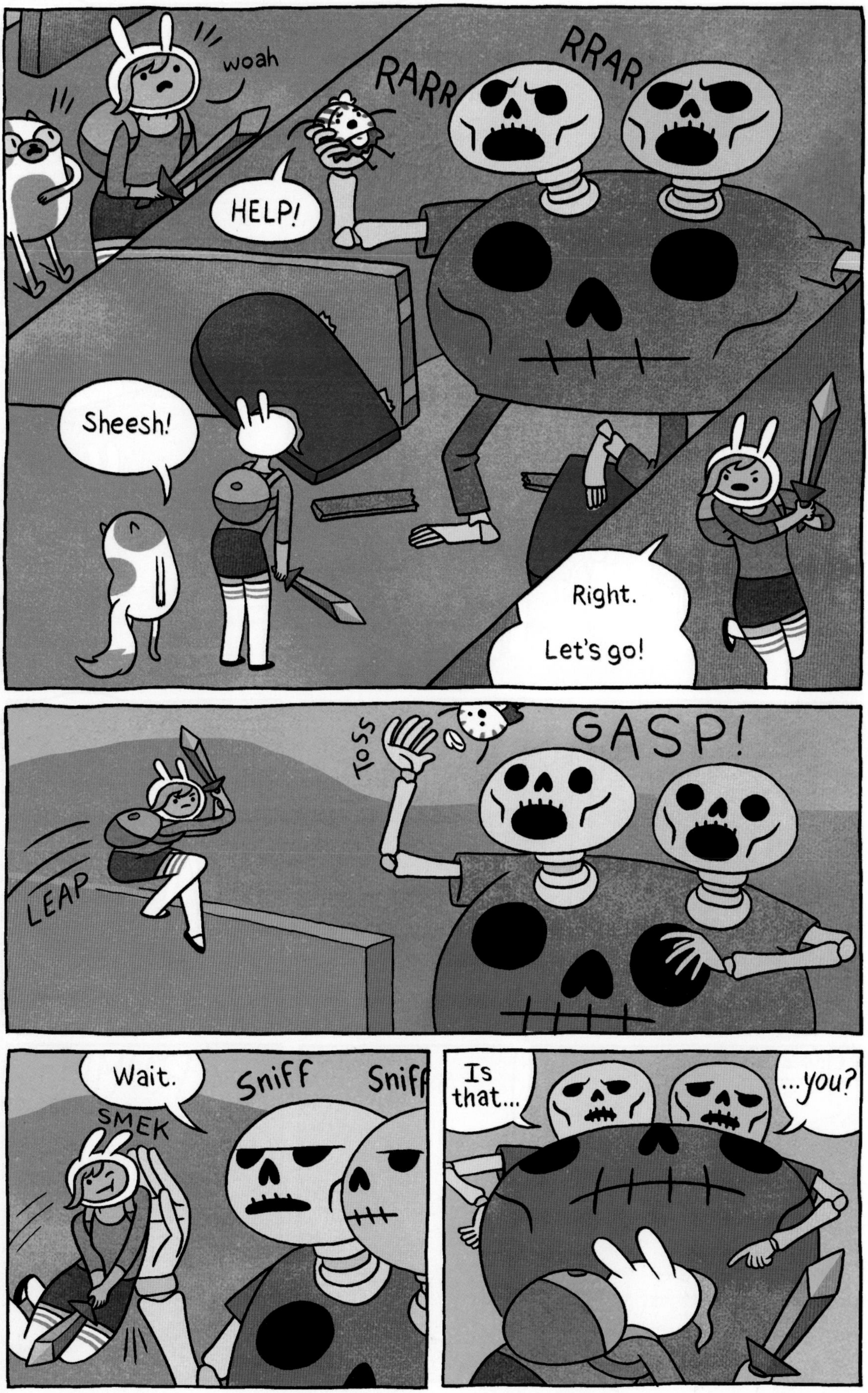
woah
RARR
RRAR
HELP!
Sheesh!
Right.
Let's go!
LEAP
TOSS
GASP!
Wait.
SMEK
Sniff
Sniff
Is that...
...you?

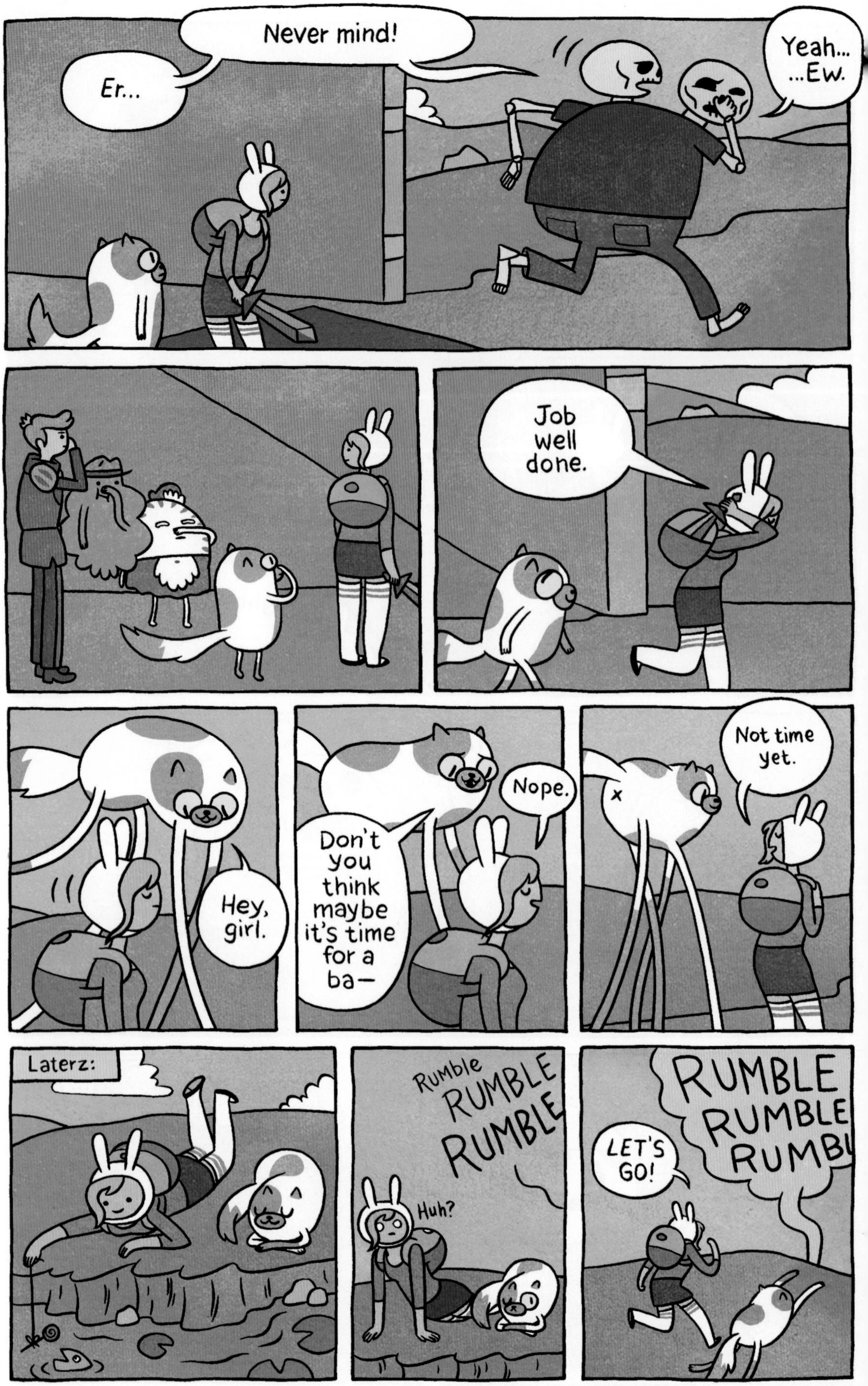
Er...
Never mind!
Yeah... ...Ew.
Job well done.
Hey, girl.
Don't you think maybe it's time for a ba—
Nope.
Not time yet.
Laterz:
Rumble
RUMBLE
RUMBLE
Huh?
RUMBLE
RUMBLE
LET'S GO!

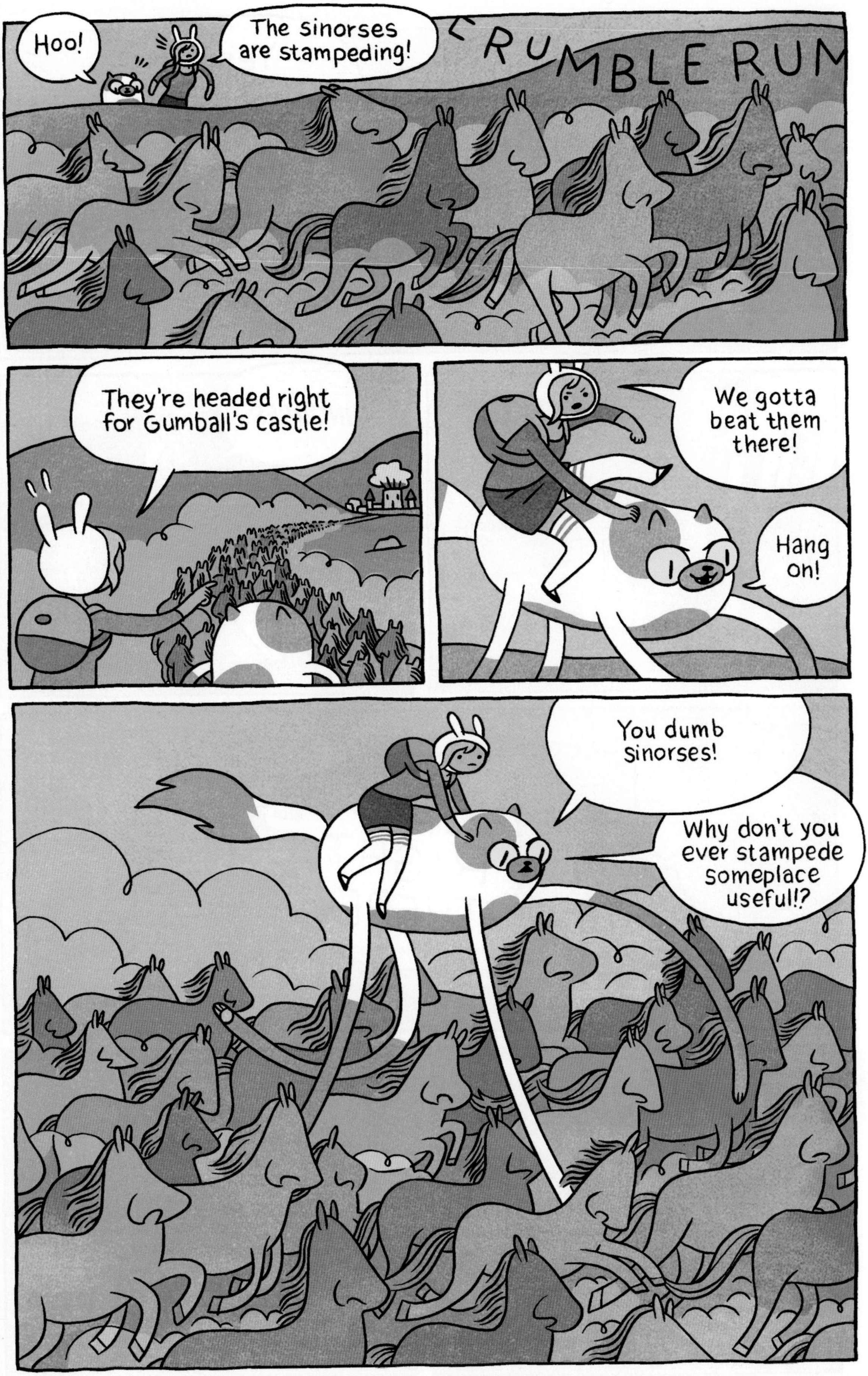
Hoo!
The sinorses are stampeding!
CRUMBLE RUM
They're headed right for Gumball's castle!
We gotta beat them there!
Hang on!
You dumb sinorses!
Why don't you ever stampede someplace useful!?

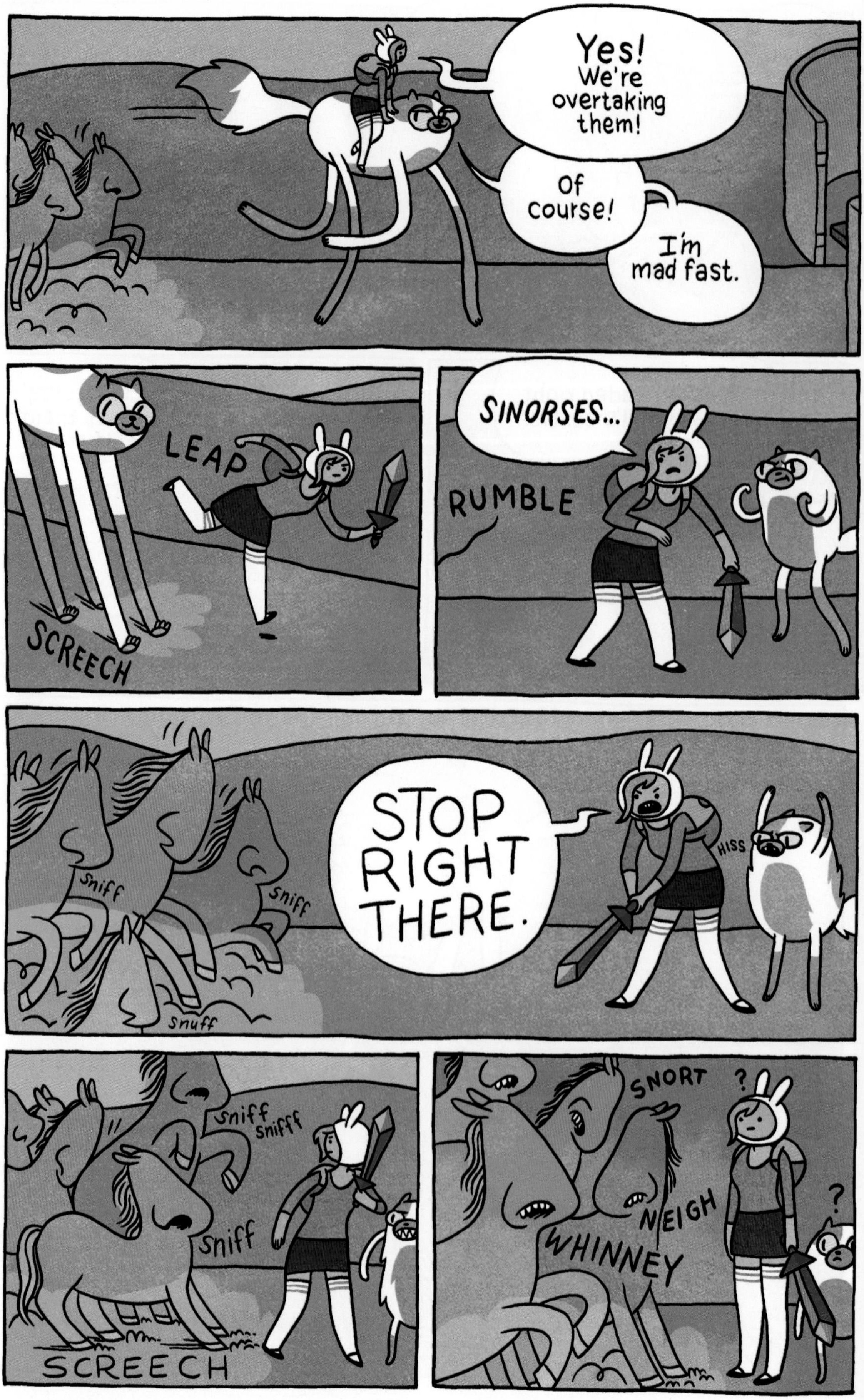
Yes! We're overtaking them!
Of course!
I'm mad fast.
LEAP
SCREECH
SINORSES...
RUMBLE
Sniff
Sniff
snuff
STOP RIGHT THERE.
HISS
Sniff sniffff
Sniff
SCREECH
SNORT
?
NEIGH
WHINNEY
?

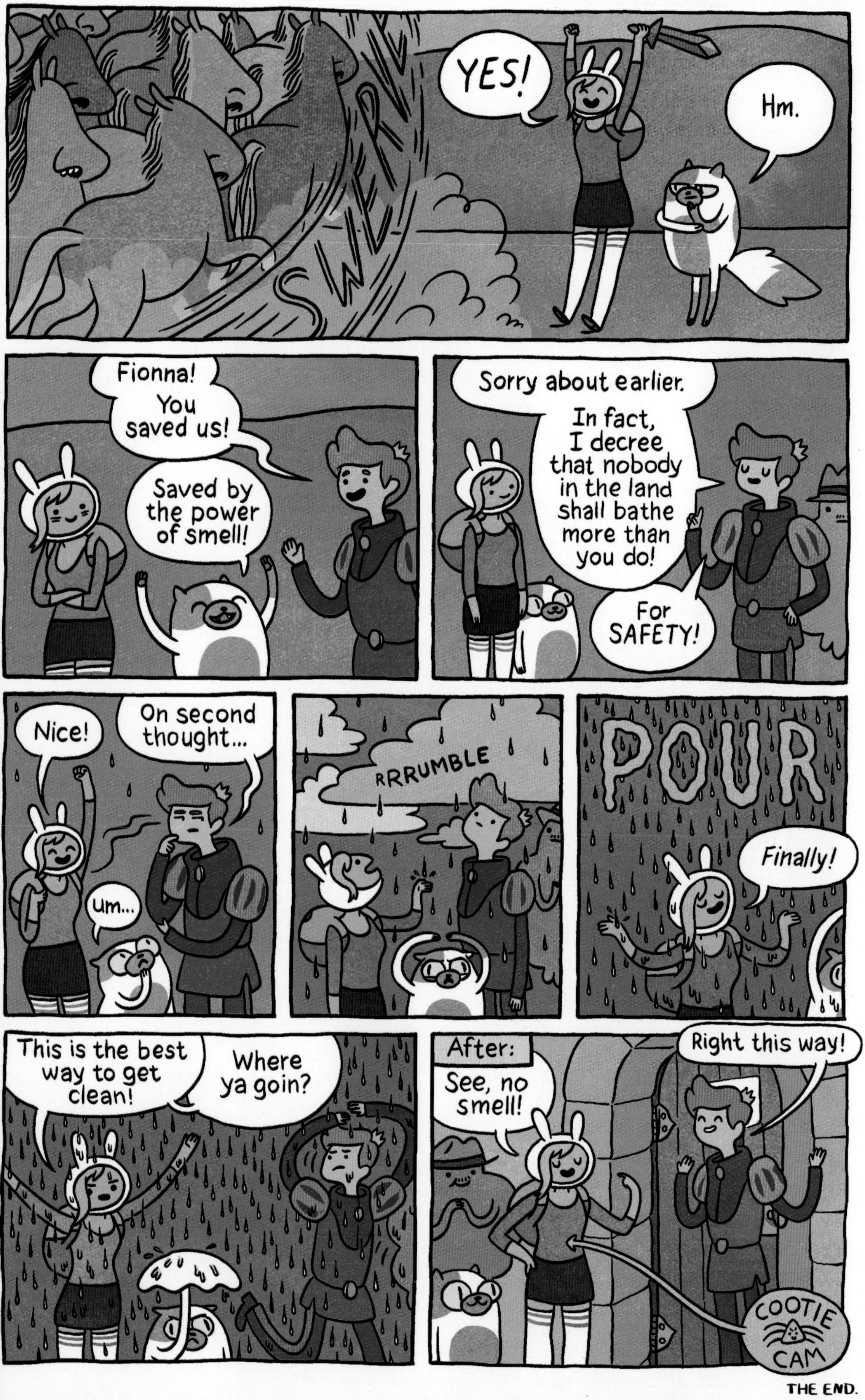
SWERV
YES!
Hm.
Fionna! You saved us!
Saved by the power of smell!
Sorry about earlier.
In fact, I decree that nobody in the land shall bathe more than you do!
For SAFETY!
Nice!
On second thought...
um...
RRRUMBLE
POUR
Finally!
This is the best way to get clean!
Where ya goin?
After:
See, no smell!
Right this way!
COOTIE CAM

THE END.

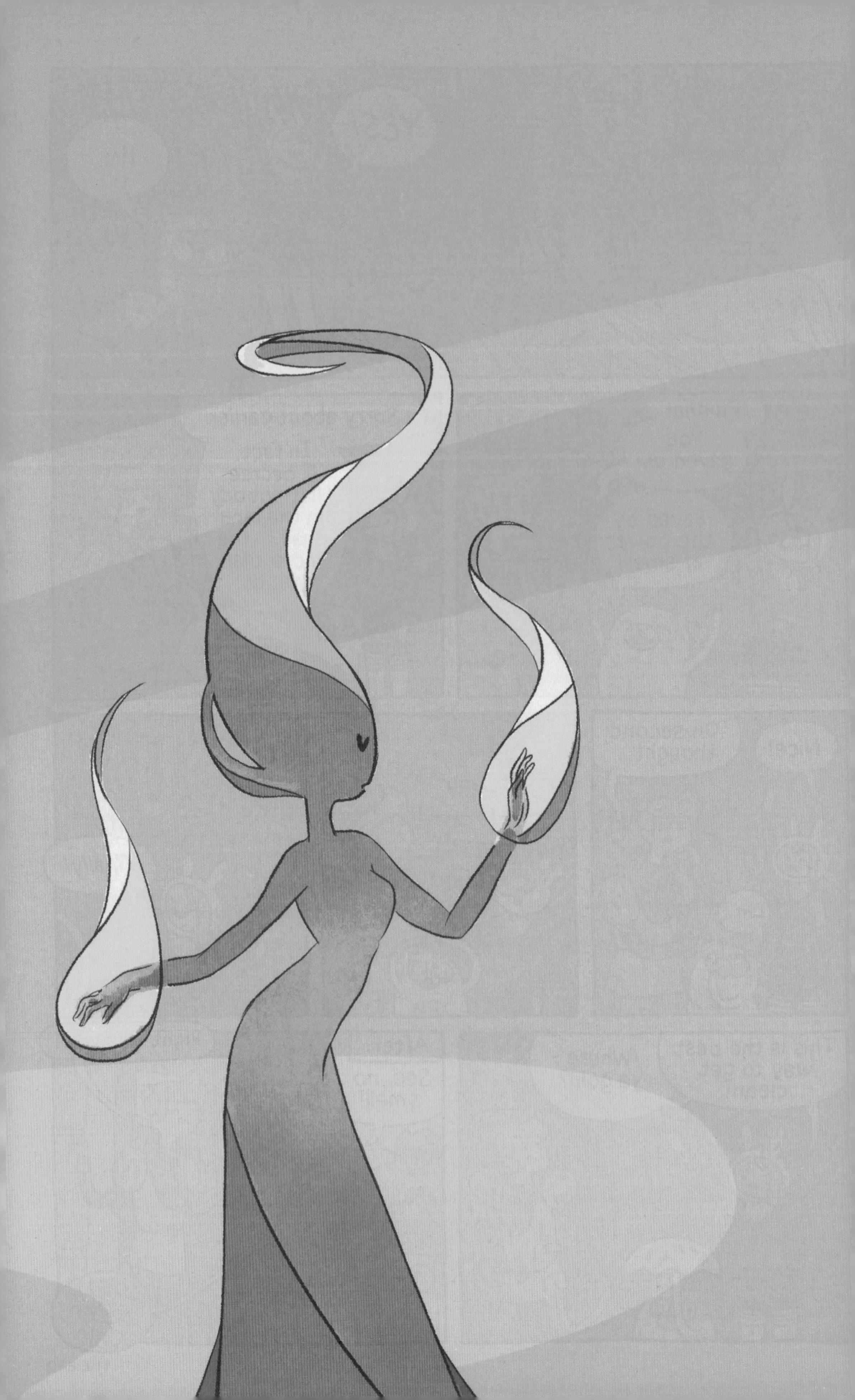

Cover Gallery

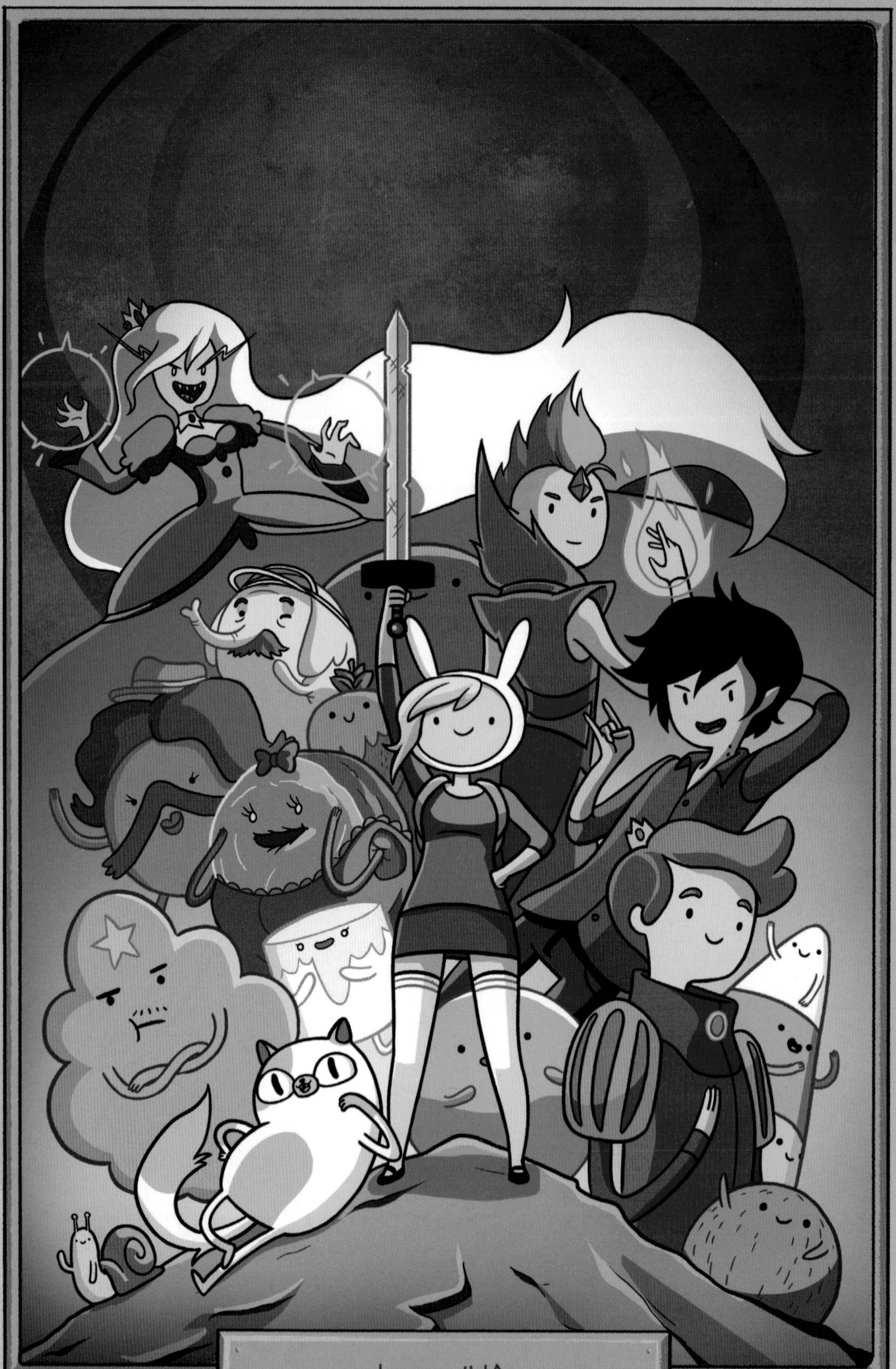

Issue #1A
Jen Bennett
Colors by Lisa Moore

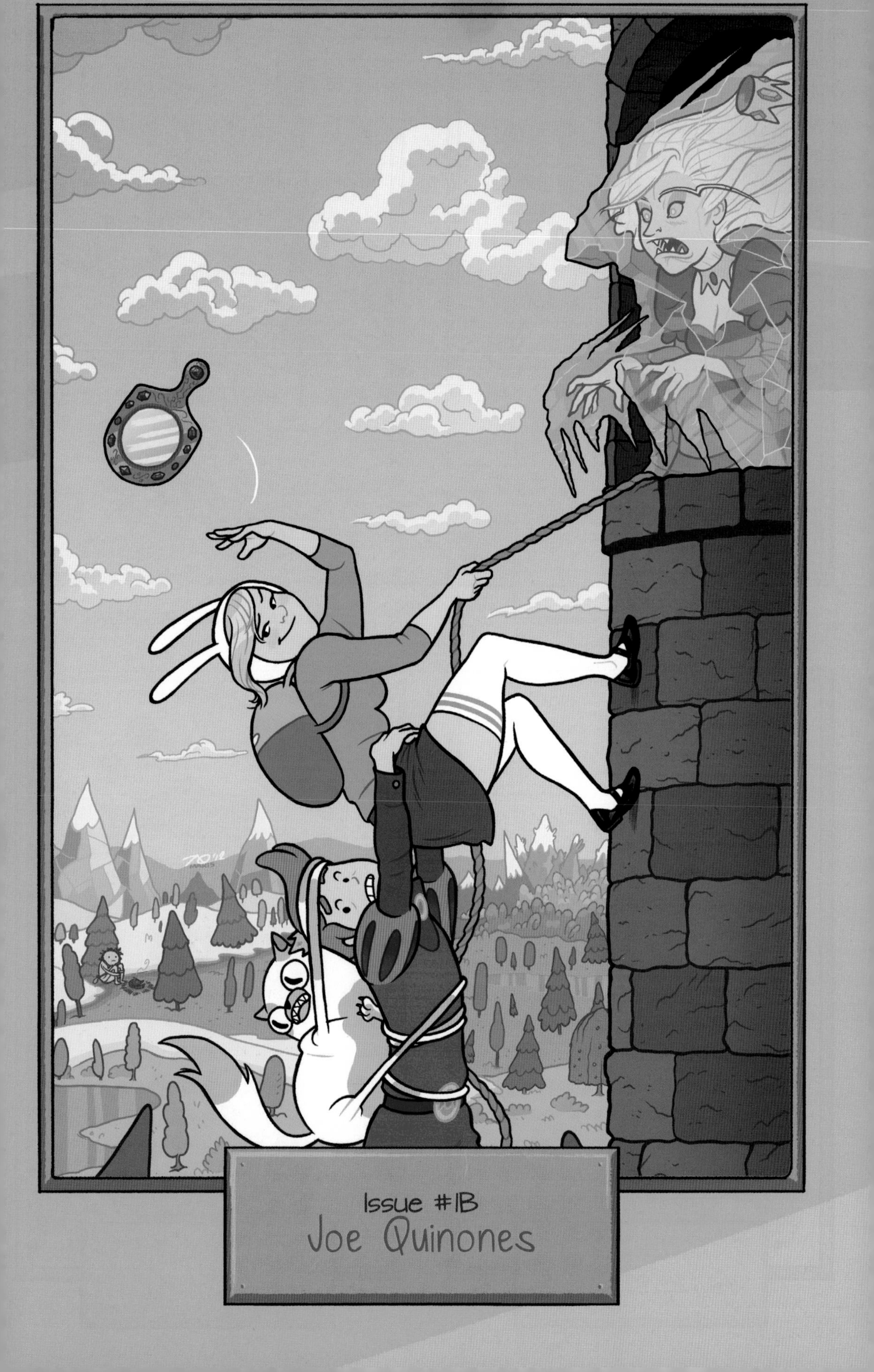

Issue #1B
Joe Quinones

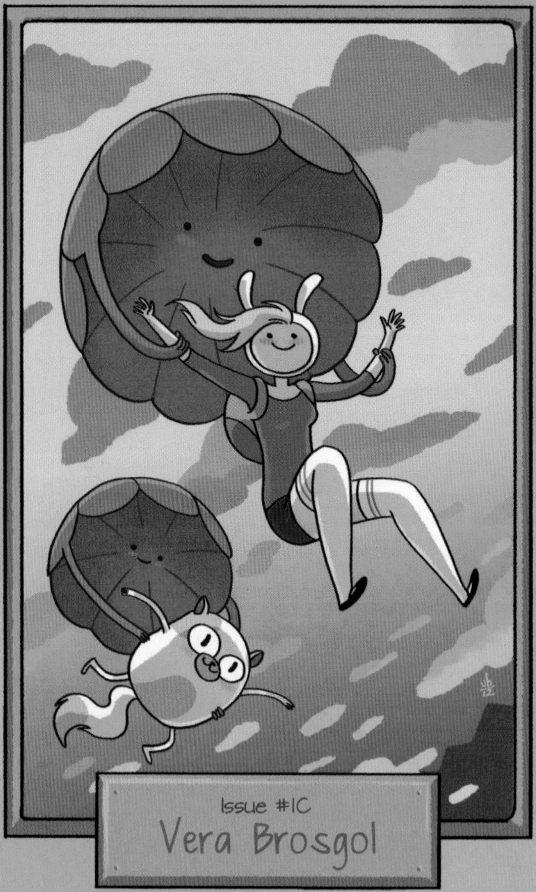

Issue #1C
Vera Brosgol

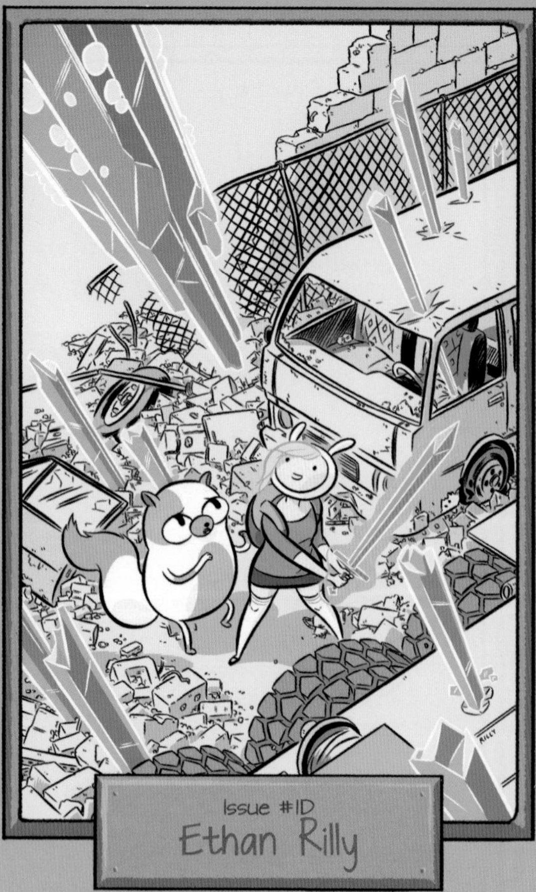

Issue #1D
Ethan Rilly

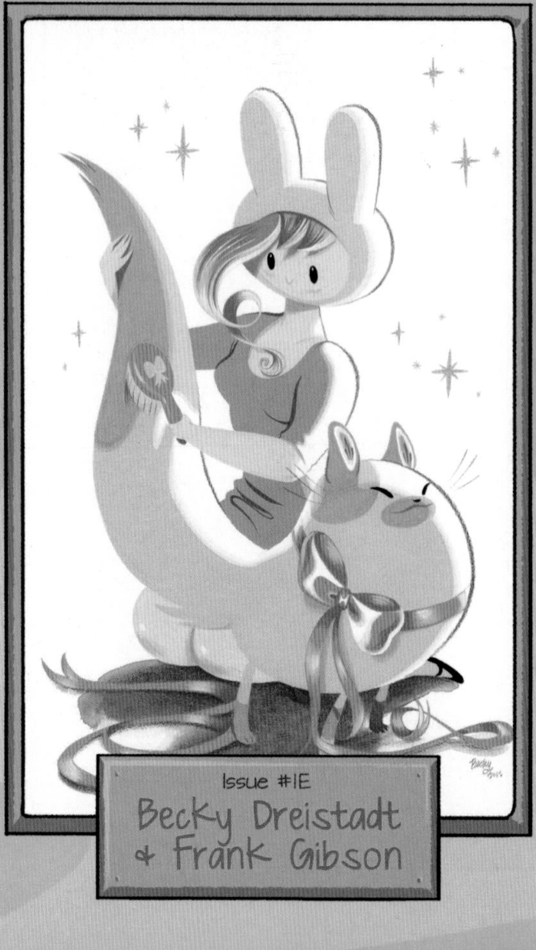

Issue #1E
Becky Dreistadt & Frank Gibson

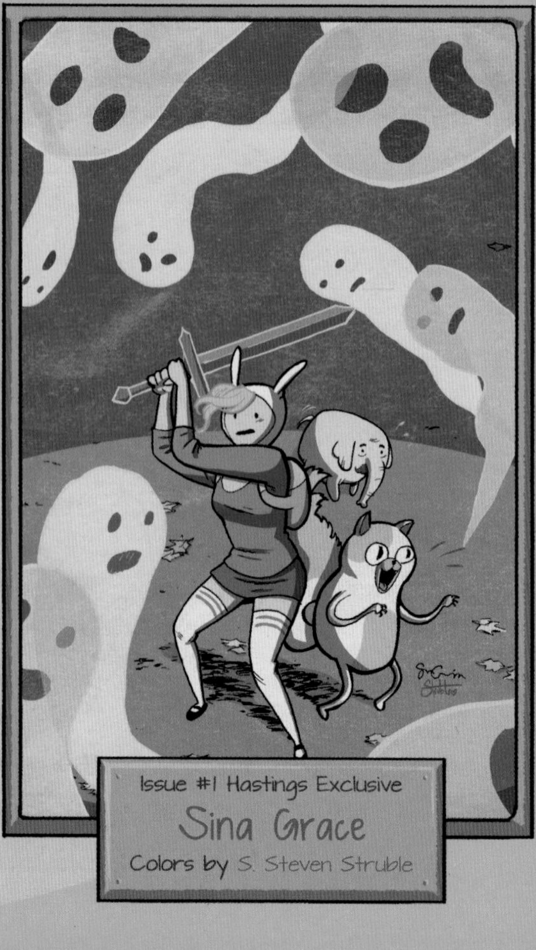

Issue #1 Hastings Exclusive
Sina Grace
Colors by S. Steven Struble

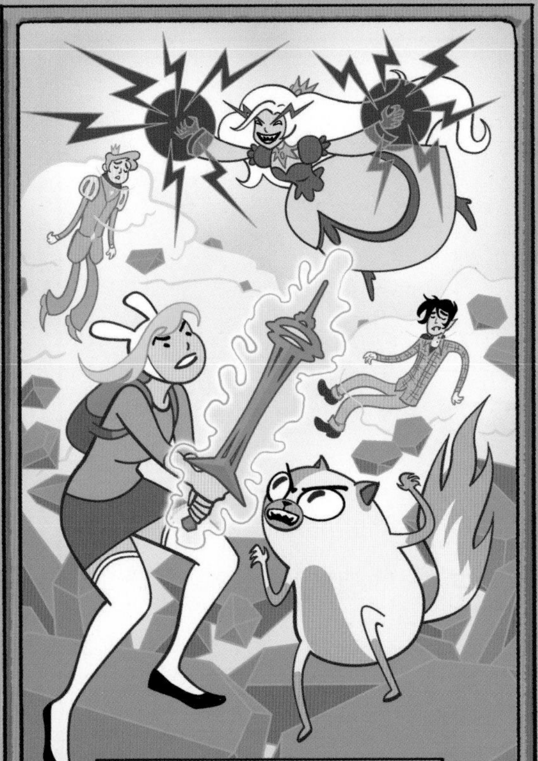

Issue #1 Emerald City Comicon Exclusive
Colleen Coover

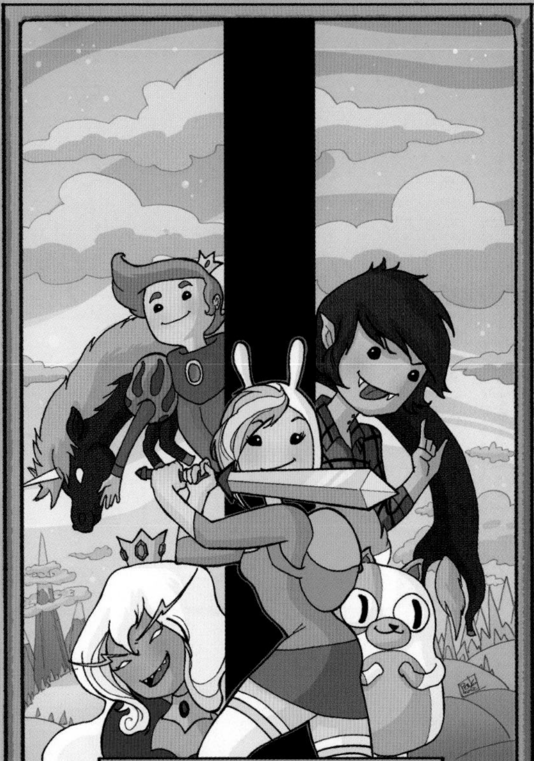

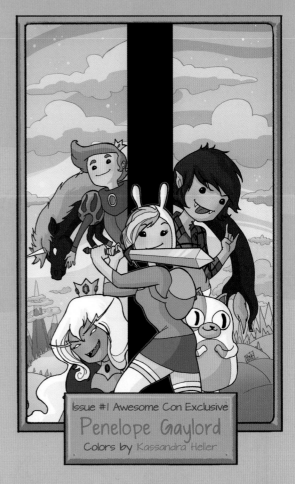

Issue #1 Awesome Con Exclusive
Penelope Gaylord
Colors by Kassandra Heller

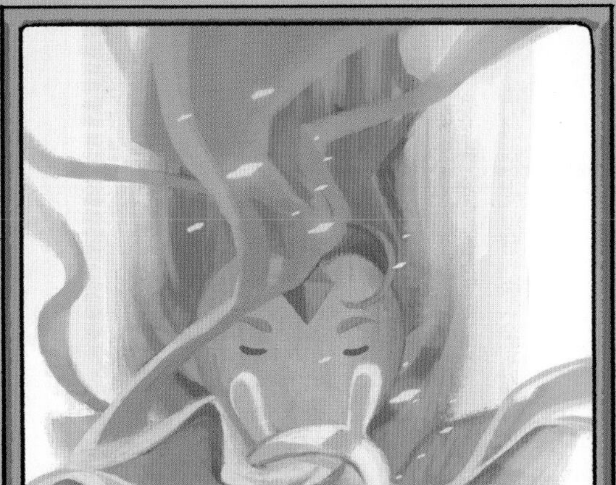
EMILY WARREN

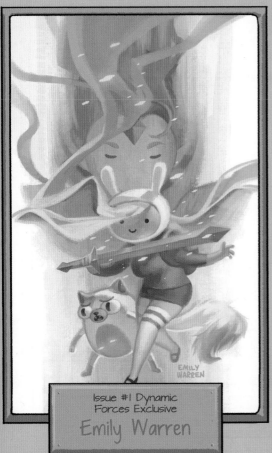

Issue #1 Dynamic Forces Exclusive
Emily Warren

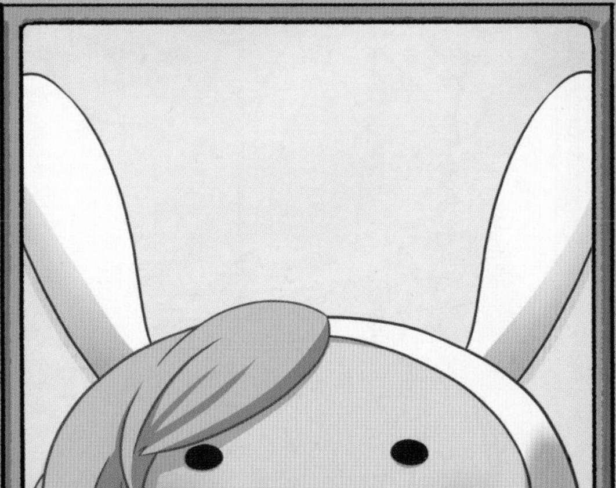

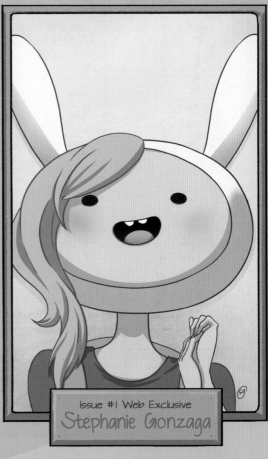

Issue #1 Web Exclusive
Stephanie Gonzaga

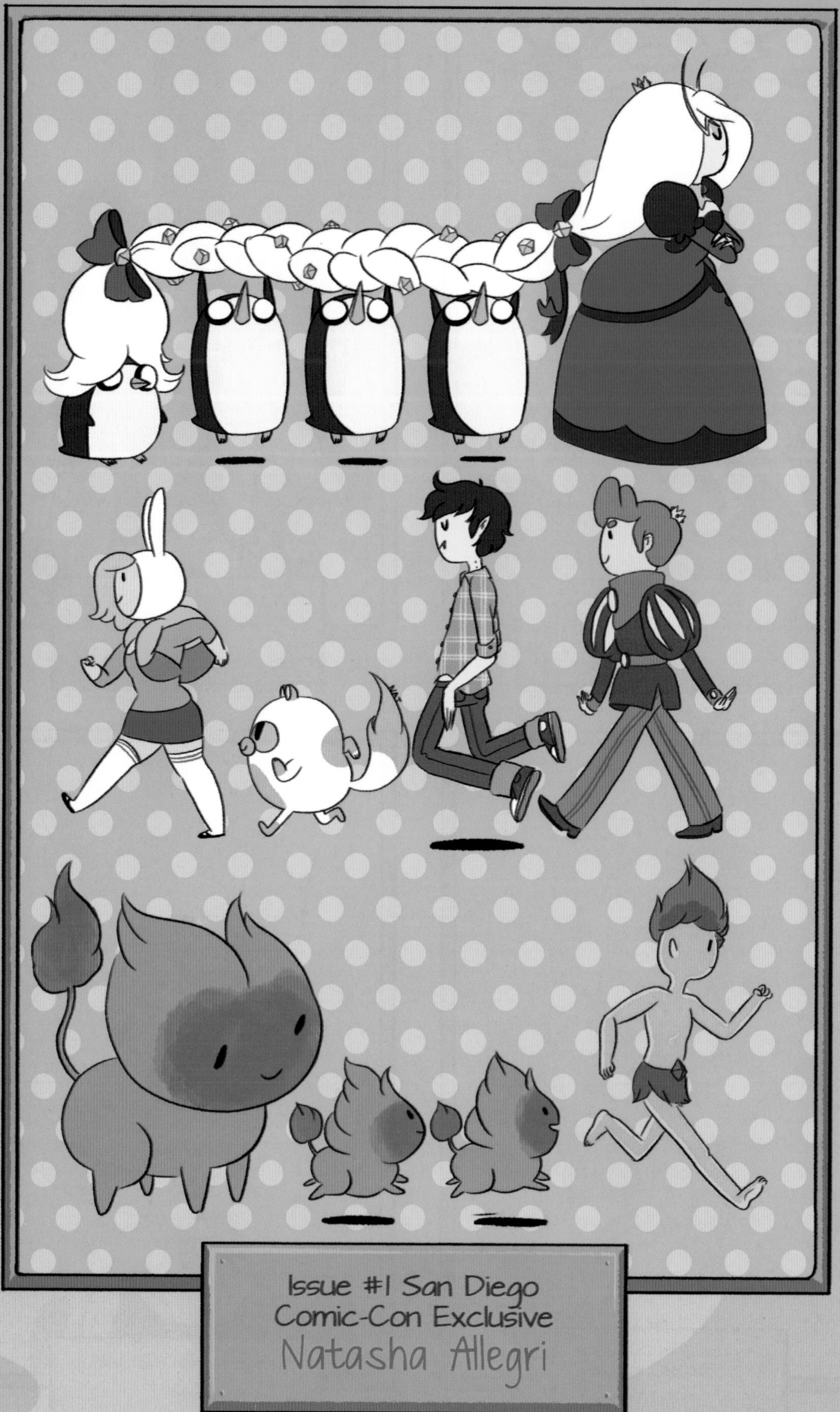

Issue #1 San Diego
Comic-Con Exclusive
Natasha Allegri

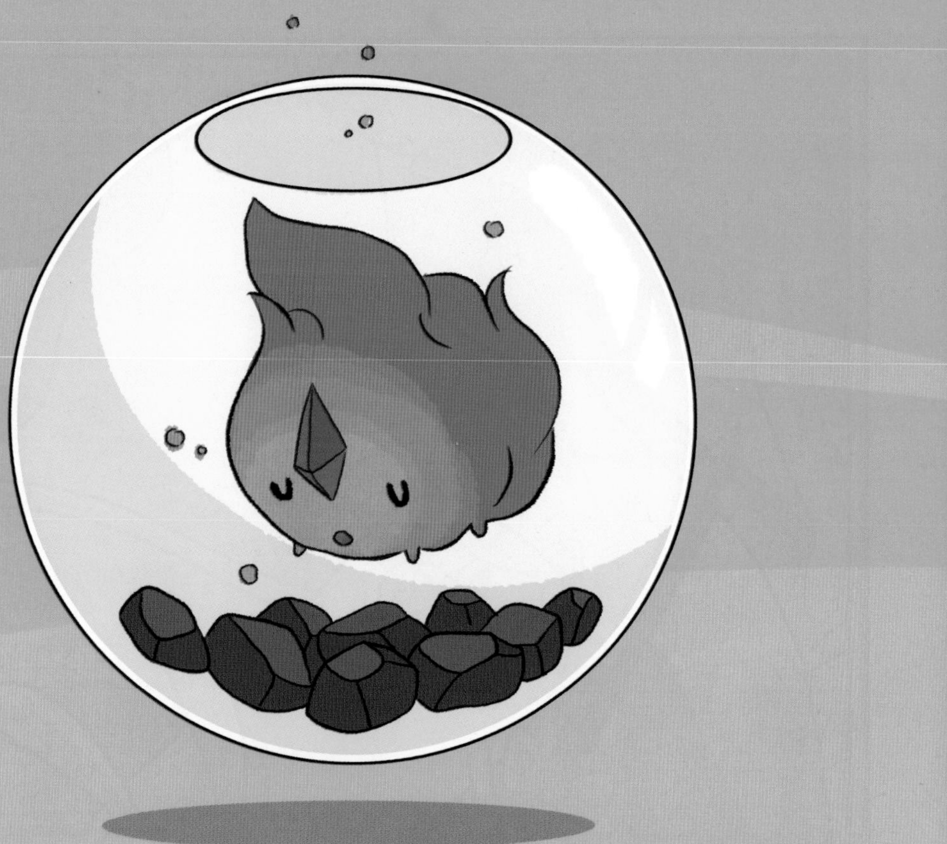

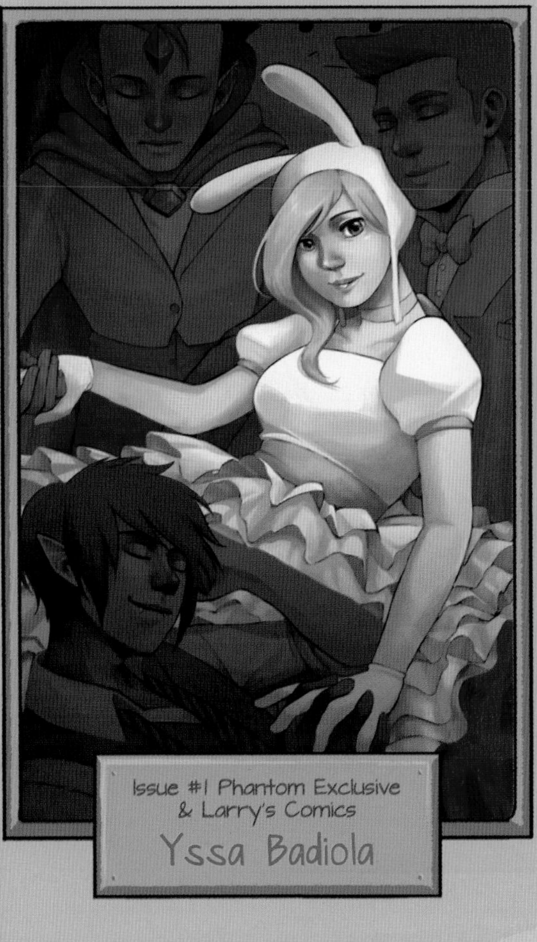

Issue #1 Phantom Exclusive
& Larry's Comics
Yssa Badiola

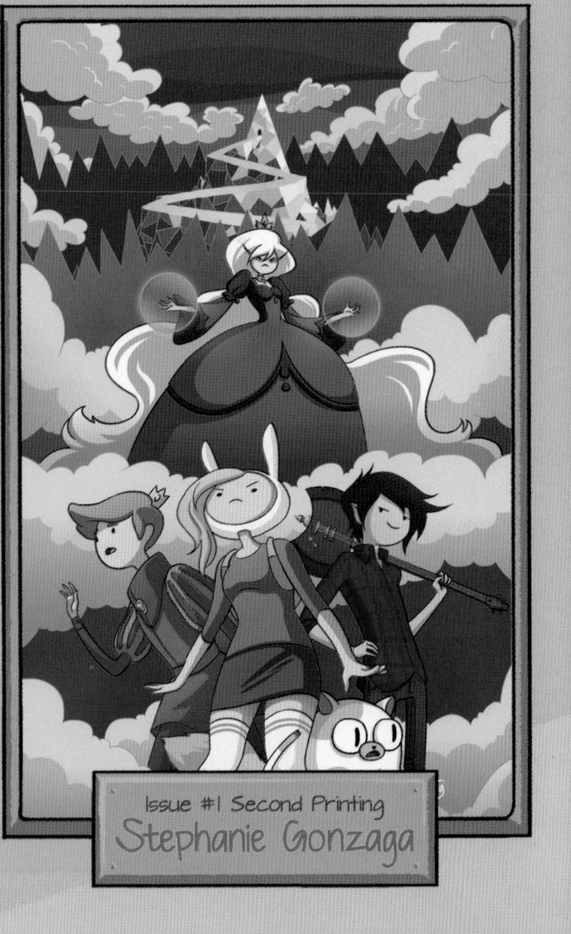

Issue #1 Second Printing
Stephanie Gonzaga

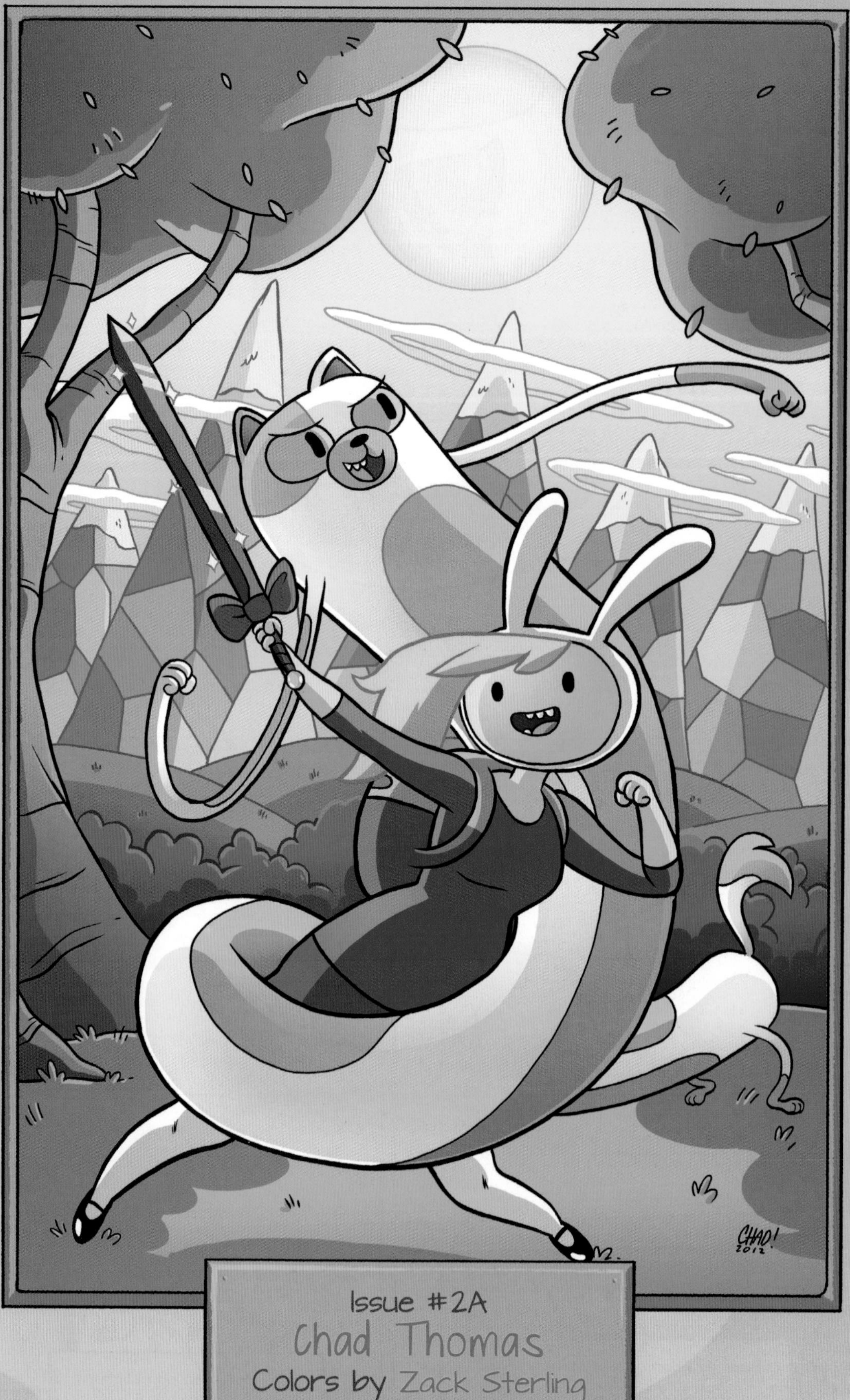
CHAD!
2012

Issue #2A
Chad Thomas
Colors by Zack Sterling

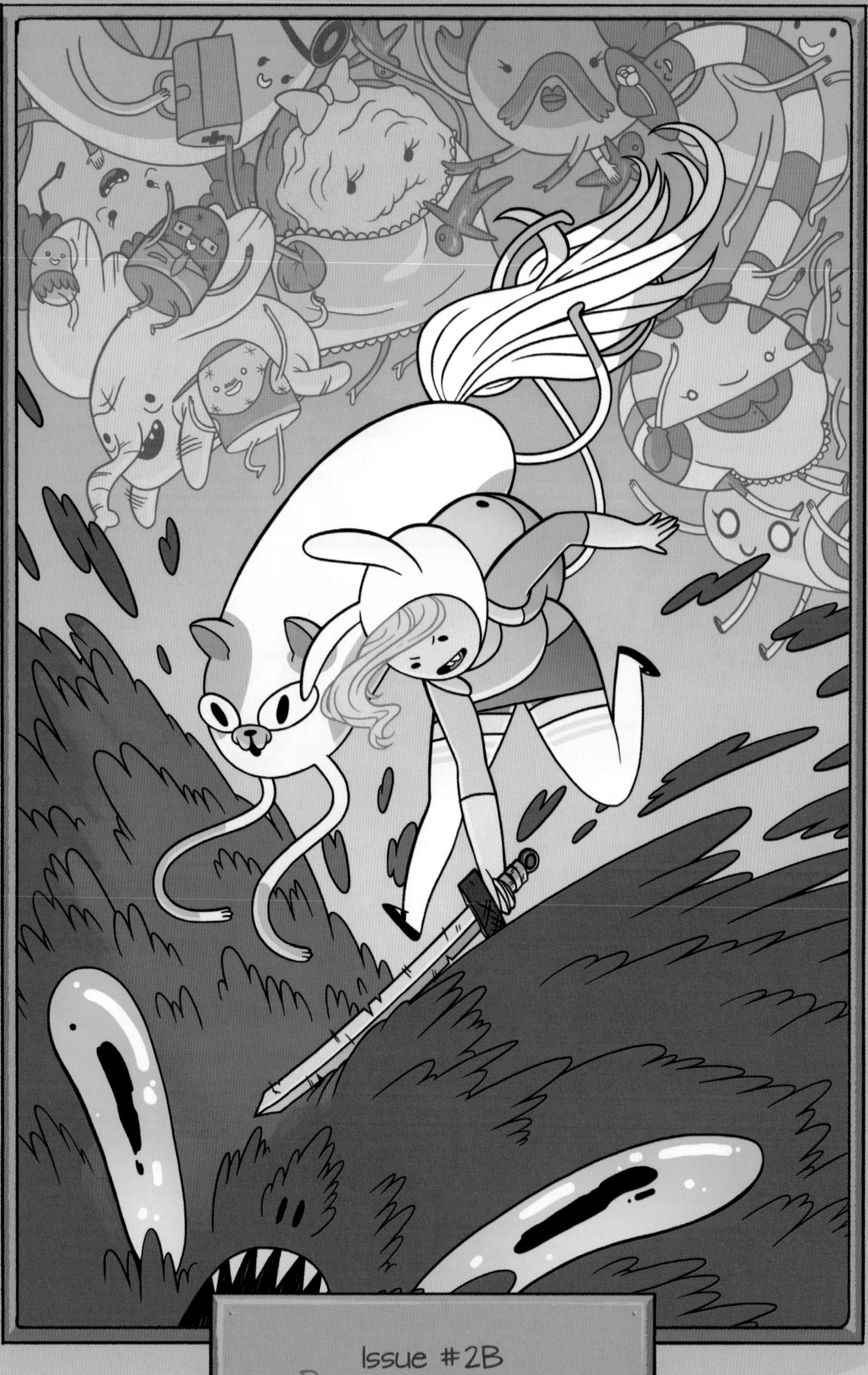

Issue #2B
Rebecca Mock

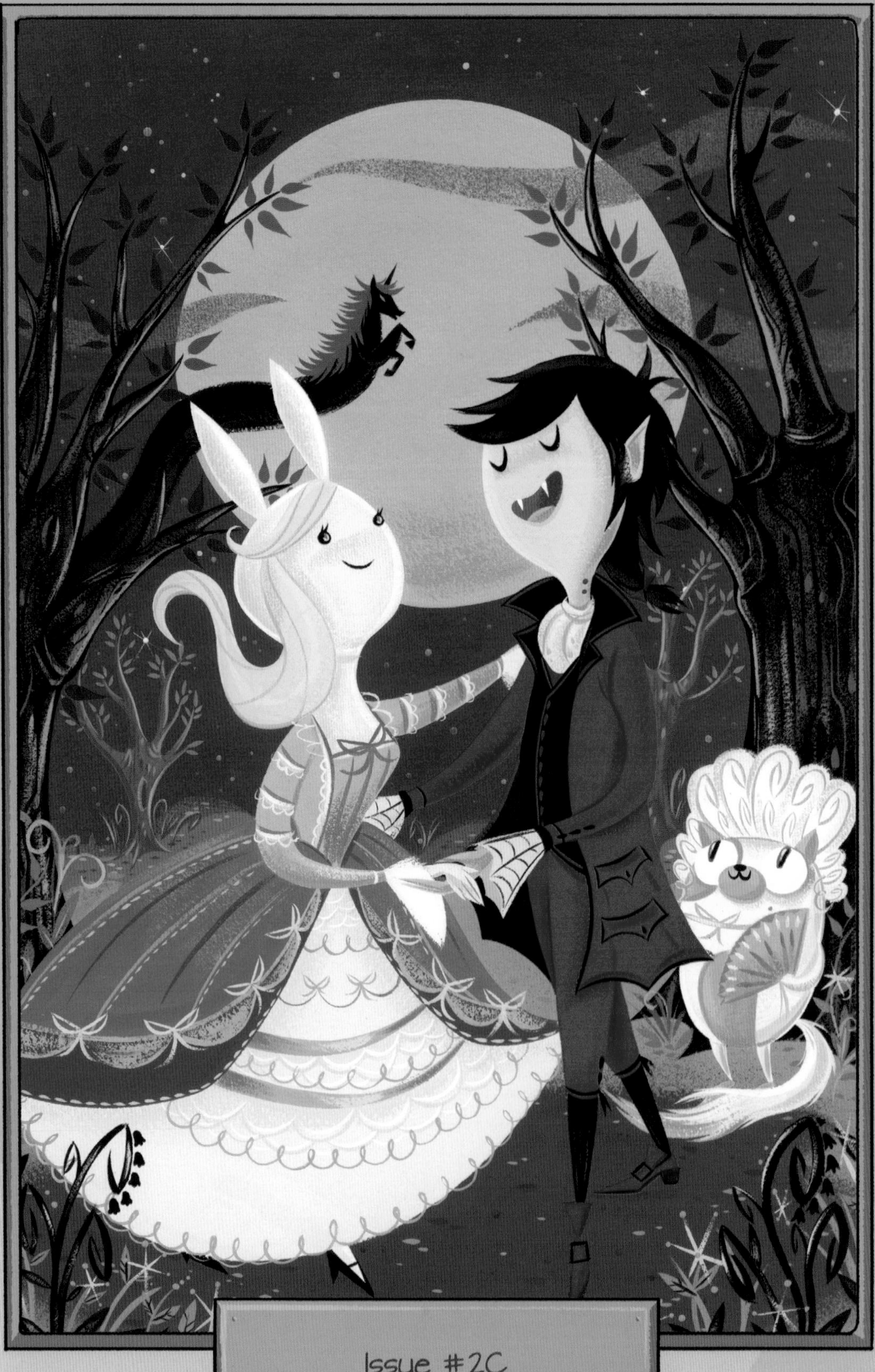

Issue #2C
Stephanie Buscema

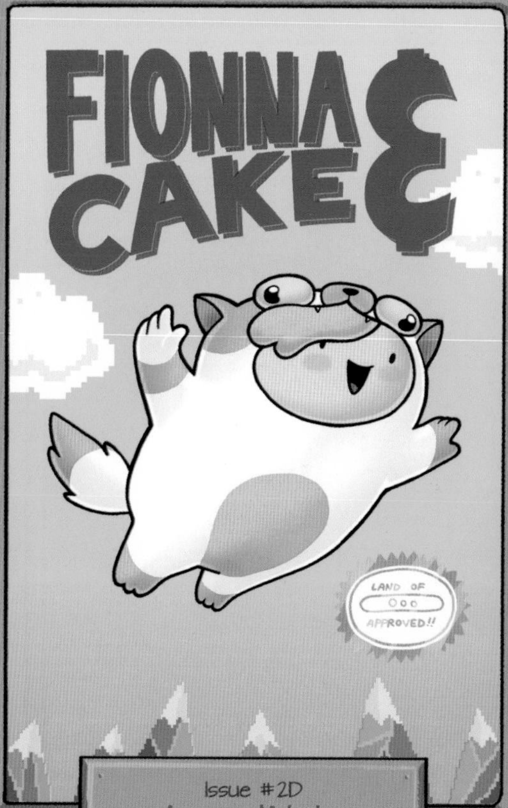
FIONNA & CAKE
LAND OF
APPROVED!!

Issue #2D
Maris Wicks

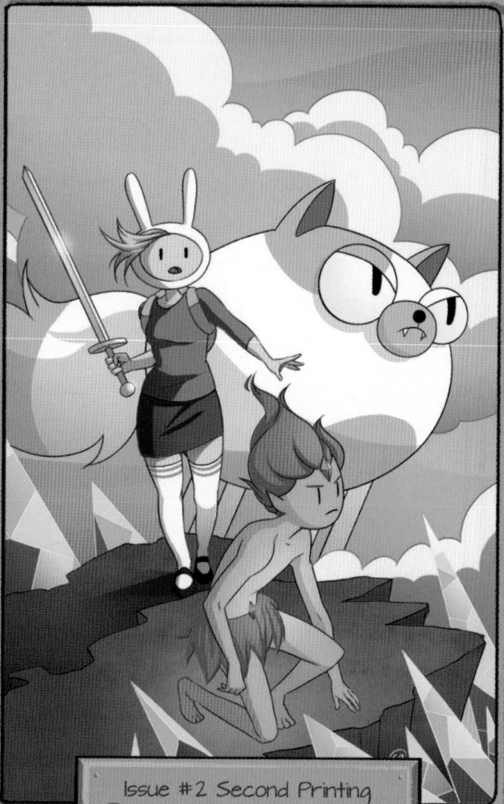

Issue #2 Second Printing
Stephanie Gonzaga

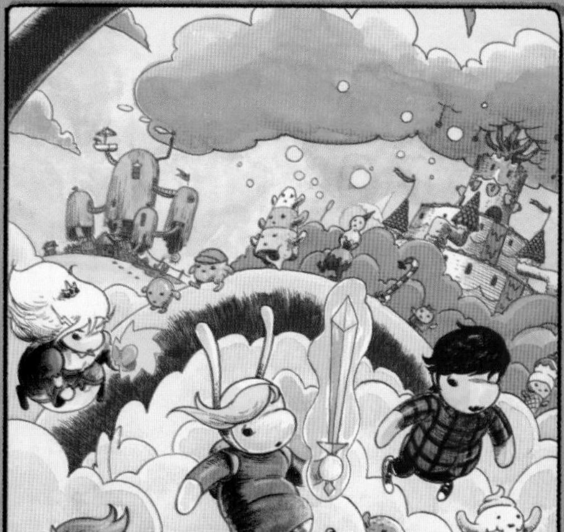

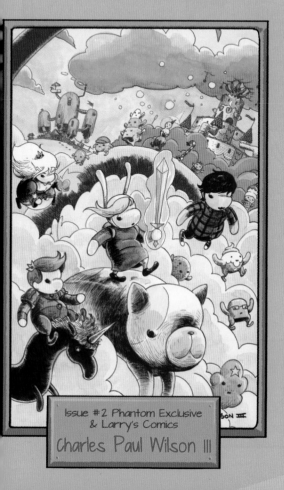

Issue #2 Phantom Exclusive
& Larry's Comics
Charles Paul Wilson III

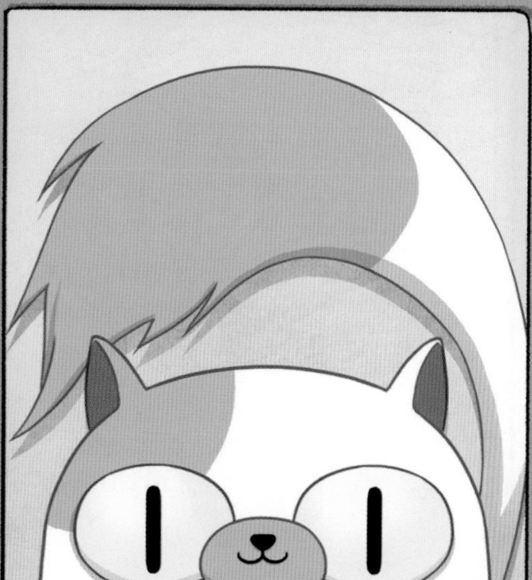

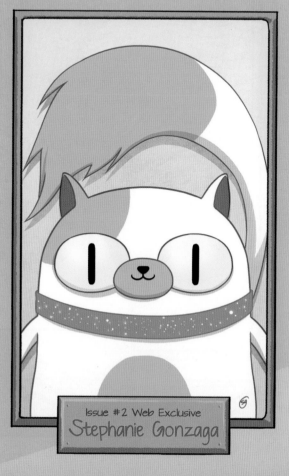

Issue #2 Web Exclusive
Stephanie Gonzaga

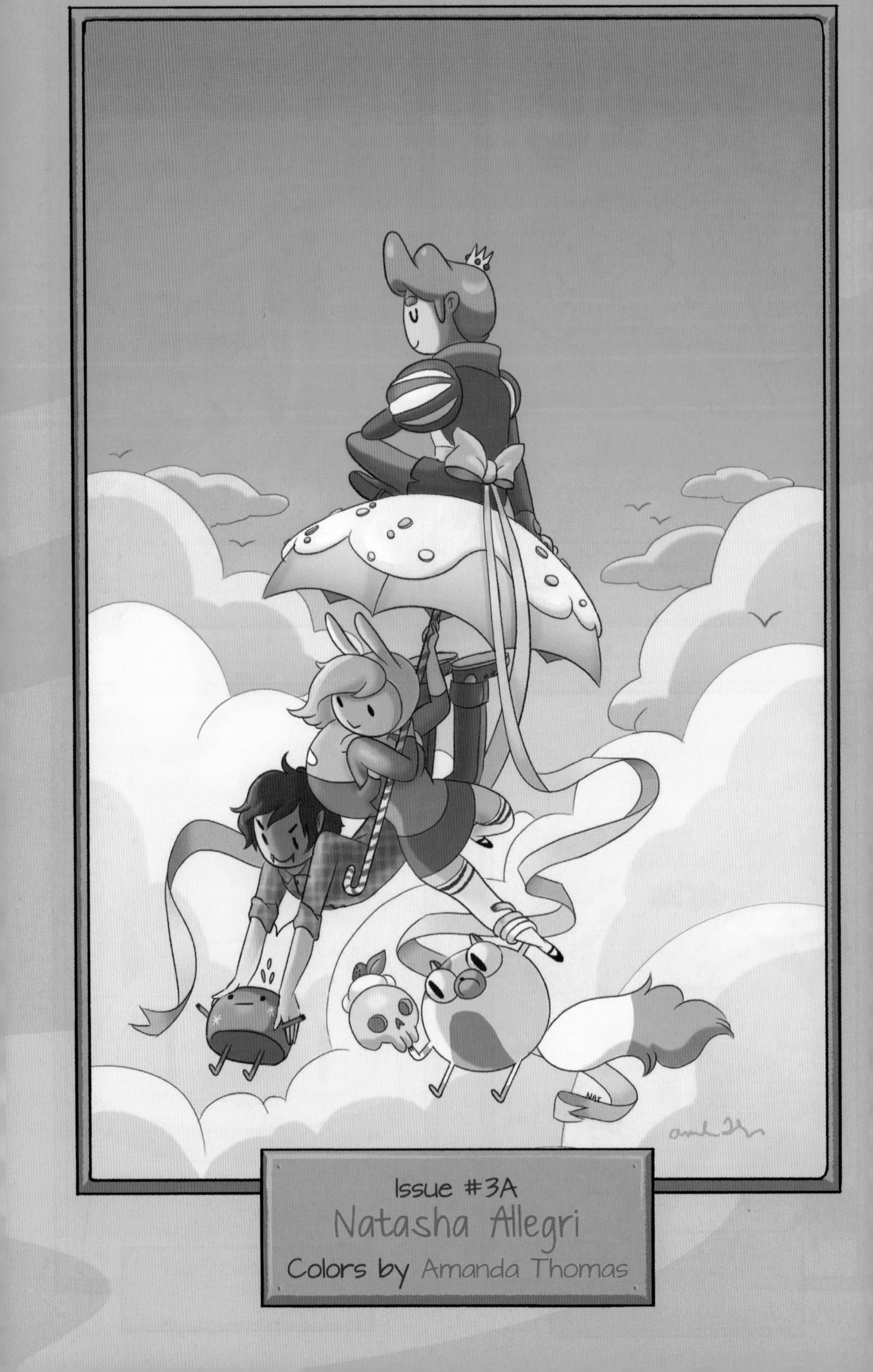

Issue #3A
Natasha Allegri
Colors by Amanda Thomas

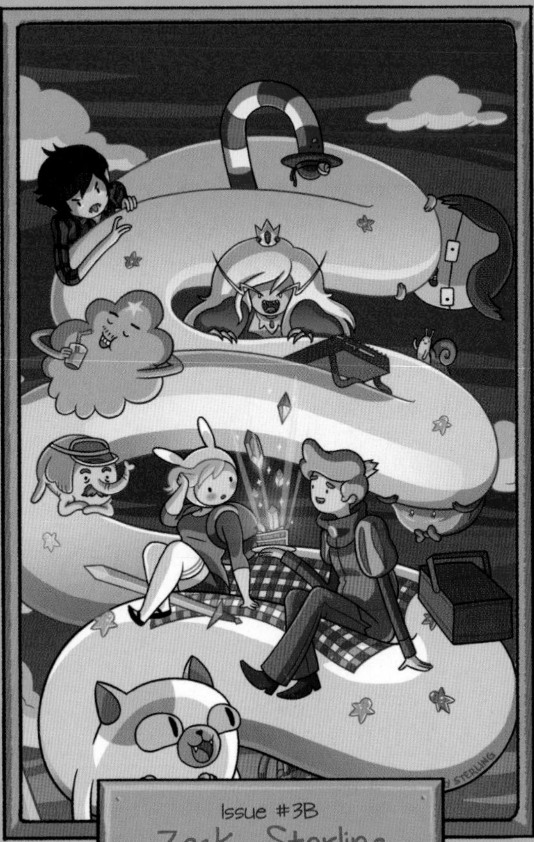

Issue #3B
Zack Sterling

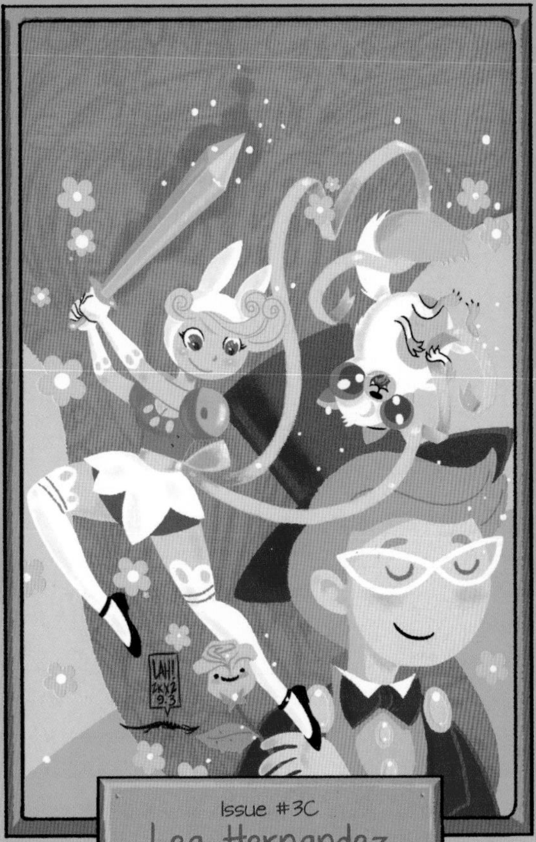

Issue #3C
Lea Hernandez

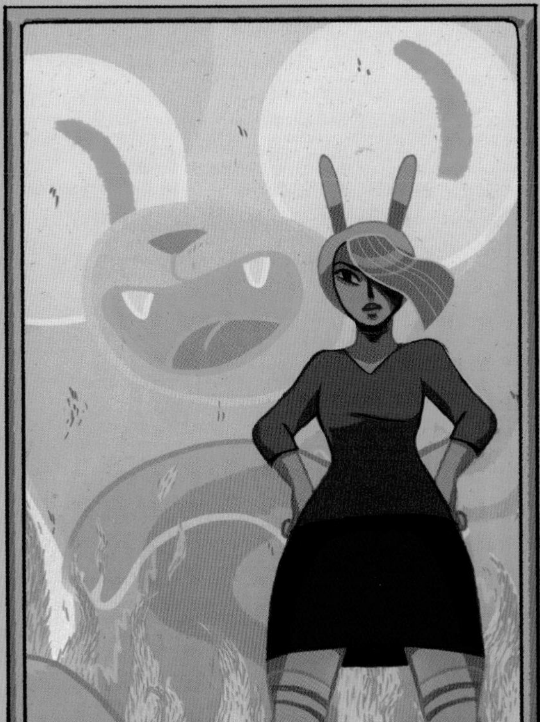

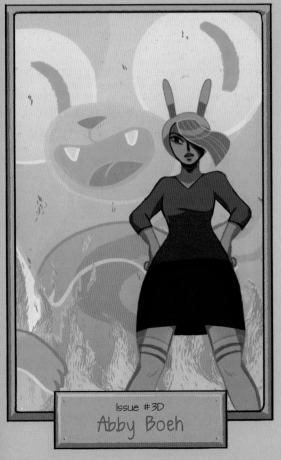

Issue #3D
Abby Boeh

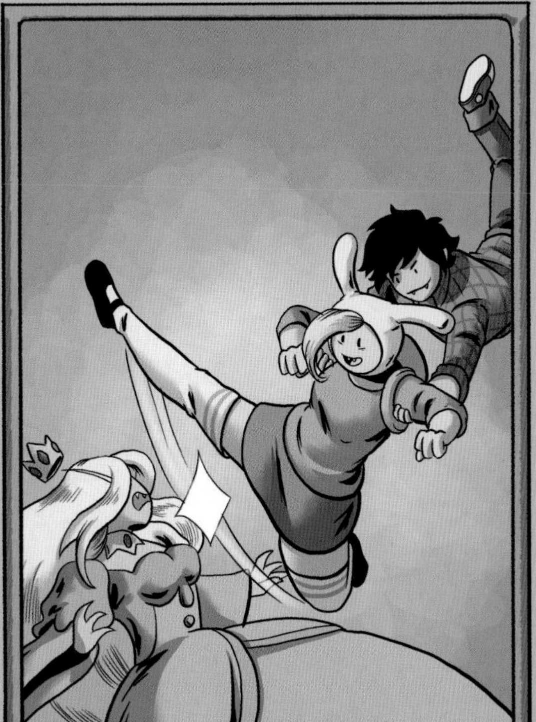

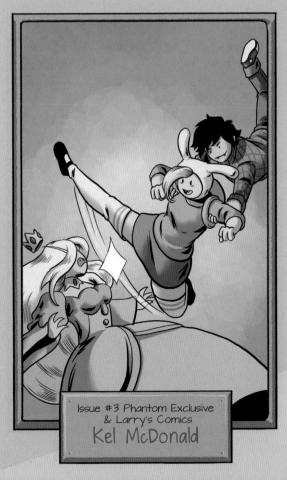

Issue #3 Phantom Exclusive
& Larry's Comics
Kel McDonald

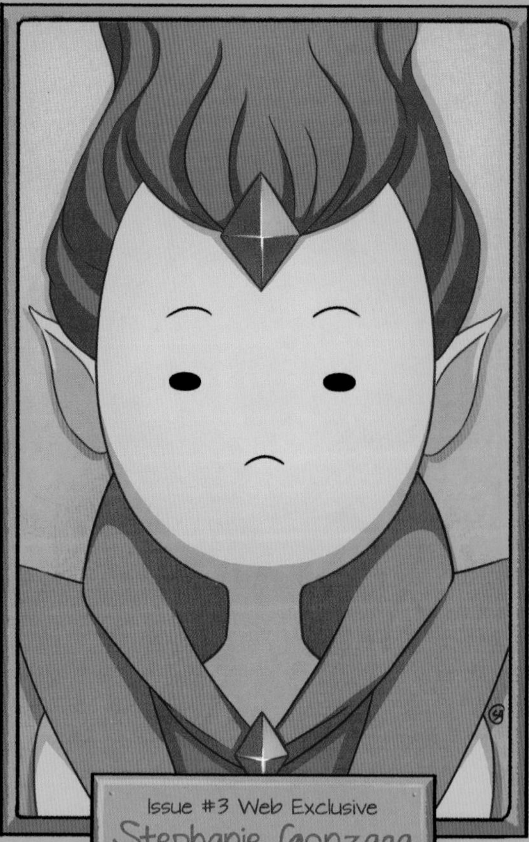

Issue #3 Web Exclusive
Stephanie Gonzaga

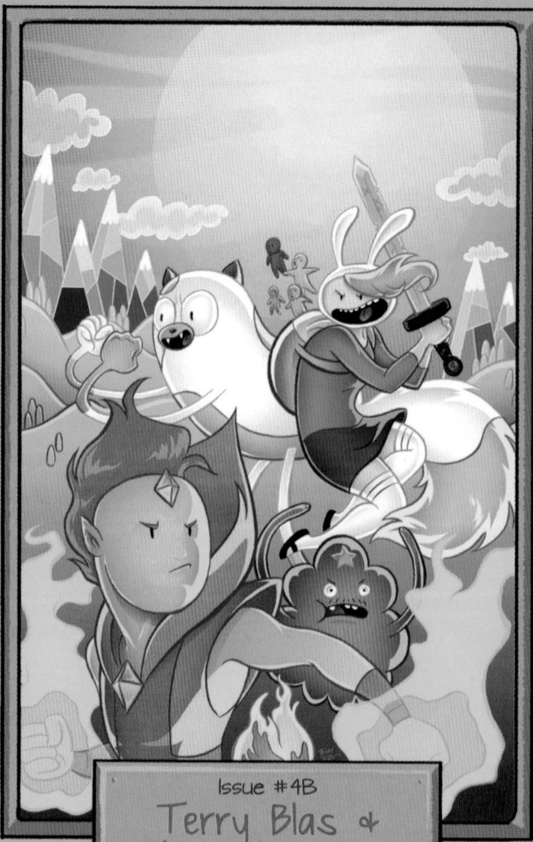

Issue #4B
Terry Blas & Kimball Davis

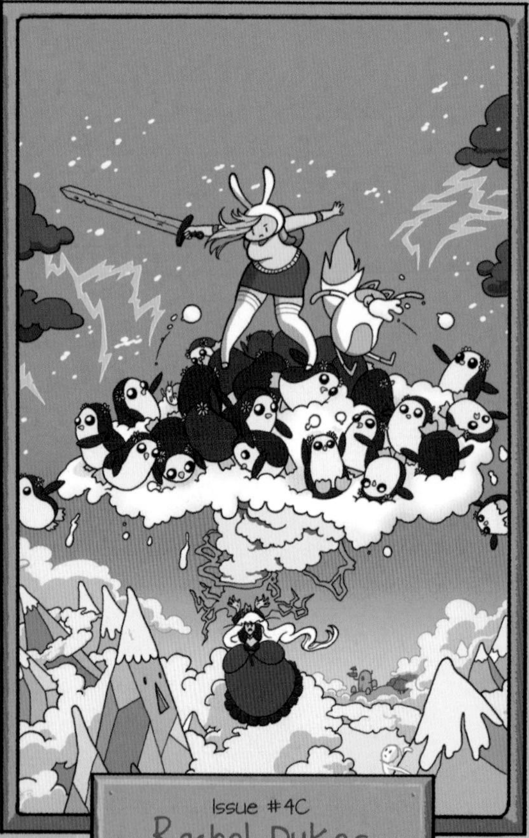

Issue #4C
Rachel Dukes

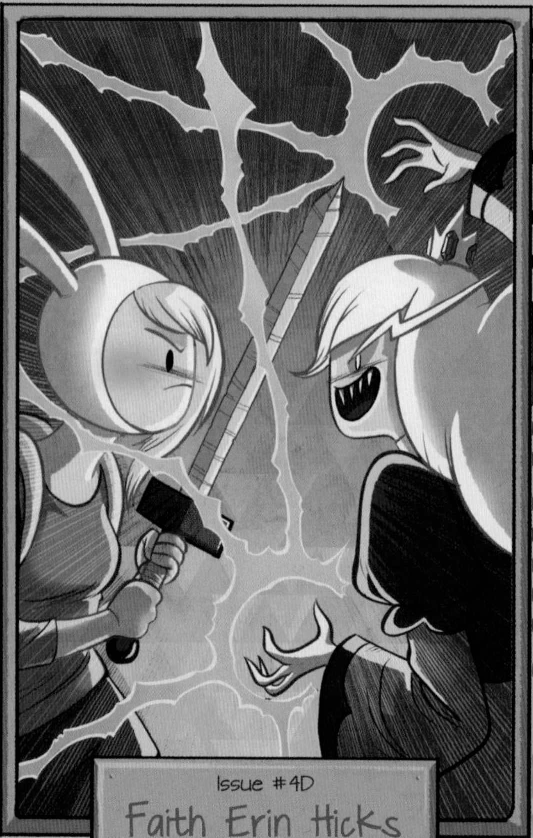

Issue #4D
Faith Erin Hicks
Colors by Noreen Rana

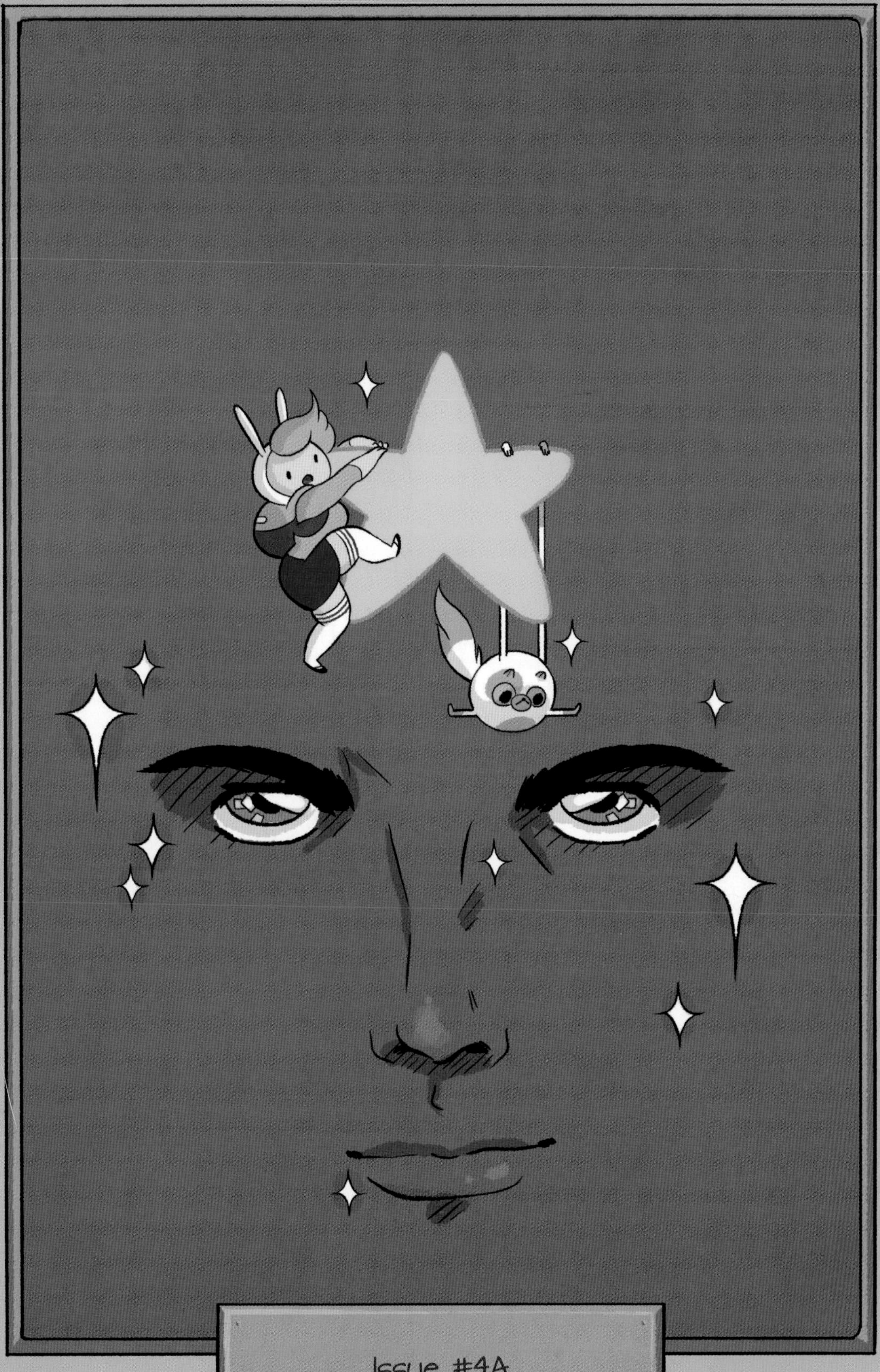

Issue #4A
Natasha Allegri

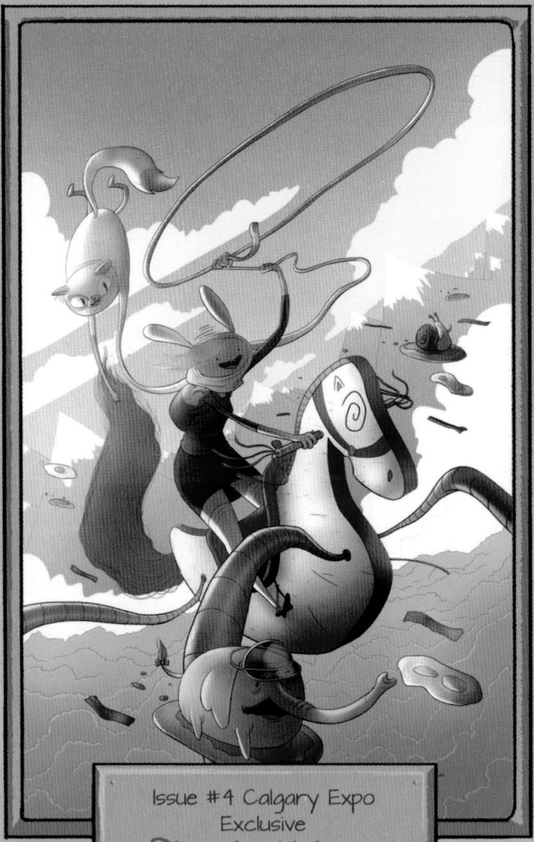

Issue #4 Calgary Expo Exclusive
Shoichi Uehara

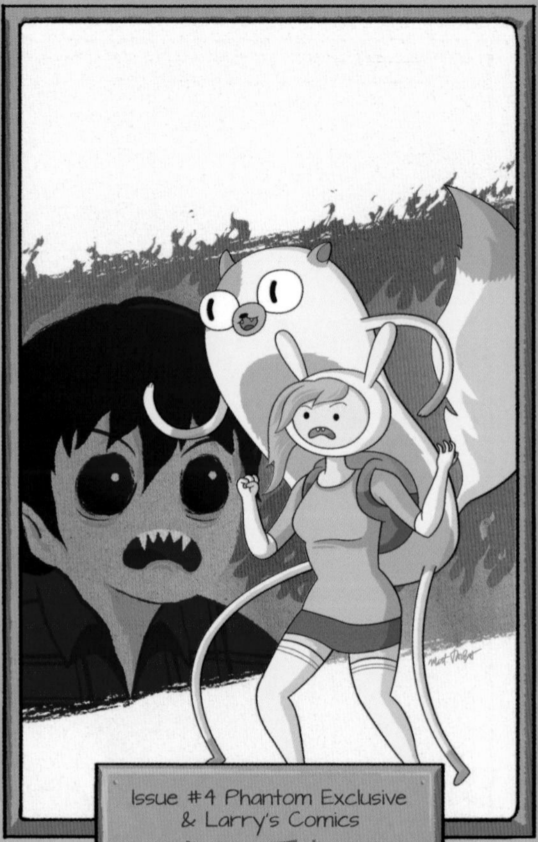

Issue #4 Phantom Exclusive & Larry's Comics
Matt Talbot

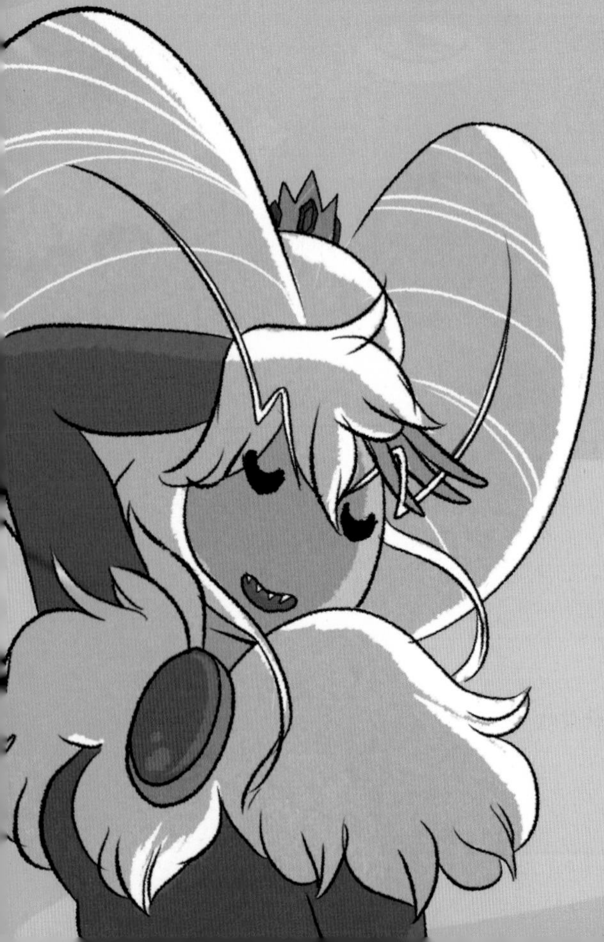

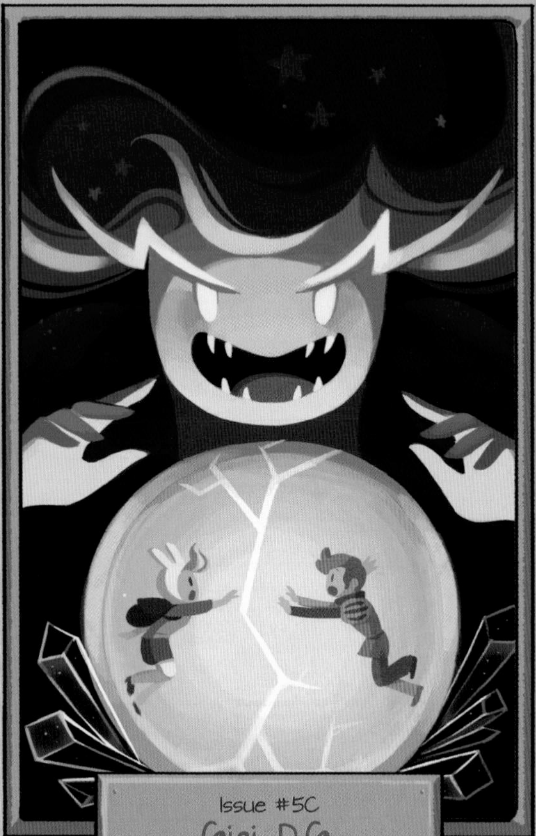

Issue #5C
Gigi D.G.

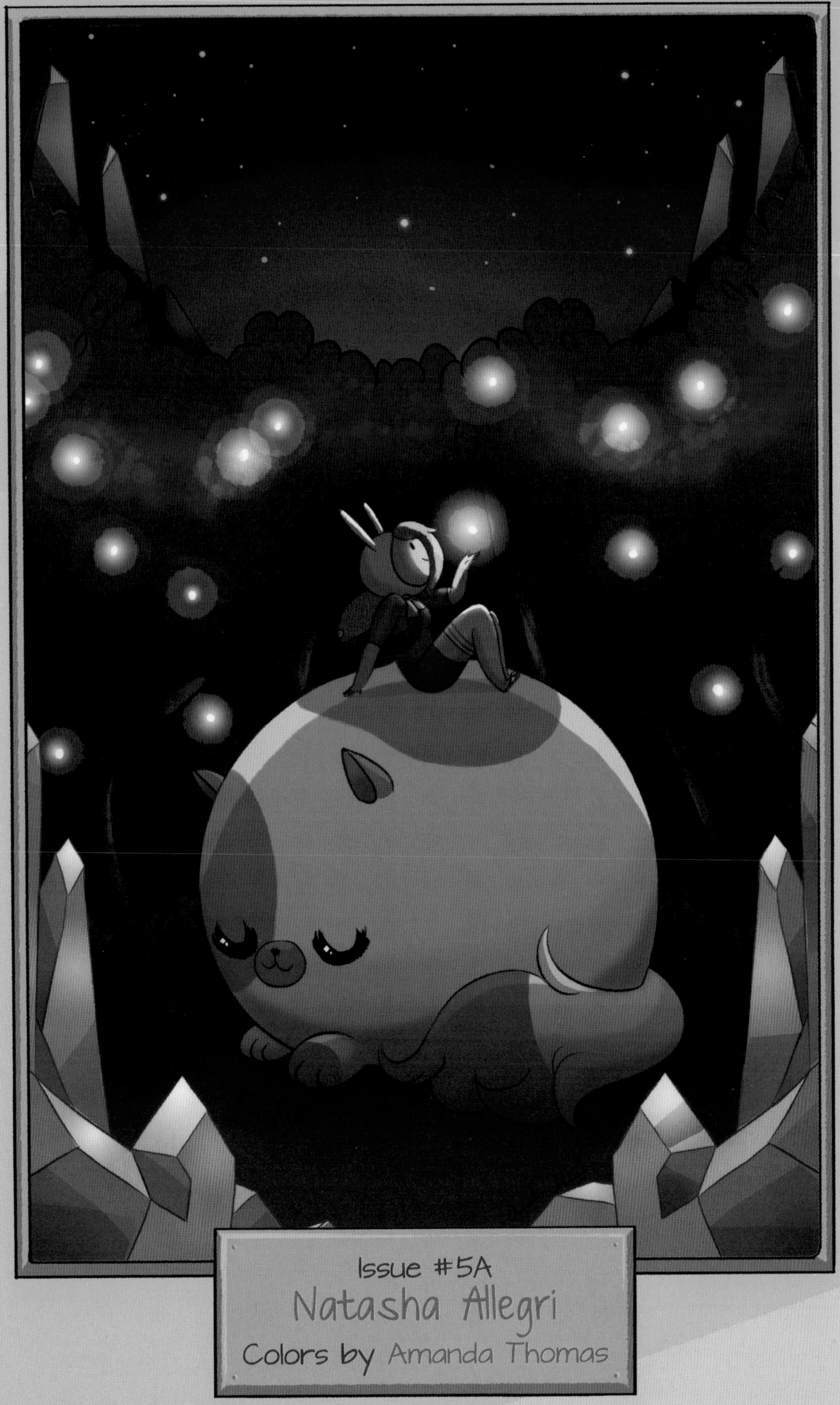

Issue #5A
Natasha Allegri
Colors by Amanda Thomas

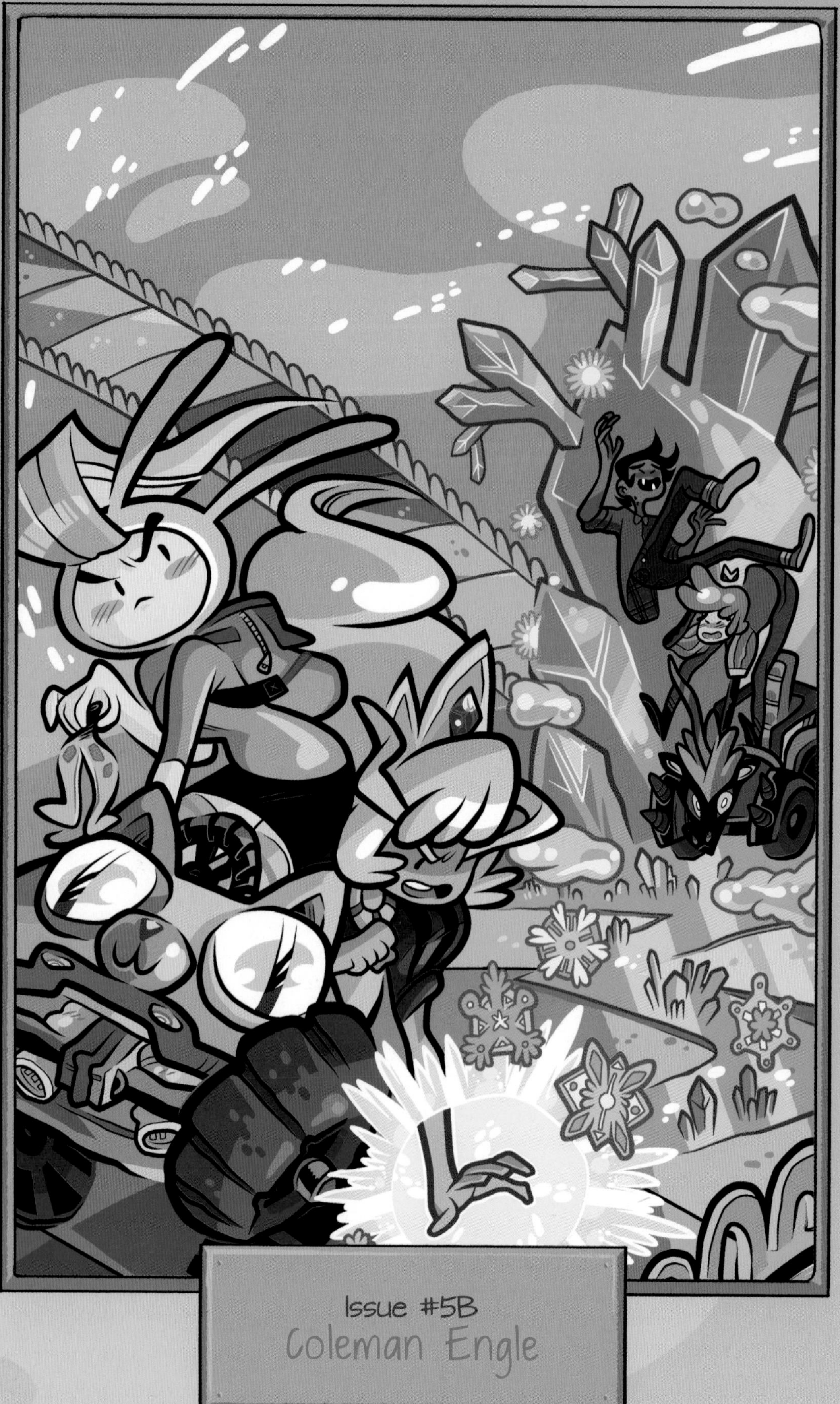

Issue #5B
Coleman Engle

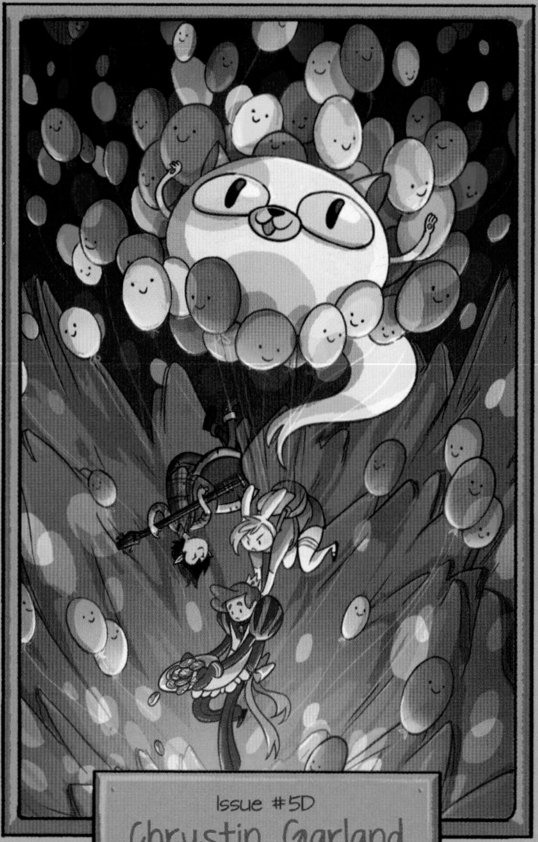

Issue #5D
Chrystin Garland

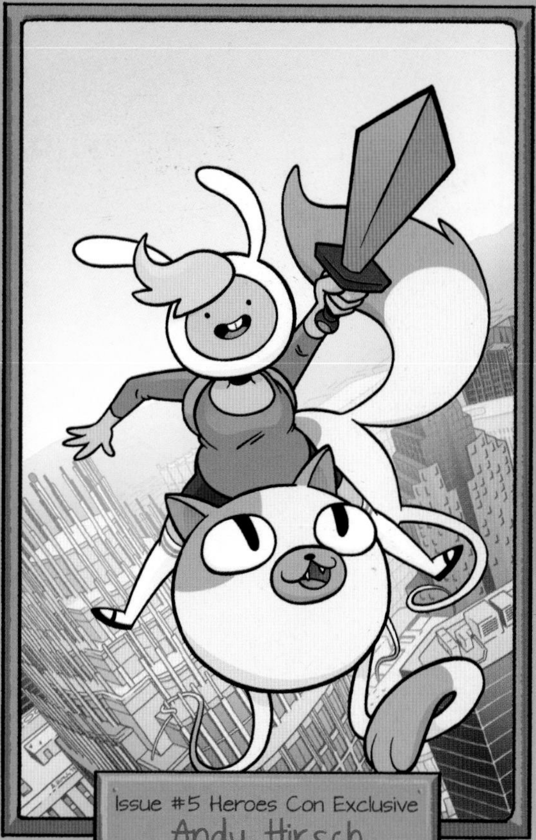

Issue #5 Heroes Con Exclusive
Andy Hirsch

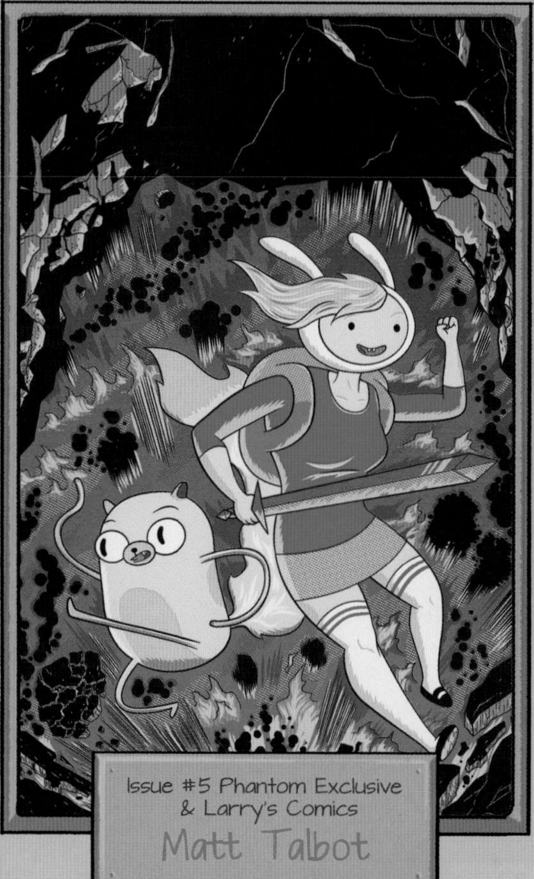

Issue #5 Phantom Exclusive
& Larry's Comics
Matt Talbot

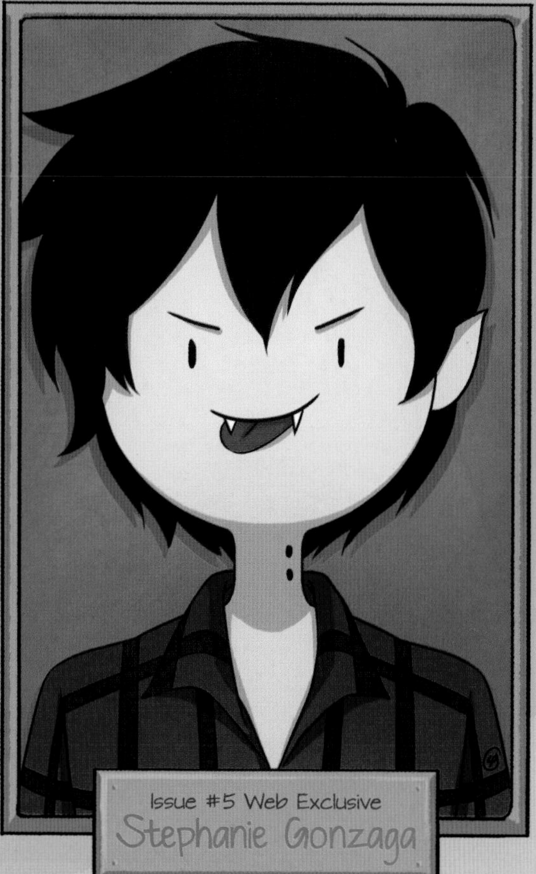

Issue #5 Web Exclusive
Stephanie Gonzaga

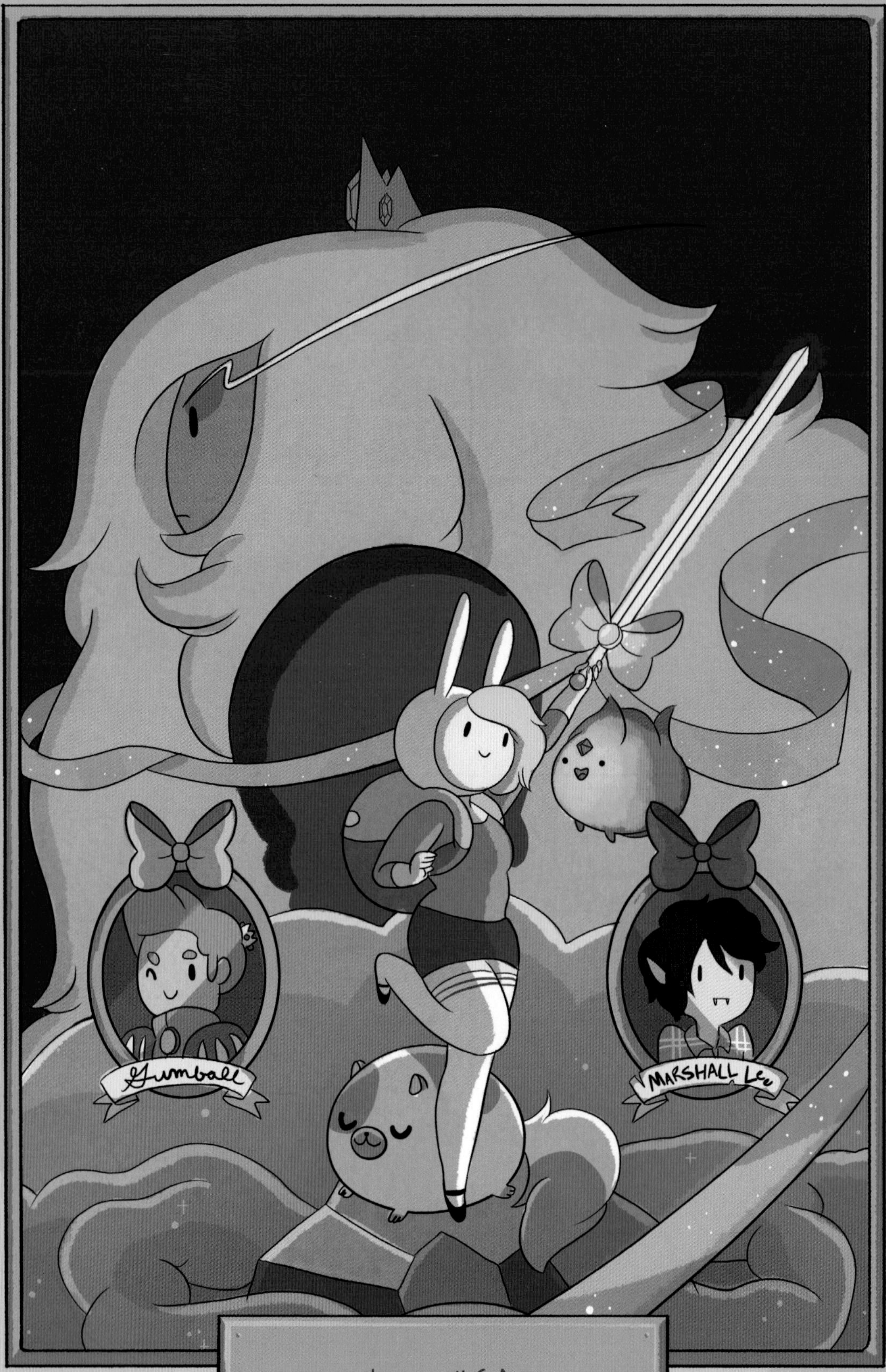
Gumball
MARSHALL Lee

Issue #6A
Natasha Allegri

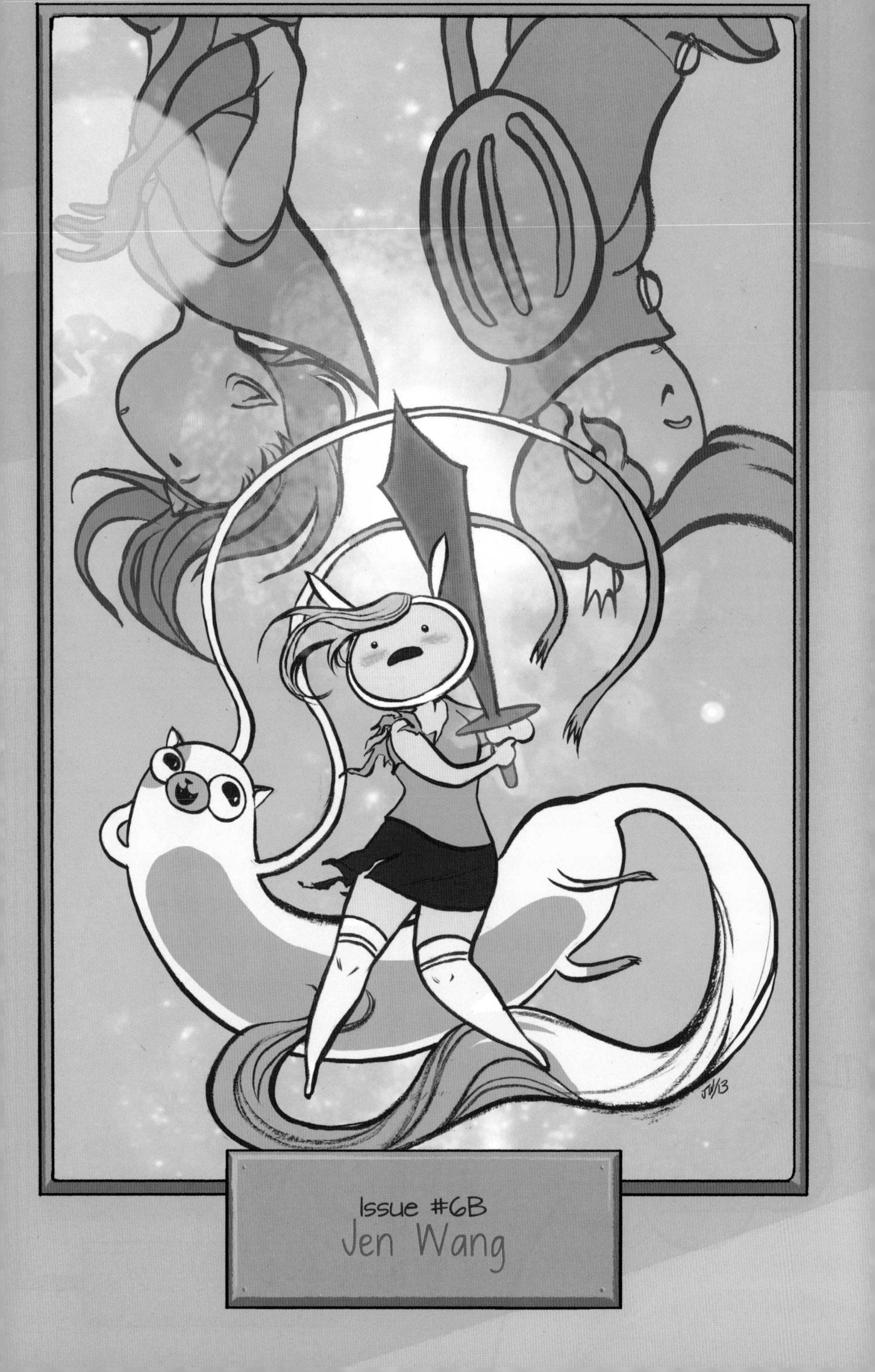

Issue #6B
Jen Wang

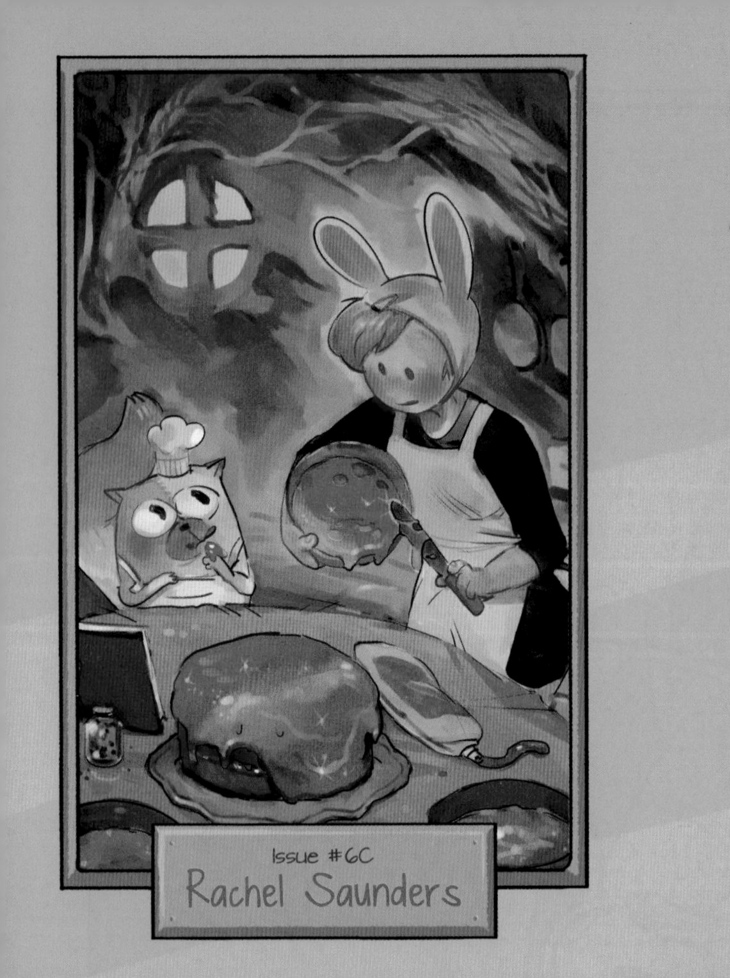

Issue #6C
Rachel Saunders

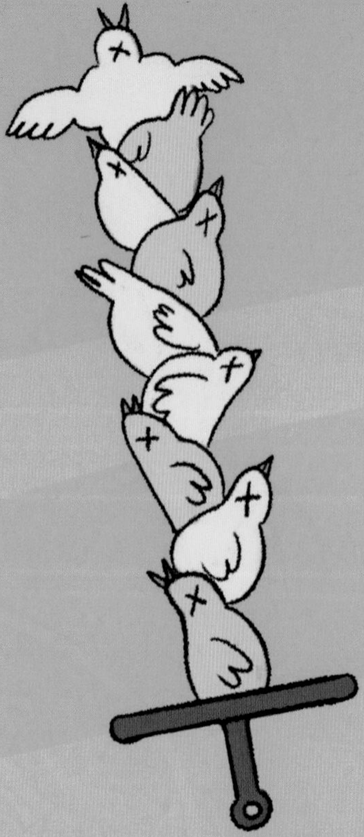

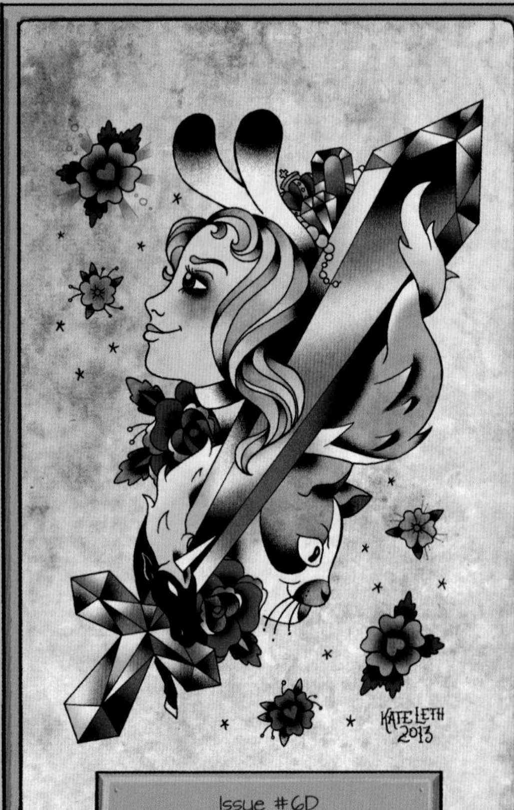
KATE LETH
2013

Issue #6D
Kate Leth

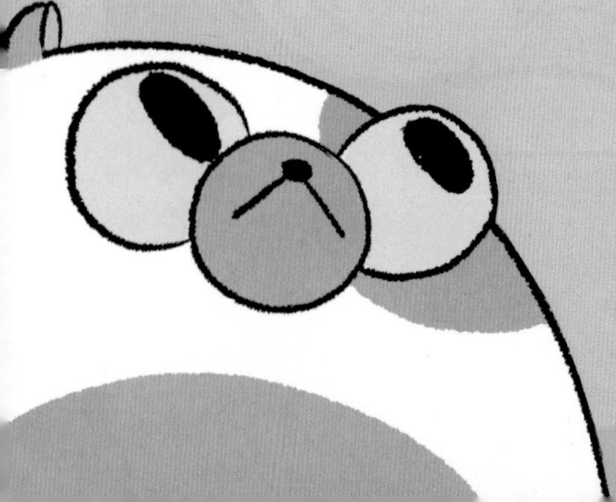

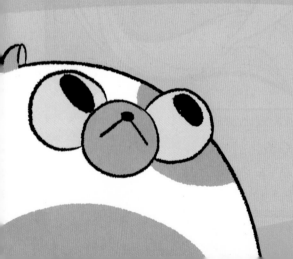

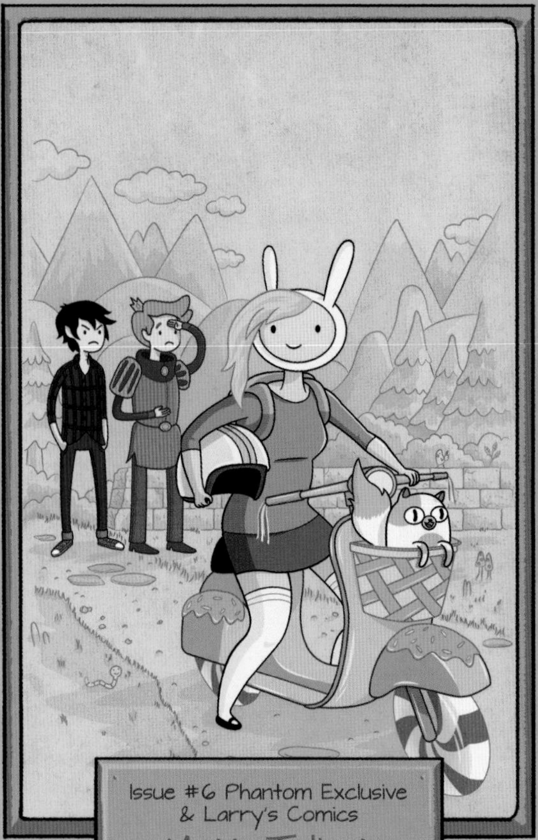

Issue #6 Phantom Exclusive
& Larry's Comics
Matt Talbot

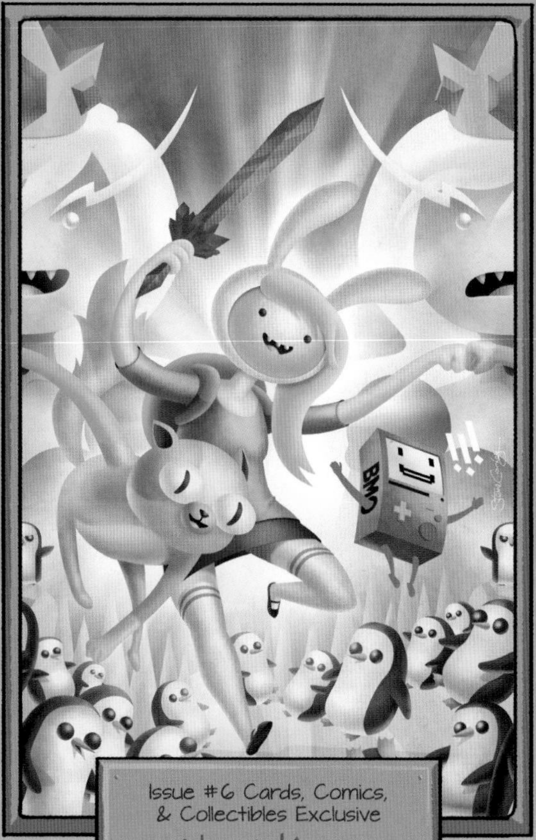

Issue #6 Cards, Comics,
& Collectibles Exclusive
Nomi Kane

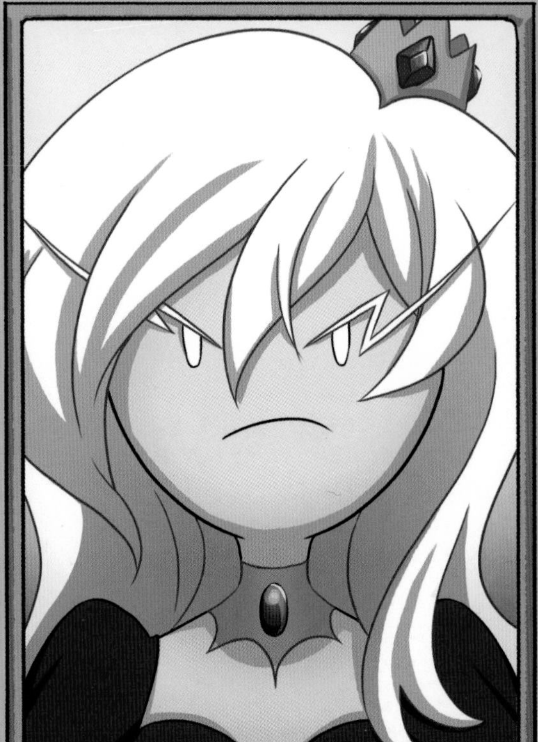

Issue #6 Web Exclusive
Stephanie Gonzaga

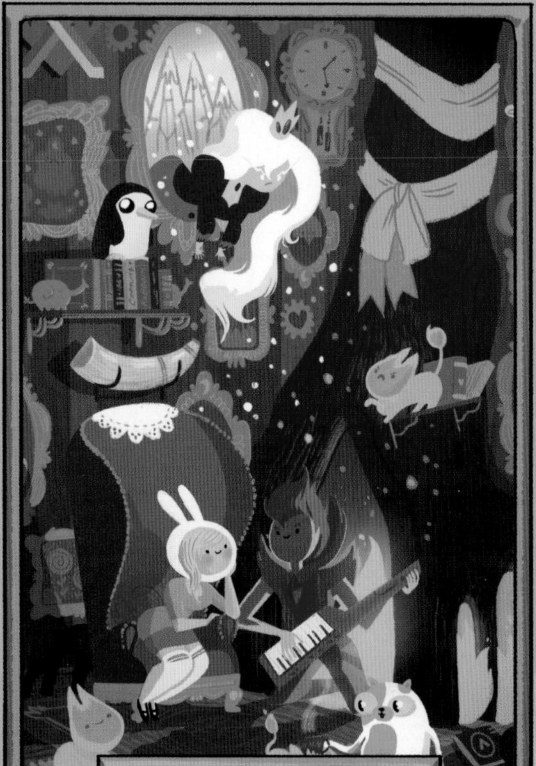

Issue #6 San Diego
Comic-Con Exclusive
Kassandra Heller

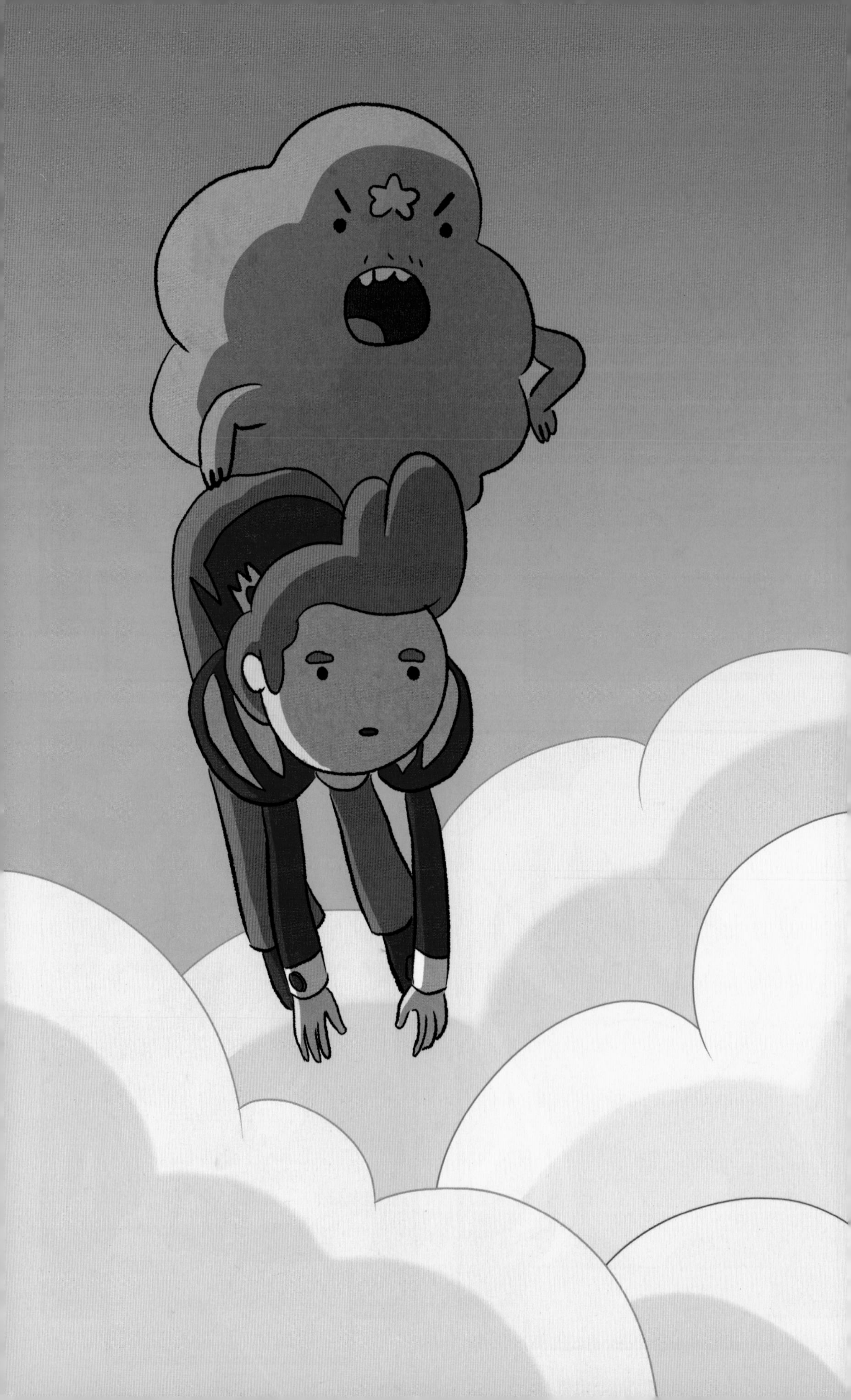